DEDICATION

I would like to express my love and thanks to my family, Joe Elvis, Isaiah and Emmanuel for standing by me through this process and loving me, even when I make that difficult. You are my heart and soul, my safety and my sanctuary. I want to thank the rest of my crazy, wonderful family and my amazing friends who not only offer me a treasure trove of material - yes, you know it's true - but have been my biggest supporters. You're all a blessing and a gift to me.

A special thanks to my good friend, Robert J. Elisberg, who edited this book and was one of the first people to tell me that it was good. You helped me believe. Thank you.

To all the people who have aided in my career that has added up to me writing HARRY, and all those who helped me since with this book and the other projects that are in the pipeline, also a heartfelt thank you.

I am a blessed man.

Bart

HONEYMOON WITH HARRY

MIRACLES ON ICE

There is one irrefutable fact. She changed my life. And nobody's life needed changing more than mine. A few foolhardy women had attempted to straighten me out, believing they were strong enough or possessed the feminine wiles to rip me from the bad behavior that I clung to tighter than a six-year-old with his blanket. But it never happened. Oh, for a few weeks - give or take - I would clean up my act. Dog and pony the good boyfriend routine so she could trot me out for her girlfriends who would all "ooh" and "aah" on cue and then furtively whisper to her that they were sure that I was "the one."

But either I got bored, or she slacked off when she thought she had triumphed over the evil empire. And like cancer no longer in remission my selfish behavior would rear its ugly head, usually worse than before. When I sink, I sink fast. She would cry. I would stop calling. Or caring for that matter. And the party was back on.

Bad habits die hard. Mine are immortal.

Until I met her.

Luther's Bar, about six blocks from the lake. It's a big-ass lake, larger than some seas actually, and when you're in Chicago living near it sums up your station in this status aware city. When you got married and popped out a tribe, you loaded up the U-Haul and moved to the tree-lined, rolling lawned suburbs to the west. But when you're a young, single professional, you'd smother your grandmother in her sleep for her condo near the lake.

I was pretty fucked up by the time she wandered into Luther's with two girlfriends. But no matter how shitfaced I am on any particular night, a beautiful woman sobers me right up. I don't even have to be looking in her direction to sense when one enters the room. It's a gift. And when she walked through the door of Luther's, I composed myself instantly as I ogled her steady stride across the crowded bar, keeping her girlfriends close to her side. She didn't notice me at all. She and her friends kept their eyes lasered in on each other, so as not to make any of the leering testosterone laden lumps hanging out think that they were even remotely interested in their company. They signaled every male that this was a girl's night out, laying out invisible landmines for those either too stupid or drunkenly brave to catch on. They didn't need the usual hassles from horny guys trying to score. It wasn't going to happen, so keep your not-so-charming patter to yourself, and your dick in your pants, boys.

Not that that stopped me. I've danced across so many landmines in my life there's little left that can be damaged.

She and her friends sneaked toward the back of the crowded bar just as a middle-aged couple were exiting a booth. They didn't wait for the mess on the table to be cleared away. One of the girls yanked a rag from the end of the bar, and the other two - including the woman that I couldn't take my eyes off of - bussed the table, dropping the plates and glasses into a plastic bin near the kitchen. The girls laid claim to their private arena before anyone else could. They knew if they didn't, someone else would. Luther's always has been inexplicably crowded. The old wooden structure built near the end of Prohibition was close to falling down. And it stank from decades of beer rotting through the wood floor. The drinks were weak, the beers always had far too much foam, and the menu ranged from tasteless fried vegetables to undercooked burgers. The only reason the place was still in business was because Luther Jr., who inherited this goldmine, paid off the city inspectors. In Chicago it's called "the cost of doing business."

Getting hammered on a week night was not uncommon for me. On a weekend it was a given. I hated my job as a futures analyst for a major brokerage house near the Stock Exchange. I mean how often do you jump out of bed in the morning revved up to get to the office and check the price of pork futures? And just in case you haven't actually pondered that question, I'll tell you. As close to never as you can get without actually applying for a new job. But I'd never quit. I make decent money doing this and I'm actually pretty good at it, which is why they won't fire me no matter how bad my attitude. Money beats anything when you're within sniffing distance of the Stock Exchange.

I had moved to Chicago two years earlier from a rural New Jersey town, which left me saddled with an accent that made me sound shades dumber than I actually was. Tony Soprano meet Lil' Abner. I didn't know a lot of folks, had few people I considered friends, and I was single. There were only two things that I liked about Chicago. At the top of that list was the women. There were a lot of them. They outnumbered the men. Good odds even for the weaker members of the herd. I'd been fairly blessed in my life when it came to women. Though not by any talent or personality asset that I'd cultivated. My parents never did much for me but they were both tall. I stood six-three and went about two hundred and fifty pounds. Like my father who was in unexplainably great shape well into his fifties, I had long, rangy muscles, a flat stomach, and an ape chest. And depending on where you caught me along my night of drinking, I could be mildly amusing in a smartassy, narcissistic, sort of way. I possess about sixty minutes of actual charm. It slept comfortably most of the time, hidden in its stable until it had to be saddled up and rode hard. Once I approached a woman, the clock was ticking. I had to seal the deal within that first hour or they would find out it was all smoke and mirrors. If you asked any woman that I had slept with what she thought of me, approximately ninety percent would use some variation of the term "asshole." I'd like to believe that I was just misunderstood. But truthfully most of the time I was just a big prick. Like most drinkers, I have a sliding scale. Two drinks and I'm all snugly and cute, the guy that girls cuddle up to and share a few laughs with. Then I take them home and fuck their brains out. Three to four, I'm still charming and witty, but the snugly guy has disappeared. Here is where I can cut to the chase. She knows she's not going to have a lot of laughs but the sex will be intense, and I'll leave afterwards and her boyfriend will never have to know. After I've put down a half dozen drinks, I'm loud and surly and behave as stupidly as I sound. That's where if I'm going to get laid it's either out of pity or she's as obnoxiously drunk as I am. At this level I'm the perfect guy to take home and screw, so she can rub it in her boyfriend's face the next day.

This is also the stage where I get into a lot of fights. With men and women. When it is with women it usually takes the form of having a drink thrown on me as they launch into a tirade of verbal insults. With men it's more about heading outside and hoping I can clear my head fast enough to block a punch. My father taught me to fight by beating the crap out of me, so I learned how to defend myself. Once I finally could whip his ass, which happened when I was just shy of sixteen, he left me alone. Since I was always large for my age, my father constantly accused me of being "too big for Jockeys." As if my size was a challenge to his own. He had a quick way of settling his fear. A smack upside my head. A kick to my ass. And my personal favorite, a sharp twist of my arm followed with a toss across the room. Yeah, he was a dick.

Boo-hoo for me. I bided my time and when I was nearly as tall as him and youthfully fast, I stole his crown. I finished the fight by twisting his arm behind his back and tossing him across the room, much to my younger brother's delight. From that moment it was boo-hoo for him. He often toyed with the idea of trying to topple the new regime which had deposed his top dog standing, but I covertly - and a few times overtly - reminded him that I was not about to let him reign again, at least, not without hurting him badly.

Bar fights aren't dissimilar. I don't step outside unless I'm serious about kicking someone's ass. And once I do, most guys aren't too keen about heading out back to take me on a second time.

The other thing I like about Chicago is the bars. What a surprise, huh? A metropolis built for the likes of me. You can get a drink in this city at any hour of any day. Coming from a place where there were three bars total, I hit the mother lode. Hello, my name is Todd and I am an alcoholic. Hello again, my name is Todd and I don't care. I'm not interested in conquering it. I like slugging it back and getting loaded. Most people are terrified of the demon hooch. Never much concerned me. Most people don't like feeling out of control when they drink. I do. Being in control is highly overrated. I don't often get hangovers, either. Another genetic blessing. There may be a slight ping in my engine, and I'm just in a pissy mood until I get my next drink. But I'm in a pissy mood most of the time so people can't tell the difference.

My two interests: women and bars. Most women wince and mutter, "What a waste." Most men won't admit it but they completely understand.

Usually when a group of women wandered into Luther's, I'd gather my sea legs and wander over, checking my watch to keep track of the time on my magical charm. I prep my initial salvo to suss out the weakest of the herd, the one most likely to end up back at my place. It never takes me more than a few minutes to know who I have a shot with and who is too much work. And then I dig into my bag of tricks and finagle my way into her good graces, hoping to finagle her out of her panties. But as I smiled at this woman, I knew dead-off she was neither the easiest of the three, nor did she have any intention of getting naked with me. There was something so unique - so completely foreign to me - about this woman that she scared the piss out of me. And just so there's no doubt, I mean that in a good way.

From that very first instant, I was completely smitten. Trapped like a dog in a well. Or more accurately, trapped like a dog in a well who was still attached to his tether. I'd been hot for lots of women in my life. Hot for a night. Hot for a week. Sometimes even for a month or so. But this was different. Scary different. I knew from moment one that I would walk through fire for this woman. The best I can compare it to is being hit by a car as you step off the curb. You only have a moment to react before you find yourself rolling across the pavement until you're out cold. She creamed me like a speeding T-bird.

Maybe I would stand for a better chance with one of her friends. I sensed that the little brunette she was with suffered from relationship problems, and if I dazzled her with enough voodoo, I would be dropping my jeans on her bedroom floor. But it didn't matter. I could not break my focus. It was locked on this woman. Those eyes. They were like the color of summer wheat on the farms near where I grew up, with dark brown lashes that gave her an aura of mystery which I would never be privy to. I wanted to know her. Only her.

Do I believe in love at first sight? Nope. I believe this started long before she and I met. There are no accidents, except possibly my birth. At least that is what my mother always told me. I was her "happy little accident." But this beautiful woman waltzed into this shit hole of a bar, the same bar I just happened to stop in that night for a face to face with my good friend, Dr. Buzz, who always showed up after a few scotches. This woman found me. It was the world's way of kicking me in the nuts and bringing me to my knees.

As I stood at the end of their table, stumbling over words, searching for a topic that would elicit some response from her, she kept playing with a salt shaker on the table. Rolling it around as I rambled on trying to find something that would spark her interest. She'd glimpse up at me as I towered over her and her friends, but she would not meet my gaze dead on. Her look didn't say go away, but it certainly didn't say sit down and make yourself at home, either. As hard as I tried to keep those amazing eyes focused on mine, she knew better than to allow me in. That would have given me too big of a clue as to how she felt about me. This woman was far too smart for that.

There was a ring on her finger with a soft blue stone that sparkled when it caught the dim light. I asked her if it was a gift from her boyfriend in a doltish attempt to uncover any competition I might have. She shook her head, "A gift from my father. For my birthday last year."

"Oh. Happy birthday, a year late," I responded with a goofy smile that sometimes passed for engaging under the right circumstances, which these weren't, "What did your boyfriend get you?"

One of her girlfriends, Gretchen, a big-boned girl with a hard stare, short temper, and a nasty attitude, piped up, "She's single, all right? But she's not looking, none of us are." And then, twisting the knife in my belly, she added, "Especially for a baboon's ass like you."

I think the reason Gretchen boiled my blood so badly was because if I were a woman, I would be an aggressive, smart-mouthed chick exactly like her.

Lucky for Gretchen, I didn't give a good goddamn what she thought. Gretchen pegged me as a big jerk, no surprise there. Good instincts. I recognized that Gretchen was the fire I'd have to walk through to get to the one I wanted. And if that's what it was going to take, I could survive any trash-talk she tossed in my direction. I was undaunted. And more than a little drunk. Besides, the beautiful girl smiled with a sedulous gaze that told me not to give up so swiftly. I sensed she thought I was just a big, harmless oaf unsuccessfully trying his best come-on. Usually, I was anything but harmless, but with her, I laid down my arms, ready to be taken hostage.

The longer I lurked around their table desperate to make a connection, the more blatant Gretchen's disdain for me became. And it rubbed off on Amy, the little brunette with boyfriend problems, because I wasn't paying her any attention. The two rode me hard, refusing to let me finish a sentence. I don't know what jerked a fat knot in my ass more, when Amy told me I reminded her of a strip club bouncer, or when Gretchen asked me if I had to take off my shoes to count to twenty.

"If she'll give me her phone number, I'll go away," I replied, not letting their venom shake me from my mission.

Her friends gave up on the hope that they could shame me into slithering my way back to the barstool I had crawled off of and decided to beat a hasty retreat to someplace with a more upscale clientele. As they slid out of the booth, I took the hand of the beautiful woman.

"Stay. Have a drink with me, please. I'll drive you home."

Gretchen and Amy traded sardonic rolls of the eyes. "Like that's gonna happen, Ted Bundy," Gretchen spouted off. "Should she supply her own duct tape and rope too?"

The beautiful woman only smiled, placing her hand on Gretchen's arm in an effort to silence her sarcasm. I wasn't sure she was doing it because she was interested in me or simply wanted to make an escape without any casualties.

"Do I at least get a name?"

"Tami."

"Do I get a last name?" I pressed.

"No offense, but how do I know you're not a stalker," she asked, which considering that I had cemented my hips to the lip of her table and wouldn't budge seemed a solid probability.

"I wouldn't sweat it, Tami," Amy fired into the conversation, "It's doubtful he could even read the phone book."

Tami refused to give me any other information. With her friends growing more belligerent by the second, I had to cut my losses and go for the Hail Mary pass. I borrowed a pen from one of the waitresses and scribbled my name and cell number on the back of a coaster.

"Please use this," I said, "A man's life could depend on it. Mine."

She laughed, jamming the coaster into her purse as she, Gretchen the Hun, and stink-eye Amy pushed a path from the table to the door and disappeared.

As I turned, everyone in the bar had spun around to watch me get shot down. They broke into applause, some laughing at me. I took a bow. "Fuck you, fuck you all very much." Normally when I crash and burn I'm not so accommodating. But because this woman held some weird mojo over me, I was actually in a good mood. All I could do was laugh at myself. As I sat back on my stool, I looked over at Dandy Dave, a car dealer who was as big a drinker as I and asked, "Did I actually utter, 'A man's life depends on it. Mine'??" Dandy Dave sniffed the air like a blood hound that had just uncovered a rotting corpse and looked away, shaking his head sadly. Whatever this virus was, it had already infected me so badly I was babbling the cringe-inducing lines of a hallucinating loser.

I grabbed my jacket off the stool and left Luther's. Pathetically, I had morphed into the guy I always poked fun at.

For modesty's sake I'd like to say I wasn't sure if Tami would call. But I believed she would. Not because I'm some phenomenal catch, but because there was no way in this world that she didn't know what I already knew. We were going to be together. Todd Cartwright and Tami Whatever-her-name-is. Straight up, there was no damn way I had experienced what could best be described as emotional electroshock, and she felt so little that she would blithely toss that coaster into the garbage.

Normally, I'm Mr. Right. For the Night. I'm not a guy who falls in love. Never in my thirty years had I experienced anything remotely resembling love. I cynically suspected love was a practical joke that poets and priests played on a naïve populace so they would propagate the species. One by one my few male friends were plucked from the pack, disappearing from my life when they tumbled into love. I couldn't understand what this was all about. Utterly amazing sex was the only reason I could value getting hitched. But none of the guys stated that that was the case. They were in love! Uh-huh. Right. Don't tell me about love, none of you sons of bitches would know love from a leper. I sure wouldn't. Well, actually I would. If your skin falls off it is leprosy. Other than that, you're on your own. Up until meeting Tami, if love had bitten me in the ass I would have crushed it and then stomped on it a few times just to make sure it wouldn't get back up.

But my heart had never spoken to me so clearly. Or maybe before that moment it never spoke up loud enough so that I could hear it over my penis. But there was something about this woman that I couldn't shake. Every time she entered my mind, which was about every seven seconds, I got both clammy and tingly at the same time, like a snarling stray that realizes it's just about to be shoved into the chamber for the big sleep. This was new. And I couldn't tell whether I should like it or be completely scared out of my mind.

Tami didn't call for two insufferable days. There were actually times I banged the cell phone off my desk, enraged that it hadn't rung. It's a miracle that it was functioning when she did call. The cell phone rang in the middle of a staff meeting, which interrupted my boss, George O'Neill, a man only a year older than me but who looked well into his forties.

"I gotta take this," I said swiftly, standing. "My Mom. Cancer."

What could he say after that? Besides, I was his most accurate analyst. For me it was more simple, common sense blended with a blind throw of the dart, but I seemed to hit more than I missed on gauging where there was money to be had. I bumped my way out of the meeting, right in front of George with apologies to my co-workers.

If I wasn't counting on a phone call from this woman, I would have turned the phone off. But like I said, I knew in my gut.

As cornball as it sounds, Tami's voice reminded me of honey. She never seemed to rush her words, as if every syllable she uttered delighted her. I hid in an alcove and talked to her for over an hour. Tami was at work. She worked in corporate for Macy's Department Stores in the Chicago area. Not so much because she loved the job but because she got great discounts.

"Every woman has her discount price," she laughed gracefully, reminding me not to take her too seriously.

Twenty-four, a Virgo (whatever that means in Zodiac-talk), she still lived in her father's house in Oak Park, a suburb a clear shot down the Eisenhower Expressway. In her father's home.

"You're a big corporate muckety-muck, how come you don't have your own apartment," I quizzed, believing most people in their twenties would cut off a limb rather than live with their parents unless they were slackers living in the basement, sleeping on a dilapidated pull-out sofa and playing in internet chat rooms all day.

"Family rule," Tami stated. "Unfortunately, I promised my father years ago that I would not move out until I get married. And he reminds me of that promise on a regular basis."

"So let's run off to Vegas and get hitched that way you can get your own place."

That got a laugh. Her laughter felt like I was breathing a relaxing sigh of relief as my body sank comfortably into an overstuffed chair.

Tami explained that she didn't normally hang out in bars. Especially a bar like Luther's. But her friend, Gretchen, thought it would be exciting to have a drink in a dive where no one knew them. Damn, I was liking that Gretchen more and more. In spite of being a mouthy bitch, she made one miraculous decision. And it played into my favor.

Surprising even myself, I was remarkably honest with Tami about who I was and what my life was about. I'm not sure why I was so forthcoming with this woman who with every fiber of my being I wanted to impress, but I felt an obligation not to lie. Feeling this profound, unexplained connection to her, I sensed she would see right through any crap. If this instantaneous desire for this woman was not going anywhere, I didn't want it to be because I was a liar. If this was just about hooking her into bed, I would have lied my ass off.

But this was different. She was different.

Tami exacted total truth. And as painful as some of my admissions were about my history, I was not going to sugarcoat it. From this first conversation, I set a precedent of what I wanted from her and what she could expect from me. My past was not a pretty picture. Especially to the fairer sex. I admitted that I had slept with many women. That I drank too much. That I got into fights. And I had both an attitude and a temper. And then I prayed that honesty would count for more than my behavior. If she could accept that, I knew that I would love this woman forever.

After laying myself bare, I asked her if I could see her, take her out to a great dinner, a movie, whatever she wanted. She laughed, again there was this honey that sparkled in my ear and kept my hope afloat. She agreed to a date but made it clear that there would be no movie, no ballgame, no museum. Tami preferred to talk. "I want to get to know you. A movie gives you the movie to talk about," she said. "It's too easy. You don't get to know the person."

I hadn't scared her off yet. Brave woman.

As stupid as it sounds, I hadn't felt like this since I was fourteen and Mary Jo Brownie agreed to be my first girlfriend. We sealed it with a kiss. I strutted about like a fat peacock, much to the jealous dislike of the other boys in my class, because she was the girl who had developed the largest breasts. And at fourteen, breasts are the most awesome constellation on a woman's body. I only had a vague conception what a stud was at that age, but I certainly knew what it felt like to be one. And here it was again, that same childish elation tickling my entire body.

And just as in the eighth grade, everybody I came into contact with noticed the change in my demeanor. For an asshole, I mellowed into a pretty bearable guy after meeting Tami. Even my co-workers in my analysts' bullpen complimented me on my "change in attitude." Hell, there was no change. What there was was a reason to get up in the morning other than making a paycheck. I felt like one of those cartoons where the big headed character sees some girl, and his head slaps wickedly side to side as his tongue and eyes bulge out, the steam coming out his ears to the sound of a train whistle. This woman had reduced me to Elmer Fudd.

We planned to meet at a small cafe in the city not far from where I worked. We could sit outside and talk under the stars. Unfortunately it was pouring rain, so Nature reminded me not to take anything for granted. I arrived first and asked the hostess for a booth. In the back. Away from the bar - just to be on the safe side. I was tense enough, and any time a bar and I are within spitting distance trouble isn't far behind. The hostess gave me a quick up and down, and spotting the rose in my hand, she smiled knowingly. "Lucky girl," she purred, as she led me past the bar to a booth in the back. I guess everyone knew. Or maybe it was the way I nervously passed the rose back and forth between my hands like a basketball player deciding whether to fake right and go left, or vice versa.

Time slogged along as I kept my eyes peeled on the door. The hostess sat me facing the door so I could spot Tami as she stepped in. I had this fear I would miss her entrance, she would look around the place, not see me, then quickly exit. I kept thinking what a dork I had become. Here I was sweating from my pits and crotch, my blood pressure heading north, my leg tapping the floor like I was sending out a Morse code signal, waiting like a loyal dog that senses the time its master returns home from work.

Fear that she was going to blow me off kept popping inside me like hot bacon grease. I imagined the conversation between Tami and her girlfriend, Gretchen.

"You can't be serious! You're not going out with that oaf," Gretchen would say, shaking her head, rolling her eyes, and huffing simultaneously.

Tami would make a sweet remark about how I was not the guy Gretchen thought I was. Even though Tami knew I was. And Gretchen had a pretty good sense I was.

"He's a pig. And all he's after is a night of sex. So if that's what you want, I'm sure he's your man and he'll be great. Just don't mistake that misfit for anything else, Tami."

"I am a pretty good judge of character," Tami would respond in my defense, "I just get a feeling about this guy."

"Me too," Gretchen would snap back, "he's one drunk night away from a prison sentence."

I hate when girls are right about me.

If I had to slip out of the booth with the rose in my hand and dart for the door, the hostess would look at me with pathos wondering what was so awful about me that a woman would stand me up. I would never make it past the bar. I would sit at the end, sullen and bruised, daring anyone to even look at me cross-eyed as I drank myself into oblivion.

Just as I'd worked myself up into a frenzy over being stood up, Tami stepped in, shaking the rain from her umbrella before turning. I felt my heart rip from my chest and lodge in my throat. I stood. Not because I was supposed to, but because my first inclination was to run to her. I was behaving like someone I'd never met before. Nor would like much if I had. What was it about this woman - a woman I hardly knew - that made me change my entire spectrum of human behavior? Maybe I was just too overwhelmed dealing with emotions jutting out of nowhere to make any reasonable sense of this. But I have the insight to trust. Go with it. Something inside me was telling me that this woman would be with me for the rest of my life.

If this was love, then I finally understood what all the excitement was about. And being as vain as I am, I was one hundred percent positive that what I was feeling was deeper, stronger, and better than any love anywhere. Ever.

Tami turned, her hair flipping around. Seeing me standing there, she smiled. And so did just about everyone else in the place. She had that kind of effect on people. The entire restaurant watched her move towards me. With every step she took, all the other people seemed to disappear into a haze, until it was only Tami and I.

But then I wigged out. I heard a voice telling me to run. Now! Get the hell out! Someone needed to slap me around good before these conflicting feelings ate me alive. My penis had been in charge for most of my life, and if I ever needed a second opinion, I always counted on my head to come through with an answer. A coup had taken over, and I was being held hostage by a different organ. One that had been often ignored. And it's scary when your captor doesn't speak the same language as you, but it controls all of your bodily functions. So here was my heart telling my lips to smile, my feet to stay put, and my penis to behave. And to my complete amazement, they all did.

As Tami had asked, we talked. For hours. I can't remember ever having a conversation that lasted that long with anyone. Dialogue isn't exactly my strongest asset. When it comes to sexual intercourse, I am on Plymouth Rock, but with verbal intercourse I'm lost in the Amazon, sinking in quicksand. Part of the problem is that I don't consider my life that interesting.

Unless I'm drunk. Or you are. Then I can spin my life until it sounds like I should be on some magazine's list of the fifty most fascinating people. Or at least fifty most fascinating intoxicated people. Most sober women accuse me of being self-opinionated, but hardly self-reflective. I am Joe Palooka from the wrong side of the tracks with a sad story that resembled every other wanna-be bad boy that I've ever known. People say that what you believe about yourself is its own self-fulfilling prophesy. Bullshit. For me it was the simple truth. You can dress up a turkey and call it a macaw, but it still gobbles and usually doesn't make it past Thanksgiving.

With that voice that entranced me, Tami drew things out I never spoke about. Much less laughed about. Talking about my parents hadn't made me laugh since I was a kid, and my brother and I hid among the dust bunnies under our beds, imitating them. Usually they would find us and whip our asses, but it was fun while it lasted. Even with sore asses, we would lay in bed and stifle teeters at their expense. For kids to know how pathetic their parents were, Mom and Dad had to be blatant losers with a constant track record of being life's also-rans. And mine were. But staring into Tami's amazing eyes with her dark lashes waving to me, nothing in my past or present seemed that devastating. In our first two conversations I had already confettied her with every piece of dirty laundry in my basket. And this girl didn't balk. If I had bigger balls I would have asked her right then and there to marry me. Then sweep her into my bed and, for the first time in my miserable life, actually make love to a woman.

I learned that Tami's mother had passed away from cancer when she was four. Her father had raised her. Her memories of her mother were vague and came more in smells and sounds than in anything she could actual tie to a solid image. The aroma of oatmeal and the bleach used to clean the floors always summoned up images of her mother. The fragrance of lilac, her mother's perfume, drew her back, as did the smell of crayons and Play-doh, the ting of a kitchen timer, and the quiver in Johnny Mathis's voice. Tami said she could barely remember what her mother looked like without glancing at a photo, but those scents and sounds placed her right back into mother's arms.

I knew I would marry this woman. No joke. My life had turned into some kind of twisted Harlequin romance. I knew the first time I laid eyes on her that I loved her. I knew the second time I saw her that I was going to spend the rest of my life loving her.

Head and penis, you better jump in here, because you are losing the war, boys. In fact, I think penis is turning traitor because he's liking this woman a whole lot too.

Around eleven-thirty she told me she had to get home. She had promised her father that she wouldn't stay out past midnight. And he would be waiting up. Her father, Harry, was protective, Tami said. Especially when it came to new guys. Laughingly, she warned me that her father didn't trust men. When I asked if she meant all men, she shook her head and grinned.

"Just the ones I date."

Without ever meeting him, I liked Harry. A woman this special needed protection. There are a lot of assholes out there that would try to take advantage of her. I could understand how leery he would be of most men's motivations in dating a sweet, beautiful woman. I've dated many. They should have been protected from the likes of me. If Tami gave me a chance, Harry would see that what was happening between her and I was different. Rare. If he loved her as much as I assumed he did, he would want her to be with a man who could protect her as much as he did. I was enlisting for that duty as soon as possible. If any other man so much as looked at her funny, I'd be all over him like a monkey on a cupcake.

The rain had slowed to a misty drizzle as I walked her to her Honda Accord. I noticed it was meticulously clean inside, unlike any other car of any other woman I had ever known. Most women's autos looked lived in. Her father, she explained. He took the car in once a week and had the car washed and detailed. The more tidbits I culled about Harry, the more I suspected I would eventually have to contend with uber-Daddy.

But if this girl's love was the prize, I was up for that challenge too. When I got the chance, I'd make Harry love me as much as I loved his daughter.

I opened her car door and let her step inside. She thanked me for a wonderful night and started the engine. I didn't ask her if I could see her again. I told her I was going to see her again. I was not letting her out of my sight without her giving me her phone number, so I could ask her out like a gentleman (another word seldom used when describing me, except, well, by me). She nodded and rattled it off quickly, smiling, testing to see just how badly I wanted it. I must have held a confused look because she quickly added, "In case you don't remember, it is in the book under my father's name, Harold Everett."

But the number was already emblazoned in every cell of my brain. Whatever information was pushed out to make room for it didn't matter.

I kissed her. Although not on the lips like I was desperate for, it was too soon, and I didn't want to take the chance it would give her second thoughts. I embraced her on the cheek near her neck, lingering close, breathing her in. The faint flavor of what was suddenly my favorite perfume filled my head. This was where I wanted to stake my claim, build my home, and live for the rest of my life.

Thanking her again, I shut the door and watched her drive away. As I strolled back to my car, wondering if anyone would think it odd that a man who was the size of a linebacker for the Bears was dancing by himself in the parking lot, it dawned on me that I hadn't touched a drink that night. Not even a warm-up scotch to relax. What an odd sensation. Sober on a weeknight. But I was higher than I had ever felt in my life.

POP GOES THE WEASEL

The romance raced into high gear. I certainly wasn't going to give her a chance to change her mind. Or even contemplate me deeply for that matter. My best shot with a special woman like Tami was to hit her like a defensive guard and keep driving her back until I had her tackled. If she discovered what I already knew, that there were a lot better guys out there that deserved a woman this unique, then I was hosed. No, the greatest assets I had in my arsenal to win this woman's heart were going to be relentless persistence and the blunt honesty that had not intimidated her. Luckily for me, those were two personal utilities that had never been overused in my lifetime, so I had a deep reserve of both waiting to be tapped.

What I was ill-prepared for was that Tami jumped into the relationship as openly as I did. She exploited both my honesty and my persistence to ensconce herself even deeper into my heart. That kept me completely off-balance. Especially at this precocious stage where I was tap-dancing overtime in an effort to keep her interested. My greatest fear was that she would get bored and politely dissipate into the ether, leaving me holding a phantom memory. But when Tami's hand slid over and picked up the check after our fourth date, explaining to me that she didn't feel when she was in a relationship that the man should pay for every meal, I felt my abs tighten as if they were ready for a punch.

Relationship? Did she actually use that word or was it simply a noun my mind shoved into place? She could have easily referred to it as "dating" but she didn't. She used the 'R' word, and my head felt like a melon that had fallen out of a grocery bag and rolled right under the tire of an oncoming SUV. The only time I could remember being as simultaneously excited and frightened was when I was thirteen, and for the first time while jerking off, I splattered a load across my bed. I didn't quite understand the power of it, but I liked it an awful lot.

I knew her girlfriends were working Tami hard not to get too involved with me. They still smelled trouble. And the stink was coming from me. There was nothing I could say or do that would change their minds. I could see it in their eyes every time we got together. The suspicion hung in their glares like wolves surrounding a lost lamb. All I could do was take hold of Tami's hand even tighter, keep her near me, letting them know that if they were going to try and pull her away from me it would get ugly. They had the upper avenue in every arena except one. Tami had my heart. And I'm sorry, just like at Macy's, once you wear it, there are no returns.

And most certainly if they were going to break it, they were going to pay for it.

After the sixth date - the sixth date and still no sex, which should demonstrate just how completely crazy in love I was with this woman - Tami actually let me pick her up at her home. It was going to be the night I met the infamous padre estupendo. By this time Tami had thoroughly cautioned me, quizzed me, and toughened me up for the gauntlet that was Harry Everett.

What I knew at this point was that he would not like me for a multitude of reasons. The main one being that Harry would consider me utterly unworthy of his daughter. But I was in fine company. "I could bring home Prince Harry and my father would want to know what he was going to do to support me," Tami sighed, something she did whenever she discussed the man that sired her. Harry exhausted her with his overprotection. Like someone smothering you with their body in the process of saving you from a fire. But none the less, Tami loved her father. She was acutely aware of what her Dad had sacrificed to make sure she had every opportunity in life.

As a Father, Harry Everett towered over mere mortals. As the father of the woman I was in love with, he was becoming a giant pain in the ass. And I hadn't even met him. When Tami first told me about Harry, he sounded like a man of solid judgment and concern in all matter labeled 'Tami'. But the more she let slivers of information eek out, the more she inadvertently chipped away at the monument I had erected in my head. Originally, I hoped Harry would love me for adoring his daughter. But I subsequently tempered my enthusiasm. By the day we were to meet, I cautiously trusted that he would give me an Ebert thumbs-up and whisper to Tami that it was all right if she kept seeing me in spite of my many hidden flaws.

I snuck out of work a few hours early that day so I could get ready. I needed to look my best. Iron my clothes, trim my sideburns, yank out those little hairs between my eye brows and on my ears. Nothing I had ever done in my life made me feel more like a girl than leaving work early to prepare for this night. My head kept telling me how loony all this was, and even my penis was a bit nervous, but my heart knew I had to make a good impression from the instant I walked in the door. My desire: to look sharp, almost militarily so. There was going to be nothing casual about this night, and I didn't want Harry to think I took dating his daughter as anything less than serious business. If this were any woman other than Tami, I would rather eat glass than put myself though this crap. Not a chance in hell. Just to piss off the girl's father, I would pull into the driveway and honk a few times, never stepping foot out of the car.

I was actually early when I pulled down her street. It was an endless row of attractive, middle class homes with ancient trees lining the avenue from both sides, offering a canopy of green. Exactly what I had expected. Even in this environment, Tami's father probably terrorized anyone who had a shaggy lawn or a grease spot on their driveway. Harry Everett's lawn was immaculately manicured. His walkway swept of any fallen leaves. The trim on the beige house painted a clean white. This image fit perfectly into the world I assumed Harry struggled mightily to maintain for his daughter. Though she had never used the word, it wasn't hard to assume that Tami was his princess. Harry Everett's daughter had been treated as exceptional since she was a little girl. Harry made sure she grew up believing that, and I'm sure this was part of the reason it came true. Tami believed in her own remarkableness. And she did so without an ounce of the vanity I suffered from. Honestly, I wasn't that extraordinary. I just treated myself that way.

The joy of Tami was that, in spite of having this strength instilled in her, she did not grow up a selfish brat like many people would have under the same circumstances. She was a willful woman, and most likely a headstrong child - growing up motherless, a female child would naturally assume pieces of that role no matter how the father compensates, or how many powerful female role models she is exposed to. Tami learned to be herself early and it carried over. And I learned this was not someone who could be talked into anything she didn't believe in. Many, if not most, women I had known could be seduced with one ruse or another, into doing just about anything I wanted. Like most guys, I fooled them into believing I was the special one in the relationship, and that they would have to acquiesce to me or move on. Hell, I once had a female boss doing tricks in bed, and she paid for all our meals and vacations. Women attempt to defend themselves against the male ego as best they can. But most are ill-equipped because they haven't been taught the same rules. Most girls are cultivated to play nice. Men play to win. Sounds quite simple, but once you mix in a couple spoonfuls of sexual politics, social roles, and kick-ass machismo, you're playing the game on a messy, muddy field. The men who are extremely adept at these dirty games often end up CEOs and movie stars. Or in prison. I proudly admit I am one of these guys. Hopefully one day I'll run my own business, because you won't be seeing my mug at the cineplex anytime soon, and I'd as soon jump off a building then let them stick me in prison for any length of time. It's only a woman who masters a substantial sense of self that is capable of standing her ground when a guy like this wants into her panties.

Tami grew up one of these women. It aided her all through school and in business. She didn't make it to corporate at Macy's at such a young age for nothing. Tami knew what she wanted and she went for it. Unlike many, Tami always used honey to accrue what she wanted. And damn, did it work well for her. It was almost as if people loved stepping aside for her because she was so sweet in her determination. But I was well aware she had strong boundaries. I memorized them very quickly and made sure not to cross those lines. Though with Tami, I never felt like I was competing to be on top. I simply knew who she was and completely respected that. I loved that she was not like the women I normally encountered. Tami told me early on she would sleep with me only when she was ready. If any other woman said that to me, the next thing she would realize was the door slamming as my ass flew past. Tami wasn't waiting for a ring on her finger - although if that was what she wanted, I would have been on bended knee in a heartbeat - but she wanted our first time to mean something. Translated, that meant when she was falling in love.

All I could do was wait for her to catch up because I was already there.

I drove around her neighborhood a few times, stopped a block from the house, and checked myself out in the rearview mirror. Earlier in the day I had bought a bouquet of lilies, her favorites, which sat beside me, as did a bottle of wine for Harry. I didn't know if he drank, but I made sure I purchased a pricey, well-known label so he knew I wasn't cheap. When it hit seven straight up, I pulled down to the Everett house and parked in front. Stepping out of my Cherokee Laredo, I straightened out my shirt and said a quick prayer that Tami was ready. I didn't want to be left alone with superfather for too long. I didn't want to give him time for anything more than cursory conversation. Box scores, cars, the Bears. I had versed myself well enough to chatter a few minutes about any of these. But I wasn't there for any other reason than to get him to like me enough to give Tami that parental nod, and then get out the door with his daughter. If he wanted to know anything more, I'd prefer he ask Tami. After we were married.

Before I could even ring the bell, the door opened. The picture I had in my head of Harry Everett couldn't have been more miscalculated. I envisioned a tall, imposing man, with squared shoulders and rope-like muscles, who stood uncomfortably straight, with a short graying buzz cut so that each hair stood at attention like a unit of soldiers. He would be fastidiously dressed in a crisp, white shirt, with the top button buttoned and creased khaki pants. The Harry that had been described to me didn't seem the type to ever be caught anywhere in jeans or shorts.

And here he was in front of me. Or more aptly, beneath me. Over a head shorter and older than I imagined. He was crawling into his sixties, a journey that most of his hair didn't make. The wisps that were left on top were longish and kinky, as if reaching out for friends who were no longer there. The lines around his eyes were deep and cautious. And I gathered from the way he winced at me that he actually wore glasses most of the time. His eyes were brown and unremarkable. Time had dulled them. This was the man who fathered the woman I was completely knocked out by? This is part of her genetic code? Her mother must have been a major babe because I couldn't spot a single feature on this guy that was even in the neighborhood of what anyone would consider attractive. Nor that Tami had inherited. Thank God.

"I saw you drive up," he said as he reached out his hand to me. Instinctively I took it and shook. The grip was strong, but his hand was small and he worked to get his fingers around my mitt before he pumped it a few times.

"It is good to meet you, Mr. Everett," I said, relieved that he wasn't some Homeric titan of a man. "Tami has talked so much about you, I almost feel like I know you."

I handed him the bottle of Merlot which he peered at for a moment, turning it around in his hand. "Not much of a wine drinker," he stated flatly, "but come in anyway."

What was he expecting, gold, frankincense, and myrrh? If he didn't drink wine then he could re-gift the damn thing. It's not Boones Farm, for Christsake. He'd look classy showing up somewhere with that bottle of vino, which I was sure from viewing the little man in front of me, was not a word often associated with Harry Everett.

Harry plopped the bottle on the table in the foyer as if to emphasize his indifference, and then his dark, murky eyes lasered in on my face. I forced a smile as I stood there, awkwardly, waiting for some kind of indication from him whether this was the end of the line or we were going to make ourselves comfortable in the tidy living room. Harry nodded, his gaze never leaving my face. He smiled. Crooked, with a medieval curl to his lips that pressed against his teeth. That was when I felt the hair on the back of my neck stand up.

Worse than not liking me, I sensed that Harry knew me. Knew who I was as a man. My less than lustrous past with women, with booze, with life. I'm sure Tami hadn't told him. She wouldn't have chanced that with the cautious prig she described. No, I felt that Harry could size people up both quickly and accurately. Especially men. Most especially men wanting to date his daughter.

As I peered down at him, his glare cautioned me from taking his diminutive status for granted; he would crack me upside the head with a hammer and chop me up for a snack just as soon as look at me if I got out of line. Then his shoulders relaxed as if to say, "I'm not worried. You won't be around long. I'll make sure of it."

I heard once that Chihuahuas will form feral packs and kill off the weaker of the group and eat them. I was sure Harry had escaped the litter after dining on the rest of his clan.

We stood in the tiny, spotless foyer, nearly on top of one another, and Harry didn't speak. I actually felt heady, like I was going to keel over and crush the midget. But if I passed out, this worm might grab a dinner fork, shove it under my eye lid, and perform an amateur lobotomy on me.

Harry knew that he had me off balance. Whatever minor victory I had won by being more physically imposing, cramped up and would never finish this race. I may have had a spectacular jump out of the starting gate, but in a blinding move he had passed me and I was sucking on his dust.

Harry turned, again without a word, and waddled into the living room. He didn't ask me to follow, didn't give me a wave; he just moved to the sofa and plopped down.

"Your name is Tom, correct?" Harry quizzed, once he was comfortable.

"No sir. Todd," I said with a smile, "Todd Cartwright." I was still standing in the foyer like Boo-Boo the Fool, uninvited into his living room.

"Tom, Todd, Tom, Todd," he muttered a few times as if he had confused me with the guy who repairs his car or his mailman. "Hmmm," he finally added, "I thought Tami said it was Tom." Then his eyes lit up and he snapped his fingers with an eye-narrowing nod. "I remember Tom. Tom, Tom, Tom. Poor Tom. You don't have to worry about him. He's no longer in the picture," Harry remarked, in a queer manner that suggested to my nervous imagination that he had Tom buried under the floorboards of the house, along with all of Tami's other past suitors.

"Sit," Harry finally commanded, pointing toward a stiff backed chair that sat at the end of a long coffee table. To me, it looked like an upholstered electric chair. All that was missing was the straps and metal helmet that he could place on my head to fire a few volts through my body.

I sat, holding the lilies. For the longest time his mean eyes sized me up silently, no doubt wondering how much effort it would take to get a man of my height and weight under the floorboards. I glanced at my crotch to make sure that my zipper wasn't down and sucked in a deep breath to make sure the mints I had popped in the car were still working. I had been dating since I was fourteen but never in my life had any girl's father overwhelmed me with discomfort as Harry proceeded to do. I thought I knew all the ins and outs of handling parents. What to say, when to smile, how to present myself. But I was out of my league when it came to this weird game of silences, slow remarks, and chattering to oneself. Even though I innately knew Harry was manipulating me, I couldn't capture him in anything specific. Maybe he was simply odd. Dottering. Slightly daft. But my better judgment kept telling me that he was far more devious than that. Harry had been protecting his daughter for a lot longer than I had been dating. Experience counts. He wanted me off balance. He wanted to squeeze my nuts and measure at what point I begged for mercy.

Or ran.

He finally spoke again, announcing that Tami would be out in a minute. "Just like her mother was," Harry muttered, looking off to the left at nothing in particular as best I could tell. "Late, late, late. Always running a few minutes late getting ready."

I suddenly flashed back sixteen years, waiting for Mary Jo Brownie, my date to the junior high school dance. While she was upstairs making sure the curl in her hair was just right, I was downstairs with her old man who sternly warned me about the dangers of alcohol and trying anything more than a goodnight kiss with his daughter. Little did he imagine that that night I would get my hand down her panties. And three weeks later, she was the first girl I coaxed into a blowjob in her bedroom, while Mr. Brownie slept down the hallway.

Harry's daughter was too old for him to have to lecture me on the perils of drinking or kissing. And if Harry knew his daughter at all, and I suspected he did, he knew she was powerful enough to say when and where. No, Harry's plans were far more insidious, and he eyeballed me like a pit bull leering at the master's pork chop, just waiting for a chance to swipe it off the plate. He was going to pull the wings off this fly while we waited for Tami. And enjoy it. Bye-bye, Tom, Todd. Nice having you. Next contestant please.

Harry took a deep sighing breath, not unlike the breath that Tami took each time she talked about him. With absolute disinterest, he launched into questions. Starting with the usuals, what I did, where I worked, where I lived. Any guy, anywhere, who has ever picked a woman up at her parents' home can knock these creampuffs out of the park, and jog through the victory lap as he waves to the cheering crowd. Foolishly, I let my guard down believing that his behavior was a bit loony but entirely benign. His tired face nodded as I answered each question quickly, but with enough joviality to keep things pleasant. Maybe this wouldn't be too bad if Harry gathered that I had come in peace.

But then he detonated the bomb, and I was pierced by shrapnel of all kinds. Before I could duck and roll I was pinned against the wall.

"I just want to tell you, Tom...Todd," Harry started in his vague, flat tone, "that my daughter is very important to me. And when she says 'no' I say 'no'. And it means no. No, no no. You're a big kid, nice looking, I'm sure you don't have trouble dating. Am I correct?"

I nodded my head with a shrug, unsure of exactly where this was going. Harry leaned toward me, his head going down so he had to look at me from the top of his snake eyes. Suddenly those blank eyes flooded with a subterranean fulmination intended to disable me. The whole milquetoast father routine was an act. And I walked into it blindly. He cracked me hard.

"I'm sure you don't even have trouble getting a piece of ass when you want it. Do you?"

I paused, my mind spinning in overdrive, like the wheels of a stock car at the beginning of a race. Not about what to say but about what would be best for Harry to hear.

"Well, I don't really look at it that---"

"My daughter IS NOT a piece of ass. I don't want you to ever think of her that way. Are you and I on the same page?"

I tried to respond. He didn't let me.

"If you treat her like a piece of ass," Harry hammered at me, no longer nebulous, no longer innocuous. "I will, repeat, WILL kill you a thousand times. My daughter was raised with dignity, and no big, lumbering, pretty boy is going to swagger into my home and think he's going to treat my daughter with any disrespect!"

"I haven't," I forced out, jamming the words between his.

"And you won't. Ever! I love my daughter more than my own life. And if you ever hurt her, do anything to cause her pain, I will, repeat, WILL hurt you. I will cause you so much agony you will wish you were never born. You will beg me to kill you just to end the torture. If I go to jail for it, so be it. I'm older, it won't bother me. But I'll make sure you won't bother her ever again. Is this something we are both clear on?"

"Yes, sir."

What am I saying? No, not 'yes sir!' I meant to say "fuck you." "Fuck you straight to hell." Why am I putting up with this shit from this sorry excuse for a garden gnome? I should have stood up and clobbered him on the head with my fist. This nutbag was obviously demented. Goddamn! Am I already that whipped by this girl that my feet have turned to clay?

Harry sat back on the sofa, looking like an ugly child in his first big boy chair. The assault was over but I could see in his eyes the war was anything but. The shitheel wanted me to grab my lilies and hightail it for the door. And for a brief moment, I thought I would. This loon job was scary crazy. I didn't want him in my life. Sooner or later this rat bastard would come at me with a chainsaw while I slept, slice my Achilles' tendons so I couldn't run, then slowly turn me into a Thanksgiving turkey, trimming off piece after piece, stopping only to revive me if I passed out, so I could feel every second of it.

If Tami hadn't walked into the room at that moment with her wide smile that seemed to throw me a life vest, I seriously believe I would have told Harry to stick the bottle of Merlot up his ass and bolted. It may have taken some doing but I would have figured out a way to convince her to see me on the sly. Hell, I couldn't be the first and only guy that Harry had kamikazed. Otherwise this woman would have been off the market long before I came along trying to weasel my face into the family photos.

Tami appeared almost relieved that I was still there, as if she knew that her whack job of a father was boyfriend-icidal and that I was the first guy ever to stick around this long. "Hey there," she said as she stepped up to me. I stood, but was struck by a massive wave of fear. I couldn't kiss her on the lips in full view of Charlie Manson's equally crazy cousin. I swiftly grabbed the flowers and brought them up between us. She didn't seem to notice that I was avoiding kissing her, as her eyes warmed even more at the sight of the lilies.

"Let me put these in water before we go," she said as she headed off to the kitchen before I could stop her, again leaving me alone with psycho-dad. I wanted to grab her and scream, "Don't leave me here with HIM," but I could hear how that would sound in my head, and I wasn't ready to appear fearful and pathetic, even though that's how I was feeling.

Now I had nowhere else to look but at Harry Everett, so I had to turn and glance at him again.

"She's my only daughter and I love her," he said, standing up, his puny size easing my nervous ire only slightly. "I want you to know where I stand now so it doesn't have to turn into something ugly later on. It wasn't meant as a threat."

Yeah, right. If you knife someone a dozen times don't plead self-defense.

I walked out without another word, stopping only to shake Harry's hand but refusing to look him in the eye. Wimpy, I know. But I was with a woman that I adored, and I didn't want that bastard to ruin the evening by prolonging the encounter another minute.

I debated telling Tami what had happened. She didn't ask. So far she had been nothing but direct with me, so I had to assume that she didn't know what a psycho her father was or she would have given me a heads up, or at least a high five for enduring little Atilla long enough to make it out the door with her hand in mine. I knew that a woman this special had to have a string of guys chasing after her. It just made sense. But when she informed me that she didn't get asked out that often, and if she did it usually ended after a couple dates, red flags went up. Now it was all crystal clear. One by one, prospective suitors had been terrorized by the gnome under the bridge, the hellish gate keeper that threatened to de-nut them if they so much as looked at his daughter the wrong way. Tami lived in the dark to her father's menace. And she was continually left wondering why guys never called her back. For most guys it wasn't worth it. For the others, they were probably too scared to attempt to see her again. Or even call. But I knew this woman and I were destined to be together, and if it meant suffering through a fan full of crap from the lunatic that spawned her, then I would put on a helmet and goggles and he could let it fly.

At this point I was in no position to lay down the law to Tami: it was either me or her father. One of us had to go. One day, though, after I firmly held her heart next to mine, she would have to choose. And I was already relishing that day.

All night I was so pissed off it caused me to itch. I thought I was breaking out in hives. But I couldn't finesse the conversation to rip on her old man. I would wager my every nickel in my 401 K that the rat bastard was going to trash me before my taillights disappeared down his neat, little block. He would cut me to ribbons, tie me to rocks, and sink me in cement. I could hear his nasally voice whining, "He'll hurt you. He'll cheat on you. He's scum." All of which may have been true with just about any woman in the world other than his daughter. But I couldn't shake that voice out of my head. My usual attitude about situations like this was to say 'fuck it' and not sweat what some chick's old man said about me. Not this time. For the first time in my life, I did care, goddamn it. And I was sweating because this guy held a card I couldn't trump. I hated someone holding this advantage over my head like the Sword of Damacles. At this early stage, his opinion counted for more points than mine. I would have to suffer through the napalm he spread over my village and try to come up with an antidote for the poison he pumped into her ear. I always enjoyed a good fight. And though I'd lost a couple, I'd never had my ass handed to me.

This was shaping up to be a massacre.

Tami sensed my moody distraction and clung tightly to my side. I loved that. She didn't know what was irking me, but it was her way of telling me she was there for me. Maybe she smelled my desperation to keep her and wanted to reassure me that it would take more than her father to kill what we had between us. Maybe she recognized how much I really did love her. Feeling her beautiful, lithe, body curve into my hulkish frame exactly as it should emboldened my belief that we were made for each other. We just fit.

"Do you want to tell me?" Tami asked, her fingers entwining with mine.

Again, I thought briefly about blathering on about her old man, literally biting the inside of my cheek to stop myself. As much as I feared losing this woman, I could hardly badmouth her father. Even if it were all true.

As I shook my head silently, Tami nodded.

"I won't push," she said, looking directly into my eyes, her hand settling on mine, her fingers wrapping around my wrist, as if she wanted to feel how fast my pulse was racing. "You're entitled to a few secrets, Todd. But whatever it is that's bothering you, and I know something is, I want you to know I'll listen."

All I wanted to do at that moment was dive over the table and kiss her.

After dinner, I debated whether or not to drive straight to my place and keep her safe with me. Away from the toxic prick who would undoubtedly try and screw this up. But how could I warn her that a snake was curled up inside her front door, ready to strike? God, this was killing me. I wasn't used to keeping my mouth shut. I wasn't even used to thinking before I spoke. I usually just let it fly and mopped up the mess later.

As we kissed that night, I let my heart do the talking and trusted that she would sense the love and fear bleeding together inside me. These feelings had brawn, and I had to believe that she felt their innate strength. If I was going to hear, "I don't think we should see each other again," the next time I called then I wanted her to know that she was breaking up with a man who would give her the world. I broke the kiss and looked into her eyes.

She touched my face and asked again, "Are you sure you don't want to talk about it?"

I took her delicate face in my hands and smiled. "You're the best thing that's ever happened to me," I said softly. Even though I wanted to scrape her father off the bottom of my shoe, I had to respect everything he had done for this woman. "We'll talk tomorrow," I said after kissing her again. She nodded with a loving smile, silently conveying to me that whatever it was it would be all right. She would be there.

I wished I could believe that once the door shut and she disappeared inside her home. His home.

As I walked back to my car, I felt eyes burrowing into the back of my head. Turning, I glanced at the house. Harry was standing in his bedroom window, staring out. He wanted me to know he had waited up. That he would be having a Come-To-Jesus talk with Tami. And I would be the only entree on the menu. I fired him one more glare, our eyes connecting, before he dropped the curtain. I got into my Laredo and drove away, completely unsure of where I stood with this woman who possessed my soul.

I wanted to do nothing but drive to the nearest watering hole, plop my ass on a stool, and flip my credit card onto the bar. But I didn't. I shot home and fell onto the sofa with ESPN. Highlights of some NASCAR race. Nothing numbs the mind faster than watching cars hypnotically circle a track, yahoos cheering from the stands as they wait for someone to crash.

The next day I stayed home from work. I couldn't drag my ass out of bed. I assumed that Harry had irreparably tainted our relationship, and I was going to suffer from a severe case of emotional ptomaine. It was bad enough that love had me by the balls and was squeezing. Now I had to endure this too.

I lied in bed and stared at the TV, flipping through talk shows. I imagined myself on one of those circus events, tearfully telling America how Harry had deliberately, and with gleeful malice destroyed my only chance at love. The audience would applaud sympathetically as the host handed me a tissue to wipe my self-pitying tears. Then they would haul Harry out to the boos of the rowdy studio crowd. He would taunt them with a cruel smile while they hooted at him. But Harry would laundry list my past sins. My nightly drinking binges. My obnoxious behavior. Rudeness. Bullying. How I left good girls who fell under my spell tearful, broken, man-haters. How I had banged every tramp in Chicago in an endless parade of one-nighters. The crowd would turn on me viciously when Harry pleaded with them to not let me hurt another woman. Especially his precious daughter.

Then I would pick up a chair and crack him across his weasely face before the show's bouncers wrestled me to the ground. It wouldn't win my case, but Harry would have a chair imbedded in his head, and I would feel a whole lot better.

The phone rang about noon. It was the girl at the office who took my messages. I would tell you her name but there is a new girl almost every other week, so I stopped trying to keep up with it. She told me Tami had called, and that she wanted me to call her back. It was urgent. I didn't even say goodbye before hanging up and rapidly dialing Tami's work number.

"Where are you, I was worried?" she asked, relief and concern melting in her voice.

I told her that I hadn't felt like dealing with work headaches that day. Which made it like every other day only more. Tami said she had called several times but no one explained that I wasn't in until the fifth call. And then they only stated that I couldn't be reached. It scared her, so she left an urgent message. I laughed. Not because it was funny, but because the worry in her voice sent that hot fear bubbling up inside me into remission. I wanted to jump up on the bed and dance.

Tami asked if I was sick. "If you were I'd bring you some soup," she added after I had prematurely said 'no.'

"Then I'm sick. I'm dying," I corrected myself. "Bring soup. Bring a blanket. Bring yourself and keep me warm."

I could feel her smile through the phone. She told me she only had fifty minutes for lunch and then asked my address. After I told her, she said, "I'll be over in ten minutes. I've been dying to see your condo and this doesn't give you much time to clean."

Or shower. Or shave.

I bolted off the bed and quickly stuffed all the clothes lying around the bedroom into the closet. I wasn't an absolute slob so my place, though not tidy, was relatively clean. I raced to the shower and was out in under five minutes. Shaving wasn't going to happen. I slipped on a pair of jeans and a T-shirt, and then quickly straightened up the living room and kitchen before the doorbell rang.

Tami stood there, a bag in hand. Smiling. I wanted to grab this girl in my arms and never stop kissing her. I had been rescued from the lion's den of self-inflicted mental torture. God, the tricks your mind plays on you when you feel this intensity over a woman. This was so new to me I had no ability to keep it in check.

As I let her in, her eyes searched the place, absorbing all the details. I took her on the quick tour...not that there was a lot to see. But she didn't care about the space. For Tami, being there, seeing how I lived took her one more step into my world. Our lives were blending together. She nodded at every room, never speaking until I was done with the mini-tour. Then she smiled widely and said that it was exactly how she had envisioned my home. "It's so you," she added.

"Is that a compliment?" I asked, not sure whether I wanted to know.

Striding through my living space, Tami spread her arms. "Black leather sofa across from a flat screen TV. Two leather chairs. Framed poster art and a coffee table." She moved to my bedroom door again, glancing in and smiling. "A king size bed and another TV sitting on the dresser."

"With surround sound," I added.

"With surround sound," she repeated, before walking to the entrance to my tiny kitchen. "I'll bet you whatever you want, Todd, that there is no solid food in your refrigerator--"

"Yes there is," I piped in quickly.

"You didn't let me finish," Tami held up a finger to silence me. "No solid food that is not growing a fur coat."

All I could do was grit my teeth and grin. "Damn," I sniffed. "I knew I should have cooked some chicken the other night instead of ordering Chinese. We'd be getting naked right now."

Tami broke up laughing and ran over to me, landing a long kiss on my lips.

"I know you better than you think I do. You're such a guy. A total guy," she bellowed with laughter.

Again, I wasn't sure what she meant by that, but I decided since she was smiling I'd take as praise.

Tami had stopped by a deli and gotten us chicken soup on the off-chance that I wasn't telling her the truth about not feeling ill. "My father always tells me he's fine when he's not," she said.

Normally with an opening like that and with just about any other woman, I would have punched in a zinger just to lay my opinion of her father out on the table. But at that moment he was the last person I wanted to talk about. It was bad enough he had burrowed into my brain and was gnawing at my better sense. But I had a balm for my affliction. Tami was there. In my home. With me. And she had come bearing gifts.

As we sat on the living room sofa, facing each other, soup cups in our hands, I relaxed. All the mind games I'd played over the previous twelve hours were figments of my imagination. Caring for someone deeply seems to come with a side order of self-doubt and psychological misery. And I'm sure that that is exactly what Harry wanted. He knew that if he scared the bejesus out of me, it would fester. The infection would spread to my brain and I would end up delirious. Good call, Harry. You sneaky cockroach. But what you didn't count on was Tami being here, in my home. She was the shot of penicillin. Even more, she had crossed that magical line, making herself a part of my domain. She was hungry to know more about me. To get deeper into who I was. And believe me, if a woman this incredible wants to know more about you, you feel unequaled.

I can't remember ever feeling that honestly good about myself.

Cognizant that the ground underneath me was more compact than I expected, I took a shot at uncovering whether or not Harry had said anything derogatory about me. Maybe he wasn't as hellish as I had assumed. He was simply a father who loved his sweet daughter. Maybe the speech was standard text. When you have a baby girl at the hospital, they give you these speeches in a bound book and tell you to memorize them for the future. I could understand why Harry would worry about Tami. When I have a sweet, little daughter, one day, my first stop will be the gun store. I guess Harry didn't own a gun. Against me, he owned a bigger weapon. His daughter.

"So," I led in as I slurped up a few noodles, "I got the sense your Dad didn't really like me much."

Tami burst into a loud peel of laughter. From the laughter's ring it sounded as if maybe I had said something completely out of left field, that I couldn't have come up with anything more absurd. Harry loved me! He knew I was a man who could protect and love his daughter like no one else!

I laughed with her, taking a reinvigorated breath, realizing I had blown this Harry thing ridiculously out of proportion.

"Didn't like you," her voice rose in a question, not a statement, "he HATED you."

I gulped hard, but there was no soup in my throat. Just my Adam's apple which I nearly swallowed. The blood rushed into my face and broke me out into an immediate sweat. Then it drained away just as quickly, leaving me with a shiver.

"As soon as I walked in the door," Tami continued in a chuckling lilt, never stopping for a breath, as if this were the funniest thing that had ever happened to her, "he was standing there in his bathrobe and slippers, this deep furrow in his brow, insisting over and over how wrong you were for me. I told him he didn't know you, but my father thinks he knows everybody. He said he knew men and he could tell that you were an example of the worst kind."

I could only hate the bastard that much more, but admittedly, Harry's instincts were keen.

"He doesn't want me seeing you anymore," Tami continued, as I felt my heart ping-pong off my rib cage like a pinball machine that had short circuited. "All the way through changing for bed, brushing my teeth, washing my face, he kept on about it. You don't know my father. He can be relentless when it comes to stuff like this."

What? Trashing me? Ruining my life?

"Finally I kissed him, said, 'thanks for being concerned' and went to bed."

Wow. That's all I could jumble together in my head. Wow. Three letters and luckily two of them were the same. So I had been sitting with the enemy. Evil incarnate. I am shocked he didn't brick up Tami's bedroom while she slept to keep her away from me. Then it hit me like a foul odor.

"Are you breaking up with me?" I blurted out, desperately needing her to throw me a life buoy before I went down for the last time.

Again, that laugh. "Are you kidding?" Tami smiled wider than I had ever seen her do before. "My father is the worst judge of men. He doesn't see what I see. The fact that he hated you so much only proves how right I am about you. Todd, I'm not going anywhere. You're the most wonderful man I've ever met."

I almost glanced around the room to see if there was someone else named Todd standing in the corner. Granted, I've got a fairly vaulted opinion of myself, but I couldn't imagine that I was the best guy this girl had ever met. Maybe she does see past my excesses. Can grasp the potency of the emotions she brings out in me. I needed a moment to catch my breath. Everyone around this phenomenal woman has warned her off of me, most painting me as some sort of omen of the Apocalypse, but she was still here delicately running her hand over my fingers one by one.

"I want you to come to dinner Saturday night at the house," Tami exclaimed, "I'm cooking dinner for you and my father."

Whoa!

Dinner. Me. The hateful troll. Her trapped in the middle. This could get dirty. And Tami would be pulled from both sides until we ripped her arms off like two kids fighting over a rag doll.

"I don't think that's a good idea," I let slip sheepishly, trying not to hurt her feelings, only skating across the upper layer of how wrong I thought it would be to put me in a room with her father so soon. Because all I could imagine at that moment was me bloodying him badly for sticking his weasel nose into the middle of my relationship with Tami.

"It's not only a good idea," Tami smiled, "it's the only idea."

Tami explained that her father was never going to see what she saw in me if I avoided him. She loved her father and admitted having "feelings" for me. I sensed her optimism that this idea would bring us all closer together. But I didn't share it. Harry may have known me. But I also knew him. He was going to pull out every piece of heavy equipment at his disposal to fuck with me. To make me look bad in front of Tami. Harry couldn't wait to point to me and announce to his daughter, "I told you so." Harry was a pro. He would slice his way under my skin until I went berserk. Little did he know just how near the edge of sanity I already stood.

"I'm going to show my father he's dead wrong about you," Tami reassured me.

No, actually he's dead right about me. But not where you're concerned.

"He's scared," she added, trying to make me feel better. "He knows how much I care for you. For the first time ever, he's got competition."

Competition. Great. That's exactly how I wanted the snarky son of a bitch to view me. If he wanted to arm wrestle, now that would be a competition. If he wanted to run a 440, or a mile, I'd take him on. If he wanted to see who was better at division, could hold their hand over a flame the longest, could spit the furthest, I was up for it. But how do you measure someone's love? How do you vie for affection against someone else when your loves are completely contrasting shapes and sizes?

Aware that I couldn't say no, I mumbled, "Sure. Sounds great." And then Tami asked one favor. "Just be yourself."

Yeah, that had charmed the shit out of the Hobbit the first go-around. Tami didn't have to worry; I didn't know how to be anyone else. But right now, it seemed that being anybody else was a safer bet.

THE FLAVOR OF QUICKSAND

Loving Tami with all my heart couldn't blind me to the reality that this face to face over pasta was a seriously flawed notion. Where Tami imagined a love fest with Harry and me holding hands in prayer and maybe singing a chorus or two of Kumbaya, I forecasted two men rolling around the dining room floor, knocking over everything in their destructive path, as they wrestled each other for control of the only sharp knife in the room.

If Harry had his way, dinner would be an excruciating experience for me. I couldn't fathom the depth of his torment over having me in his daughter's life. What distance would he travel to prevent me from anchoring myself to her? It is not much of a revelation that Harry's attentiveness to his daughter bordered on obsession. Did I say bordered on? Hell, Harry dove into the pool of obsession with a triple reverse in the pike position. I didn't know much about Harry. But I did know that his campaign to drive the prince of unworthiness from my quest for his daughter's heart would be endless.

But if he thought I was going anywhere quietly, Harry was about to face off with a junkyard dog. This battle would be waged until one of us ended up with the other's head in his jaws. Harry's opening salvo to wreck this relationship hadn't worked. But in that little mind of his he was already cultivating plan B. And C, and D. I had to be ready for anything.

I prepped for the obvious. He could grill me on past girlfriends. Worse yet, it wouldn't be much of a challenge for Harry to unearth a woman or two--or three--that I had balled and never called again. There were a lot of them. Inviting them to join us for dinner would make for an interesting evening. Fortunately, Tami and I traveled in different circles. Meeting her at Luther's was a fluke, a blessed act of fate. I racked my brain trying to recall any woman that I had slept with who could be connected to Tami in any way. Thankfully, Chicago is a big, fat city. Though I am sure many of my past conquests weren't but a few degrees separated from the woman I love, I didn't believe any were close enough to cause me a severe case of the sweats. Beyond the array of one-night stands, there were a few bars I'd trashed during drunken fights and guys I'd sent to the hospital who had a bone to pick with me. Would Harry dig? How far would he search? Sad to say, it would not be hard to prove to a jury of my peers that I was as big a sack of shit as he believed I was.

But the forewoman on the jury had the only voice that counted.

Saturday, Tami spent the entire day in the kitchen preparing the feast she intended to feed myself and her father. If she had any concern that the evening wouldn't be perfect, it wasn't in her voice when she spoke to me that day. Perhaps she planned to dump a little Vallium into the sauce to keep things mellow? I wondered if she had taken all the expensive breakables out of the dining room. If we were dining with plastic utensils, I would know what she really thought the chances of a peaceful evening were.

Tami always believed the ancient myth that food created a common ground for humans to gather and share. And she was fairly certain that both her father and I were human. For centuries, even rival warriors sat together at the same table and broke bread, often before they killed each other, but sometimes it's better to just ignore facts. In her heart, Tami, an amazingly non-cynical woman, hoped against hope to please us both and give Harry and myself 'us' time.

Like two cats in a bag.

I will forever be in awe of Tami's optimism. I don't have an ounce of it. Where she saw the glass as half full, I wanted to know which son of a bitch had had the balls to drink out of my half-empty glass. Maybe her outlook came from having a tyrannical father who sheltered her from life's harsher worries. And if she and I were to carry our relationship forward, I would step in and make sure that the world's hurts were never laid at her doorstep. I had never met anyone in my life with a purer heart. And that is something I sincerely wanted to protect with my whole being, because I knew how rare it was in the world. Rare not only to see the goodness in her, but her belief that everyone holds goodness within them. If Harry and I could agree on one thing, it would be that Tami needed to be protected against all the creeps in the world. And there were a hell of a lot. Hell, I knew half of them by name. Simply put, I feel most people in the world are full of shit and shouldn't be trusted. Tami was the first person in my life I felt I could trust implicitly. And that included my parents. I knew Tami was not out to hurt me, and it felt strangely wonderful to have that in my life.

As corny as it sounds she really had made me a better man. I laughed at lines like that when I heard them in the movies or in a wedding toast. Couldn't happen. No one had that kind of power over another soul. But for the first time in my life it became absolutely clear to me. Without her in my life, I'd have had no desire to be a good person. I functioned well enough being a jackass. But Tami gave me reason. You may call that a breakthrough. In actuality it's a fucking miracle.

In theory, Tami was correct. Harry and I would sooner or later, someday, in this lifetime, have to sit down in the same room with each other. Although I would have preferred the meeting to take place at his funeral. I feared sitting across the table from Harry at this point in my relationship with Tami. Wriggling around inside me was this gigantic apprehension that this terrific girl would get spooked. With enough impetus from her father or evidence that I was even less of a man than I had already copped to, Tami would shut me down and move on. I couldn't shake the very real itch that Harry still had a vote over my fate. It was no secret that if given the opening, he would feed me to the lions.

While I was ready for the obvious and aware there were hidden icebergs below the surface, I wasn't sure I could navigate through them. The more I prepared myself, the more I felt completely clueless as to how to play this. I was suddenly back at my first football game my freshman year in high school. Since I was big for a freshman, and faster than almost everyone in the high school, the varsity took me. My inaugural game, I was thrown in at linebacker against a team that had been together for four years. I didn't know my ass from my elbow. Well, at least until after I played. My ass was handed to me, and my elbow was what was broken.

I needed coaching from a professional because I was unaccustomed to caring what others thought about me. And since I had concern about what Tami thought, I had to have regard for what her slippery father said about me too. I was not versed in caring, and it altered everything about me. Did I sit silently at dinner and not say anything if he started badmouthing me? Did I get together before the meal to try and come to some peaceful middle ground? When he snarked out the first remark, did I level the prick? What does someone do when they are worried about losing someone they love? And how come I had never learned how to deal with this situation before?

As I drove over to her house I kept hearing Tami's words ringing in my head. Be yourself. Be yourself. And then it hit me. I actually had to pull over and take a couple deep breaths. "Who the hell am I?" I said wondering aloud, asking a paradoxical question for which I had no reasonable answer for. I knew who I was to Tami, but that was not the me most people knew and hated. In the few months we had been together, I had kept Tami away from the places I usually haunted. I had introduced her to a few peripheral friends but made sure that it never went any further than pleasantries. I didn't want Tami to associate me with the past she had a big hand in separating me from. There was this new Todd, who even I liked a lot more because he actually did give a shit about things other than his primordial needs. This new Todd laughed more, was actually tender, and he worried. There's that Christian saying, 'What Would Jesus Do?' I never much concerned myself with religion, convinced that if there were a hell, I had a hot rock emblazoned with my name on it. But I began to look at the world through Tami's eyes. 'What Would Tami Do?' She was about as close to Jesus as anybody I'd ever met. People that I normally came into contact with on a daily basis: old co-workers, bar flies, women I had dated, or more aptly, knocked boots with wouldn't recognize me as the man who held Tami's hand. She began to infuse me with a sense of calm. That general pissed-offness that had resided in my belly for as long as I could remember evaporated when she came into my life. And I didn't want it back. There was a serenity - well, as close as I would ever get to serenity - that dominated my soul. I'd been the villain in my own life for too long. It was a major revelation to finally be the hero.

Stepping from the car, I again pulled out the bunch of lilies I had bought at the little shop near my condo and took a deep breath, searching the windows of the house to see if Harry was peeking out. Possibly with a rifle. As I strode toward the front door, the aroma of Italian food lured me closer. My stomach gurgled. Since Tami had never cooked a full meal for me, I arrived ravenous on the off-chance that if the meal sucked I didn't want to be grabbing at excuses why a big guy like me was only picking at his plate. Tami already knew I was an eating machine. So even if it bordered on inedible, I'd wolf it down and ask for more. This was a skill I had learned at a very early age. My mother knew how to cook three things. Pork roast, Polish sausage, and brisket of beef. All of them tasted exactly alike. Salty. And my brother and I ate them in one form or another every night of our lives growing up. If you were going to make it to the next day, you learned to suck it down. It was never going to get better than what was sitting on the table.

I rang the bell and waited. It took a surprisingly long time for the door to open. Had Harry taken Tami and fled? Was he busy drilling screws into her bedroom door, locking her in until I disappeared? Perhaps he was duct taping a pistol under the dining room table? Just in case. Finally, the door swung open and Tami was there with a welcoming smile. She pushed open the storm door and let me in. There was a sheen of sweat, which caused her skin to glow. I found it incredibly sexy and wanted to lay her on the floor and lick it off of her.

Tami always seemed surprised when I brought her flowers, although I had done it every time we went out. I even sent them to her office a few times. When she caught a bad flu and was in bed for three days, I sent over a couple bouquets a day to keep her spirits up. The little Chinese lady who owned the flower shop treated me like royalty since I had been buying so many flowers. She always called me Mr. Cartwright, which made me chuckle every time she said it because it sounded like 'car ride,' and had personally introduced me to her husband, her parents, and all six of her children, each of whom bowed whenever I entered.

Tami took my hand and led me to the kitchen where pots filtered an aromatic steam into the room, and something in the oven smelled even better than what was on the stove. I leaned back against the counter and watched her work as she recounted her day of shopping, chopping, stirring, and baking. It was clear that this was a true joy for her. And it fit her so well, creative but with a purpose. I asked her if there was anything I could do to help, but she gave me a coy wink, "Just stand there and look pretty." Pretty. Not handsome, not studly, not hot. Pretty. Hey, if this girl thought I was pretty, then I was going to stand there and be as pretty for her as I could - which in reality wasn't very pretty at all, but what the hell. I was happy to oblige her anything.

Harry stepped into the entrance of the kitchen in a freshly-pressed, button-down shirt, dress pants, and his tie half-tied. He glanced at me, the sides of his lopsided mouth turned down. "Oh," he moaned with a tired nod, "Hello." I moved over and shook his hand. "Mr. Everett," I said forcing as much chipperness into my baritone as possible.

He called Tami over to help him do his tie. Looking at him all dressed up, I felt a little odd. I figured casual was the way to go and had dressed in a light blue Polo shirt and navy blue Dockers. Tami evidently found it odd too that her father was going to this much trouble, and when she asked him why he was putting on a tie for dinner, Harry replied dryly, "We have a guest. I wear a tie for guests."

Tami rolled her eyes as she finished the Windsor knot and raced it up just below Harry's Adam's apple. I would have tightened it until his cloudy eyes bulged out of their puny sockets, then swung him around the room and launched him out the window like the hammer throw. With Harry's emphatic sharpness on the word 'guest', it was apparent that he meant I wouldn't be around long. I would be banished from his castle as quickly as he could arrange it. His remark set the tone for the evening. Not that it came as any surprise that the night was going to be a royal pain in my ass. Although how majestic a pain was still a mystery. The 'guest' remark was subtle for Harry. And as I soon learned, he didn't like to rely on subtlety too often. Or wit for that matter. He was more of an in-your-face kind of ferret, chewing away until he hit a vein. The dining table was set with Tami's mother's good china and glassware. Heirlooms. As I eyed the beautiful table, I imagined that I would be seeing this china and stemware every holiday for the rest of my life. It made me nostalgic for something that hadn't even happened yet. Tami set the lilies in the middle of the table, which caused Harry to wince visibly. He waved me to the 'guest' seat, which happily was across the table from him. Tami sat between us. Wasn't this cozy? The other seat was where Harry's wife, Winnie, had sat when she was alive. Luckily, the lilies partially blocked Harry's view of me. Tami knew exactly what she was doing when she placed them on the table. It would take some effort on Harry's part to fire off an acid scowl or toss a pissy remark directly into my face.

Tami floated in and out of the kitchen, carrying platters with the redolent meal she had prepared. Left alone with Harry, I knew I had to struggle all the harder to make it through this night without letting the rat bastard get to me. Be strong, Todd, be strong. So much was riding on this evening working out nicely. For myself, as well as Tami. For her part, Tami kept a vigilant guard on the temperature in the dining room, which yo-yoed back and forth between silently icy and silently molten.

But every time she disappeared into the kitchen, Harry went to work using his evil mojo. His squinty, milky eyes would peek around the lilies, his nose and lips scrunching up until he resembled a wild rodent caught in a trap, willing to bite off its own leg to free itself. I never gave him the satisfaction of looking directly at him, or even speaking to him, hoping that he would get bored with this game. Whenever Tami entered the dining room, Harry's face abruptly shifted to a smile, then once she left, the two-faced, mini-monster's scowl returned.

And he could sense he was getting to me. Drip by drip, like Chinese water torture. Though I wouldn't make eye contact with him, I found myself again biting the inside of my mouth in an effort to keep it shut. Another couple months of this relationship and there was going to be a hole in my cheek the size of a golf ball. I knew this stupid game, I had been Prince of the Pricks for years and glared at guys in bars until they would come unglued. It's a dog's way of starting a fight without starting the fight. Sit there and bear your teeth with a low growl until the other mutt feels he has to defend himself before he's attacked. It was a real bitch having the tables turned on me like that. He was using my own powers against me. Everything inside screamed at me to jump up and knock his block off like a pinata. I wondered if Tami would believe it was an accident if she returned to the dining room to find Harry lying on the floor with a fork buried in his forehead.

Tami pulled out the stops trusting that a great meal could dissipate the tension between her father and I. How much fighting could there be if we were stuffing delicious food into our faces?

The salad was served on plates she kept in the freezer like a pricey restaurant. I don't know how Tami did it, but the veal was the most tender piece of meat I've ever had. She even made the sauce from scratch. If I didn't love this girl enough before, afterwards she was not only everything I wanted, but she could cook too! Images of myself in ten years tipping the scale at three hundred pounds danced in my head.

But as long as Tami loves me, who cares, I thought, letting down my guard for a moment, unaware that the tiger had slipped through the bars of his cage.

"Tami, my God, this is terrific," I complimented her with a big smile.

As she smiled back, we heard from across the table, "No, it's more than terrific. It's the best I've ever tasted. I would hazard to say probably the best veal parmagiana in this city."

We both turned. Harry smiled at us, his mouth full as he pointed to the veal with his fork, nodding less than innocently, and then went right back to eating.

Then with my next endorsement of the meal, Harry chimed in, topping my compliment again with another of his own. Every adjective finished with an -est. If I said "great," he said "greatest!" If I hummed an "Mmmm," he trumped it by nearly fainting from pleasure. When I told Tami she was the best cook I knew, Harry had her opening her own restaurant, making millions from her recipes, and on network television starring in the first prime time cooking show, "Tami's Kitchen".

Maybe when I have a daughter and detest the pantywaist she is dating as much as Harry hated seeing me sitting across the table with his baby, I'll behave the same way. I'd like to think I wouldn't, but I'd find some way to make the little puke squirm. I felt like taking notes because Harry was a professional. And with every bite of food I chewed I knew this night was only going to get worse.

Harry didn't even try to couch the compliments in a way that wouldn't come off as anything but playground one-upsmanship. Poor Tami, her head spinning back and forth between us like a spectator sitting center court at a tennis final. And that snotty grin on his face brazenly displayed his glee at what he was doing. He actually thought this bullshit was funny. The entire dinner was a litany of Harry peeing on trees, marking his property like the Schnauzer he resembled. This was his house, the food was cooked on his stove, and the chef was his daughter. After dinner, he would be the one kicking off his shoes and retiring to the living room to watch the nightly news. I would be the one climbing into my car and leaving. He didn't want me to forget that.

Tami slipped apologetic glances in my direction. But she said nothing. This was not a fight she wanted to referee. She had toiled all day creating this meal. Stepping into the middle of this sophomoric fracas would only serve to ruin the night completely. She had to let it play out and hope for the best. Agitated silence was her only option.

And it became mine. Rather than continue playing patty-cake with the father from hell, I just stuffed my face with the meal Tami had made. If I couldn't out-praise Tami, I would prove to her just how much I thought of her effort by letting my fork do the talking. If there was something I knew I could do, it was out-eat a guy who weighed in at about 150 pounds soaking wet. I had him by just damn near a hundred pounds. There was no way that little sociopath was going to out-gorge me.

By my third plate of veal, Harry's gnarled gray matter caught onto my angle. Realizing that I was expressing my love with my appetite, Harry jumped in to do battle. My size didn't matter. Harry wasn't willing to concede defeat on any front.

Every slice of veal I requested, he asked for one. Every piece of fresh baked rosemary bread I ripped a bite out of, Harry was right there jamming a chunk into his mouth. New plate of salad for new plate of salad. Forkful of pasta for an equal forkful. I don't know where that dwarf put all that food; he must have had a hollow leg or colostomy bag or something, but he was putting it down just as fast. And just as much. My only hope in out-eating him was that he would actually explode and die. He couldn't let Tami believe that he loved her less because he digested less.

When it came down to the last piece of veal on the massive platter, both of us requested it. Tami glanced from side to side, stood up, and announced, "Figure it out for yourselves," then scraped her chair across the wooded floor and stormed into the kitchen.

Harry eyeballed me through the narrow slits that housed his eyes. Then his fork went for the meat. But his tiny arms were no match for my reach, and I drove my fork under his, stabbing the slice and ripping it right off the platter, the sauce dripping onto the table cloth.

I held it up triumphantly, an icy grin on my face, and then shoved the whole thing into my mouth and chewed slowly with a long, orgasmic, "Mmmmmmmmm."

I contemplated running a victory lap around the dining room before sliding into the kitchen and checking on Tami, but I couldn't pull my ass off the chair. My stomach was bloated as if I were pregnant with twin calves. If I stood up, I feared that dinner would come up with me. I felt horrible for Tami. She had labored all day to make the meal spectacular, and it was. But the ogre had done everything to make the evening as cutthroat and uncomfortable as possible, and I had bought into it by stuffing my jaws with everything on the table short of the napkins.

Tami returned from the kitchen with a gorgeous three-layer chocolate cake that she had labored on earlier in the day. She removed the lilies from the table, and then, without uttering a word, dropped the cake into the middle of the table. It bounced once and landed like a building in an earthquake, its cocoa frosted walls collapsing in on each other. Tami jammed two forks into the middle of the mess and announced, "Eat up, boys. If that cake is not gone by the time I am done with the dishes, I'm not speaking to either one of you."

She then cleared all the dishes off the table, leaving only the cake and the forks between Harry and me. Tami marched back into the kitchen, the dishes crashing against the swinging door as she went.

Harry and I glowered at each other, both aware that neither of us was physically capable of eating another bite. Much less an entire chocolate cake. Harry was actually turning flush from just looking at the pile of dessert. His gaze rose from the cake and locked into mine.

"This is your fault," he enunciated in a soft, high-pitched snivel.

My fault? Yeah. For not putting the kabosh on his crap from the get-go. I kept my eyes locked on his, because I wanted to see his reaction. And then I smacked him right between those beady eyes.

"I am in love with your daughter, Mr. Everett," I announced as clearly as he had, speaking in a deep, no-bullshit, deliberate voice.

His eyes widened as he sat back in his chair. Harry opened his mouth trying to form some retort but all he could do was sputter. I believe he came damn close to having a stroke. He was prepared for me to berate his behavior at dinner, but I clocked him with a roundhouse punch, nailing him with my true feelings. For the first time all night, the decision for the round went in my favor.

"You ARE NOT in love with my daughter. You don't know the first thing about love," Harry finally spat back at me.

"Yes, I am," I continued calmly, enjoying watching Harry have a meltdown, "I love Tami with my whole heart and soul. And there's not a damn thing you can do about it because these feelings are mine."

The old man staggered like a bloodied prize fighter who had just realized he was past his prime and there was an arena full of young bucks ready to take the title. His mouth bent down at the ends in what could best be described as a frown, though I really believe it was the only thing preventing him from crying. Then he curled up his face again. I struggled not to bat an eye. Not to twitch. Not to sweat. I'm absolutely positive that if he could have gotten his hands on me, we would have ended up wrestling on the table. I could easily kick his sorry ass, but this mongrel certainly would have gotten in a few mean licks.

Harry slammed his hands on the table so hard he sent the mound of collapsed chocolate cake leaping into the air once again, this time landing on the table cloth while the forks spun off and skipped across the floor like they were running for cover.

The clatter brought Tami flying back into the room. Her eyes landed on her father who was now standing, strangling his napkin, while I sat back in my chair, still coolly refusing to blink.

"What happened now?" she barked out, though clearly afraid to hear the answer.

Harry pointed at me, wagging his finger across the table while I held my eyes steady, unflinching. This was going to be interesting. What could he say? That I told him I loved his daughter? What if Tami began to cry and then rushed into my arms? I had never said the words to her...not exactly anyway. Harry would not only lose the battle, he would have to surrender the war. He couldn't chance that. And Harry was too good at this kill-the-suitor game to fall into that set-up.

But I bet I'm the first guy who has ever had him dangling from the ledge.

"Your guest is the rudest young man I have ever let set foot inside MY home. He disrespects me, and he's not worthy of you," Harry launched in, muscling his way back up from the ledge. "There are plenty of other young men out there, more than plenty, who would give their eye teeth for a wonderful woman like you. That deserve a woman like you. This is not one of them. Not even close. What could you possibly see in this....thug? Do you want to know what I see? An unfaithful, cheating, lying, selfish, goon. How could you even think this man is right for you? Your mother would be crushed if she were alive. Crushed, crushed, crushed! To think you brought this hoodlum into our home, Tami..." Harry then turned his acrimonious glare back on me. "I want you out of my house. And don't think of ever stepping foot in here again. You are not welcome!" And with that Harry threw down the napkin to punctuate his overly dramatic monologue.

So that was his next move. Throwing me out of the house. I wanted to cross my arms over my chest and tell him that if he wanted me out, he was going to have to pick my big ass up and carry me to the door. Put up or shut up, Harry. But confronting Harry in his dining room wouldn't have elicited much sympathy from Tami. Harry was taking the gamble that if I sulked and walked out with a devastated look on my face, Tami would not run after me. But he would have had to crawl out on some kind of limb if this hysterical outburst was going to succeed in causing the slightest doubt about me in her mind. And even more, Harry was betting that in this pique he had worked himself into, Tami would fear leaving him alone.

From the look in her eyes, Tami was so off-balance she didn't know which of us to turn to. This ached me. I could have yammered on with a rebuttal, but I refused to cause this woman any more pain than she was already in. The next day I would try to explain my side of things. The rub was that that would allow Harry twelve extra hours to destroy me with an emotional chainsaw, ripping through flesh and bone. But if it meant salvaging at least a moment of peace for her, then I wanted Tami to know I had done it.

I slowly stood up, taking a deep breath to try and force the food further down into my stomach, so I wouldn't look like I was walking with a bowling ball in my pants. That was when lightning struck. I had one ace. I told Tami from the beginning that I was going to be nakedly honest with her about everything. And I had been. It didn't dawn on me that my truth hadn't been spoken. And if it saved this girl from being locked in the tower for another hundred years by the evil gnome, then all the better.

"I'm sorry," I said to Tami, searching her face for some sign that she was not too disturbed to make sense of what I was about to say. There was a tiny glimmer in her eyes, perhaps it was tears, but I took it as an indication that she needed to hear me out before Harry shot me out of a cannon. And out of her life.

"I'm not sorry for upsetting your father. I did that by walking in here tonight. I expected it and congratulations, Mr. Everett, I was not surprised. But I'm never going to apologize for what I said to you." I took a pause for effect, my eyes glancing at Harry as he waited like a panther eager to pounce, but unsure of the direction in which I was heading. With my voice cracking slightly, I said, "I told your father that I love you and I realize I've never actually spoken those words to you." And then an even longer pause for the coup de gras as Harry visibly shook, unsure of whether to jump in and work some damage control, or let me finish and leave, I added, "Tami, I love you more than I ever thought I could love anyone."

Three-pointer from the outside of the court. If I could have high-fived myself, I would have.

Not that I want to make light of this. Saying "I love you" to anyone was not something I had had much practice in, nor would ever say if I hadn't meant it. Even drunk, I never uttered those words to seduce a woman into bed, and consequently lost out on a lot of great sex, because I pissed off more than a few crazy, needy women by refusing to say it after a wild night of hot passion. A lot of people mistake the two. I've always been quite clear. Hell, after the age of seven, I never even said it to my parents. These were hard words. I believe the most difficult and maligned in the English language. Love was rare for me. More than rare, love was a living, breathing part of me I didn't even know existed until Tami.

I began walking toward the front door.

With each step, I grew more confident about the outcome of what was about to happen. And then I heard the magic word: "Don't."

As I slowly spun around, Tami's eyes held on me as her father hovered nearby, his face twisted as his hope that she would let me walk out the door crumbled like the cake on the table.

"You are my guest," Tami stated. "And if I want you to leave I will ask you to."

Damn straight! When we get married, I know who will be wearing the pants in our family. Me. But I will still end up acquiescing to her every wish.

Then she turned to her father, the look in her eye not defiance but one of decisiveness. Harry glanced from Tami to me and then back. His own daughter had cut him off at the pass, swiping victory from his sharp talons. He shook his head bitterly as he spun on his heels and clomped out of the dining room without another word, like something out of an old Bette Davis movie.

Damn if this wasn't sweet justice.

After the moment passed, I wanted to break out laughing, but I knew that wouldn't win me any points, and it looked like I was about to collect my championship ring, after all. Instead, I glanced down sheepishly, embarrassed, and waited for Tami to make the move. I expected her to step over to me, wrap her arms around my neck, and look deep into my adoring eyes as she said, "I love you too." She was leading this parade. I was just happy to still be on the float.

Once the sound of Harry's bedroom door slamming shut echoed down the hallway, Tami stood completely still, closed her eyes tightly, and muttered softly, "How could you do that to him?"

Wait a second. What just happened? I won! I'm still here and he left. And now she's going to knock me off my skates during the victory lap? What the hell is this about? I mean, telling her father that I loved her was wrong? It's truth. And truth rules. Doesn't it? Okay, telling him before I actually said the words to her wasn't exactly the best strategy, but I should take home the trophy for admitting my feelings.

"He's so freaked out about you," Tami continued. "I've been very clear about my feelings for you, Todd, and he's scared to death that he's going to lose me. He doesn't have anybody else. I don't want to hurt him. My father has given up so much so I could have the best. I never, ever want to hurt him."

Okay, leave that to me. Because I want to string him up like a pig.

"I didn't mean to hurt your father," I spoke, defending myself. "But he had to know what I was feeling. I didn't like the way he was treating you. Or me. You worked too hard on this night to have it turn out like this."

Tami came over and sat me down, then climbed onto my lap. Not the most comfortable position considering how much food was lodged in my stomach, but when she kissed me so softly, her hand running through my hair, I forgot about all discomfort. "He's scared," she said quietly. "Try and understand his side. It has been me and him for as long as I can remember. I'm not sure what he'll do if he loses me. And he is going to lose me. Because I love you too," Tami said.

Could you go back and say that again? I like to be warned ahead of time that statements like that are coming so I can truly savor the moment. I prayed for this. Wanted to hear it. And now I was just happy that my big ass was already sitting down, or I would have fallen over.

As she opened her mouth to continue, I put a finger to her lips. This woman I wanted to give the world to had said she loved me. I didn't need to hear any more. This was my victory. I pulled my hand away from her mouth and locked my lips on hers, pulling her body into mine. I never wanted to break this kiss. Let Harry shuffle out of his bedroom in the morning and find us still here sucking face.

"Next time I'll try and be more aware of your father's feelings and not to rub it in," I whispered to her, my arms still wrapped tightly around her tiny body.

Tami giggled, nodding. "Good. Then maybe I can survive this."

"But there's one more thing I want to ask you," I continued, seriousness deepening my voice.

Tami waited, loving concern crossing her face.

"Will you marry me?"

MISERY'S COMPANY

That wasn't what I was going to ask. The meal had been so great, she had worked so hard to make it special, I wanted to do something wonderful for her. What I wanted to ask was if she would come back to my place for a while. I would turn on some old Savage Garden, lay her back on the sofa, strip her out of her shoes, and rub her feet. Besides, I had eaten so much I desperately needed to get out of these pants so I could breathe again. And even though Napoleon-lite was locked in the master bedroom licking his wounds, there was no possible way I could feel comfortable in his house.

The startled glow in Tami's eyes was matched by the wide-eyed startledness in mine. What had I just asked??? And if the question I think flew off my lips actually had, where the hell did it come from? It's not like I hadn't been thinking it almost from the moment I met her, and if I had been drinking I would understand how I could blurt out a question that bold. I always said the first thing that blew through my warped mind when I was hammered. Good or bad, hostile or friendly, whatever darted between my ears was pretty much fair game to come out of my big mouth. But I had only had one glass of wine. I wasn't remotely intoxicated. No, this had to be sheer madness. Again my heart took over, and I suddenly found myself Christopher Columbus entering a brave new world.

And it wasn't like I could scream, "Psyche!" and take the words back. If it was too soon for her, entirely off the wall, or completely inappropriate after what had just gone down, the words hovered between us like a hummingbird flitting around a jasmine bush. Tami remained completely still; all I could feel was her heart beating against my chest.

The longer the silence, the more I recognized the beauty of what I had asked. My heart was right. Why should I wait to marry this woman? I knew I would never love anyone else like her. This was a no-brainer. My heart was even more impatient than my penis when it came to what it wanted. I concede that Tami and I hadn't been dating that long. We hadn't even slept together. But there wasn't any doubt that could cast a shadow on my feelings for her. I was going to marry this woman. Be it that day, the next, or whenever. And if I didn't marry this woman, I couldn't see myself marrying anyone else, ever. I wanted only one woman. I had had the rest, I got the best. And I was staying.

A tiny pond of tears rimmed the bottom of her eyes. At this moment I prayed she wouldn't blindside me like she had earlier when she told me I should have never told her father I loved her. I suddenly felt a wave of cold clamminess surge through me. Please tell me you're not freaking out. That you're not pulling away with some lame excuse why we should break this off right now. That things were happening too fast. This happened quickly because it's real for me. If she wasn't ready to commit to a guy who had balled half the single women in Chicago and never met a glass of scotch he didn't like, if she needed more proof that I had changed, that it was only her that I wanted to spend my life with, what the hell would I do? Oh shit, could I have screwed this up? Big time? My head was motoring overtime trying to wrestle power away from my heart and clean up this situation. But it wasn't happening soon enough. She was crying. Shit, shit, shit!

I don't believe that tears are ever a good omen. You want to think they are, that they are an emotional response to something joyously wonderful, but it usually means that there are two shoes that are about to drop. In cases like this, a satin slipper drops first as she explains what a great guy you are and how much you mean to her, blah, blah, blah, but then a size-thirteen boot lands on your head and crushes the feeling right out of you. I had moved too fast, and I was going to pay for it.

Tami reached up to my face, tracing my brow and cheekbone. "Todd. You are the greatest guy in the world," she began. I felt all my internal organs shutting down, rebelling against my heart, which had lead them all astray. It was anarchy.

"If I told you I would marry you, will you promise NOT to say anything in front of my father until I get the chance to sit him down and break it to him?" she asked.

Huh? Did she just say yes? I shut down after hearing the statement, "you're the greatest guy in the world." Every male older than twelve knows exactly what that means. Why even bother with the rest of the speech? Guys stop listening, their ears filling with blood to protect what's left of their ego. If you're going to break up with me, I don't need a reason.

"Did...did, did you say yes?" I stuttered.

"I said 'yes,'" Tami repeated with a giggle. "As long as you don't say anything to my father. I need to break this to him, Todd. Not you." And for emphasis again she added, "Not you."

I couldn't hide my smile. I didn't want to. "Anything you want...as long as I come with the package." My lips moved closer to hers, her body cradled in mine. As we kissed, I realized that this woman who had completely knocked me on my ass had just told me that she wanted to spend the rest of her life with me.

I was not unaware that I didn't deserve a woman this good. For damn near the past thirty years I had not been a good man (I'm factoring in a year or so on the off-chance I was a good baby). I've left a lot of carnage in my wake. Harry is so goddamn dead-on about me. But for some reason Tami picked me. Of all the men she could have had, she pointed at me. And if you think I'm altruistically giving her up because I'm not worthy, think again.

Tami stood. She took my hand and signaled me to remain as quiet as possible, as she pulled me to my feet. Grabbing a sweater from the hall closet, she led me to the front door, creaking it open. "What about your father?" I whispered. Tami shook her head and then smiled slyly. "He's pouting. He won't come out of his room until morning."

She didn't say a word the entire time I drove back to my place. Nor as I let her into my home. Tami walked straight to my bedroom and stood at the door. "Are you coming?" she asked.

Hell yes! That's if I don't trip over the gigantic woody that slingshot from my groin as soon as she moved to my bedroom door and gave me that look.

I bolted across the living room, fighting my shirt off over my head. Her laughter filled the room as she yanked me toward her, jumping into my arms. We kissed hard without the usual romance. This was about something else.

I had never been scared about having sex. Not even the first time when I was fifteen and the tramp of the senior class thought it would be a big joke to take the overgrown freshman into an empty classroom and make a man out of him. Right away I knew what went where and exactly what motion gained the most pleasure. Some kids are like fish the first time they are thrown into water; some can hit a ball without any coaching. At sex, I was a natural. From my first experience, I knew this was something I would only get better at because I liked it better than I liked swimming or baseball. Or breathing for that matter.

But that night with Tami I felt out of my element. A novice. To me the words 'making love' had always been a polite euphemism for humping like Rhesus monkeys. And I had a Masters degree in hump-ology. I knew every position. Every kinky, freaky, crazy, turn-on, but when it came to using sex to express my love for this woman, I must have skipped school that day because I was at a loss. The palette of my experiences was vast, but I was about to learn to paint with a new color. To give my soul to a woman in the bedroom. To give my love.

Since I had waited five months, I had planned the scenario for this night a million times. And like most things I plan, it was perfect. In my head. Lenny Kravitz on the stereo, candles, pillows, champagne; I had even bought satin sheets that I was saving for the big night. The only element I hadn't outlined was Tami picking the time. She told me she wanted to wait until she was sure. I guess a wedding proposal pretty much threw that over the top.

Tami shoved me back to my unmade bed with my normal, cotton sheets and knocked me over. I tried to pull myself up, hoping she'd at least let me grab the satin sheets and shove in a Kravitz CD, maybe light a candle or two, so the night could at least partially resemble all my extensive plotting. And even though I was more than a head taller than her, this little lady pinned me to the bed and crawled onto my chest. She pressed her lips to mine, her tongue exploring my mouth. Excellent. But she needed to get these Dockers off me. Unfortunately, my stomach was still bloated from my lamented eating contest, and now my penis was rock hard, and there just wasn't enough room for everybody in my pants.

Tami whipped off my belt and unbuttoned my pants. I nearly sighed. After unzipping them, she stood up and grabbed the bottom hem, yanking them off me like a magician snatching a table cloth off a table, while still leaving all the dishes in place. Damn nice move! At least I was wearing my good underwear.

Once I was naked, Tami let me undress her. Since this was my first night with her, I wanted that Christmas effect. I unwrapped my present slowly. Kissing her. My hands wafting down her body as I exposed each piece of new skin. I wanted to show Tami that she was in solid, gentle hands. If I had a history, at least here it counted for something. I was going to give her more pleasure than she had ever thought possible.

I refuse to give details of what happened the rest of the night. I have spent many hours on a barstool, bragging endlessly and in detail about my conquests, but even I know when to circle my wagons and leave something private. For the first time in my life, my heart lead the charge during sex and opened up a new vista to me. It was beyond everything I had imagined. Because nothing I ever imagined held this much love.

I sneaked Tami home around midnight, locking lips with her once more. After the kiss I looked at her silently for a long moment.

"What are you thinking?" she asked, her hands sitting on my chest, feeling my heartbeat.

"Why me?"

Tami blinked, unsure of exactly what I was asking. But the glimmer in my eye expressed to her that I needed to know why, of all the men she could have, she had picked me. What did she see that I didn't even know existed inside me? Because for the life of me, I had no idea.

"For some reason you think I'm perfect," Tami whispered, "but I'm not."

"But I'm--," Tami stopped me, putting her hand over my mouth.

"You asked me a question. You deserve an answer," she stated softly, looking away, shaking her head with a tender shrug of her shoulders. "I know that you're not perfect, Todd. But I know in my heart that you are perfect for me."

Without another word, Tami kissed me one more time and then disappeared inside.

I stood on her stoop for a moment, reliving the night. What started off as possibly one of the most demented and tormented evenings of my life had ended beyond my expectations. I was now engaged to be married to a woman who was far superior to me in almost every aspect of my life. And for someone who thinks as highly of himself as I do, that's saying a busload. It's quite common for most men to mistake their own stinking machismo for manhood. From the exterior, they are painted exactly alike. And I don't believe that any man learns the difference unless a very strong woman enters the picture. If Tami hadn't been dropped into my narrow, self-gratifying universe, I would never have understood what now seemed so basic. And how blessed I was to have this woman fall in love with me.

I pitied Tami for having to devise some way of breaking the news to her old man. No matter how she sugarcoated it, it wouldn't be pretty. And there wasn't anything I could do to help her with this audacious mission, besides respecting the restraining order that I was sure Harry would put out against me once he found out that Tami and I were engaged. With any luck, this news would cause him to spontaneously combust and I could sweep him up into a dustpan and use him to fertilize house plants.

While I let Tami deal with the brewing tantrum, I focused my energy on a task of greater importance: finding her the most beautiful engagement ring that I could afford. If I had to travel to Africa, bribe a dictator, and dig in the mine myself, I was going to find her a diamond that would call out to the world just how much I loved this woman. Tami would not demand anything extravagant. This was where she and I were vastly different. I could have slipped a twisty-tie around her finger and she would giggle and tell me how special it was. I wanted her to have the world, the red carpet. Big ring, short engagement. There was still this oozing fear that she would be sitting at her desk at work one day, and it would suddenly fall on her like a piano from the fifth floor. "What am I doing marrying this mook?!" No, I wasn't taking the chance that whatever voodoo had worked to get her to agree to marriage would wear off, and she would realize she had gone temporarily insane. Most people would believe her. At least most people that knew me. I didn't ever want to hear the words "colossal blunder" associated with this engagement. Speed was going to have to be my friend.

Especially since Harry was going to be grinding her down twenty-four/seven.

But I was in love. Five months earlier, I couldn't picture myself in bed with the same woman for more than a couple weeks. And, even in that short time, chances were I'd cheat on her. Now, I was committed to spending the rest of my life with Tami. For a man like me to reverse directions so radically, to be so stupidly head over heels is not a minor miracle, it's a supernatural phenomenon. I felt invincible, just like I had when I was a kid. I never believed anything could hurt me. And now because of this love I was impervious even to pain. My entire life seemed so much easier. I didn't feel that rawness in my heart that made me so angry. That's not to say that things no longer sent me over the edge. But there were new changes. For instance, guys would often bag on the women I had slept with, though more out of jealousy than merit. And I would laugh along with them. Since there was nothing at stake for me, a joke at some girl's expense was fair game. But when I spoke about Tami, I lost all posturing. I didn't know another man who spoke of his girlfriend or wife the way I spoke about Tami. I knew how freaking lucky I was. When a schmuck I ran into accused me of being "pussy whipped by some bitch I was banging," I had a major league wig-out. Grabbing the smartass by the throat, I chokingly warned him never ever to speak of Tami again in his miserable fucking life. I knew that he had meant it as a joke; it's how he had always known me, it was how we had always spoken about women. But not about this woman. Never about Tami. Whatever this was between Tami and me, it demanded respect. I now owned it and I wasn't going to let any man tread on it with boy-talk bullshit. Any man who tried risked swallowing his teeth.

And you wonder why I have so few friends.

I hadn't talked to Tami since lunchtime which concerned me. We always checked in with each other four or five times a day, at least, usually just to say we were thinking about each other. We never had much to share, our daily routines weren't that rousing. I just needed to hear her voice. It had such a settling effect on me. It was now six-thirty, and I was microwaving a couple of Lean Cuisine meals for dinner, since one never filled me up. As I waited for the microwave to ding, my mind started fucking with me. What if she told her father and he kidnapped her, rushing her off someplace to have her deprogrammed? Or in a jealous rage he killed himself, and now Tami was crushed and would never recover from the blow?

It was nearly eight o'clock when the doorbell rang. I had downed the Lean Cuisines, a protein shake, and a bowl of Corn Chex, and was just settling in for a night of Sports Central, still debating whether I should try Tami at home or wait for her to call me. Tami stood in the doorway with tears rolling down her cheeks. I didn't have to be a member of Mensa to figure out that she had had her campfire chat with Harry. And he popped a gasket.

Without a word I pulled her to me and let her cry into my chest.

"He completely lost it. Just lost it," she began after the sobbing subsided enough for her to speak. "He came up with every possible reason he could think of for me never to marry you. My God, I think he's been writing a list."

I'm sure he had. Written in blood.

The litany tumbled out of her as if the list had been permanently emblazoned into her frontal lobe. "It's too soon, I don't know you well enough, you're not good enough, you're going to cheat on me, hurt me, and eventually leave me. It got so bad," she paused, trying to catch her breath as she fought against the tears, her body trembling, "my father actually got down on his knees, crying, pleading, begging, doing everything he could to get me to say I would never marry you."

Holy shit. Got down on his knees. Cried. Pleaded. Begged. I only wish I had been there. With a golf club. Could this snarky bastard manipulate his daughter any worse? How do I compete with a father on his knees, crying?

Tami was completely wrecked.

I fought the urge boiling through me to race over there and throttle Harry into unconsciousness. He had used thresher shark tactics on a goldfish. I was sure that he was now on his feet, dancing a jig in the living room, congratulating himself on demolishing his daughter's happiness and raising serious doubts that she would continue with the engagement. I hid my own fear as best I could. Tami didn't need any more drama. I am not big on drama either. I'm big on getting even. And I was nearly out-of-my-mind pissed off. I didn't want her to know just how badly I wanted to hurt her father. I had to conjure up a formula for setting the world back on his axis so it would spin in my direction.

But first I had to recapture the faith of the woman I loved. Reassure her that she was doing the right thing by accepting my offer of marriage. Then I'd get a bat and go weasel hunting.

Gently, I reminded Tami that it should come as no revelation that her father was going to react this way. I attempted to neutralize all the drama by calmly stating, "You knew he didn't like me. Hell, he wanted to throw me out of the house when I told him I loved you." There was more I wanted to say about Harry, names to be called, threats to be made, but I knew that there was no benefit in trashing her father. It would seem desperate and vengeful. Not that I wasn't both, but I could afford neither at that moment. Besides, she had twenty-four years of evidence that her father cared for her. I couldn't counteract that in a few bitter sentences.

I exerted every ounce of willpower that I possessed to prevent Tami from witnessing just how freaked out I was that Harry could rattle her so much that she'd contemplate breaking it off. And I did sense she was wavering. The best equipment I had at my disposal was my little-used ability to bite my tongue and extol her father's virtues, while I slyly ripped at his jugular. Needless to say, this was goddamn, painfully difficult and for two reasons. One, I had no idea what virtues Harry actually possessed, other than having had three minutes of carnal pleasure with his wife that lead to the birth of his daughter. And two, I had to be slick. I was not very good at indirect; I was more a sledgehammer than a scalpel. And I hated trying to pull one over on this woman. It was just plain wrong. But if it meant she'd stay with me, I had to focus on the greater good.

I trumped up Harry's unwavering love for her. She was the apple of his eye, and he did an amazing job of raising her single-handedly. It raked my throat to compliment Harry but I continued, lauding his wishes for his daughter, his desire for her to have the best life she could with a man who loved her. I applauded Harry's concern for his daughter, his 'adoration,' which were surreptitious avenues for stating Harry was an obsessive freak with an insatiable domination complex. I didn't care if this man had raised her since she was four; he acted like he had sat on the egg for nine months to make sure she'd hatch. And now the vulture wasn't about to let her leave the nest without picking her to death.

I gibbered on about Harry, the wonder-father, until the tears subsided and Tami calmed. All the while I kept kissing her. Not because I thought it would help but because I wanted to. And it made her smile, which was all I wanted. If she was upset, I was upset. But I wasn't about to let that worm upset me anymore.

Finishing, I told Tami, "The only problem your father has is that he can't see that I'm the guy who will give you everything. I'm the one who loves you and wants to spend the rest of his life with you."

We slipped into the bedroom and curled up on the top sheet. She was completely exhausted from the battle with Harry. She laid across my chest, closing her eyes. As she dozed off, I knew this was a moment that Harry and I shared. I was sure there were many nights after her mother had died that she fell asleep across her father's chest. And I'm sure Harry would stroke her hair softly, just like I was doing, and wonder how he was going to raise this little girl.

I suddenly had an awesome respect for Harry. I still didn't like him but I understood. They had years of history together just like this. Tami and I had five months.

When we woke, it was six a.m., Tami freaked.

"Oh, my God, my dad's probably got the police out looking for me! I'm surprised that no one's kicked down your door with search dogs," she rambled, only half-joking, as she pulled her hair back and rushed into the bathroom to splash some water on her face.

When she stepped back into the bedroom, she stopped and looked at me still on the bed. "Why does he have this kind of hold on me?" she asked.

"He's your old man. Been the only one there for a long time. And even though he hates me, I envy him for having you in his life. I envy you for having him in yours."

A whisper of a smile came to her lips as a shimmering rim of tears came to her eyes. My words drew her to the edge of emotion. Not something I was used to. But I was rewarded with a long kiss and the words, "I love you," before Tami fled from my house and raced home to what was surely going to be a tornado of panic and anger thanks to Harry's chronic case of overreaction.

So I decided to follow Tami home.

Harry was literally waiting at the front door. He had parked his easy chair near the entrance to the living room, so he wouldn't miss her when she came in. When Tami walked in, he swallowed her up in his arms and kissed her head, relieved that nothing horrific had happened to her. Then he launched in. He had called her cell phone over a dozen times but all he got was her voice mail. Where had she been, why hadn't she called, didn't she know she had nearly killed him with worry?! And then he finally noticed me standing at the storm door, peering in. Harry sneered. "I should have known." He walked out of the living room to the kitchen.

Tami turned to go after him, but I stepped in and stopped her. I had to get this torture over with sooner or later, and he was already steamed and I was already pissed off, so the time was ripe.

I followed Harry into the kitchen. He was pouring himself another mug of coffee as I entered. When he spied me, he frowned, turned back, and finished slopping the coffee into the mug.

"What kind of man asks a girl to marry him without a ring? Did you even think of asking me for her hand? Have you no respect for me whatsoever?"

"No, I don't," I responded, causing Harry to spin around to face me, armoring up for battle.

"You play Tami like she's your personal puppet, trying to force her to do exactly what you want. I don't respect you. I don't respect you because you don't respect me, or the love I have for your daughter. The love she has for me. You want my respect, Mr. Everett?" I declared, without a hint of apology. "Give a little."

"Wake up, young man. You don't love my daughter," Harry shot back, shaking his head. "You are in love with the fact this wonderful, young woman loves you. That is all. You don't fool me for an instant. I know exactly what kind of man you are. You think you're so wonderful, some big catch, but you're nothing but a big dope who doesn't deserve the love of any woman, especially my daughter. Who trusts and cares and treats people with kindness and respect. None of which you deserve. You shouldn't marry any woman, but I am absolutely positive that you WILL NOT marry my Tami. I know where this relationship will lead. You will either break her heart or break her down. And I won't let that happen."

Even with my thick skin, I gotta say, that shot through my body like a hypodermic full of battery acid. Not because he had me all wrong. But because my past declared that he had me dead to center.

I was never one to believe that people change. My theory is they become more of themselves as they get older. An asshole is an asshole, and as he grows older he will only become a bigger asshole. Someone has to be metaphorically struck by lightning to make drastic, life altering, changes. What Harry Everett was blind to was that his daughter was that extreme jolt in my life.

I didn't respond to Harry's assault. I wasn't going to change his mind. And me being me, my first thought was tough shit. If he didn't like me too goddamn bad. I didn't love him, and as far as I could remember I hadn't asked Harry to marry me. I loved Tami and I had asked her to marry me. End of story. He was going to have to learn to put up with me, or he was going to find himself staying home with a turkey TV dinner on Thanksgiving because he sure as hell wasn't coming to my house.

Tami appeared at the entrance to the kitchen as Harry started for the door. I stepped into his path, blocking his exit. Being as big as I am, he was forced to pause. Though he tried not to express any intimidation, he didn't know me well enough to know I wouldn't punch him in the face. Or maybe he knew me well enough to know I would. I felt Tami's hand on my shoulder. "Todd. Don't do this."

But I didn't move. I glared down at Harry as I spoke with every ounce of directness I could gather. "I am going to marry her, sir. Because I love her and I want her in my life forever. And we are going to have to find some way to tolerate each other, or we're going to drive Tami over the edge. What do you say?" I asked, "Can you do that? Not for me but for her."

Harry took a long moment and then sighed. Thank God, I thought. Maybe, just maybe, we can salvage a sliver of consideration and allow it to grow into something more.

I stuck out my hand so we could shake. But he walked right by me as he huffed out, "Stick it up your ass. You will not marry my daughter."

THE DMZ

The line had been drawn in the sand. Marrying Tami was going to have to turn into a clandestine military operation. Shock and awe.

I knew this whole thing was terrible for her. She loved me. But she also loved her father. And he had seniority. It was never my intention to make this a "me or him" situation. I was looking forward to a "me and her" situation with "him" somewhere hovering dotingly on the sidelines. But if Harry was going to do everything in his power to drop dynamite down my pants, I had no choice but to defend myself.

The first thing I did was spend three days shopping for an engagement ring with Gretchen. Since I never thought much about jewelry, it didn't even occur to me to ask Tami what she wanted. But I knew what I wanted. And more to the point, Gretchen knew what I should buy. Once I had proposed to Tami, Gretchen and Amy both shifted their attitude towards me. Especially Gretchen. She had been Tami's friend since they were kids, and there is a remarkable bond that lifelong girlfriends have that men cannot understand or penetrate. When I called Gretchen for help, I became her new best male friend in the whole wide world. We spent afternoons barnstorming through jewelry store after jewelry store, until I knew I had found the ring in this tiny, family owned store that Gretchen had dragged me to way the hell out in Elk Grove. The fact that it was eighteen hundred dollars over what I had to spend didn't matter. Perfect mattered. Gretchen backed me up on this, rubbing my back as I whipped out my credit card, my hand shaking as I signed the receipt. This ring was as close to perfect as I had ever seen. The way the light hit it, the gem lit up like a fireworks display. It was spectacular. And it was as big as my feelings for Tami, and all I wanted was for her to love it, which Gretchen promised me she would.

And Tami did. Until she found out how much I had spent. I had promised not to lay out more than two grand. Tami did not want to start out our life together in debt. "It doesn't need to look like a paperweight," she instructed me when I began my search - to which Gretchen rolled her eyes as she pulled me aside and sniffed out, "That's bullshit, Todd. Complete bullshit. Most girls are afraid to state the simple truth but I have no hesitation. Size ALWAYS matters."

I knew Tami wouldn't force me take it back. She wore it proudly.

We nicknamed the ring 'diamondzilla.'

Yeah, it was way too big for her delicate hand...hell, it was probably too big for even my paw, but it stood out like a beacon. But it wasn't nearly as big as everything she had given me. And if it wowed old Harry enough that he couldn't come up with a snarky remark, then that was icing on the cake.

No luck there. Tami told me that when he saw the ring for the first time, he took a lingering gaze and then sniffed, "He must be making up for other inadequacies."

I figured that at this point the best way for me to deal with Harry was to keep my distance. Tami began spending the night at my place more often and stayed every weekend. She would call her father a half dozen times a day, but it was better than her being there with him. Or even worse, me being there with him.

To my grateful amazement, in the middle of World War Harry, I was not without my fans. And they came from the unlikeliest of places.

I thought I knew everything about women but I actually knew nothing. It wasn't until Tami that I even had a scintilla of an idea how to treat one. But though Tami couldn't have cared less about the size of the engagement ring, her tight crew of girlfriends were all over that big rock. Especially Gretchen, who proudly boasted that she helped me pick it out. When her girlfriends who had shown nothing but ugly distrust for me caught sight of diamondzilla, I suddenly metamorphosed into Prince Charming.

One evening, when we were out and I went to the head, I overheard Gretchen talking to Tami in the ladies room, which shared a wall with the men's. "Your father is not marrying Todd. What are you going to do, live with your father all your life? God Tami, look at him, he's tall, great body, great face, and he loves you! He loves you! Look at that ring and tell me that that man doesn't love you. I mean hello! That's what I call love."

You go, Gretchen. And if I ever meet a good guy who could put up with your constant needling, I'll hook you up. Until then, I'm glad you're on my side. I'm glad they're all on my side. And since I had never slept with any of their friends, there was no one around to drag my reputation through the muck. I'm sure most of her girlfriends had heard stories about me, but as far as I could tell they kept them from Tami. Her friends were more inclined to hone in on how protective and loving I was toward her. That wasn't something I had to fake. And they became my secret ace in the hole.

At a gathering at her friend Amy's home, Garth, the boyfriend of another of Tami's girlfriends, wandered over as I was pouring us some wine. He looked at me with wounded eyes and said, "Dude, what are you doing? I'm going to have to buy Cathy a ring the size of my fist or she's never going to be happy."

There wasn't much comfort I could give, other than to recommend getting a second job. But I knew the real secret of his discontent. Cathy was no bolt of lightning for Garth. He figured that she was the best he could do, which was probably true. Cathy didn't bust his balls too much, and they had sex enough to keep him interested, but not interested enough to want to slide a small ice rink onto her finger. And it was killing him to know he was going to have to face some grief over it.

With Tami the next to get married, her friends swarmed around her, making plans, filling her head with ideas for dresses, cakes, bands, and babies. This was her time and she accepted the attention warmly. Her girls were tight.

And they neutralized a lot of Harry's poison.

"I want to set a date," I told Tami, as we laid in bed after having sex on a very sunny Saturday morning.

"How many men have ever said that to a woman?" Tami laughed, kissing my chest.

Probably not many. But the sooner Tami and I shared "I dos" the happier I would be. This had nothing to do with Harry. I just wanted her in my life, no questions. The fact that it would distance Harry from our lives was simply a plus.

We spent the morning discussing what it would take for Tami to pull together a wedding. The only thing I knew about weddings was that they were akin to planning a military invasion. And could cost as much. Without a mother, all the arrangements would be left to Tami. And without her father's blessing, paying for it would be left to me. I would have shot myself over the stars if she would agree to run away to Vegas with me, but that wasn't going to happen.

"I want a wedding, Todd. A real day. I want a memory to last our whole lives."

If that's what she wanted, then I'd move heaven and earth to make that happen.

Then Tami asked the $64,000 question. "I wonder if my Dad is going to pay for this?" I had figured we'd be lucky if he even showed. I couldn't imagine that Harry would actually buck up for something he believed would ruin his daughter's life. Tami knew that Harry had a not-so-secret account set aside for her wedding. He had been adding to it slowly over her entire life, and had told her since she was a young girl that she would have the wedding of a lifetime.

All bets were off now.

What worried me was that she was going to go home and talk to her father. And again, Harry held the better hand. He had something we needed. Cash. And he would make us bleed for every penny. Well, no, he wouldn't bleed Tami. Me, on the other hand, I was ready to jam a needle into my arm and start shipping pints over every morning as a down payment.

By the afternoon, Tami and I had picked a date. Three-and-a-half months away. I made her a solemn promise that I would be right there with her on every detail. Though I knew the best thing I could do was stay out of the way until she needed something negotiated, tried on, or carried.

Tami cooked her father his favorite Hungarian meal, and once he was fat and happy, she asked him about bankrolling the big day. I was positive that there would be concessions, but as long as the negotiation didn't include knocking me out of the picture, I would support anything Harry demanded.

Sorry. Almost anything.

I waited up until late that evening, knowing Tami wouldn't call me until after Harry went to bed -- that is, unless she showed up at my door again in hysteria, and we had another night of her tears and me biting back my rage. But, hallelujah, I had one night without Tami trapped in the middle of two warring tribes because the phone didn't ring until after eleven. I was already lying in bed when the caller ID told me it was Tami. I smiled and pulled the phone to my ear.

"I'm in bed, naked, and every time I think of you my Johnson gets his marching orders," I purred playfully in my sexiest voice. "So what are you wearing, beautiful??"

There was dead silence for a moment, then fumbling, and then I heard, Tami say "Hello?" I was slightly confused but happy to hear her voice so I repeated what I had just said.

"Tell me you didn't just say that before," Tami groaned.

It didn't take a baseball bat smacking me upside my head to realize what had happened. "That was your father who called, wasn't it?" I gulped.

"Uh-huh."

Oh, shit. Oh, shit.

More than oh, shit. My heart dropped into my ass. I am paying karmically for past sins. But even I couldn't remember doing anything bad enough to deserve that. I hadn't killed anyone. Yet. Because it is very possible I just gave Harry a massive embolism. I explained to Tami that I saw the caller ID and assumed it was her. She laughed, which made me feel a little better. But the laughter didn't last long. Harry had called to tell me he was paying for the wedding because he wanted Tami to have the wedding she deserved.

"And he didn't want anything from me?" I questioned.

"He didn't. But that may have changed. He handed me the phone and walked out of the room."

"What do you think pissed him off more? The thought of me being naked with a woody, or me asking him what he was wearing?" That at least got another laugh out of her before she told me she would call me back later.

That call came three hours later. Exhaustion strained her voice. Immediately after we had hung up earlier, Harry announced that he would still pay for Tami's wedding. To anyone BUT me.

"I will not invest one dime in your future if it includes him," Harry barked at Tami, as her mind hunted for the best way to plug this leak before the dam crumbled and washed out the entire village.

She spent the next three hours trying to work him back around. A task on the same mythic level as the Labors of Hercules. And I hadn't given her much to work with. But Tami was the only person who could create hairline cracks in Harry's indignation. Harry was a man of his word, except with his daughter. Tami had twenty-four years to learn how to twist her father around her little finger. She held a master's degree in paternal pathology.

"I can't even imagine what you said to him," I said, lying in bed, my arm over my eyes in bewilderment.

Tami chuckled. "You don't want to know, Todd. You don't want to know," she said with an exhausted sigh. "I've had a lot of practice with my father, but this was probably the largest, full-scale persuasion I've ever had to work on him. I honestly wasn't sure he would come around."

In awe of her patience and skill, I sheepishly added, "Will I, uh...be owing you for a long time?"

"Oh -- forever. Count on it."

I wanted to laugh. But I couldn't. My mind was still swirling from what I imagined Tami had suffered through to return Harry to the fold.

One hundred-and-eighty minutes of daughterly management, but Tami had screwed Harry back around. And in having his daughter come crawling to him, Harry got exactly what he wanted too. At that moment, he mattered more than me. That was a massive victory for Harry. If he could rank higher on Tami's sonar than the S.S. Todd Cartwright, Harry would sleep very soundly.

But I knew this fiasco would cost me a lot more than three hours of begging and pleading. I wasn't Harry's daughter.

The next time I picked Tami up from her home, Harry was waiting.

Harry hadn't answered the door since the first time I came to pick her up, usually avoiding me. It was now time for me to pay the piper.

Following him into the living room, Harry sat. He didn't offer me a seat. I stood -- not that I needed the height advantage, but if Harry was going to make me suffer I might as well at least feel like I towered over him.

"Since I'm paying for your wedding," he began, each word spat out rather than spoken, "a wedding I don't approve of, but my daughter seems hell bent on defying my wishes. There are some things that I expect."

Here we go...

"My daughter says she loves you, for reasons I cannot for the life of me understand. But...love is unexplainable. And often wrong. I know this is wrong. I know it with every fiber of my being. So, as her father, I'm here to make it as right as it possibly can be. And since what's wrong with this relationship is you, you are the one I have to focus on. It's no surprise that I don't like you."

Duh.

"Even if you weren't engaged to my daughter I wouldn't like you. You're just...a creep."

Thank you, sir, may I have another?

"So, if you ever hurt her in any way, I will hurt you. If you break her heart in any way, I will break your head. If you cause her pain, I will cause you pain. If you cheat on her, it will be the last thing you ever do. I know you're a manipulative boy, so I know you see where I'm going with this."

"No, Harry, stop beating around the bush," was what I wanted to say but I chose to nod instead. It was similar to the first talk he had given me on the night I met him. Harry's one-track mind needed a new speechwriter; they were all beginning to sound alike.

"Good. I want to be absolutely crystal clear about this. Because these aren't idle threats. I may not be a big man, I may not be a rich or powerful man, but I can be very, very, mean when it comes to my daughter. And I have been around long enough to know a few people who would be happy to help me. So don't stand there with that stupid look on your face and think I'm fooling around with you. Or that you're too big for me to take down. I'm not and you're not. Tami is my life. I love her more than anything else in this world."

"So do I," I said, though I knew I should have kept my mouth shut and let him get through his Future Father-In-Law lecture and moved on with my life.

"You think you do. But you don't. Your type isn't capable of love. Because if you truly loved my daughter, you would have walked away from her a long time ago and let her go on to find a man who is worthy of having her. That didn't happen. And sometimes I think you stayed with her just to spite me."

No, but that was certainly an added bonus.

"Here's what I expect from you," Harry continued, starting to tap his fingers together in front of him rhythmically, as if he were some evil scientist counting the minutes until his experiment took over the world. "Tami will handle your family's finances. Tami will make the plans for holidays and special events, all of which I will be invited to. Tami will be the one that sets what you do on the weekends. Tami will tell you when to jump and how high. Are we clear?"

I could feel my pulse pumping across the veins in my head, each beat of my heart slamming against my chest. But even despite what I was feeling, I found myself more fascinated to see how insanely far he would take this. If he continued to push this toward the cliffs, I'm sure he thought I would explode and he could then turn to Tami with an 'I told you so' shrug. At that point in the play-offs, he needed an 'I told you so' moment to bring him back into the game, so he was painting this red in big, broad strokes.

But I kept my trap shut and just stared at his bald head, imagining that if I painted a dark line down the middle of it it would look like his ass.

"It's killing me to know that you are going to be part of my family. I cannot give Tami my blessing in her marriage to you. But I can and will bless her happiness. And she believes that will happen with you. You do have some hold over her. But I don't see anything special about you other than that someday you'll end up on that TV program, America's Most Wanted."

Without a doubt for killing you, Harry.

"Once you say 'I do', your life will belong to Tami. That's the way it will be. And I am going to be watching. You screw up, even a breath, you will think the wrath of God fell on your head. Because I will be there, son. And there will be hell to pay."

And with that, he was done talking, sitting there on the sofa like some swami after a spiritual proclamation.

I was done listening long before he was done talking. None of what he was saying rocked my world anymore. I was still getting married. Tami was still mine. I was glad Harry had gotten it off his chest. It could have been a great deal worse. I was just going to have to get used to it. This was a package deal; he came with Tami. And I loved the woman enough to eat his shit. It's not like I ever expected him to have an inspirational moment and suddenly realize what a terrific human being I was. Not after Tami and I bought a dream house. Not after we gave him grandkids. Not after we celebrated our 25th wedding anniversary. The only thing I had to look forward to when it came to Harry was the day I danced on his grave. Other than that, he was going to be a pit bull in this marriage that I had to constantly fend off.

That night, Tami and I planned our honeymoon. Well, she planned, I listened. As far as I cared, we could have spent a rainy week at the Motel 8 in Pensacola, Florida. But Tami had something more exotic in mind. She had her heart set on a place. A place that was magical to her.

There was a small island in the Caribbean, St. Carlos, that Tami knew intimately. Her mother's mother owned a home there, and Tami visited often as a little girl. Even after her mother's death, Grandma Ginny had her there every summer until she passed away and the house was sold. Tami's memories were idyllic, and it was a place she could see us retiring to. Ever since our second date, she had filled my head with stories about "the most beautiful spot in the world."

"When you make your way out of the jungle, your first step is on the whitest sand you've ever seen. There are these amazingly tall green reeds that sway in the breeze, sort of waving you down to this sparkling turquoise water," she would recall. "You've never seen anything like this, Todd. It is the most beautiful place I have ever seen. I cannot wait for us to be there together."

My imagination wasn't strong enough to visualize it, but the overwhelming sense of peace and beauty on Tami's face as she spoke expressed volumes about this special place she wanted to share with me. The shimmer in her eyes as she created this world for me allowed me an inroad to the most special place in her heart.

Tami told me that when she died, she wanted her ashes spread on the beach so she could live there forever.

And across the island was the Saint's Club Resort, which catered to honeymooners and couples on romantic getaways. This was Tami's dream. And ten days would be perfect.

It all seemed within reach. The wedding, the honeymoon, a life with the woman I loved. There was always the Harry Factor, but at least the train was moving now. If I could get it up to speed, I'd run his sorry butt right over the moment he stepped onto the tracks. Choo-choo.

Harry wasn't about to concede defeat. He even unearthed an old boyfriend of Tami's -- forever known as 'poor, dumb schmuck' -- and invited him home for dinner. Tami wasn't oblivious to her father's shenanigans, but this had reached a new nadir. She told me later that when she pulled the poor, dumb schmuck into the kitchen and told him the real reason her father had asked him to dinner, he kissed her on the cheek and asked her for a plate of food to go.

Every time I ran into Harry when I was picking up Tami, he would mouth off which of my twenty allotted guests hadn't returned their RSVP. "Even your parents still haven't RSVPed," Harry would announce as I walked past the living room.

"You probably forgot to put a stamp on their return envelope," I would respond, never stopping to look at him. "Don't sell their seats. They're coming."

Not that I was entirely sure. My parents, God bless their pointy little heads, were never the best at making plans. My first communion, they stumbled into the church just after the ceremony ended and I was marching down the aisle with the rest of my second grade class. Same thing when I played Abe Lincoln in the third grade. They arrived in time for the Martin Luther King "I've Got A Dream" speech. Abe had long been dead in the theater. They never saw me play a football or basketball game in high school, working out their busy, busy schedules -- usually doing a whole lot of nothing since my father never had a steady job and my mother was also dubiously unemployed -- was simply too great a task. By the time my high school graduation rolled around, I'd grown so accustomed to them never showing up for things that I didn't even bother to tell them the date and time. I got up in the morning, showered, ate a little breakfast, and walked out with my cap and gown under my arm, adding, "I'll see you after I graduate."

My mom simply waved as she shoved the dirty plates into the dishwasher. My father didn't look up from the sports page where he was busy scribbling down the favorites for the college basketball play-offs so he could call in his bets.

They never even asked if I actually received my diploma.

My guest list for the wedding was short. My absentee parents back East, my younger brother, Kyle, who I had finally tracked down in Seattle and asked to be my best man, a couple guys I used to dog the bars with, and a few work associates, including my boss, George, who furtively wagered five hundred dollars in an office pool against me ever making it to the altar. Prick. Tami questioned why I hadn't invited more guests, but this was a very special day in my life, and I held so few people close it made this experience with Tami that much more important to me. Many of my old guy friends had fallen away in the last few months since I met her. I wasn't keeping bar seats warm anymore. It's shocking how little you have to say to drunks when you aren't drunk yourself.

The rest of the hundred plus guests were Everett invitees.

As anybody who's been in a wedding party knows, it's customary for the groom's parents to buck up for the rehearsal dinner. But unlike Harry Everett, who would do anything for his offspring, my old man made it vivid that once I was out from under his roof, never to hook him for money. Ever.

For anything. "I don't care if you need a kidney," he said to me as I packed up to go to college. So I didn't waste my breath inquiring whether he was going to pay for the rehearsal dinner. If he wasn't going to chip in for a body part, anything associated with my happiness certainly didn't stand a chance. It's not like he had much dough anyway. My dad resented paying his bills, except his bar tab. He had priorities. When I was twelve, he actually sold his car to keep drinking. He ripped a cardboard lid off a case of beer bottles and wrote: 'For Sail. $500.' No lie. 'For Sail.' But when you're marketing your wheels to other drunks that's a perfectly acceptable spelling.

My hard drinking didn't occur in a vacuum, but I was a virtual saint next to my father. If there were going to be any added dividend to marrying Tami, it would be that moment when my drunken father cornered Harry in the bathroom to discuss the newlyweds, love, life, and whatever future failed business venture he was presently involved in. My father was always loaded with sage advice and offered it unsolicited. Harry and he would be the most happy couple at the wedding. Until Harry made the sign of the cross and plunged the cake knife into his chest to escape another of my father's incoherent soliloquies on the multi-million dollar deal he's got in the works.

My parents are a funny lot. And not ha-ha funny. They're working class, though my old man would never admit to that because, as he always put it, "I have dreams. Look around. You think any of our neighbors have dreams? That's why I'm not like them." Now I'm all for having dreams. But I'm much bigger on having dreams that have a shot in hell of amounting to something. My dad would rush head-long from one grand scheme to another, pouring in what little savings he had or could con out of someone next to him on a bar stool at the Legion Hall. Then, for a few days he would be flush with the white-hot excitement of a gambler on a streak and fill our heads with all the prizes he'd be buying once his dream took shape.

He might as well have pissed the money down the toilet in some crappy bar. Which is what he did after each and every dream went down in flames. Yet his endless failures didn't stop him from sticking his nose back out there to get it bloodied one more time.

Why my mother stayed with him was always a mystery to my brother and me. She was beautiful but grew old before her time. Like a tragic character in a Tennessee Williams's play, my mother was this young girl who fell for the good-looking dreamer and would cheerlead for my father as he blew their meager savings on his next sure-fire bonanza. As I got older, I accepted the fact that my mother wasn't very bright. It was relatively simple to convince her of just about anything. An imperfection that both Kyle and I exploited through most of our teenage years. Later, my we struggled to persuade her that our father was a chromosome short of ever being a winner. A mutant loser. But God bless her, my mother was nothing if not loyal. Still is. And they're still flat ass broke in everything but bad ideas.

I put myself through college working as a bouncer in a discotheque and running a small campus gambling operation. Having a father who bet nearly every game, every weekend, I picked up a thing or two. Usually I simply thought, what would my old man bet on? And then I went the other direction. Neither gig made me rich, but it kept me enrolled and fed. Another great thing about having a father who is a perennial loser is that you have to work if you expect to own a pair of shoes that fit. It was only my father's privilege to dream. The rest of us had to earn a living.

It wasn't until I met Tami that I finally had dreams of my own.

The closer it got to the wedding, the more it became apparent that this was a Harry Everett production. For his daughter. ONLY for his daughter. The silver lining was that he was too overwhelmed to run roughshod over my ass about anything. I would like to say that he had finally accepted that the wedding was a foregone conclusion with me as the prize at the bottom of the box. But rather than acceptance, I believe it was simple resignation.

And then we were there. The finish line was a lap away, and I felt my stride long and solid. I was hardly even winded. The practice was far more difficult than the race. Harry couldn't deny the love in his daughter's eyes. As much as he resented it, the bond between us glowed stronger the more the wedding became real. Unlike my father, my dreams were only a reach away.

Finally having my name stare back at me from the invitations made the wedding a reality for me. I ran my finger over my name in raised lettering. Then I drew my finger across Tami's name. I could feel it. And I began dreaming of the first night Tami and spent on the beach in St. Carlos. Married.

I had won. For the rest of my life.

THE BIG DAY

The last few months jetted by in a blast of feverish activity that bordered on panic. For me, though, it was all pretty easy since I happily kept away from the planning. My major concern was moving Tami's furniture, clothes, and life into my place and figuring out where to put it all. My condo was not built for two people. Especially when one of them owned a massive array of clothes for all seasons. Just in case I'm not clear, that would be Tami. Her recollection of every single item in her wardrobe borders on savant genius. After stuffing as much as I could into the closet, then the guest closet, then the hall closet, and then piling everything else in the living room, I decided I'd let Tami deal with figuring out where to put what after the honeymoon. We were going to need a huge storage unit. Or a stadium.

All I was looking forward to was waving adios to my newly acquired father-in-law at the airport and acquiring major tan lines. Ten kick back days in the sun, drinking, dancing, and dining. And lots of sex with Mrs. Todd Cartwright.

Tami had already made it clear that she intended to redecorate the entire condo. My black leather furniture, all of which I had bought at a divorce sale - something I should have never told Tami - was not only jinxed according to her, it was mannish, oversized, and "icky bachelor ugly." She knew exactly which pieces of furniture her mother had delegated to her and just where she was going to place them. What Tami didn't count on was the renegotiation that Harry put her through to get the furniture. He would have gladly given her every stick of furniture in his home but for the fact that the U-Haul in the driveway was then escorting each and every piece over to my home. Each chair became a bargaining chip, a sofa was another negotiation, the bedroom chest declared a potential deal breaker. Harry needed to be reassured that Tami wasn't walking out of his life forever once she walked down that aisle. Tami would have dinner with him every Wednesday. Need I point out that it wasn't Tami and Todd who would have dinner with him every Wednesday. I was excluded from the meal. Much to my delight. Tami had to promise to be there if Harry needed help out with chores as he got older. Which really meant that the man marrying Tami would eventually end up as Harry's own personal Kunta Kinte. And finally, Tami agreed to call him twice a day, every day, even if she was coming by that day to see him.

Whatever you want, Harry. She's still going to be sharing a bed with me. And as hard as you try to put that out of your head, I'll be around to remind you with a devilish twinkle in my eye.

While the personal negotiations were in summit, I moved most of the furniture and boxes myself. When Harry wasn't eliciting promises from his daughter, he tailed me through the house, making sure I didn't ding his walls. But the highlight came when Harry deemed I needed his help moving Tami's bedroom furniture. Apparently, after moving all the heavy boxes and bulky pieces of furniture alone, I was suddenly unable to carry bedroom furniture without his assistance.

Harry outlined detailed instructions on how we were going to handle this. He hadn't spent thirty-five years as an operations manager for an airline parts manufacturing company for nothing. Or so he kept reiterating. Tami patted me on the arm and whispered, "Think of this as a bonding experience."

Oh yeah, Harry and I were going to bond over this. Like nitro and glycerin.

"Use your legs! If you hurt your back you're worthless to me," he hollered each time I went to grab something, as if each time I picked up my end of something this was all brand new to me.

Harry ordered me around like a lackey, snapping out panicked directions, which were usually the exact opposite of what he meant to say. We rammed Tami's headboard into his hallway wall, nearly snapping off one of the long bedposts. Harry eyed the damage and the direction he had ordered. Right or wrong, and he was wrong, there was no way he was going to take the blame for the dent in his wall.

"Do I need to write an L on your left hand and an R on your right?" he huffed.

Yeah, so I know which fist actually dropped you to the carpet.

Tami held a silent gaze on me, begging me not to erupt. By the time we were done, Harry had bloodied his knuckles on a doorjamb and scraped his shin tripping down his front stoop. Both, of course, my fault: I mustn't have been carrying my weight. Right Harry. It's me. I'm the problem. Even if I couldn't have done it solo, I would rather have ruptured both my nuts and compacted my spine than endure his sweaty, huffy, puffy whininess throughout the move.

I couldn't escape Harry. The last few days we were together more than ever. Tami wouldn't admit it but this was her last ditch effort to force us to find some common ground. Couldn't she see we had found one: mutual loathing. It may not have been what she had in mind but it was working pretty well for us. Harry went as far as forbidding me from depositing the wedding gift checks in the bank. He hid them, allowing only Tami to take them to the bank and put them in her personal account. Just in case I decided to run off to Vegas for a bachelor party with that massive dowry.

That's if I were actually having a bachelor party, which Harry also forbid. "How can you tell me you love my daughter and then think of having a bachelor party?" he lectured.

"Dad," Tami interjected, "Todd can have a bachelor party if he wants. I trust him."

But Harry was having none of it. "Which just proves my point about your naiveté, honey. I know what goes on...hookers, drugs, booze." Harry turned to me, wagging his finger in my face. "I didn't have one out of respect for my wife and neither should you."

This played to my complete advantage. The idea of spending the night getting loaded with a bunch of other drunk chuckleheads was way too dangerous for a man with my history. Besides, battling my body to recover before the wedding wasn't something I wanted to deal with. I had sewn all of my wild oats. And those of at least ten other guys. So acquiescing to Harry's demand, I feigned the wounded party, allowing him a hollow victory and granting my bride-to-be a respite of peace.

"I so appreciate you doing what he asked," Tami whispered to me later while we were in bed. "It gave my dad a little feeling of partnership in all of this."

Partnership? More like complete domination.

But Tami reiterated that she knew how hard this was on me.

"And I love you even more for doing it," she added.

Just as we pushed the bachelor party out of the picture, Harry announced the 'tuxedo conspiracy.' Tami had selected the style of tuxedo she wanted me and the groomsmen to wear in the wedding. And if I do say so, I was styling in the damn thing. For the father of the bride, Tami selected a more traditional style. And with only three days left before the wedding, Harry suddenly decided he hated it. "I don't understand why he looks so good in his tuxedo, and I have to look so frumpy in mine," he complained.

Yeah, Harry, it must be the tux.

All of these escapades were Harry's way of keeping Tami's attention focused in his direction. But the big day was just too close, and his attempts at staying near the center of Tami's world reeked of sweaty desperation. For Tami, it was more exhausting than damning. Harry was going to have to rethink his game. The playing field slants a different direction when you have the home field edge.

Advantage, Todd.

But I would have to work overtime to keep that advantage. I respect Harry as a worthy adversary. Without a doubt he would strive mightily to undermine my marriage until he was stiff in the ground. Even then, the odds were better than four-to-one he would come back from the grave to haunt me.

Tami's girlfriends were thankfully growing more excited the closer the wedding loomed. Their love for Tami overflowed toward me, and they were the biggest champions of us making it to the altar. Gretchen and a few other girls conspired to throw a ladies-night-out for Tami's bachelotte party. This was completely okay with Harry. "There are no hookers at bachelorette parties," he insisted.

It was completely fine with me. If I had had friends as close to me as Tami's were to her, I would have flipped Harry the bird when he demanded I not have a bachelor party. Tami's friends were so tight, I knew they wouldn't let anything get too out of hand. And she kept me apprised of the plans. The girls were going to meet for dinner at the Grill near the lake, and then a limo would pick them up for a night of club hopping.

Tami drove to Gretchen's apartment so they could gossip like excited little girls as they got ready together. But by the time they arrived at the Grill, Tami's other girlfriends had already cracked open the champagne and were in a party mood. The girls ordered expensive dinners and then opened the gifts they bought to "enhance" the honeymoon. One of the gifts was a gargantuan purple dildo they nicknamed the 'Toddmeister.' "If he ever tells you he's had a long day, whip out the Toddmeister and tell him you're going to bed early," her married friend, Rachel, explained. "He'll come running.

No man wants to be outperformed by a giant dildo," she added, speaking from experience. Tami sipped a glass of champagne and laughed as the girls passed around the Toddmeister, stroking it and talking to it as if it were a huge, pet lizard.

Then the girls piled into the limo with Davis, their driver, and cruised to the clubs up the street. They made a pact that they would not buy a single drink all night, keenly aware that every club in Chicago would be loaded with hopeful, needy, guys spilling money out of their wallets in an effort to get lucky. Useless. These women took too good of care of one another. They could be "daring" because there were five other girls there to back them up.

Tami stuck with bottled water. This made her feel like a party pooper, but she had too many last-minute details to handle. I chuckled to myself because I knew the real reason. Liquor made her puffy, and there was no way in hell she'd chance not looking her absolute best on her wedding day. As she kept reiterating to me, "Those pictures last a lifetime."

Phoning me every two hours, Tami filled me in on the evening.

"Right now we're dancing on the table," Tami bellowed into the phone and then held it out and commanded her friends to say 'hello.' All I heard was a monstrous group scream my name garbled in there somewhere.

Tami kept me updated on who was getting stupid, who was working on some unsuspecting male for more free drinks, and who was dirty dancing with some poor sap destined to go home alone. She laughed as she replayed the evening, and the fun in her voice gave me access to her world. I envied Tami. Her girlfriends were true and lifelong. Something I had never made. Tami was the first person in my life that I knew would be with me forever.

I lounged back on the sofa and thought about the last close friend I had. David Presley. His father got a decent job, and they moved out of my neighborhood when I was eleven. That was my last intimate friend. Because I was bigger than most of the kids, they were either scared of me or naturally hated me. And I never bothered to try and change their opinions. I felt safer keeping everyone at arm's length, especially as I developed demons I didn't know how to deal with. Both in my head and at home. I acted the role of the toughass without comprehending that I was sentencing myself to a life without the ability to make close friends.

Hell, I was hard-pressed to come up with enough guys to be groomsmen. I tried talking Tami into a smaller wedding party, but she refused to exclude any of her girlfriends. I found myself calling in the second stringers to stand up for me because I didn't have a starting line-up. But given the chance for a free dinner and the possibility to meet chicks, I knew they'd at least show up.

Tami called again as they were heading home in the limo. She passed the phone around to her girlfriends, all of whom told me she had behaved like a dutiful fiancée all night. They teased me about the Toddmeister and lauded me with each bridesmaid's tales of debauchery and excess. I howled with laughter. I was not used to women talking so intimately with me. Even stranger, I knew that these women would be my friends for the rest of my life because of my love for Tami. But more importantly, I knew I had their respect for exactly the same reason.

I can assure you that if they had met me six months before I met Tami, they would have hated me with every fiber of their being. So that respect meant a lot. It marked me as a changed man. A happily changed man.

I told Tami I loved her, and she repeated the words back to me and then told me she would call before she fell asleep. That had become a nightly thing for us. We never went to sleep without sharing the day and telling each other that we loved each other. We had vowed to carry that over once we got married. It was a beautiful way to never go to bed mad. I had spent most of my life going to bed mad. Half the time I didn't even need a reason. No wonder why I never slept well. But lying on my bed with the phone to my ear, my eyes shut, listening to the woman I loved recalling the joys, triumphs, and hurts of her day was like someone rocking me in their arms. She allowed me to dream. And sleep. Because there was something in my life to wake up to.

I waited for the phone to ring. Maybe she was sitting with Harry, relaying pieces of the evening, omitting any details he would disapprove of; she knew better than to set him off. Since he wasn't going to have her for much longer, Harry monopolized more and more of her time. I knew Tami wouldn't forget about me. She would wait until she was under the covers and then call. We would laugh our asses off for about an hour and then finish with "I love yous" before we both hung up and went to sleep.

But two hours after she should have been home, there was still no call. It was now nearing three in the morning. I felt a pinch of hurt that Tami may have fallen asleep without calling me. I dialed her cell number but got her voice mail. Damn it, the cell phone was either turned off or in her purse and she couldn't hear the ring. It left me no option other than to call her home number. Inevitably Harry would pick up, pissed off that I had woken him. I didn't need to poke the tiger through the bars now that I was on the downhill slide to the finish line.

Problem was I couldn't fall asleep. My body tossed from side to side, front to back. I dozed but couldn't actually slumber. I needed to hear her voice. She should have called. It was like an itch I couldn't scratch. It was nearing four in the morning. I sat up and again pulled the phone to my ear. Fuck Harry. If I woke him up, I woke him up. He couldn't hate me any more than he already did. I dialed Tami's home number. The phone rang. And rang. The answering machine picked up.

A wired chill ran through my body, and I broke into a sweat. This was wrong. Even if Tami was fast asleep, Harry would have shot up in bed at the first ring and been barking at me through the receiver seconds later. I dialed again, and again, the answering machine picked up.

I was out the door in three minutes, pulling a shirt over my head and carrying my shoes.

I don't remember driving over to Tami's. My head was gyrating with too many scenarios. Harry had kidnapped Tami to prevent her from marrying me. Harry had slipped over the edge and tried to kill himself in order to stop the wedding. Every scenario I envisioned involved Harry doing something stupidly wrong or blatantly evil. The closer I got to their home, the faster I drove. The faster I drove, the more pissed off I became.

I jerked the car to the curb in front of the Everett house. Tami's car wasn't in the driveway. I walked up and peeked into the garage through the dusty window. Harry's car was gone too. What the hell was going on?

I pounded on the door, but there was no answer. My patience snapped, and I threw a shoulder into it, just under the tarnished silver door knocker. The door shimmied but the locks held. My brain finally shot a few sane impulses across its bow, and I remembered that Tami always slept with her window slightly ajar; she liked the fresh air no matter how cold it was. When she first started sleeping at my place, there were a few nights I almost froze my ass off.

The curtains were drawn, and I called in, but Tami didn't answer. Yanking the screen off, I shoved the window open wide, throwing myself through, falling to the floor with a house-shaking thud.

Her bed hadn't been slept in.

There were clothes strewn about, hinting that she had gone through a few dresses before deciding on which to wear to her bachelorette party. But it wasn't like Tami to leave clothes strewn about before she went to bed. She had already trained me not to leave a mess for the morning. "Put it away or put it in the hamper," she would tell me.

Her wedding dress hung in a bag on the back of the door. Nothing was out of the ordinary except for that bed, the comforter pulled up neatly, the pillows placed tidily on top. I felt my heart pounding hard in my ears.

Something had happened. Something bad.

Making my way down the hall, I peeked into Harry's room. His bed was a rumbled mess. I knew where Tami got her freaky neatness, and his bed being unmade hinted that something extreme had occurred. I stomped down the hallway and into the kitchen, flipping on lights, searching for some clue as to where Harry and Tami had disappeared to. I called my place, hoping there was a message.

None.

Breath-shortening panic was congealing inside me. I tried to keep myself from unraveling, clinging tightly to any shard of rational thought so I could hold my shit together. I didn't know anything was wrong. Not really. But with Tami, I had earned this connection. And I sensed the worst. There was someplace I needed to be. I just didn't know where.

As I was about to head out the front door, the phone rang. Harry's house or not, I answered it. It was Gretchen.

"Is it true?" she demanded in a voice that was hostile and panicked.

I didn't know what the hell she was asking. And I was frightened down to my balls to find out.

"What?! What?! What are you talking about?" I questioned quickly, trying not to let her hear the panic rising in my voice.

"Nancy called. Tami was in an accident after picking up her car at my place!"

"Is she sure!? How does she know this?!"

Gretchen began to cry. "I don't know, I don't know," she repeated.

"Where is she?" I was breathing so hard the blood wasn't making it to my heart.

"University."

I dropped the phone and ran.

AND THEY LIVED HAPPILY EVER AFTER

I don't remember stopping for traffic lights or stop signs. At that hour there weren't many cars on the road. I buzzed around the ones there were, my head spinning, my eyes unable to put images into perspective, as if everything were being viewed through a kaleidoscope. I remember chunks of time. Chunks of spatial images. But nothing in its entirety. All I wanted to do was wail like a fire-trapped wolf, calling to his mate to come and save him. But I held it back, keeping a tight rein on my imagination. I couldn't let it take over, or I would have driven my car right into a brick wall.

I whipped into the first parking spot I could find in the hospital lot and sprinted into the building.

"Tami Everett," I said, pounding on the desk, causing every nurse within twenty yards to jump. The nurse manning the desk pointed down the hallway. "Check ER," she said. If she said anything else, I didn't hear it. I raced in the direction she pointed. I could feel tears starting to break through my best effort to keep myself together. ER. That was bad. Worse than my emotions could manage.

The ER waiting room was packed. People with all sorts of ailments and wounds, waiting silently with an aura of helplessness and pain. This only fueled my delirium. I shoved around the injured at the checkout counter and pushed to the front of the line.

"Tami Everett!"

The harried woman behind the counter glanced up at me. I didn't like the look on her face.

"Are you family?" she asked.

Oh, shit. Why is she asking that?

"Fiancé. We're getting married in two days."

Her face dropped even further, the sides of her mouth curling down. This was a woman who saw terribleness every day and enured herself from its ravages. But she was giving me a wounded look in preparation for what was to come. Even the injured people in the line reacted, sensing that this was going to be a much worse night for someone else. The woman literally reached out and grabbed my hand. "Come on," she said, leading me out of the line and through a door.

I wanted her to tell me what had happened. How bad it was. But I was too terrified to ask. Not knowing was better. This couldn't be that bad. Just couldn't.

Once she had me in the ER area, she pointed down a long hallway where doctors and nurses shuffled quickly, like disoriented ants after a six-year-old has crushed their nest.

"Listen to me," she began. "Right now she's in surgery. Her father is down the hallway. There's a small chapel..."

"Chapel," I huffed out, tears flooding my eyes, my vision blurring. "Why is he in the chapel?!"

She didn't want to tell me. "Go," is all she said.

I felt myself moving down the hallway as if my feet were moving but the rest of my body was melting with every step, leaving me dizzy and cold. The doctors and nurses didn't stop me, didn't talk to me, didn't even seem to notice me. They were too busy on their quest to save lives. Was one of the lives that needed saving Tami's? I was this lumbering shell who moved like a phantom to the end of the hallway and toward the chapel. As I passed one of the emergency operating rooms, my eyes landed on something that froze me.

I couldn't see anything. The medical team crowded around tightly, moving almost hypnotically trying to save a life. The endless plethora of tubes pushed into a body, sustaining it, signified the direness of what was. As a nurse moved away, a woman's hand was unveiled. The ring. My gift to Tami. The motionless woman on that operating table was my fiancée.

"Sir, you cannot be here," a woman's voice said, as a hand gripped my forearm. I looked over at a tiny nurse.

"Is that Tami Everett?" I asked with a raw fear in my voice, while all emotion inside begin to freeze to save myself from the truth.

"Sir," the tiny nurse said again, "either go to the waiting room or the chapel. But you cannot be here."

My eyes locked on her engagement ring one more time. My expression never changed, my eyes going dead. I could no longer hear my heartbeat. I turned and plodded toward the chapel in an agonizing stupor that was fighting to save my sanity from an all-too painful reality lying in that emergency room.

Inside the chapel, Harry was on his knees. His head rested on the pew in front of him, his hands clasped over his head in prayer. He didn't hear me enter, but as I got closer he sat up rigidly, his eyes open in fear, thinking I could be a doctor. Seeing me, he relaxed briefly but quickly grew tense.

It took me a moment to form any words. All I could force out was, "What?"

I can't remember what he said. It was beyond surreal. Words slapped me like the sting of a wet rag. Accident. Drunk driver. Trapped. Skull. Brain. Hemorrhage. Broken. Ruptured. Torn. Firemen. Ambulance. Surgery.

I stood. For a long time. Not moving. I couldn't puzzle the images together into anything I could understand, as if from a bad night of drinking where I knew I had done something atrocious but couldn't remember exactly what. Harry never took his eyes off me. They were rimmed with tears, dark red, as if he had been crying blood. I peered deep into his tired, old, and now damaged eyes. It was the crimson tint that seemed to finger through my fog and touch me inside, letting me know exactly how grave this truly was.

Then I felt it, a clawing rage. A fear. It grew like a wild tumor from the bowels of my soul. I began to heave. My entire body shook like a swelling earthquake. I lost all feeling in my legs. I couldn't control it. Shaking, I suddenly sensed my knees tighten up, and, without warning, I toppled. I grabbed the pew as I fell. Harry jumped, more from fear then assistance. But as I hit the pew, crushing it into the one in front, Harry took hold of me from behind, trying to steady me. I knocked down three pews like bowling pins with Harry attached to my back.

I let go of a scream that ripped my soul from my body. Harry crashed on top of me, disoriented from the fall and scared of the immense pain that vibrated from my body. In that moment, I understood helplessness clearer than any emotion I had ever known. It owned me. I wasn't going to shake it. I couldn't rage against it.

I punched the floor over and over as tears blinded me, my body still trembling uncontrollably. Slowly, Harry lifted himself off my back. He stepped back as I tried to crawl away but I couldn't do it. I couldn't move. I wanted desperately to huddle in a corner and lick the deep wound that was threatening to slowly bleed me to death.

Harry stood over me as I suffered on the floor, unsure of how to deal with me. My pain, like his, was too personal to infringe upon. The woman I loved more than my own life lay on a table in a room not twenty yards from me, as doctors tried to piece together her broken body.

When I finally sat up, Harry didn't speak. Just stared. As if I wasn't entitled to the depth of my anguish. I leaned back against a pew and stayed there. Without a word, he walked away, moving across the small chapel to kneel again in one of the pews I hadn't crushed in my fall. Once more, he dropped his head and folded his hands above it.

I never much believed in prayer. It wasn't that I didn't believe in God. I just didn't believe that God bothered with us individually. And events like this proved my point. God would never let anything bad happen to that wonderful woman. Yet it did. God was not to blame. The blame landed squarely on the young drunk driver lying down in the morgue of the hospital, who had run a red light going nearly seventy-five miles an hour, just as Tami had pulled into the intersection.

When I was finally capable of comprehending what had happened -- and what was happening -- Tami was in her third hour of surgery. They had moved her from the ER up to OR, and Harry and I were ushered to another waiting room. Tami's girlfriends had begun to gather. They rushed to us, hugging, crying. I never spoke. What could I say? I couldn't make them feel better when I felt like my life had caved in and buried me. I let them hug me, but it felt like they were holding onto someone else. Someone I didn't know. I felt their bodies aching for some kind of support, but I had none to give. My limbs trembled, fear seeping through me. I knew I may never hold the woman I loved again. I was not ready for that. I was not ready to give her up.

The longer we waited without a word, the more aware I became. And the more anger I sensed welling up inside me. It was old anger, rage I had entombed when I met Tami. For many years it was the emotion most at the surface for me. Lying dormant, it had only become more potent. Vital. Vengeful. This was an unleashed demon that was quickly spreading through me like a super-virus. I abruptly stood and rushed down the hallway. With each step I felt a fuse inside me burning closer to the explosive.

"How do I get to the morgue?" I demanded from some white lab coat. He gave me quick directions. I jumped into an open elevator and pressed basement.

The basement smelled like clinical, clean death. There were small labs with stainless steel tables on either side of a florescent-lit hallway. My steps echoed off the narrow walls. I found the morgue at about the same time a chubby, baby-faced attendant wandered out of a back room.

"Whatchu doin' down here?" he questioned, his eyes narrowing suspiciously as he swallowed what he had been eating.

"They brought in a guy a few hours ago. Auto accident. He was drunk."

"You here to identify him?"

"Yeah, I'll identify him," I said emotionlessly, my fury in check.

I knew the attendant didn't believe me, but he also could tell that it was in his best interests not to fuck with me. He hobbled towards the wall in the back where they housed bodies in stainless steel, refrigerated apartments and yanked one of the handles. He pulled out the body covered with a white sheet.

"He died upstairs in ER. He's been cleaned up, but they're going to want to do an autopsy before they release his body."

Flipping down the sheet, I stared into the face of this young guy who couldn't have been older than twenty-five. He had a gash on his forehead and massive bruising. I held my hard gaze on the youthful, almost fresh face of the man who had damaged the woman I loved.

"Could you leave me alone a minute?" I muttered to the attendant.

"I'm sorry, I can't really do that--"

But I turned with a glower so intense it nearly scorched him. He took a step back. Realizing that my request wasn't really a question, his eyes locked on my heaving chest. Quickly, he mumbled something about getting an ID report and told me to take my time. He left me alone with the body.

I balled up my fist and began punching. Over and over again, I wailed on the guy's face and body. The sound gave me an instant sense of relief as skin smacked skin, ribs cracked, nose broke, bones snapped. Punch by punch, it released gallons of the ungodly pain that pulsed through my body. I couldn't truly hurt this kid, but I knew that if he were alive, I would have killed him. No hesitation. I can't say I'm proud of what I did, but I needed some course of action other than tears.

As the attendant wandered back in with papers on a clipboard, I flipped the sheet back over the battered body.

"This isn't who I thought it was," I said, pushing by the attendant, rubbing my bruised knuckles.

Back upstairs, everyone sat. Tears had given way to terse silence among Tami's friends. Except for Rachel, who was sobbing inconsolably, succumbing to the melodramatic effects of the liquor still in her body, and Gretchen who was telling her through pursed lips to "pull her shit together and shut up." But everyone knew that the longer this took, the worse the news would be.

I wanted to be left alone, but if there were news, I needed to be right there. I allowed Tami's girlfriends to hold my hand or lean on my shoulder. For their comfort. Not mine. Every time my eye caught Harry, he was scowling at me with a glaring blame. A dark simmer which I couldn't understand. I wanted to ask him what his goddamn problem was, but I couldn't do that. Not there.

Five hours after she'd gone into surgery, the lead surgeon, Doctor John Frankel, stepped into the waiting room, exhausted. His heavy brow knitted together in a perpetual frown.

As I stood, Harry pushed past me and right into the doctor's face. I was a head taller than Harry so it didn't matter. The doctor looked at me. I needed to watch the doctor's lips because I was so distorted; I would have to see what words his mouth formed to make sure I understood exactly what had happened. What to expect. I held my breath.

"I don't know how this girl is alive," Dr. Frankel said, his eyes darting toward each of us, but never seeming to land on any of us. "She has massive internal injuries. She broke her neck, her right leg, and both her arms. But the biggest problem we have right now is that the right side of her skull was smashed. We had to remove a piece of her cerebrum."

"Her brain," Gretchen questioned with a gasp from somewhere behind me.

Dr. Frankel could only nod. "Right now I would have to give her a less than fifty-fifty chance of making it through the next twenty-four hours. If she is able to hold on, her odds go up."

"What does that mean?" Harry forced out with what I knew had to be nothing but utter agony.

Again, Dr. Frankel shook his head. "We have to wait and see."

When he finished speaking, everyone seemed to collapse into one another for support. I caught Harry and held onto him. He actually turned and hugged me, needing to feel that someone was there. I simply felt anesthetized, completely frozen in limbo.

My world was being erased as if it had never existed.

As Harry pulled free of me, he glanced up, catching my eye. Again, bitter culpability. I felt my hand ball up. I wanted to smack the shit out of him for even fantasizing that any of the blame for this was mine. But Harry needed to strike out. I understood that feeling. I acted on it. But he assigned blame to the person he knew was even closer to Tami than he was. Blame Todd. Otherwise he would have to face the reality. There would be plenty enough months ahead while Tami healed for Harry and me to tangle, to spit insults at one another, and cast accountability over her injuries.

All day we sat in that waiting room, reaching out to any hospital employee for news of Tami's condition. The hours dragged. One by one, Tami's friends left to shower and change clothes, while a few of Harry's buddies arrived to sit with him. As I sat there, I believed with all my soul that Tami and I would still be married. Cynical as I was, I still counted on that miracle that would allow her to walk down the aisle on Harry's arm that Saturday. Miracles happened. I had believed in them ever since Tami had entered my life. And I couldn't see any reason why there couldn't be one now.

As the day progressed into evening, and the giant orange globe sank before my eyes, I fought the parasitic despair that was digging under my skin. Each doctor or nurse that came out to talk to us followed the same pattern: a shake of the head and then the words, "No news."

Fuck.

How did I battle this?

The waiting room was packed with Tami's friends and family. I felt like an interloper, not the man she was to marry at the end of the week. I didn't fit in with these people. My only connection to them lay in another room somewhere battling for life. They had history. I was the outsider, the one who only came coupled with Tami. I couldn't shake the irrational feeling that their pain was more valid than mine. They had a right to a deeper anguish. Mine didn't rank. Time mattered, intimacy did not.

As the night ticked on, one by one people disappeared. Harry told Tami's girlfriends he would call them if there were a change. They gave lingering hugs and left in a group, leaving only myself and Harry to wait for news.

"Why don't you go home and get some sleep. I'll call you if there's any news," Harry demanded rather than suggested. His first words to me since that morning in the chapel.

I held a silent gaze on him. Who the fuck did he think I was? Some kid who had had a crush on Tami once in high school and happened to catch wind of her accident? I was her goddamn fiancé, the man with whom she was to spend the rest of her life. Fuck him. Fuck him.

Responding darkly, I asked, "Just like you called me this morning?"

Harry stiffened, his tired eyes narrowing. He had to know that was coming, but I don't think he expected it then.

"I was going to call you when I knew something," he snapped back.

"I am marrying Tami! She is going to be my wife! You don't have a goddamn monopoly over her, and you're not the only one feeling like shit, Harry. I should have been called right away. You may hate me, but she loves me. When are you going to get that through your thick skull? What you did to me is fucking cruel. And I won't ever forget it."

Harry hyperventilated. He stayed in the chair for a long beat and then stood.

"If you weren't marrying her, none of this would have happened," Harry uttered through his clenched teeth.

So this is what tied his intestines into knots. He actually did hold me responsible for this psychotic nightmare. He couldn't blame God. Or fate. But I gave him a focus for condemnation. I had knocked his world off its axis by falling in love with his daughter, and now he had a tragedy to cast upon me.

"You're damn right. We should have eloped. Kept you away. Then this would have never happened."

"How dare you talk to me like that, you little bastard," Harry barked out, injured, as he took a threatening step in my direction.

I stood quickly, ready.

"You come at me, Harry," I growled, "I will put you down. Tami's father or not, I will knock you out."

It was the first time I'd ever physically threatened him. Part of it wasn't him. Part of it was my own crushing fear. But enough of it was warranted. My words were meant to hurt Harry. Yeah, it was his daughter lying in a bed somewhere in that fucking building, fighting for her life, but she was my future. I was the man she CHOSE to spend the rest of her life with, so he couldn't dismiss me like I don't matter in this goddamn equation. I wanted it to sting. Deep.

From where I stood, Harry earned my threats. I was done. I'd been silent for far too long, taking a bath in his shit for the last half a year. I wasn't playing any longer. Especially now that all bets were off. I wasn't worried about his feelings. I was worried about Tami. Period. Do not pass go, do not collect two hundred dollars. I almost wished he would have kept coming at me; I could have ended this competitive horse crap once and for all. But Harry knew better than to challenge me.

"You selfish piece of shit," Harry slurred out between his tight lips. "I'll have you barred from this hospital. I can make sure you never see her again," he threatened idly, before trudging down the hallway, going nowhere but away from me.

I was finally alone. For the first time since I had dashed into that hospital and gone searching for the woman I loved, I was by myself. It allowed me to do what I had been waiting to be alone to do. I wanted to keep crying until I knew Tami was well. As long as it took. In penance for my sins, in case they were the reason she had to suffer. I didn't know what the future would be for us, but with everything the doctors had said, and hadn't said, it was undeniable that the forecast was far different than the life she and I had planned. We would have months, if not years of recovery. And with issues of brain surgery, who knows what Tami would or would not be capable of after it was over. Even the doctors couldn't tell us that. I had to prepare myself for almost anything. Including the fact that she might not even remember who I was. That the last glorious six months of our lives would be a complete void to her. Or she could be an entirely different woman. Not the one I was going to walk down the aisle with on Saturday. I had no clue as to what was coming.

Other than that it wasn't going to be what I had expected. That dream had passed.

DAWNING BEFORE DARK

I prepared myself for what was coming. As long as Tami was with me, I made a vow to deal with whatever was thrown at us. Medical, emotional, psychological, I would grit my teeth, tense my muscles, and slog through it, if it kept Tami on the road to recovery. But I wasn't sure exactly what Harry could deal with. His daughter had been a twenty plus year project for him. Tami, his sun and moon, his morning, noon, and night. If she couldn't remember him or the life he had given her, it would destroy him.

All night, Harry and I wandered the hallways. Sat in the waiting room. Paced the floors. Prayed in the chapel. Dozed now and again. But mostly we waited. Just never in the same place.

The parking lot filled with cars, doctors and nurses returning for the morning shift. Patients arriving for their morning appointments. Dr. Frankel stepped outside into the coolness of the morning, where I stood sipping cold coffee from a Styrofoam cup and staring blankly at nothing. His eyes were tired, his shoulders slumped low. I didn't have to be Kreskin to know the news was going to punch me in the face.

"I want you to come in and see her," Dr. Frankel began as he shook his head. "Her EEG is still flat. Todd, the damage to the cerebrum is deep. Now that the swelling has gone down, we can see that her brain stem was nearly torn in half."

I waved my hand in his face, closing my eyes hard and shaking my head. "I don't know what---I can't think. What-what-what are you saying? Just say it."

Dr. Frankel leaned against the post near me, trying to get me to look him in the eye. Finally, I mustered the strength to raise my head, allowing my bloodshot eyes to lock into his. "There's no brain activity. There hasn't been any since she came in. Her body is being kept alive by the machines, but..."

He paused, giving his words a moment to latch onto my own gray matter. He waited patiently for an answer. But what could I say? What did he want to hear? My ears felt like they were filling with blood, and all I could hear was my own pulse beating in my chest.

"Son, it's not fair to her, to her memory. Don't make the decision to keep her alive. She's not going to recover. She's never coming back."

I didn't blame God. But at that moment I hated Him. I hated Dr. Frankel. I hated all of Tami's girlfriends. I hated Harry the most. As if everyone didn't already know that. I despised everybody and anybody who breathed on their own. I had never comprehended why anyone would want to take their own life until that moment. Because I wanted to take mine rather than deal with that reality.

There's strength in numbers. And right then I was a big, fat, fucking zero.

I combated tears. I kept repeating the mantra, "Stay strong..." Which is far easier repeated in your head than when you're standing in the path of an emotional tsunami.

Would this doctor completely freak out if I wrapped my arms around him, buried my head in his shoulder, and cried like a little girl? Because that's exactly what I felt like doing.

"Tami and I aren't married yet," I struggled, "We are...we were...we are. Fuck!" I didn't know how to say this. "We're supposed to get married Saturday," I finally forced out. "This decision isn't mine. You'll have to talk to her father."

He had. Harry said he would not allow Tami to be unhooked from the machines. Harry refused to believe that God would take his only daughter from him.

"He shouldn't do this to his daughter," Dr. Frankel stated. "I've seen this too many times. If there was any hope, I wouldn't be asking. Please, you have to reason with him."

I almost laughed. Reason with him? Harry? I couldn't do that if the topic were the color of the sky. But this? Shit. I had no clue how to explain to Dr. Frankel the insanity of what he was asking me to do. Harry and Todd's Traveling Circus

From Hell. Talk to Harry? Get fucking real. I might as well have cut off my head and handed it to the bastard. That would have been the only way Harry would've talk to me. Especially about Tami. And most especially about me asking him to let his little girl die.

Painful as it was, I logically wrapped my head around why it was the best thing to do. But I couldn't ask Harry to pull the plug. At that moment, having Tami alive, even if only via a machine, allowed me some hope. He wanted me to ask her father to do what I couldn't.

"Doctor, Harry Everett hates me," I said, stopping there as my voice cracked.

"You love his daughter. I can see that. You have to do what's right for her. Not for you. Not for him. She is not coming back, Mr. Cartwright. Tami is dead. Please, speak to him."

Nodding was all I was capable of, as my focus seemed to explode in a thousand different directions like a Chinese bottle rocket.

After being outside, I found the dead air inside the hospital stifling. The florescent lights cast everything in an eerie, dull pallor. I kept gulping breaths as if I were wearing scuba gear, walking into the waiting room, searching for Harry. He wasn't there. Which meant he was in the chapel praying for the miracle that he would never see.

He sat in the first row. In the same prostrate position I had found him in previously. I moved up and sat in the pew behind him. He didn't look at me, though he knew why I was there. He wouldn't give me the benefit of turning. I reached out and touched his back. I felt him tense.

"Harry, the doctor says that we need to take Tami off the machines. That she's gone."

He didn't answer.

"Harry, talk to me. This is killing me too."

But he refused to budge from his prayers.

"You're not going to do this to her. I won't let her lay there like a vegetable just to give you some feeble reason to live. Give them the okay and let her go with some dignity."

Harry jumped up, spinning around, his finger pointing at me, his eyes wild with fury. "You ARE NOT her husband! You have no right to tell me what to do. This is my decision. My decision! I will tell them what to do!"

"Then do the right thing for Tami."

"You don't count in this," Harry snapped.

"Neither do you," I shot back. "This is about the woman I love. And I'm not letting you keep her body alive because you can't face life without her. I don't give a shit about you, Harry. You want to kill yourself after this, I'll buy you the bullets. I care about Tami. I love her! So fuck you! If what's best for her is letting her go, then I'm going to do it with or without your permission, you miserable son of a bitch."

Even though he logically knew I couldn't follow through on my threats, my words pierced him. He shook. And then he broke. He grabbed the pew and began to sob. I don't know what compelled me to stand up and pull him to me other than I knew exactly what he was feeling down to the last tingling thread of anguish. We were never connected before this moment -- and doubtfully would ever be again. Not on that level. I sobbed too, my tears falling on his shoulder. A bond forged from a pain so raw that it seared both our souls into one.

"How do I...?" Harry couldn't finish the sentence, though I knew what he was asking.

"I don't know. But you have to," I said softly in one breath.

Harry pulled away from me. Neither of us spoke as we strode down the hallway to the nurse's station. We asked to see Doctor Frankel. They paged him and he arrived quickly. Harry couldn't bring himself to say the words, leaving the agonizing deed to me.

"Do it," I said to Doctor Frankel, the only words I was able to finish.

His hand shook as he signed the documents to take Tami off life support. I could feel Harry's body harden, almost as if it were involuntarily sweating out scorching heat. Once he finished signing his name, he closed the pen, and out of habit, slid it into his shirt pocket, just as he probably had every day of his work life.

Leading us to Tami's room, Dr. Frankel didn't speak. I was hoping he would give us a morsel of what to expect, of what to do once we were in the room. Is there no goddamn protocol for killing someone you love? I felt completely isolated with Harry walking ahead of me, as if he were stepping closer and closer to his own death.

At the door to Tami's room, Harry turned and stuck out his hand, stopping me.

"I don't want you in there. She's my daughter. I should do this alone."

I was frozen, as if someone had shot dry ice up through my feet and was filling my body. My eyes caught Dr. Frankel's, begging him to come to my rescue. But he remained silent, distancing himself from this personal war.

"Don't do this to me, Harry," the words tumbled out slowly in a tone that nearly whined like an injured dog. "DO NOT do this."

Harry kept his hand up, his head shaking. My pleading eyes fastened on him, like a drowning man grasping at a small float he knows isn't enough to keep his head above water.

"Harry...you keep me out of this room, you will take everything I have. I love her more than my own life." I paused and then said without malice, "You do this to me, I will spend the rest of it making your life a fucking hell."

The flicker in Harry's eyes shifted darkly. He knew I wasn't kidding. I would make this bastard suffer. He had tapped the deepest well of my inhumanity and was dangling his feet in a pool filled with the most awful monsters he'd ever encountered. Whether he was doing this to hurt me or because he truly felt it should be a private moment between he and Tami didn't matter. This would wreck me. And I would unleash a jihad on his ass from which he would never recover.

Slowly, Harry's hand fell to his side. Without a word, he turned and walked into the room where Tami lay. I followed, moving past Dr. Frankel.

As I walked into her room, I closed my eyes. My memories of this woman who had held all of my adoration lapped just under the surface. I could hear her voice tell me she loved me. When I heard a whimper rise out of Harry my eyes popped open. I grabbed the bed to keep from buckling as my body shuddered.

It took Harry and I a long moment to cognitively grasp that this battered and bandaged body was actually Tami. Nothing in my life, and I had seen a shitload, had prepared me for this. Logically, I could see. Emotionally, all I could feel was a snarling, snapping rage coursing through me.

Harry shuffled around to the far side of her bed, keeping his grip on the mattress, woozy from the sight of his battered daughter. I stepped up on Tami's right side. We held her delicate hands in ours; her engagement ring was still on her finger. I knew that even in death she loved me. Harry and I took turns whispering in Tami's ear, telling her that we loved her, how much she meant to us, all those little things that we hoped she knew but you don't say as often as you should. We both wept until we couldn't breathe.

Mr. Everett, Mr. Cartwright...hold her. Send her off," Doctor Frankel said.

Harry and I wrapped our arms around her tiny, broken body. We tried being gentle but couldn't hurt her. We could only love her.

I buried my face into Tami's neck, smelling it for the last time as I heard switches being clicked off. Struggling acutely, I focused my senses so I would always recall everything about the last time I had felt my lover's body moving. The rise and fall of her chest continued for a brief moment and then it ceased. I could literally feel everything about Tami shutting down, as the tattered vestiges of her life stopped.

Her death was so non-epic it was almost confusing in its simplicity.

I don't know how long we held onto her before a nurse asked Harry and me to step out of the room. Neither of us wanted to but we had no fight left in us.

Walking out of the hospital, I realized that for the past day my life had stood in suspended animation, but the rest of the world had carried on, unaware of what I now had to survive. For the first time since meeting Tami, I felt insignificant. Having Tami in my life, I proudly fashioned myself into the role of her boyfriend, her fiancé, her lover. It blessed me with a golden sense of purpose. Now I was thrown into the life raft and cut from the ship. Left to drift right back into real life. Real life, only worse.

As Harry and I shuffled across the hot asphalt parking lot towards our cars, we knew we would have to administer the arrangements like a military operation when your platoon is under heavy fire. Do it now; cry later. I told him that I would call Tami's girlfriends. He would call family. I volunteered to cancel all the wedding plans. He said he would take care of the memorial and cremation. It was utterly matter of fact. Neither of us allowing sentiment to interfere with the job. Though Harry and I were psychologically bankrupt, we could not sink under the ballast of emotion.

Other people tried to help out. They dropped off food and offered comfort. Some assisted with the arrangements. Gretchen sat with me for hours, not speaking. With her girlfriends she could cry and reminisce, but she knew that my wound was vastly different than hers. As was my love for Tami. I knew Gretchen was looking out for me, cognizant that I could hurt myself or someone else if left alone. But she was a smart girl. No small talk. No tearful comfort. No melancholy memories in an effort to get me to smile. My nature was to lash out when wounded. Gretchen sensed that any contact would cause me to explode. The shrapnel would have shredded her to bloodied ribbons.

I didn't want sympathy, didn't want anyone to hug me. My skin actually hurt. Even a shower stung. And at least five times every day I needed to release my unearthly moans and punch the walls.

In the lobby of my building, as I was coming back from returning my unused tux, the mailwoman smiled at me widely. "Congratulations," she said.

A freakishly long moment of silence later, it dawned on me that she wasn't talking about Tami's death. She was talking about my wedding. Tomorrow. She held out a stack of what were obviously wedding cards sent in the mail.

"And only one bill," she smiled again. "When's the big day?"

She must have thought I was semi-retarded because, again, it took me a gaping beat to answer her. What the hell do you say? And she was smiling so sincerely.

"Tomorrow," I responded, taking the stack of wedding cards.

"Are you nervous?"

I blinked. "Scared to death."

"You'll make it. It's one day. And then you'll have the rest of your life to laugh about all the craziness," she added with a laugh of her own, touching my arm warmly. "Just remember, enjoy it. Hopefully, you'll only do it once," she added with a wink.

How absurdly interchangeable marrying a woman and having her die are, when you're making small talk.

I canceled the reception hall, the band, the cake. The woman making the cake turned belligerent when I told her we wouldn't be needing it but it would be paid for, demanding to know why we weren't using her 'creation.' As if I had insulted her artistic integrity.

"You want to know why? Because my fiancée was killed yesterday, and it's REALLY fucking hard to marry a dead woman," I screamed into the phone.

And it felt terrific to say it. Even better when she mumbled out a horrified apology. I told her I wanted the cake donated to the homeless mission on 63rd, before slamming down the phone.

Most of the other vendors didn't even bother to ask. I'm sure they all assumed the bride had changed her mind. Which was all the better since I didn't want to actually say the words again. I kept the chapel. The day Tami and I were to be married would now be the day we held her memorial. If this were happening to anyone else, I would find the irony. Actually, I did find it. I was just really pissed off it was at my expense.

Meeting this girl had become my moral compass. All I could do now was keep flying until I ran out of fuel. Then I would crash. The only thing I didn't know was what kind of obliteration would be left in my path. But I could guarantee there would be carnage.

I spoke to Harry periodically over the two days, but usually I left that to Gretchen. Harry and I would do nothing more than exchange information on what had been taken care of, what still needed to be done, and then hang-up without so much as a goodbye. Even though we shared a brotherhood of anguish, Harry and I still tasted like poison to one another.

The morning I should have been slipping into my tuxedo, I was tugging on a dark suit and mentally preparing myself to brave a horrendous day.

There was nothing more to keep me occupied. After today, it would be over. My never-to-be wife would be ashes. And I would be...that was the damnedest thing. I didn't know. But the coiled snake that Tami had tamed in me was rattling its tail again. I could feel it slithering around in my belly. I no longer trusted happiness, did not believe in forever after. I wasn't just falling off the wagon, I was jumping off. Ready to freefall straight for whatever trouble I could find.

I craved relief from this horror. Itched to feel my ass on a barstool and get a drink in my hand. Keep them coming until I felt nothing but the relief of hazy nausea. That would be a reward next to what I had withstood in those few days. I can't say I had missed the old Todd, but he was back.

BODY SHOTS

I asked my parents not to come in for the memorial. My father, in a grand act of self-sacrifice, agreed once he found out his airline tickets were refundable. My brother stayed in Seattle. The friends I contacted were also told to remain home. There were enough people I had to put up with. Too many asking me how I was feeling.

"Just great, thanks! Boy, I sure dodged that marriage bullet, didn't I?"

It wasn't within my realm of belief that this woman would ever go away before me. I was the crazy one who would overdo it one night and run off the road into a ravine. I was the asshole who would mouth off to someone packing a forty-five. The hot wire who would have the heart attack. Not her. Never her.

As I arrived at the chapel, there were already too many people milling about outside. All dressed in dark clothes, hugging, crying, talking in hushed tones as if this would wake Tami up if they spoke any louder. As I staggered into the masses, I recognized some as Tami's friends, some as her co-workers from Macy's, the others I suspected were relatives I'd never met. Women hugged me. Men shook my hand. All offering lame condolences. It wasn't fair to judge their pity, which I am sure was genuine, but what the hell could it really do?

I couldn't help but think that Tami would enjoy it that everyone had been there. Together. This was her big day. The mood may have shifted but it was still hers. And she would want me to be nice to her guests. I could hear her say, "If you want to be alone at your funeral, that's fine. We won't invite anybody. In fact, nobody even has to know. But I want all these people there. For me, and my dad. And for you. So be nice."

Honey, you know me. This is nice.

"You're not going to punch me if I ask how you are?" Gretchen said to me with Amy standing by her side.

"No. But if you want to bring over someone you don't like I'd be more than happy to knock them out," I responded without a drip of humor.

Amy knew I was dead serious and had a few people in mind.

After that wretched day, I would never see any of these people again. To Tami's family I was the almost-was. By the next day I'd be an afterthought to the catastrophe. On the anniversary of her death, they would lament the fading tragedy, "Whatever happened to that guy she was going to marry? Tom." To Tami's friends, I would be remembered as the poor schmuck who stood at the altar waiting for a ghost. Unless I was loaded in a bar one night and tried to pick one of them up. Then I would be the cretin ex-boyfriend who never deserved her from the get-go.

As I made my way up the steps and into the chapel foyer, Harry was off to a corner surrounded by his relatives. Spotting me, he broke free of his sister and shuffled in my direction. He didn't offer his hand but flicked out, "Good, you wore a tie."

Kiss my hairy ass. What did you think I was going to wear, sweat pants and a dirty T-shirt?

"The Minister thinks you should say a few words," Harry stated with a paralysis in his voice that had drained him of any emotion.

I jolted back a step. I couldn't do that. Shit, I was having a hard enough time keeping things straight in my own head, much less try and make any kind of sense of this odiousness for other people. And I refused to share those special moments that Tami and I had created to make her family and friends feel all warm and fuzzy. No, they could cry and feel like shit, just like me. They could sit there confused and lost and wonder why this had happened. And if anyone could come up with a goddamn answer that made even a scintilla of sense, they could clue me in. My misery didn't require their company, but it was sure glad it wasn't alone.

"No way," I stated without hesitation, my eyes locking in on Harry's.

"I don't care whether you do it or not. You tell Reverend Terrman you're uncomfortable with it," Harry shrugged indifferently, walking away.

Is it just me, or does that little fucker sometimes need a good smack to the chops?

I slipped into a pew behind everyone else, closer to the back in case I needed to make a quick retreat. Harry and his family walked by me, holding each other as they moved up to the front of the chapel, where sprays of lilies and white roses surrounded the photo of Tami. The flowers I recognized. They must have been the same flowers we were going to have near our table at the reception. Nothing like recycling. There were candles surrounding the photo, giving her face a softer, dreamier appearance. Looking at her photo, I was sure Harry hadn't made the arrangements. One of the family must have stepped in. In fact, I was positive Harry hadn't done much of anything other than call me once or twice a day to make sure I'd taken care of the repulsive tasks I had.

"Todd," a voice called as a thin hand with rings on every finger reached out to me. I looked up at Gretchen. "Uh-uh. You are not sitting back here. You need to be up front," she commanded, grabbing my hand. I shook free. I didn't want to move, especially now that the place was filling up. But Gretchen wrapped her fingers around my wrist, refusing my protest as she yanked me up and slid her arm around my waist. She understood that I was fused, so she moved me gently without her usual forcefulness. It wasn't a matter of whether I would erupt; I was only waiting for the time. As Gretchen escorted me up the narrow aisle, people whispered as we passed. I attempted to make no eye contact, but many of Tami's girlfriends stood up and reached out to me. As I got to the first row, Harry glanced over with an unquiet scowl, before turning away as if he hadn't noticed.

"Forget him," Gretchen whispered as she pushed me across the aisle from Harry, "he never knew a damn thing about what Tami loved."

True or not, I needed to hear that. Once in the front row, I actually felt safer. If I broke down, no one could stare me in the face. With Tami's girlfriends lining the row behind me, I had a barrier that protected me. If anybody knew the love that Tami and I had shared, it was her girlfriends. I was sure they'd discussed it to death over the course of the past six months. And now it would be spread with her ashes.

Reverend Terrman, the minister Tami had selected to do our wedding, appeared from the back of the altar in a black robe, a purple alb draped over her shoulders. We had only met twice. When Tami insisted that a female minister perform the ceremony, it really stuck in Harry's craw, reason alone to give her the thumbs up.

She gave me a smile that I couldn't read. Compassion? Understanding? Motherly nurturing? Who the hell knew? As she spoke my mind drifted. My eyes stayed on the dreamy photo of Tami. The longer I held my gaze, the more I felt I'd been had. Like a magician's sleight of hand, my relationship, my love, disappeared, only to leave me questioning whether or not it had actually existed. All I had now was an enlarged photo smiling at me dreamily. It wasn't enough.

After the minister spoke, Harry's sister, Nancy, stood up and remembered Tami. I tried not to listen to the eulogies, but there were moments that caught my ears. It wasn't until Tami's girlfriends spoke that I lifted my head. One by one, they stood and told stories, each more hilarious than the next. Recounting secret moments of Tami's life, crazy stunts they had pulled, and the deep bond they all shared. I actually laughed out loud, especially when Gretchen stood, her hand on her hip in a pose of defiance to Tami's death.

"I'm going to tell everyone what happened when my ex, Bob, cheated on me," she stated firmly, causing a giggled gasp among her friends. Bob was some asshole Gretchen had dated for about a year-and-a-half. And cheated on her for about a year of that. When she found out, she was destroyed. She had truly believed he was "the one."

"Tami hatched a sinister plot to even the score and remind dear Bob why he should never mess with one of 'the girls'." She met him in the bar at the Radisson Hotel and got him hammered on martinis and vodka shooters. After nearly cleaning out his wallet, she easily coaxed drunken Bob into getting a room, so as Gretchen put it, "she could rock his world." Unfortunately for the poor asshole, Gretchen and the rest of the female posse were lying in wait. The girls stripped Bob naked, gagged him with his own Jockeys, duct taped him to the mattress, and then shoved the mattress upright against the sliding door leading to the balcony, taping him to the glass. "He was on display for every passing car on Michigan Avenue for three hours, before the hotel management came and released him," Gretchen sneered. "Thank you, Tami. I'll owe you forever for that one."

The horror on Harry's face as he listened to the story was worth the price of admission. But when Gretchen winked at Harry, finishing with, "You didn't know everything about her, Mr. Everett," I wanted to jump up and kiss her on the lips.

For those brief moments I felt Tami's presence.

"I've asked Tami's fiancé, Todd Cartwright, to say a few words," I heard Reverend Terrman say, as she stepped up in front of me, reaching out for my hand.

I looked up and she smiled at me. She knew how difficult this was. I would have rather gnawed off my right arm than turn around and face all the people that had packed the chapel, but I was already unsteadily standing on my feet, so there was little choice. I bit down on my tongue to keep from crying. Turning on my heels, I refused to look at anyone but then her girlfriends caught my eye. Their eyes glistened with tears but they all smiled. Rachel looked directly into my eyes and mouthed the words, "the wedding dress."

Taking a deep breath, I looked at the crowd in the chapel, now packed to overflowing. I nodded.

"I think Tami would love this. I may not have known her as long as a lot of you, but I knew her better in many, many ways. And when she asked me to help her pick out her wedding dress, I thought why not? What's the harm?" Pointing at her friends, I added, "It's your fault. If you could have agreed on a dress, I would not have had to go through that."

As the girls chuckled, I grabbed the pew and looked out. "Nobody ever told me that it's a really, really bad idea for the groom to help pick out the wedding gown. Or to say much of anything for that matter."

The crowd laughed.

"Tami actually said she was going to leave the final decision up to me," I shook my head, remembering. "This is why they say a groom should never see his bride-to-be in her wedding dress prior to the big day. But I figured that Tami had already decided on which dress she really loved. I just needed to stay on my toes and catch a signal as to which dress she secretly wanted more. Then all I had to do was agree. Easy enough, you know? She would be happy, I would be happy, and we could go eat, which is what she promised. Once we were done, we would go eat. So I didn't eat anything before we left."

Tami's girlfriends were all giggling as they wiped away tears. They had heard this story from Tami. But now they were getting my side of the action.

"While I parked my big butt on this freakishly uncomfortable, little chair in the bridal shop, Tami tried on each dress. Twice. I thought I was going to die. And she wasn't giving any signal as to which she liked more. She kept saying she loved them all for different reasons. Now I don't know what it takes to get in and out of a wedding dress, but she was in that dressing room forever each time she changed. And I was getting super hungrier and lightheaded. The sales ladies hated that I was there. I think I may have been the first guy ever in their store. They gave Tami a scone and tea. I had to ASK for a glass of water," I laughed.

"It wasn't rocket science to know which dress Tami looked best in. There was one with a sexy V-neck that showed off enough, you know, cleavage...and cinched in at her tiny waist. She sort of looked like a comic book heroine in a beaded wedding dress."

Everyone laughed out loud.

"I dug that. What guy hasn't wanted to bed Wonder Woman at some point in his life?"

Everyone laughed again. Except for Harry.

"Well, as we headed into our second hour of trying on dresses, I kept being non-committal because I couldn't tell which one she liked best. But my stomach was growling and I actually felt faint. I needed some food. But I was afraid to say anything until Tami decided to try on ALL four dresses again! My head was swooning, and it was like I heard this voice blast inside of me, and it said, "Forget trying them on! You look like a sexy superhero in that one." And when I opened my eyes, I was pointing at the dress I really dug."

I paused, the memory now so vivid. I couldn't help but to smile even wider.

"The saleswomen did this slow turn like the Three Stooges. 'Slowly I turn, step by step, inch by inch.' And Tami gave me this look...this sympathetic, loving look, like I was her five-year-old son with A.D.D.. And then she picked up the dress I liked, looked at it for a long while and then said, 'This one's out.'"

The place erupted into laughter, some people applauding. They all knew. It was so Tami.

"Tami gave me twenty bucks and told me to go get something to eat."

Her friends were all holding each other now, laughing.

"I guess cartoon vixen isn't the image she was going for on her wedding day," I said.

It buoyed me to see everyone smiling, laughing, nodding. But then it slammed into me like a tsunami. There would be no wedding day.

I choked back the growing lump in my throat, closing my eyes tightly. "Her wedding day," I repeated, battling my emotions as the crowd hushed. "Tami should be walking down this aisle on her father's arm..." The Reverend squeezed my hand as I heard a collective sob fill the chapel. I took a deep breath and forced myself to continue. "I can't hold her hand. I can't kiss her. All I wanted was to spend the rest of my life with that girl."

I heaved hard, my body shaking wildly. Reverend Terrman moved closer, sliding her arm around me. Gretchen stood, steadying me. They were both big women but not big enough that if I went down, I wouldn't take both down with me.

Once the service was over, I slipped out of the pew and dashed out the chapel's side door without a word to anyone. I crawled into my truck and shut the door. There I took the deep breath I had been holding for the last hour of the memorial. I cranked the stereo as loud as I could and cut out the world. Car after car drove past, heading for the wake, which was being held at Harry's American Legion Hall. My body ached like I had gone eight rounds with a fighter toying with me for his own sadistic pleasure. I wished someone would put me out of my misery and drop me to the canvas.

Arriving at the Legion Hall about six blocks from Harry's home, I strode into the building and straight to the bar. "A shot of Cutty," I requested from the bartender, who looked like he'd been keeper of the spirits at the hall for longer than I had been alive. If I had to accept another round of condolences, I needed as much scotch in me as possible. With the first sip, I felt the genie muscle out of the bottle, ready to reek some havoc. Slamming three quick shots, I felt the amber liquid doing the deed.

It would help me be nice. For the moment.

The scotch allowed me to talk with Harry's family members without getting surly, to accept the hugs without freezing up and turning myself inside out. I hadn't drunk that much since I had met Tami, and I gotta say it opened a pressure valve. Tami had been the balm on most of my internal wounds. But now I had to lean on some old habits to survive.

But as I swilled my sixth glass, I began to feel a wedge weigh down on my shoulders. It always happens the same way. It starts in my shoulders, as if someone is jamming a shank of metal between them. My shirt doesn't fit correctly any longer; it's tight, binding. I try to relax my shoulders but it's fruitless. The muscles continue to knot up until I'm unable to turn my head. Then there is this prickling that runs up the back of my neck. You can't scratch it, making you even more edgy. And the more I drink, the more volatility surges through my arms and legs. Paranoia sets in. I pick out potential enemies. Problem people. And given enough scotch, I will make a preemptive strike. Like the President, I can manufacture a reason to invade and justify it later. With a reputation as a nasty brawler, my phantom enemy will usually apologize for the imaginary wrong of which I've accused him. Even without an altercation, the sense of victory for the imagined sin brings a wave of relief. Sometimes it will last all night. Sometimes it doesn't last an hour, and I'm off to thwart another fabricated evildoer.

Since I was at my fiancée's wake, I stayed cognizant not to lay a trip on any of Tami's girlfriends or get aggressive with their mates. No benefit in having them hate me this soon. I had a lifetime ahead to accomplish that feat. Though a group of guys I didn't know kept eyeing me as I drank, furtively hissing secrets to one another. Undoubtedly about me.

Beyond making me paranoid, alcohol enhances my omniscient powers. And there's nothing more interesting than an overtly suspicious mind-reader with a few under his belt.

I stayed on my stool, preferring to drink alone. If I could stay isolated, I'd make it through the day. I knew some there were aware of my hard-living past. As another gulp of scotch trickled down my throat, I wondered if the whispering boys were slapping money down on the moment I would meltdown. When you're notorious in clubs for being an asshole, the stink doesn't rinse off in six months.

Thanks to Tami, I was a changed man. But changes change.

As I sat on a stool at the bar, finishing scotch number seven, someone approached me. Spinning, there was Harry's mug, his forehead all furrowed, glaring at me from the top of his eyes, as his chin sat on his chest.

"How many of those have you had," his question more accusing than inquiring.

"Not enough to make this easier."

"There are people here that are worried about you."

I chuckled hard. "Point them out. I'll buy them a drink," I responded, taking another slug of scotch.

"You're not driving yourself home."

"I'll take a cab, Harry. I can handle myself, thank you," I replied, dismissing him by giving him my back.

But Harry wouldn't go away. "You're not the only one who misses her," he stated loud enough to draw attention from those standing nearby.

The words took a moment to sink through the booze and my thick skull. Goddamn, why wouldn't he just go away? Why wouldn't someone there pull his face out of my reach? A master of stating the obvious, Harry seemed oblivious to the fact that I wanted him far, far away from me.

"Fuck, Harry," I laughed cynically, "there's plenty of misery to go around. If you don't think you're carrying your load, I'd be happy to give you as much as you can handle."

"Why do you have to behave like this?! Don't you have an ounce of respect for Tami?"

"Why, Harry?" I raised my glass, the snake in my belly ready to strike. "Because this is my wedding day," I continued, feeling the venom spitting in Harry's direction. "Only right now, when I should be dancing the first dance with my new wife, she is being disintegrated at about a thousand degrees."

Harry's head snapped back, verbally sucker punched. "Don't you dare talk about my daughter like that!"

I raised my hands and waved them in defeat as Gretchen raced between Harry and I in order to save the day. Or at least salvage a little dignity for us both. But this wasn't her fight and whatever puny amount of dignity Harry and I had left wasn't worth rescuing.

"I'm not trying to make you feel any worse than you already do. But let me feel like shit if I want, Harry. I'm dealing with it as best I can. I haven't punched anybody, or called them an asshole, or tore up this poor excuse for a place to have a wake. I think that's pretty fucking good since that's all I feel like doing!"

"Todd, don't, please," Gretchen nearly begged, seeing that I was about to shoot off into orbit.

The sorrow in her eyes caused me to back down. But Harry inched closer to my face, speaking under his breath. "Don't do anything to embarrass Tami. I'm warning you. Don't do anything that will cause anyone to think less of her because of your actions!"

Gretchen glances around for some back-up but the cavalry stayed a safe distance back. "Enough, guys. Mr. Everett, Todd, I am asking you to stop," she pleaded, the tenor of her voice now overtly nervous.

Harry and I held burning glares on each other for an excruciating minute. Eat me, I thought, letting a nasty smile slide onto my lips. "Lighten up, big guy" I sniffed out. "After this, you never have to see me again. You sidestepped a landmine, Harry. I'll never be your son-in-law."

Harry's eyes narrowed, in no mood for my shit. "Lucky me," he growled.

Gretchen let her hands drop from our chests, relaxing. Big mistake. I wasn't near done.

I gave Harry an ironic wink and then laughed harshly, the aroma of scotch filtering from my throat. "You wished too hard, Harry, you got exactly what you wanted. Only it cost Tami her life."

Harry reared back and, as quickly as he could muster, dove over Gretchen and socked me in the jaw. It didn't knock me out of the seat, but it certainly caught me off guard. A collective gasp whistled through the Legion Hall. People rushed toward us as Gretchen fell back against the bar, snapping off one of the heel of one of her shoes. Grabbing her and pulling her back to her feet, my eyes caught hers. She had tears. It was actually startling for me to see her start to cry over this. Was she that embarrassed for us? Was this so completely unwarranted and irrational that it cracked her emotionally? Her tears silently implored me to stop this insanity. But insanity was all I had left to hold onto.

"All right, all right," I said, as I rubbed the right side of my face, suddenly surrounded by a lynch mob of friends and family. I stood in front of Gretchen who kept her hands grasped my shoulders as two of Tami's uncles held Harry back. I staggered forward a step and then mockingly grabbing up a bar stool and holding it between myself and everyone else as if I feared them stringing me up. No one spoke but they all glared at me as if I had provoked the altercation. Good guess.

"You don't have to apologize," I said to Harry, impressed that he would actually have the balls to pop me. Not that he hadn't been craving to do it since we first met. "I deserved it. But I'm not about to apologize to you either. I meant what I said. You did everything possible to keep Tami from marrying me. You got it, Harry! I hope you're happy." I slammed the stool back to the floor and kicked it at the whispering boys, cautioning them that if they made a move at me I would not hesitate to hurt them.

"So fucking long, Harry."

I turned to Gretchen and mumbled a contrite apology before pushing through the guests that had encircled me, unsteadily moving toward the door that led out of the dank room normally filled with dying men.

"You're right," Harry spoke as I neared the door. "I didn't want Tami to marry you. This is exactly why."

I turned slowly to face Harry, who was still being held back by his relatives.

"You didn't deserve her. She was way too good of a soul to marry a selfish, callow, low class hoodlum." Harry continued, his disgust and rage spewing like acid, "For some reason, Tami was blind to who you are, but I've known more than my share of guys like you. Garden variety slugs. I am sickened by you. But I AM glad Tami's been saved from the life full of heartache that you would have put her through. I hope she's looking down right now and seeing the type of man you are. You never deserved my daughter's love. Never."

All eyes fell on me. Half of the guests believed I was going to charge Harry and beat him bloody. The other half thought I would crumble to the floor in a puddle of drunken self-pity. Me, I would have taken one of their bets. But I didn't move.

"What kills you, Harry, is that Tami picked me over you. I loved her unconditionally. Your love came with a will-call slip. You pay for it now, you pay for it later, but you pay for it. She paid for it all her life, and all she wanted to do was be with a man whose love overflowed without a goddamn price tag attached. So fuck you."

Once outside, I headed for my truck, but my eyes caught sight of a dumpy, little bar down the block. Screw going home. I already had a head start on a really ugly drunk. Why waste it?

"Are you sure you want to do that," a recognized voice asked, knowing right where I was heading.

Turning, Gretchen stood behind me, her body tilted by having only one shoe with a heel. Shit, why couldn't she just make apologies for my near psychotic behavior and let it go? I didn't need this. Not now. Especially not right now.

"Gretchen, I aim to get so completely shitfaced that I will black out. If it could last until I'm over Tami, I'd be grateful to God in spite of what's happened. That was my only chance to forget what the last few days had been. I needed them gone."

"It won't change anything," she spoke in a soft, damaged tone.

"I couldn't survive any more change..." I half-whispered, shaking my head. I closed my eyes tight for a moment, wrestling the overwhelming urge to breakdown. When I looked back up, I said, "Go back inside, Gretch. Be with your friends and leave me alone. The way you look at me now, like I'm some three-legged mutt at the pound you just know no one is going to adopt, is killing me even deeper."

She watched with tears dropping from her cheeks as I staggered to the bar down the block and vanished inside.

I woke up covered in my own vomit.

Nice, huh?

I don't know how I got home, I don't know how I got into bed, I don't know how long I slept, because I had no idea what time I actually crawled onto my mattress, or what time it was when I woke up.

As I stood up the room spun wickedly, causing my stomach to feel like it was on a cheap ride at a traveling circus, and the midget carny wouldn't let me off. For a man who seldom had a hangover, this was vile. I pulled the sheets off the bed and wadded them up. I had a thick pad atop the mattress because this was hardly the first time I had gotten sick in bed. Five years earlier, in fact, I had ruined a $500 mattress right after I bought it and swore I would never do that again. I couldn't trust myself not to do that again so I bought the thickest mattress pad I could find in hopes of saving the poor, defenseless bed. This time it did the trick.

After I pulled the mattress pad off and stuck it in the same garbage bag as the sheets, I sprayed the mattress with Lysol. Not sure why, with the amount of alcohol I had consumed the night before no germ could possibly survive.

I fell into a chair at the kitchen table. Pushing away unopened wedding gifts that had been sent to the condo, I closed my eyes, trying in vain to keep the room from orbiting.

When I finally opened them again, I stopped seeing double. I'd been afraid I had drunk myself into a state of permanent multiple vision. On one of the wrapped boxes lay the plane tickets to St. Carlos. That day was the start of my non-existent honeymoon. We were leaving on an evening flight. Our honeymoon night plan was to unpack in our suite at the Saint Club, make love until we combusted, and then sleep on the balcony overlooking the ocean, wrapped in each other's arms. Funny how things change. Instead I would be sleeping in my old sheets, still battling a monumental hangover and the remaining stench of Lysol.

The plane pulled from the gate at O'Hare at six-forty that night. In theory, I could make the flight. Of course, the last place on earth I wanted to be alone right at that point was the Caribbean. No, that wasn't true. The last place I wanted to be alone was my condo where Tami and I had made love. If I could have pulled my ass from that chair, by evening I could actually be lost in the tropics, sipping booze in a shanty bar within spitting distance of the ocean. Why the hell not go? Escape all the bullshit in Chicago, invade a place where the liquor flows freely and people don't know me, thus chances are, don't hate me. Yet. I could go on a nightly bender without pathetic glances from people who have "heard the bad news." No judgment. Just a ten-day drunk to banish myself from the immense pain I find in every corner of my own home.

And then I realized something else, something even better. If I could wrest Tami's ashes from her rat bastard father, I could find the magical place, the treasured site that brought Tami so much joy as a child and release her there to dance on the beach forever.

Not that I held a chance in hell of Harry handing me Tami's ashes. I knew that, at that moment, he was probably lying on his sofa, hugging the canister. He would sit the can across the table when he ate, talking about his day. And then carry the ashes upstairs, kissing the can goodnight before he crawled into bed. No, Harry wasn't about to let those ashes go, no matter what Tami's wishes were. He was hell bent on owning her in life and now he could in death. If I wasn't good enough to marry his daughter, be damned sure I wasn't good enough to help send her into eternity at a place she loved.

The longer I sat at the table, surrounded by wedding gifts and Tami's furniture and clothes stacked around my condo, the easier it became to convince myself to leave that place and disappear. Maybe I'd even be able to gather my head and figure out where the hell I was going in my life? Who was I kidding? I'd be incoherent and sunburnt the entire time. But what the fuck. Inebriation stood heads and tails over the grief I was suffering.

After emptying all the wedding cards with cash, I yanked a few pairs of shorts and a couple T-shirts out of my dresser and tossed them into a battered duffel bag. Traveling light. The new beige linen suit that Tami had bought me wasn't making the trip. Neither were the polo shirts. The pleated slacks. The unblemished slip-ons. There was no one to impress and nothing to do other than lock lips with a glass of scotch.

There wasn't a soul alive I wanted knowing where I was hiding, so I didn't call anyone to announce my covert plans. A few people would grow concerned, maybe a few would worry that I did something stupid to myself, but they would figure I escaped to lick my wounds. In my condition, anyone around me was asking to be bruised. And I already owned enough regret. The dog fight I had had with Harry in front of a packed audience left a sour taste in the mouths of friends and family. Not that I had made it onto too many Christmas card lists to start with.

The cab dropped me off in front of the American Airlines terminal at O'Hare. It was just after four. Plenty of time to check in, get through security, and stop by the bar for a warm-up. I had my duffel bag over my shoulder and a wallet full of cash and credit cards. What more could I need for a ten-day drunkathon in the Caribbean?

Plodding along the cattle line that weaved toward the ticket counter,I got a grin on my face. It was the first time in the last five days I'd smiled, other than when Harry had punched me in the jaw. Which I still found amusing. The gnawing pain of Tami's death still squeezed the few ounces of life remaining in my vacant soul, but a cool breeze of anonymity was but a plane ride away.

Who says you can't run away from yourself? I was looking forward to it.

That is until a nasally, high-pitched voice caught my ear over the airport din. I shook my head, hoping it was the hangover. How many past sins was I paying for? Goddamn, didn't having Tami stolen from my life break me even, or was I going to be indebted to the fates forever?

I spun side to side, peering over the heads of the people shuffling along in the line. Kill me now. This can't be true. Standing at the counter, arguing with a young female ticket agent was none other than my never-to-be-father-in-law from hell, Harry Everett. He of the weak right hook. I couldn't hear what he was saying, but his hands were gesturing wildly on the verge of losing control.

If this was a bad dream, I preferred blacking out.

Harry's actions continued to grow more irrational by the moment. He was pounding on the counter, barking nastily at the young woman, who was tersely trying to remain in control. I hung back, hoping to witness Harry completely losing it, causing the airport police to pounce on his ass and beat him bloody with their night sticks. That would be a joyous beginning to my vacation. Everyone in the line was rolling their eyes at the crazy asshole whose squinty face was turning an off-shade of plum. There was plenty of awkward laughter at Harry's expense and a number of people calling him names.

Poor bastard. If only these people knew he had just lost his daughter.

Not that I was feeling sorry for Harry. He brought most of the shit in his life on himself. Not that I'm immune to that either. But I knew the reason why Harry was at the airport standing at the ticket counter, barking at this young ticket agent. And this was going to be ugly.

Taking a deep breath and wishing I had brought a flask, I threw a leg over the rope and climbed out of the line, slipping through the crowd until I was right behind the nagging Harry.

"I'm telling you, he's NOT using the tickets. Has he checked in? No! I don't understand why this should be so hard. He's not going to be here," Harry insisted, his hand running through the wisps of hair dying a slow, lonely death on his shiny pate. "Look, I paid for the tickets. I have the receipt right here." Harry patted his pockets until he found where he had stuffed the credit card copy from the travel agency, and shoved it in the young woman's face. "See, see, Exotic Travels. I ALREADY paid for the tickets, and I'm willing to buy one of them again! I don't know why you won't sell me one when they aren't going to be used."

The girl tried forcing a smile but she was past that point. She was tired of being nice to this cantankerous curmudgeon. I know verbatim how she felt.

"Sir, as I've already explained, that's not how it works. Any empty seats will go into the pool and be passed out to standby passengers on a first-come, first-serve basis. Now, if you would like me to put you on standby..."

"That doesn't make any sense," Harry continued, hoping to wear down this young woman. "They're not using the seats. Okay? That's why I'm here, I WANT to use the seat. It's very simple. Just sell me one of the seats, it'll save all that standby silliness."

"We can't give any seat away until fifteen minutes before the departure. That's airline policy."

"But I'm telling you, they are not going to be used," Harry hammered again.

"You may be 100 % positive about that, Mr. Everett," the girl sighed, "but we aren't. I have you on the standby list. We'll contact you if a seat opens."

"But---"

"Jesus Christ, asshole, leave the poor girl alone," I spoke loud enough for everyone to hear.

A few people in line applauded.

Harry turned, his eyes narrowing furiously at whomever it was butting into his business. But when he saw it was yours truly, his eyes grew wide from shock and then narrowed again like a pissed-off cobra. Yep. There I was. Right behind him. In the flesh. In the airport. With the tickets.

Not missing a beat, I stepped around him and handed the agent the ticket and my ID. "I'm the guy not showing up," I said with a smile, ignoring Harry.

The agent punched in my information. The girl glanced at Harry with a satisfactory sliver of a smile, and then turned back to me, handing me a boarding pass with my passport. "Gate 26," she said. "You will make a connection in Miami."

I fired Harry a sneering look as he peeked around my shoulder, then turned back to the woman. "How many people are waiting for seats on this flight?"

She told me there were already sixteen, including Harry.

"Any chance he'll get on the flight?" I quizzed.

She gave me a knowing smile and said, "Doubtful. We're overbooked and most of the passengers have connections in Miami. On this route we have a low percentage of no-shows."

I grinned at Harry like a fat dog who had just figured out how to open the pantry.

Harry was livid. "He's got another ticket! It was my daughter's but she's not going," he cried to the agent, and then turned to me, literally grabbing at my boarding pass, "Give me that! That's my seat, I paid for it!"

"Holy shit, Harry," I said, almost laughing as I held my boarding pass out of his reach, "pull it together. You're in public. If you punch me here, I'm punching back."

Harry took a step back, straining mightily to calm himself. But the anxiety was imprinted on his face, and his head was pulled into his shoulders like a snapping turtle. "You have Tami's ticket," Harry spoke distinctly, as if that would help him keep his cool and end the sideshow he was performing for those waiting in line. "She was my daughter. I want it."

"Not happening," I said, turning to leave. But Harry is nothing if not a resourceful little gnome. And though I held all the aces, he held all the wild cards. Unzipping his suitcase and digging his hand in, Harry extracted a plain metal canister. The mere sight of it froze me.

"Tami wanted these spread on that island," Harry stated, noting the instantaneous change in my demeanor, which I was incapable of hiding from him.

"Unless I go with you, you won't be any part of that."

I felt all the air escape my lungs as if I'd been booted in the nuts. The ass wipe was going to do this to me? I couldn't blame him, as shitty as I had been to him, but he had me cornered. And like any trapped animal, I wasn't going down without a fight.

Unfortunately, I was defenseless. And that only made me more rabid.

My first thought was to swing my duffel bag and crack him so hard I'd send his sorry ass over the ticket counter. I'm sure everyone in line would have cheered wildly and then carried me to my gate on their shoulders. But the police would have to arrest me on principle. And if I was going to spend time in jail, I would have preferred a view of the ocean over some cinder block dungeon under O'Hare Airport. I had spent a couple nights in a Chicago jail a few years earlier after a bar fight. Stinky, ugly place with the gnarliest mutants I ever had the misfortune to meet. Two butt-ugly brothers wanted to kick the shit out of me, but when I vomited all over one of them, I pretty much established that I was not someone anyone wanted to mess with.

I looked back at the poor ticket agent behind the counter with a bitter, hangdog expression. She knew I had lost. I slapped Tami's ticket on the counter.

"This was my wife's ticket. She died. This piss poor excuse for a man is her father. Is there any way we can redo the ticket so he can use it?"

So much for running away.

VACATION PICTURES

I wasn't sure if the ticket agent could change the ticket, and I was half-praying she couldn't. But God hadn't answered too many of my prayers recently. From the glint in her eye, it was no secret she had had enough of Harry too. Since I looked like a man who was making mental plans to kill Harry once we got to our destination - which wasn't out of the question - she gladly reissued the ticket under Harry's name for only a fifty dollar charge and her condolences.

"I don't want you sitting next to me," I said to Harry, as we neared the security checkpoint.

"The seats are together. But I'll see what I can do when we get onboard. Spending time with you isn't a bundle of joy for me either," Harry countered.

As we stepped to the back of the snailing line, he shook his head. "I can't believe you're actually going on your honeymoon," he said, half under his breath.

"It's not a honeymoon without a wife," I snarled. "And with you here, it's more like a trip into the ass of a gorilla."

"Until we get Tami's ashes spread, you're stuck with me. So just suck it up."

"What makes you think I won't kill you down there? I got nothing to lose. I've already lost it all," I said, and then fired him a psychopathic grin as I added, "Never forget, I'm a desperate man."

"What makes you think I won't kill you?" he shot back. "I've had a lot of time to consider it over the past six months. And believe me, I've figured out a way to get rid of you that no one could pin on me."

The glimmer in his squinty eyes told me it was no bluff. I needed to get a scotch into my hand. Quick.

As a result of our glaring hostility at each other, it was no surprise that we were both pulled out of line and searched.

After having a security guard stick his hands down my pants, I pulled my shoes back on and marched straight to the airport bar. Harry hunkered down in a seat near the gate. As I slammed down my first scotch, I mused about fate. Fucking bitch. I was hardly a saint but goddamn, what was happening to me was beyond vindictiveness. Yes, poor me. But damn it, I had a right to self-pity. I was on my honeymoon with Harry. If God had any mercy he would send a 747 crashing through the window of the bar and impale me against the wall. I can say that because I know He's not listening. The time with my never-to-be father-in-law was flat out hell to pay, all to make sure the woman I loved rested in the place she wanted to be. I loved Tami. And I would do anything for a chance to consummate her wish.

I just didn't imagine I would ever have to do it.

By the time I finished my second scotch, they were boarding the plane. I tucked my duffel under my arm and made sure to keep my distance from Harry. I needed every nanosecond of reprieve I could amass before this ordeal. If I was lucky, the scotch would put me to sleep for most of the flight to Miami. I was a champ when it came to snoozing on planes. The liquor only greased the road to dreamland.

The plane was packed. I was happy to be in first class where the seats were bigger than in coach. With another scotch in my hand before the flight took off and two pillows under my head, I allowed my body to relax. I twisted around, leaning against the wall of the plane, away from Harry who, surprise (thanks again, God!), couldn't get his seat changed on a packed flight. Harry pulled on his reading glasses.

The boarding passengers passed by Harry, the complaining psycho at the ticket counter, grumbling to each other that the lunatic got seated in first class while they were being herded back into coach. Harry didn't seem to notice. And if he did, he didn't seem to mind. He read his magazine, clucking and tsking in disagreement with whatever it was he saw. Even with all the bodies packing the plane, his

bothersome ticks were like having a hole bored into my skull.
And since it was Harry, the drill bit was just that much bigger.
Why couldn't he just down a few vodka tonics and crash out
like a normal person? No, Harry was going to torment me the
entire flight with his cloying, annoying habits.

If I killed him while we were still on the tarmac, would
that be a federal offense or a local crime?

As I tried my best to doze, with Harry annoying the shit
out of me and the scotch sizzling in my head, a horrible
thought occurred to me. What if Tami had never really loved
me? What if she had agreed to marry so quickly solely because
she couldn't hack living with Harry any longer? What if she
was so fed up with his ticks and oppressive bullshit that she
would have married anybody just to escape his bothersome
tyranny? Hell, I had been with him less than thirty minutes,
and already I wanted to ram my head into the side of the plane
until there was a hole big enough to crawl out. Finding my
headset, I jammed the ends into my ears, not bothering to plug
in the other end. I didn't want music; I wanted Harry on mute.

Maybe I would fart a lot when I fell asleep. Alcohol
gas. That would even the score.

Just as my eyelids were dropping, an elbow poked me in
the bicep. Twisting around, I saw Harry facing me.

I pulled the headset from my ears and mumbled,
"Whatever it is, I don't care."

"Do you know where Tami wanted her ashes spread?"
Harry quizzed, ignoring my remark.

My eyes narrowed, processing the question. Was this a
test? Or did he really not have a clue?

"Yeah. A beach," I muttered, not willing to give much
more away until I knew where he was going with this.

"I know that much," Harry grumbled, "but there is a
beach ringing the entire island. I'm asking you which beach."

My eyes narrowed further until his face squished in my
view. "You don't know which beach?"

"Would I be asking you if I did?"

"I don't know, Harry. I don't know why you do half the things you do. Except to annoy the crap out of me," I snorted. "If you didn't know where she wanted her ashes spread, then why did you come to the airport to try and steal my tickets?"

"Why did you come to the airport? At least I came with good intentions for my daughter! Why are you going to St. Carlos, huh?"

My eyes narrowed even further until they actually closed. Jesus, I'd never noticed just how much the pitch of his voice sent a chemical impulse straight into my adrenal gland. But if Harry couldn't understand why I needed to escape Chicago, he certainly wouldn't understand my plans for a ten-day bender.

"Harry, as long as you can point out where her grandmother's house once stood, I can find the goddamn beach," I growled, turning away from him.

"You better," Harry answered, staring at my back, "or I'll spread them where I see fit."

I wanted to whip back around with a Bruce Lee chop to his Adam's apple but kept my back to him. Antagonizing him only pumped up my blood pressure and fucked up my buzz.

The flight attendant shook me awake as we prepared to land in Miami. As I sat up and pulled the headset out of my ears, Harry's eyes again narrowed at me until they looked like nickel slots.

"Wipe that mess off your chin. Good Lord, you drool like a Saint Bernard."

Apparently, I had a few ticks of my own.

Miami International Airport is a monstrous conglomeration of terminals that seems designed by someone from a Third World country to confuse the shit out of someone from a First World country. Harry and I had to switch airlines, and Harry had checked his luggage. Including Tami. I'd have kept her in my arms the entire way. But Harry explained that he had carefully wrapped the container holding her ashes and placed it in the middle of his bag, snuggling it amid all his clothes where she "would not be disturbed." What, was she napping in that can, Harry? Disturbed? She's dust, for Christsake.

Chiding Harry about his luggage being sent to some socialist country in South America and him losing Tami forever, I got him thoroughly rattled. He waddled his ass down to baggage claim and stirred up enough of a scene that they brought him his bag and told him to check it through himself on Air Carib, the airline we were taking to St. Carlos. In the scheme of things, it was a smart move. If we had arrived in St. Carlos without Tami's ashes, I would have spread the broken pieces of Harry's body in a St. Carlos alleyway.

Harry was nervous that I would steal Tami from him and take her ashes to this secret place she loved and release her spirit without him. I hadn't told him that I only had a vague idea of where this place was and probably could not find it without him. Without Harry, I wouldn't know where Tami's grandmother's home once stood. I would be forced to do a lot of detective work in a foreign land. Something I neither wanted to do nor would probably be able to do if I were as drunk as I intended to be. Without that information, I'd never find the beautiful cove she had described in such detail that it became real for me. And I was simply not up for a treasure hunt.

We packed into the flight taking us to St. Carlos. This was a puddle-jumping plane that seemed to be built for tiny Japanese women, not a brawny American man who didn't like feeling closed-in. The ceiling was low and the seats so tight that I felt like I was flying in a coffin. As they sealed the door shut, a nauseating wave of claustrophobia flushed through me. And I didn't have a drink in my hand. Harry sat next to me, oblivious, clucking his way through another in-flight magazine. I struggled to keep it together, not wanting to freak out in Harry's presence, allowing the little man to blame my horrified behavior on the scotch. I broke into a flop sweat as the air vents went dead and the small aircraft began backing up from the terminal. Too late to bolt from the flight until I was outside, hyperventilating in the evening air. And I didn't have the balls to pound on the ceiling until the oxygen mask fell or the flight attendant brought me a mobile oxygen tank. I would just suffer until I passed out or ate a chunk out of the side of my seat.

Gripping the handles, I closed my eyes, hoping that I could erase the cramped physical space and regain some composure. But the sweat trickled from my hairline and down my face. I grabbed the magazine from the pouch that my knees were jammed into, fanning myself, desperate to stave off this panic attack.

"Are you getting sick?" Harry asked.

I shook my head abruptly but said nothing.

"If you get sick..." Harry started, but then stopped mid-thought, changing directions, "I'm calling the stewardess."

As he reached to signal the flight attendant who was strapped into the jump seat near the door, I grabbed his hand.

"Flight attendant," I huffed out. "They haven't been called stewardesses since Nixon was president."

"Forgive me," Harry remarked sarcastically. "I'm just not as tuned in as you are. If you're going to get sick or pass out, I don't want to be next to you. All right?" Harry finished with a sigh.

"Thanks for the concern," I wheezed, keeping my eyes closed, the sweat now running down my back, soaking through my shirt.

"You're probably having some kind of reaction to the scotch you've been drinking. You stink of it," he continued.

I told you this was coming.

"If it was the scotch, I wouldn't feel the need to backhand you, Harry," I snorted. "I'm fine. I'm just hot. You're not hot?"

"No. Perfect temperature in here. A little humid but not hot," he said, looking back at his magazine, flipping a few of the glossy pages.

"Ladies and gentlemen, we've been cleared for takeoff. Flight attendants prepare the cabin," the pilot announced over the intercom.

"See. Flight attendants," I sputtered, working hard to keep my mind off of the crazy-making feeling that was pulsating through my body. "You should step into the 21st century sometimes, it's nice here. You can actually see the future."

"You are so smart," Harry prattled. "Now I know what my daughter saw in you; your big brain and your, what do you call it, political correctness. You're so politically correct. I don't know why I didn't notice it until now."

Maybe if I did puke all over him that would do it. It would certainly freak him out. I'm sure then he would move seats. But with a jammed plane and me seemingly suffering from some foreign disease that usually started in the jungles of Southeast Asia, I didn't think anyone else would dare sit next to me either.

The plane lurched forward, racing down the runway. The air snapped back to life, whistling through the vents. I shot the air nozzle straight down on my face and opened the aperture as wide as I could force it. The air rained down and I took three deep breaths. I could feel the registration of panic slowly ebbing. The more I breathed, the deeper it sank inside until I could feel it unclench the hold it had on my chest. Thank you, Harry, the inane discussion kept my mind off of the panic attack that had me in a bear hug. Now I could sleep until we landed in St. Carlos.

"Goodnight, Harry," I said as I nestled against the window.

Harry shook his head with a sneer. "I don't know why I bother," he snapped under his breath, turning away from me.

Stepping off the plane in St. Carlos, you could feel a sparkle, an alchemy that only one who has been gifted with a visit to the Caribbean understands. I immediately grasped what Tami had told me about this special island. The air was thick with moisture that only enhanced the wonderful aromas of lush fruitiness. The sole thought circling through my mind was what a magical place this would be to visit with the person you love.

I glanced over to see Harry almost leaning on me.

So much for magic.

Harry and I caught a cab from the one-runway airport to the Saint Club Resort. Our driver was an older man named Tomas. Tomas was born and raised on the island. In fact, according to Tomas, he had never ever left in his fifty-seven years. Part African, part indigenous Indian, part Spanish, he felt blessed that he owned one of the seven working taxicabs on the island, and that it supported his wife and their eight children.

When Tomas began peppering us with questions about our trip to the island, Harry's eyes shifted in my direction to see if I would pop-off a smart-ass remark, but my mind was elsewhere.

"Just a little get away," I stated, giving nothing else away.

I was more focused on the impending sleeping arrangements. Harry and I wouldn't make it one night in a hotel room together. I didn't care what it cost, we had to get two rooms. Preferably on different floors. I was not giving up the honeymoon suite that Tami and I had reserved. It was the largest in the resort, on the top floor, and had an ocean view. Mine, mine, all mine. Harry was interloping on this jaunt to paradise, so he could get the scraps.

Tami knew what she was talking about when she said the Resort Club was the best. Palm trees crackled in the breeze, lining the drive up to the resort's plaza. I almost felt a tinge of repose. Okay, not really but it was as close as I could get. The fragrance of the sea breeze nearly knocked me out.

The natural stone lobby with its rich greenery gave way to glass walls. The huge outdoor pool spread into the night, seeming to fall off into the ocean. The muffled sound of distant dance music throbbed through the building. And I could smell food. I didn't realize how ready I was to eat. After which, I could finally start the alcohol poisoning clinic that I was scheduled to demonstrate to all the other vacationers.

Couples milled in and out of the lobby, all young, all happy, all in love. A tingle of jealousy shot through me as I stepped up to the desk and was greeted by a beautiful woman with a melodic Caribbean accent. She punched my name into her computer and then handed me a door swipe.

"I got a little problem," I told her as I took the key. I explained that I did not want to share a room with Harry, who was hovering behind me like a shadow, examining a brochure. Yeah, like he was going parasailing.

Harry didn't fool me, he was staying back so I would be forced to pay for the second room. I told the woman we didn't need anything fancy. Just a room with a bed. They could even put a rollaway in a broom closet. Harry was a small guy, he'd fit. But she shook her head. Not a good sign. There were no extra rooms. The resort was filled to the max this time of year.

Come on, God. Throw me a bone.

I asked again, this time without a smile. If she came out from behind that counter she could actually smell my desperation. I certainly could. But again, she shook her head, this time with a 'what can I do?' shrug and added, "I'm sorry, Mr. Cartwright. There's nothing. We could call around, see if we could find a room at another hotel."

As much as this sucked - and it sucked big - I didn't want Harry staying at another hotel because he still had Tami locked in his ugly burgundy Samsonite luggage. I needed him to locate the place where Tami's grandmother's home had once stood. And he needed me to find Tami's secret place. Scary as it was, we were stuck. Together. At least until we spread Tami's ashes. Then I could boot his ass. But I could not share my living space with him. He had driven me insane on the airplane ride. I had to draw the line because if they put us in the same room, the line would be drawn around his lifeless body as they hauled my murderous ass to an island prison.

Begging got me nowhere. And the woman at the front desk wouldn't even entertain the idea of me offering her money to take Harry home with her and bring him back in the morning. Though she did laugh. Harry was still milling about, eavesdropping, making sure he wasn't getting the short end of the stick on any of the arrangements. Tami told me this place was popular, but you would think there would be at least one room left open for emergencies. Like when you show up with another man who's supposed to be your father-in-law, but isn't. It looked like I was stuck with Harry in my room for the night.

"Please tell me there are two beds in the room," I sighed to the receptionist.

She gave me a weak smile and then shook her head again.

A rollaway?????

None.

It dawned on me that maybe Tami hadn't died. I had. And this was hell. If there was a hell designed exclusively for me, Harry would undoubtedly be there. Could there be a greater perdition for me than to be blessed with an oceanfront suite on one of the most exquisite islands on the planet, only to find myself sharing it with Harry Everett?

Oh, yeah, and the woman I loved more than my own life in a can locked away in his luggage.

I cussed all the way up in the elevator and grumbled all the way down the hallway. Harry mumbled under his breath, making sure he stayed a step behind me just in case I decided to take a swing. We passed a lovey-dovey couple who did a double take as Harry and I brushed by in our mutual snit and stopped outside the honeymoon suite. I just wanted to get into the room and rip open the minibar. With my teeth.

To add insult to injury, the honeymoon suite was exactly as I had envisioned it. An awesome room where a man could spend hours making love to his bride to the sound of the distant ocean. Yipee. We entered through an expansive living area decorated in Dutch Colonial - I know this because it says so in the brochure - the room flowed toward a pair of French doors, which lead into a massive bedroom with yet another sitting area and a balcony overlooking the pool and the ocean. Spectacular. And, oh so painful. The bathroom was huge with a Jacuzzi tub and a steam shower. Both may get a lot of use, but instead of lingering bubble baths with my wife, I'd be lying under a stream of cold water trying to sober up. I guess if I had to get drunk anywhere, I could survive ten days of this. Especially if I could get rid of Harry the next day. I could spend my nights in a bar or club getting ripped and then stagger back and fall into this massive bed. During the day, I could sleep off the liquor in the sunshine of the balcony and get my body ready for another night of scotch.

If I wanted to forget the last week of my life this was the perfect place to do it because no one knew my name.

Well, except for him.

"The bed is mine," I declared as I dropped my bags on it. "And I'm not sharing it with you, Harry. So don't ask."

Harry sat on the bed and bounced a few times. "I have a bad back from moving that furniture with you," he stated, as I felt my eyes rolling to the back of my head. "I couldn't sleep on that sofa."

"I couldn't FIT on that sofa," I shot back, not about to give him that king-size bed with my name on it.

One more time I reminded Harry that this room was registered to me. If he didn't like it, he could march his ass back to the front desk and see what he could do about getting another room. But since we both knew how that would go, he should shut the hell up and get his droopy butt comfortable on the sofa. He was not, no way, no how, never getting my bed. I explained that there were two things in this room that were mine. The bed and the minibar. Anything else he wanted, have at it. But I wasn't giving up the two items necessary for my island survival.

I opened my blessed minibar and pulled out a couple tiny bottles of scotch. They were damn small, and once I had the little metal caps twisted off, they were both down in three gulps. Harry scowled. I gave him a 'live with it' shrug.

"Tomorrow morning, you are taking me to where Tami's grandmother's house was, and I'll find the beach where Tami wants to be spread," I announced. "Then you can fly home."

"Fine. Eight o'clock," Harry responded. "Be dressed and ready."

Eight o'clock? Was he out of his goddamn mind? He'd be lucky if I was back in the room by then, depending on how loaded I got.

"Don't push it, old man," I snarled, traipsing into the bathroom to take a piss, wondering how late the bars were open on this island and if there was someplace other than this resort to hang out. Since this was a couple's resort, I figured any real action for me lay outside the perimeter of the resort. A club with single women gyrating on a dance floor wearing next to nothing would warm the cockles of my heart. I certainly didn't want to stay here and surround myself with a gaggle of happy couples. Because I was neither happy nor a couple.

When I came out of the bathroom, Harry had already changed into his pajamas and climbed into the bed. My bed. He grinned smugly like the smarty-pants kid in school who clued the teacher into everyone else's transgressions and then sat back smugly while they received their punishment.

"Enjoy your little nap because when I get back I'm picking your sorry ass up and tossing you," I stated matter-of-factly. The night was young, and I was hardly going to spend it in the room scrapping with Harry. Let him get a few hours of shut-eye. I'd get a few hours of Cutty Sark. After that I would be drunk enough to do what I threatened to do. Toss him on the sofa. Or off the balcony. Depending on just how drunk I was upon my return.

I slapped on some deodorant, pulled on a clean shirt, and hightailed it from the suite. As I strutted out, I was sure Harry thought he had won this battle. I reminded myself that this entire mess would be over soon. The next day we could spread Tami's ashes, and I could wave adios to Harry as he hopped a plane back to Chicago, knowing I would never ever have to see his lemon-sucking face again.

As I strolled through the resort, it seemed even more spectacular than at first view. Off of one side of the pool deck the building wrapped around toward a glassed-front night club. The music pounded from inside, literally vibrating the wall. I could spot couples dancing on a raised dance floor as a collage of lights bounced around the large room.

I checked my watch, and since it was already nearing midnight, I figured I'd save my search of the hangouts until after Harry left. My need to get another scotch in my belly superseded any desire to go hunting for a better place to drink. Besides, this was actually the ideal location to start my binge. I knew I could make it back upstairs from there.

You could feel the backbeat from the club bash you in the chest, like a small sports car backing over you. Yes, that has happened to me but that's a story for another time. I never much liked club music. Same tempo. Same backbeat. Same indistinguishable vocals. And the pounding practically shoved you around the room without your consent. Good news, it was loud, cutting down on any chance for conversation. And there were a few hot women in tight skirts shaking it on a dance floor with their boyfriends. Good. Eye candy to enjoy while I slammed back a few. And since most of their mates suffered from a chronic case of white man's disease on the dance floor, the amusement factor rose considerably.

I found a lone stool at the end of the very busy bar and waved a twenty in the direction of the bartender who had her back to me.

"Double scotch," I announced as she spun in my direction.

She was a striking woman, somewhere in her late twenties, with a mane of dark hair tied up in that consciously messy 'do that women seem to favor. Her olive skin shaded all that much more cocoa by the island sun. Even her nondescript uniform - white shirt and black slacks – could not hide the fact that this woman had one hell of a body.

I slid the twenty across the bar to her, working my best smile. Maybe drinking in this place wouldn't be as unbearable as I first believed. Without ever taking her eyes off of me, her hand slid under the bar and came up with an empty glass. Her other hand came up with a bottle of scotch. She poured. Slightly more than a double which drew a smile from me.

"Thank you, sweetheart," I nodded as I saluted her with my glass.

Her dark eyes remained locked on me. She took a long moment before she spoke. "My name is Katherine. You can call me Kat but don't ever again call me 'sweetheart'."

I threw my hands in the air as if I'd been busted on felony charges by the Feds. "My apologies. I don't want to piss off my favorite bartender. Not on my first night. You and I are going to be exceedingly tight this week."

Kat returned with my change and the same nearly-hostile attitude. A five. Damn, drinks weren't cheap, but this was a resort and they had a captive audience. And with the average age at the resort around thirty, it was going to be a drinking crowd. Jackpot. I assumed after calling her 'sweetheart' she expected me to spot the five on the lip of the bar for her as a tip or she would have returned with singles. She had me by the short curlies. I needed to show her love throughout my first night's drunk so she got herself a healthy tip right at the starting gate.

Money's always better than an apology.

About midway through my third double scotch, my old drinking buddy showed up. Dr. Buzz. As he settled into my body he felt warm, comfortable, familiar. Hello, Dr. Buzz, I missed you.

I noticed an attractive bottle blonde eye me from a table where she sat with a group. At one point, they all turned and glanced at me in unison. All I could figure was that someone at the table knew me from Chicago and had heard about Tami. Fucking great. If that was the case, Harry could have the room because after we released Tami to the ocean, I was heading for another island. But the more the woman eyed me, I found myself actually praying she recognized me as the asshole that had slept with her and never called.

The blonde slipped from her seat and maneuvered her way through the tables, standing at the bar within arm's length. She couldn't help but fire me prying glances. I sensed she wanted to say something but didn't know if she should. As curious as I was about what this was about, I really didn't want to get into a conversation. Finally, she gave me a big smile, leaned in close, and said, "I think what you're doing is so brave," in an accent so Southern-fried it almost sounded like a cartoon put-on.

I nodded with a vague smile. What the hell was she talking about? Between the accent and the liquor, maybe I didn't understand what she had said. Brave? I checked in with Dr. Buzz, but he didn't speak hick, so he was no help. I held my gaze on her, helpless as my eyes slipped furtive glimpses toward her cleavage, awaiting an explanation. Realizing that I was either too drunk or too stupid to catch on, the girl giggled and touched my hand with a familiarity that is probably a friendly custom in the deep South but, in Chicago, signals you're ready to strip naked and get down to business.

"Your...boyfriend. You. Here."

Boyfriend? Could see she Dr. Buzz? I actually found myself glancing around to see if there were some guy next to me, possibly with his arm around my shoulder or nibbling on my ear, that I wasn't aware of. I shook my head with a hazy smile and muttered, "I'm not following you, hon."

"I saw you heading into the honeymoon suite. You two were fighting. It was so cute," she said with another giggle, squeezing my hand.

But I didn't giggle. I didn't even smile. Was she was referring to Harry? My mind fritzed out, the syntax shooting across my cranium causing dangerous sparkage in my skull. This dim bulb thought Harry was my boyfriend?!? I glanced around her toward her table. Her entire party was focused on us. And then an ugly realization thundered through my besotted mind. This was a couple's resort. It would have been embarrassing enough if I had showed up by myself, but now I was sharing my honeymoon suite with a walking, talking, snarling bridge troll, while all the couples who had spied us as we entered were asking the $24 million question, "Who's on top?"

Dr. Buzz got up, gave me a pathetic shake of his head, and told me he had other patients to tend to. I tried to stop him, hoping he'd give me a lethal dose of, oh shit, anything! I needed to die, here, now, this second.

She stopped her giggling as a very serious look trickled across her face. "Oh," her tone twisted from amused to startled, "he's not your boyfriend, is he?"

Uh, no, darling! He's not my boyfriend. Jesus H. Christ, she actually thinks... This trip really is turning into a boat ride down the river Styx. If this wasn't so completely out of left field, I would probably pick up the scotch glass and smash it into my head. But that was the funniest thing anybody had said to me all week.

I howled. Slugging a hearty gulp of my scotch, I waved over Kat and asked if she would be kind enough to pour the funny lady a drink. With an icy sideways glance, Kat did as I requested and walked away with my money. Even after tipping her each drink she still didn't want to be my friend. Oh well, there were bigger fires to extinguish at the moment.

"You think that little freak is my boyfriend?" I finally responded, laughing again at the absurdity of that image, which was funny sober but even funnier drunk.

"I'm sorry," she cut in, giving my hand another little squeeze in apology. "I should have known. I mean, you and him..." She laughed at herself. "I'm so nosy. I just have to know everything about everybody." She took a smiling sip from the drink and then proceeded to kick me in the nuts. "I feel so silly. Gosh. You all aren't boyfriends, you're just dating, aren't you?"

This broad was as dumb as a turkey in a thunderstorm. Now I could have lived with her thinking I was gay if maybe she had seen me swapping spit with some Calvin Klein underwear model. But she saw me with Harry. Even if I was gayer than a thong on a Frenchman, there wasn't enough alcohol on that island for me to get drunk enough to get naked with Harry Everett. Even gay men must have a line they won't cross, and trust me, Harry's wrinkly, hairy ass would be a deal breaker. Damn, Harry and me?! Did this chick think I was that big of a loser? That I couldn't do anything better than Harry? Did she get a look at Harry? I mean, maybe she didn't get a clean view of his little mole face and badly-dressed potato sack of a body. Maybe she was into men who resemble rodents. I didn't care how stupid this woman was, it was really insulting. Nothing like kicking a guy when he's down.

Before I could rebut her obnoxious presumption, she scampered back to her table and went into a head-to-head conference with her friends.

Ain't this a special day?

If God had a sense of humor, after that he was doubled over. If I had had a revolver in my pocket, I would've splattered myself across the bar. They thought I was there on some hot rendezvous with a gremlin in a Members Only windbreaker and Sansabel slacks. How quickly would that spread around the resort?

"Kat, I need a favor," I bellowed at her over the music, causing her to lean over the bar to hear me. "How much for a whole bottle?"

"Can't do that."

"Can't or won't?"

She smiled sharply. I was a mind reader.

"You've had enough, Todd. Go back to your room, to your wife, or girlfriend, or your right hand, and call it a night. You don't need to be wandering around the resort with a bottle of scotch. That could get a guy like you in a lot of trouble, not that I really care. But you getting in a lot of trouble could get me fired. And that I care about."

Eww. Honesty. I just hate that when I'm drunk.

"You don't know me well enough yet to call me trouble," I fired back, buying time as I grasped aimlessly for any legitimate argument that would make her see the light and agree to sell me a bottle.

But she laughed in my face. "I've been working in bars since I was twenty-one. Trust me, you I know."

I pulled out a hundred dollar bill, crumpled it into her hand and then kissed her hand before begging her to meet me at the back door of the bar with the bottle. Her eyes again held mine for a moment. Great eyes. It was the frigid glare in them that I could have lived without. But the longer I kept hold of her hand, the more I could see her breaking down. My perception certainly wasn't that she was growing sort of sweet on me; it was more that she felt I was pathetic and she wanted me gone.

Hey, whatever works.

I skulked out of the bar with my tail between my legs. The gay loser was going to get even more shitfaced before he staggered upstairs to his snoring never-to-be-father-in-law-now-assumed-lover, who was hogging the king-size bed with his goddamned stubby limbs.

"Thank you," I said to Kat as I reached out and took the bottle from her.

"Don't do anything stupid. And if you do, you better not mention where you got the bottle."

"If you're that worried, why don't you come have a drink with me when you get off," I queried, with what I thought was a come hither glimmer in my eye but I'm sure only made me appear more asinine to her.

Again, Kat allowed a dark smile onto her face. I'd like to say it scared me but actually it made her more attractive as if it were a dare. "You saw all the men in the club tonight," Kat said. "Married. Engaged. Newlyweds. With their girlfriends. Doesn't matter. All of them have one fantasy. To have sex with someone else other than the woman they came with," she continued, seemingly standing taller with each word. "I could have any one of those guys. What would make you even remotely think that I would choose you?"

Ouch. Damn. Why didn't she just stab a cocktail spear through my temple and put me out of my misery? Some of the other women thought I was a gay also-ran who couldn't do any better than Harry and now she was telling me even on the straight team I was sitting on the bench.

Before I could think of a single bitter remark to campaign for a bit of my ebbing pride, the back door shut in my face and Kat was gone. Well, at least I had my bottle. Beggars can't be choosers.

Walking out onto the pool deck, I kicked off my shoes, leaving them. I threw a lounge chair onto my back and hauled it down to the beach. The club's strobe lights illuminated the white caps in flashes, as the waves tumbled onto the shore with a growl. On that moonless night, the ocean extended into an inkiness that seemed wrapped around the entire globe. An obscurity that I wished would envelope me until I disappeared into its endlessness.

Staggering through the sand, I dropped the chair where the ocean finished its foamy ride onto the beach. The tide sank my feet into the wet sand. I cracked open the seal on the Cutty, took a deep breath and then an even deeper slug. Lying back on the chair, I watched the stars. No moon but so many stars. A road map to somewhere else.

SUNNY AND WARM WITH A CHANCE OF MONSOON

"Excuse me, sir, are you a guest at the resort?"

My eyes slithered open to see a dark-skinned man staring into my face. He smiled. Glad he felt like smiling. I felt near death. And why the hell was I wet? When it finally focused, I realized the tide had come in and my chair was now under two feet of water.

Stepping into the tide, the man picked up the chair and carried it out of the surf. I glanced around for my bottle of Cutty but it was gone. Out to the ocean, I assume. The sea is a cruel mistress. Wandering up the beach behind him, I followed my guide's steps back to the pool deck. Early risers were swimming laps. Christ, couldn't you people do that at home? You don't come to a resort to swim laps. Go out at night, get crazy. Stay in bed all morning. If you want some exercise, have sex.

Glancing up, resort patrons stared down from their private balconies. Including Harry, who was sneering down at me. I waved up. "Sleep good, Harry?" Embarrassed, he slipped back inside and drew the curtains.

As I shuffled through the expansive lobby, heading for the elevators, I overheard a guy about my age comment to his friend, "He's the one. He and his lover got into a huge fight last night, and the old homo locked him out of the room." Glad to see that the rumor hadn't passed away overnight. Wouldn't want that. I was used to having a terrible reputation, but it was lovingly deserved, not based on gossipy misinformation. I wonder if anyone had sent Harry up a bottle of champagne with a note that read: Good going, Tiger. Bagged a young one.

Entering the suite, Harry's muted scowl expressed volumes about me passing out on the beach. Ignoring him, I marched into the bathroom and kicked the door closed. My teeth felt like they were wearing little sweaters, and I smelled like I had gone a few rounds with a fishmonger. Stripping out of my clothes, I noticed tiny bites all over my chest, stomach, and legs. Sand fleas. Great. Now I looked like I had the measles.

After an hour of leaning against the tiled wall in the shower, I felt semi-human again.

As I brushed my teeth, there was a knock on the bathroom door. "What?!" I barked out, hoping that there was enough gruff in my tone to dissuade even an army from bugging me further.

Harry pushed open the door a shade, peeking his squished face in. "Are you dressed?" Spying the towel around my waist, he stepped into the bathroom. "When are we going to spread Tami's ashes?" he asked, looking away, embarrassed that I wasn't completely clothed.

What was his rush? It wasn't like Tami was in a hurry. But then again, Harry did everything by the clock. His punctuality was another one of his plethora of annoying habits. If you were even a few minutes late, he would be glaring at his watch and making snarky remarks under his breath or sighing heavily. Harry planned his life to the second. No grace period. It got so bad during the last week of wedding preparations that every time he told me to be at a certain location at a certain time, I would nod and then add "give or take five or ten minutes," just to piss him off.

"Why? You got other big plans today?" I asked dryly.

"I'm not staying," Harry stated with definitive authority. "Once I am sure Tami is where she wants to be, I am going home."

That was the best news I had in a week. My boyfriend was hightailing it out of here, allowing me to spend the rest of my time on St. Carlos getting drunk in peace. And if I got obnoxious (which was probable), got into a fight (possible), or even got laid - something that was highly unlikely given that everyone thought I was into antiques - Harry wouldn't be there to give me stink eye and evoke the memory of his dead daughter, reminding me of just how unworthy I had been of her. No shit, Harry. But the difference is, now I don't give a shit. I used up my quota of good grace. So, if you thought I was unworthy before, strap your ass in, this ride is just getting started.

I told Harry that once I was out of the bathroom we would seek out Tami's special place and give her to the elements. As he exited the bathroom, I added, "Call the airlines, find out the next flight home, and reserve yourself a seat," and then kicked the door closed.

I took my time shaving, squeezed some drops into my eyes, and rubbed gel into my hair. I dug through Harry's shaving kit and found something to put on the bites. Luckily, the maniac carried something for every possible disaster.

The joy I felt at Harry's anticipated departure was fleeting. As I stepped from the bathroom, Harry had the phone to his ear, in the midst of an argument. What was it with Harry and the airlines? Was his photo hanging at every ticket counter right next to the mug shots of potential terrorists? "Potential Pain in the Ass." I dropped the towel around my waist and slipped on a clean pair of shorts. Glancing over my shoulder, I saw Harry staring in my direction. It was either the panorama of my big, white ass or his heated conversation, but his face was tensed up in a knot and punctuated with a frown. He kept peering at me, his eyes imploring me to help him out. You gotta be kidding. There wasn't a chance in a Chinese restaurant I was taking the phone from him and dealing with these airline people. I had only done it in Chicago because he held my fiancée hostage. You're a big boy, Harry. Handle it. Granted, I had a lot at stake if I was forced to stay with the human enema for another twenty-four hours, but no matter what arrangement I made for him to get off the island, it would be wrong. Better Harry make his own mistakes and I focus on my task: sobering up so I could get drunk again later.

I crossed by Harry, completely oblivious that he was barking at some poor airline employee on the other end of the line, and stepped out into the sunshine that warmed the balcony. I fell into a lounge chair, my eyelids slamming shut almost before I hit the chair.

"I don't believe you! You're just trying to get more money out of me. There has to be at least one seat on a flight before then," Harry's voice raised an octave, getting thinner the angrier he became. "No, I am not going to stand there every day for the next week-and-a-half to see if I can get on a standby flight! I understand you only have two flights a day off the island. But they can't all be full!"

Was my luck holding out or what? Not that I was surprised that Harry couldn't get off the island. The only planes that could land at the airport didn't hold but fifty people. Lots of tourists, two flights a day. Do the math. As I listened to Harry harangue the reservation agent, trying to bully his way onto a flight, I figured that if my luck continued to hold, there would be a giant comet screaming toward my room any moment.

Harry could complain to his heart's content. His return flight was nine days off, and unless he was willing to hang around the airport in the hope that someone overslept or decided to extend their holiday, he wasn't getting off this island until he stepped onto the flight that was originally booked.

Harry was now a captive on the island. Which extended another problem. It was one thing that we were on the same island. But the bed-hogging munchkin shared my honeymoon suite, and he wasn't about to leave. I wondered if the airlines would put Harry on the next flight out if they knew the mitigating circumstances. Harry had a medical condition. Chronic son-of-a-bitch-itis. He needed to see a specialist back in the States or he would die. Probably at my hands. Or those of an airline ticket agent. Because this was turning out to be a homicide in the making.

I had to think. And that was a chore. The shower helped but my brain was still bleeding information rather than absorbing it. There was no way in hell I could deal with this until later, when I was more sober and focused. Or at least more focused. My butt was embedded into the lounge chair, and my body wasn't going to let me get off.

Harry slamming down the receiver echoed through the room. Seconds later something was blocking my sun. Wrenching open one eyelid, I looked up at Harry silhouetted by a ring of fiery, island sun. It appeared as if flames were coming out of his head, which, given his ever present pissiness, may actually have been the case.

"You aren't trying hard enough, Harry. Maybe you should head to the airport and talk to them in person. You know how much better that works for you with your winning personality," I said, defeating my own argument for the sake of sarcasm.

"Are you being a smart ass?"

Of course. Being a smart ass has always come naturally to me. It's a gift. I had abandoned it while I was with Tami, but there was no longer a reason to stifle my innate abilities. "What the hell do you want me to say, Harry?" I asked. "'I'm sorry you can't get off the island?' Believe me, no one is sorrier than me. I would suggest you call around and find another hotel room." After we released Tami's ashes in the afternoon, I'd have no need to keep an eye on him. "Because as fun as it has been," I announced, "You're out of this one today."

"Why?" Harry fired back quickly, his eyes narrowing suspiciously. "What do you have planned that you don't want me knowing about?"

"I don't know, Harry. A drunken debacle. A bacchanal. Maybe an orgy or two or three. So unless you want to join in some pretty kinky shit -- Find Yourself Another Hotel."

Harry's face squeezed tighter than I had ever seen it. Like a giant red kiwi with a nose. I drew my knees up; in case he attacked I could kick him off of me before he got his fat fingers around my throat.

"Tami is barely dead, and you're already talking about having relations with other women," he spouted, outraged.

"Tami is barely dead," I said slowly, trying to make sense of whatever the hell that meant and pissed off that he had missed my obvious sarcasm and was using it against me. "Barely dead? She's been burnt to dust and is locked in your goddamn luggage, Harry! How much deader does she have to be?!"

"My daughter's memory does not deserve that from you," Harry persisted.

Soaring at hyperspeed into territory in which I was unprepared to go solo, my head was awash in images and words. It was as if I were still speeding, but everything else around me had grounded to a slow, dead silence. I tried to make some kind of sense of the man I was staring at.

"Don't talk to me about memories, Harry, when all I'm trying to do is escape mine. Tami's gone. She left me, Harry. And I'm still here with nothing but my goddamn memories." My eyes gripped him, and with the warmest smile I could muster, I purred, "So fuck you. Don't you ever fucking tell me how to live my life from here on out. It's my pathetic, screwed to shit, lonely life, and you don't have a goddamn thing to say about it." Then I leaned forward just to drive home my point. "Ever. We clear on that?"

He remained silent for a long beat, his face hidden in the darkness of the shadow cast by the sun behind him. Then he stated with sarcastic authority from on high, "If you can forget her just like that, then she must have meant as much to you as you keep spouting off."

Closing my eyes once again, I stretched out in the chair. I was sure that Harry thought I'd shut him out and was trying to find some place of Zen so I could sleep. But sleep didn't come that easy and there was no longer such thing as Zen for me. And worse, it was flat impossible to shut out Harry.

"I bet she's forgotten me too," I said, never opening my eyes. "She moved on to a better life, or so everyone's told me in the last fucking week. And I hope to God she has. Away from you, away from me. Because we would have made her life miserable. But I'm still here. And I can't love someone who isn't. Doesn't mean I've forgotten, Harry. If I could, I wouldn't be in this much pain." Finally, I opened my eyes. "But I'm going to do everything possible to hide from these memories. Because if I don't put something between me and Tami's memory, I'm going to die."

I sensed that my words had registered with his heart, but Harry wasn't going to let me suffer in silence when a few more words could start the launch code. "I guess I just can't move on as quickly as you," he added, frosting my ass completely.

"You're the champ at running in place, aren't you? You've been doing it for twenty years, since your wife died," I snapped back, pointing at him. "You made Tami pay for your inability to move on from that tragedy, but don't think you're going to make me pay for your inability to move on from this one."

I focused hard on Harry. He gritted his teeth, both of us enraged, neither backing down. The only sound you could hear was the incessant pounding of the ocean in the distance, accompanied by an occasional splash in the pool below.

"When was the last time you got laid?" I asked, in an effort to do even more damage. "You haven't had any pussy since Tami's mother died, have you? Jesus. You gave up your life and blamed it on her. Believe me, she knew it. You threw it in her face every chance you got. Well, she's gone Harry. Bye-bye. So long. And you're standing here with nothing. Nothing but your pud in your hand. What are you going to do now, champ? Go to Disneyland?"

Harry grabbed the rail behind him for support. This dark question had to be something that had been haunting his soul. But having it savagely thrown into his face by a mean prick was more than he could deal with. I saw the tears before I fully realized just how profoundly my words had wounded him. I'd talked a lot of smack to Harry, especially in the past few days, but nothing I'd regurgitated decimated the man more than that tirade.

Harry dashed back inside, keeping his face away from me. He then locked himself in the bathroom, unable to muffle his excruciating sobs.

Goddamn, sometimes I hated myself. It was so wrong on so many levels. Fuck me. I didn't mind poking at Harry with sharp objects. He deserved it. But he'd never merited some big jackass ripping his heart out of his chest, then squeezing out the blood while he watched helplessly. I buried my head in my hands and fought back tears of my own. Straight up cruel and there was nothing I could say now to stitch the wound.

Pulling my ass from the lounge chair, I stormed through the suite, yanking a T-shirt from my bag and wrestling it on over my head. I stopped outside the bathroom door, shoveling through my trunk of apologies, but there was nothing. Nothing good anyway. "I fucked up, I'm sorry," I said through the bathroom door, before stomping out of the room in self-disgust.

I hadn't eaten anything in almost a day, so the scotch surged magically to my head. The resort's club was nearly empty. A few couples tucked themselves into corner tables, sipping Bloody Marys and noshing on appetizers, but I was the only serious drinker on a bar stool. And behind the bar, Kat was restocking the inventory between orders. She didn't look happy to see me. Hard to imagine, huh?

"The usual," I called to her, the music now much mellower than the techno-shit they played the night before.

Kat stepped up and set a glass on the bar. "You haven't been drinking here long enough to have a regular, Todd."

"But I've been drinking long enough for you to remember my name," I countered.

"Yeah. Congratulations," she stated as she poured me a scotch. "You're the biggest drunk I've had in here in quite a while," Kat finished as she settled the Cutty bottle on the bar nearby.

"What do I have to do to become the all-time number one?"

She turned, her eyes examining me as if her x-ray vision was searching for the cancerous tumor that had turned my brain so acerbic and ridiculous. Then she squinted like she was looking at the sun. "Is your life that damn bad," she quizzed, continuing with her work.

"If you lined up all the days from the last week of my life, me getting completely hammered last night and feeling like dog crap today is heads and tails above the rest of the pathetic bunch," I answered, tipping the scotch bottle towards my glass for a refill.

Kat didn't respond but she would glance up from her chores, her ebony eyes holding court, waiting for my opening arguments. Fine, you want to hear, lady, you want to understand, to share in my damn drama, I'm all mouth. As I drank, I sweated out what had passed for my life through the last several months. Closing my eyes, I recounted each developing wave of my world after Tami entered. What she had done to me, how this woman had shredded who I had been and then rebuilt me into this new man. A guy I didn't recognize when I looked in the mirror but certainly liked a hell of a lot better than the miscreant I saw before. I recalled all the great moments, the little joys, and a few of the private moments. Kat continued to work, saying little. A good bartender knows when it is best to let the drinker blather rather than to offer any insight.

The more I rattled on, the more I noted a distinct shift in Kat. I knew she didn't like me. It seemed that began even before I sat down at her bar. I have that effect on people. They pre-despise me by the mere thought of some guy like me showing up. I am sure that Kat had dealt with all kinds of creeps in this line of work. A woman has to develop a tough skin. Especially a damn fine woman. The benefit was you get tipped better, but it also arrives with a shit storm full of hassle you don't ask for. I'm just rougher pavement than most of the asses she had to serve. But as I exposed my soft underbelly I'm sure she didn't fathom existed, the glower in Kat's eyes faded. Not to pat myself on the back but I think I actually became human to her. Not just a drunken prick with a chunk out of his heart that was even bigger than the chip on his shoulder. Her sultry eyes offered me muted solace and welcome understanding.

The little girl held out a flower to Frankenstein's monster.

Laying out the last few months in a chronology provided me the opportunity to make some sense as to why I was now sitting on this resort bar stool snuggling intimately with a bottle of scotch. I followed the dots right back to the place I hate the most but felt the safest. When I had Tami, she was my haven. Through her I understood my role in the world. Without her, the only way I believed I could battle through the rest of life was drunk, surly, and carnivorous.

Kat dropped her hand onto mine, offering me the first bit of sympathy I didn't feel like throwing back in someone's face. "I have to go to the back in the office and get cash. Stay put," she said with an honestly affectionate smile. I nodded only once before she disappeared into the back.

Sitting there alone, I searched for some relief I felt I could only grasp if I kept my hand tightly around the scotch glass. As I poured myself another, I turned to find a freckled brunette lost somewhere in her mid-forties settling herself onto the bar stool next to me. She was unconventionally beautiful, with a wild mane of hair that couldn't be tamed in this humidity. Her breasts beaconed from the low-cut V in her one- piece swim suit, and she had a small sarong tied around her waist. This was once a woman who once could turn every head in the room but was now at the age where it wasn't happening as often as she remembered, or desired.

There were plenty of other stools at the bar, but she selected the one only a seat to the right of me. I assumed she was a hooker, saw me alone, and figured that while my girlfriend or wife was out sightseeing she could interest me in a blowjob. Pick up some quick spending money before the overgrown frat boys or naughty husbands came out to play at night.

She gave me a smile. I was captured by the darkness of her eyes as they crinkled around the edges. They were a deep tone of chocolate and mysteriously needy. Then again, after four-and-a-half scotches almost everything is a mystery to me. I returned the smile, and then twisted in my seat away from her, pulling my glass with me. If she were a hooker, I didn't want this to go any further than a smile. A professional hummer was the last thing I needed. What would weeping, wounded, Harry have to say about that? My money was better spent at the bar.

"May I ask you a question?" the brunette said, her voice deeper than I expected, as if she had smoked most of her life. "That guy you are with, is he--"

"No, he's not my boyfriend," I replied with as much dexterity as my tongue had left. Stringing together two syllables was starting to give me trouble.

"I didn't think so. I mean people are into all sorts of things. Whatever makes them happy, I say. But you and he," she shook her head, her flowing curls bouncing side to side, "I just didn't see it. You're way too good looking to be with, well, I don't want to offend your friend. But I figured there must be something more going on," she said.

Kat had returned, her eyes widened as she saw me now nose to nose with my new friend. The brunette also spied Kat's return and raised a finger in her direction, ordering herself a Tom Collins and offering to pay for my next scotch, even though my fifth wasn't even half empty.

With a deliberate iciness, Kat snapped the cash off the bar, shifting her glare back and forth between the brunette and myself as if she were meeting the other woman for the first time. I locked eyes with her for just a moment, tilting my head as if to state, "I'm as tired of pouring out my pathetic problems as you are tired of pouring me drinks. I came down here to forget all this shit. Leave me alone. Messing with this chick is a lot more fun!"

Kat gave me her back and began to count money into the cash register.

"Since I didn't get to finish my question, can I ask you another?"

"You're buying," I responded, raising my glass to her.

She smiled. She knew the way to my heart. Through the bottom of a glass.

"So, in your profession, are you exclusively into men or do you," she stopped a beat, searching for the right phrase, "entertain women too?"

So, she thought I was the male equivalent of what I first thought she was. I could pretty much assume that everyone at the resort now had me pegged as Harry's boy toy or a male hooker. At least being a hooker, people thought I was receiving something for spending time with Harry. Not that there was enough bullion in Fort Knox for me to climb on to Harry and make him call me 'Daddy,' but it beat thinking people believed I was doing it for enjoyment.

"Yeah, I do women," I said, eyeing her up and down just in case she wasn't getting the message, "Actually exclusively."

She eyed me oddly, trying to do the math in her head. If that were true then what was I doing with the old guy? Was it a non-sexual thing? Was I being paid simply to be a companion? Or was I lying to her? I knew if I worked this woman long enough, she would stay curious and at the very least buy me another scotch. Or more.

Nothing positive or healing could come from making up an alternate life as Todd Cartwright, male hooker. But it certainly beat being Todd Cartwright, asshole with the dead fiancée. I'd bared my soul to the beautiful bartender a few minutes earlier, and all it did was lead me to the conclusion that my life was currently about as fucked as it had ever been. And it has some pretty sorry moments in the past. I had put down enough Cutty in me to make the tales of bedding-for-dollars colorful. But more importantly, I controlled the game. My life was so completely out of control that feeling like I had some minutia of power over anything was a blessing.

"How much do you charge?" the dark eyed, exotic woman asked, leaning into me as she took a sip of her drink.

I again smiled, my eyes watching Kat who continued to ignore me as I relayed to the interested brunette that I never discussed my 'fees' because so much depended on the client, their needs, and the situation. As boiled as my gray matter was, my evasion of her question echoed with extreme professionalism. Hell, I was a businessman. I knew how to talk the talk and walk the walk. And it was a simple matter of plugging it into my newfound male whoredom.

In a twisted way, it was a compliment that a lady this overtly good-looking thought I made a living schtooping women. Not that in any real sense I ever could. As much as I liked sex, turning it into an occupation wasn't in my make-up. No, I was the perfect futures analyst for one reason. Because I hated it with every fiber of my being. As my father used to say when I was little and we actually still had conversations, "That's why it's called work and not called fun." I labored at the Stock

Exchange to pay my bills and to finance the other pleasures of life. One of those being sex. Even if someone offered to finance my drinking, I didn't think I would enjoy tying one on as much as I did. Once it becomes business, it is cast in a tin shell and loses its appeal.

I continued to regale this brunette with stories of traveling the world, magnificent estates, extravagant parties, and pricey gifts from satisfied clients. As I continued my tale, I discovered that I owned a loft in New York and a Malibu condo but made my home in Chicago because I preferred to invest my money in the Chicago Stock Exchange. I convinced her that my average income was the mid-six figure level. And to add some veracity to my yarn, I kept seriously inquiring whether or not she was with the IRS or any laws enforcement organization, to which she insisted she wasn't. She was simply interested on an 'academic level.'

Academic, my ass. This was pure salaciousness. And pleasantly, there was enough scotch in my veins to keep me entertained by my own bullshit. As I drank the free glass, I wove a luxuriant tale of my paramour lifestyle, starting in college when I was a double major in finance and psychology. I paid my tuition with my escort earnings. My reputation flourished as a well-heeled, well-versed, well-hung date. The 'well-hung' remark got the biggest rise out of the brunette. Amazing how money, travel, education, all take a back seat when you toss in that you've got a fat Johnson. And damn it, if I was going to make my fortune as an escort, I needed to have prime equipment.

"When did your drinking problem begin," she quizzed.

That drew a sharp, side-eyed glance from Kat but made me laugh. And it wasn't a ha-ha laugh, it was a 'give me a break' laugh. Drinking problem? Really? Me? This wasn't about drinking. This is a dying problem, lady. And I drink because I'm not the one who died.

But I passed along to the brunette that I only drank when my services were not required. I never drank on the job. Only for my own enjoyment.

"Then you drink to escape?" she added, with that intense brow most bar stool psychoanalysts get when they're hammered but are working overtime to sound soberly coherent.

I lied, stating matter of factly that there was absolutely nothing from which I needed escaping. I liked my chosen profession; it afforded me travel, contact with interesting people, and creature comforts. And I bragged, "In another couple years, I'll have invested enough to live a certain lifestyle without relying on my body." Man, I had to have been drunk to get that malarkey out of my mouth.

But she nodded, accepting my obnoxious boasting as truth. The brunette soaked it all in as if she were talking with someone who had walked on the moon. I was waiting for her to ask for my autograph.

Hey, if they're going to buy the lie, run with it.

"Then what's the story about the man you are with?" she asked, leaning back against the bar.

I told her that I had accepted the job with Harry because it was supposed to be a purely companionship arrangement. And he was a huge tipper. "Don't let his dumpy, rumpled look fool you," I confided, tripping over the words dumpy and rumpled, "that little circus clown is worth millions." But I told her the downside of Harry was that he was a horny old bugger and now that we were on the island, I discovered that he had only booked one room.

"I don't know how to get through to the oversexed, little devil that it's just not going to happen. He doesn't want to take no for an answer. And then today, he tells me he's in love with me and asks me to move into his estate, telling me that when he dies, he's leaving his entire fortune to me."

"Wow," she exclaimed, wide-eyed as if I had just given her my address and the combination to my home safe. But then something in her eye shifted. The awe disappeared and a more desirous glimmer took its place. She turned and faced me full on, as if she wanted me to get the full view of her body and her face.

"How much would you charge someone like me?" the tabaccoed deepness of her voice mewed alluringly.

This drew Kat a few steps closer to hear the answer.

For a man who got stiff when the breeze blew the right way, this was heady stuff. Tami used to shake her head and giggle because I was always ready to raise the sail. "Is there anything that doesn't make you horny?" she would always ask me. And I would always give her a brazen smile and shake my head.

But I had found something. My fiancée dying in a car accident.

I hadn't felt like being touched since Tami had passed away. I had known the greatest of intimacies. Overwhelming affection from a woman that I adored on every level. Down in my gut, I knew I would never fall so completely in love. There would never be another soul that would change the essence of who I was, as Tami had done for me. I had given my heart away.

Prior to Tami, I had always been the guy that women slept with before they got serious with someone else. And that was all right with me. I was getting what I wanted and I fulfilled a need for them. It was win-win. From that point forward the best I could ever expect from sex was an escape. There was a great deal to be said for fornicating away a few hours, forgetting who I was and what the last week of my life had been.

"I would never charge a beautiful woman like you," I spoke in a low, gruff, voice, which caused Kat to return to the far end of the bar with a shake of her head. "I would do it because I think I'd have a good time," said Todd, the male escort, who wanted desperately to snuff out the other, angry, injured Todd.

Her eyes widened with intrigue. She was enjoying this coy game even more than I was. I'm not sure she believed a single word that came out of my mouth but that wasn't the issue. It was the frivolous, sexy fantasy that intrigued. For both of us. I got to be someone else and she was happy to be with that other person. Truth be damned because truth hurt. This woman was probably trapped in a marriage where her old man, who was most likely off playing golf, ignored her most of the time. Now some professional dick-meister a decade younger was turning her back into a desirable piece of ass and wouldn't charge her for his services. And even more incredible, when she returned home, she'd pass along the secret of her late-morning tryst with the island gigolo to her most-trusted girlfriends. They would gasp and giggle, and in their eyes her worth would be raised. And in her own eyes, as she took in her aging figure in the bathroom mirror, she could smile and remember the male escort who hadn't charged her for a roll in the sheets.

I was about to take her hand when I felt this monkey on my back. Literally.

Turning, I spotted Harry behind me. After the verbal whipping I handed him up in the suite, I didn't think he would ever talk to me again, much less come looking for me. The brunette shifted uneasily on her stool as my whole demeanor shifted from Todd, male stud, to Todd, roommate of Harry, man who had the love of my life locked in his ugly suitcase.

The tone in Harry's voice immediately made it clear that this wasn't a social call to see if I was having fun on my vacation. "I want to do what we came here to do," Harry uttered, glancing at the brunette who inspected him closely, mentally ticking off the distortions I had painted about the man.

"You mean now?" I quizzed, knowing that my dick was on the launching pad and Harry was trying to shove me back to my own ugly reality. I was way too buzzed to want to trek across the island trying to find a magical place. I was already in my own special place courtesy of Cutty Sark and my own bullshit, which was about to get me laid.

Harry had privacy issues and wasn't about to respond, not with Kat making no effort to hide the fact she was listening again and the brunette sitting next to me with her nipples pressing through her low-cut top and her sarong wrapped around her fleshy hips, eyeing him like an alien delicacy.

"Harry," I slurred for effect, clueing him into the fact that I was too drunk to go beach hunting, "let's do it later. I'm busy here."

His face tightened up and he spun around, his shoulders knotting. But he wouldn't walk away. He still wanted to spread Tami's ashes, even after all the shitty stuff I had said, even after finding me drunk in the bar with a woman willing to pay me cash for an afternoon of sweaty bedplay. Assessing the pros and cons of getting laid over fulfilling Tami's final wish and possibly getting rid of Harry for the rest of my time on the island, I decided that my ego was going to have to wait. Todd, the bereaved boyfriend, took total precedence over his new persona.

I stumbled off my stool and gave my auburn-haired drinking companion a warm nod with a wink. "The boss calls," I murmured with a shrug. "Another time."

But she didn't seem to hear me. The brunette still couldn't take her eyes off of Harry, having trouble juxtaposing the image I had created of him in my stories as the horny, multi-millionaire muppet with that of the badly-dressed lump with the sour scowl standing in front of her.

Kat stood stiffly at the far end of the bar, methodically wiping the inside of a wine glass with a rag. As she caught my eye, she mouthed words that took me a moment to decipher. Without a drip of irony she mutedly enunciated, "FULL-OF-SHIT."

My breath shortened as if I'd slammed hard in the breadbasket with a roundhouse kick. What was she saying, that my pain was a fraud? Because I decided to entertain a woman who seemed to need a diversion as much as I needed to cause one? Because baring my soul didn't lead to anything but the realization that I hated being me? And for someone who has always loved himself, that's a pretty drastic drop in the polls. I wanted to snap back at Kat, to snarl, to scream in her face, "You don't know anything about the shit in my life, so keep your fucking opinions to yourself!"

Instead, I shrugged with arrogant nonchalance, not allowing her to see the slicing wound she opened up near my aorta. Damn it, she was just a hotel bartender, how could I allow her to nick me so deeply? Yeah, I'm full of shit. Hell, everybody has to be something when they grow up. Full of shit was fine with me.

I downed the last of the scotch in my glass and tossed some cash on the bar. "Keep the change...sweetheart," I brutally cracked in Kat's direction before weaving my way out of the club.

"What was the matter with that woman you were talking to?" Harry asked as we made our way through the resort. "I didn't like the way she was staring at me."

"Maybe she thought you were cute," I answered, almost laughing before I got the words out.

"If you're going to start this again, I will do this alone. I'm not letting you get me upset again. You understand? I won't allow you to do that to me anymore."

"I'm sorry," I said with inebriated contrition. As much as I didn't like Harry, I did not want to make him cry again.

We returned to the room and Harry unlocked his suitcase. In the middle, wrapped in sweaters - yes, sweaters - something you often need in the Tropics, was a brushed metallic canister. Harry hadn't housed Tami in anything ornate.

No urn or carved box. Just a glorified coffee can that looked like spring snakes would pop into your face when you opened it. But he was ready to do the deed and then vanish from my life.

Maybe there was hope for Harry.

I took the canister from him and held it. I didn't have a clue how much it would weigh. Tami had been about a 110 pounds, but now she was in a canister that felt like a few pounds, give or take. The love of my life had been reduced to something I could toss around in one hand like a football. It didn't seem right.

I shoved the canister back into Harry's hands as I felt tears rim my eyes. I thought that holding her ashes would be cathartic. I suffered only pain. Harry knew why I turned away. The very same feelings probably overcame him the first time he held the canister in his hands. "Let's get this over with," I said flatly, trying to reinforce my own commitment to opening that can and dumping Tami, like an overflowing ashtray, into the sea breeze. For a couple hours downstairs in the bar I forgot who I was. The rage surging inside me dissipated while I performed the fantasy role of gigolo for my audience of one. And now I was back to being me. And it sucked. It sucked sober. It sucked drunk. Holding my girlfriend in one hand didn't bring any closure, just more resentment for everything in my life, with a special bitterness added for what we were about to do.

Two cabs waited in front of the resort. Peeking into both, I spotted Tomas, the gentleman who drove us from the airport. Liking the familiar, I pushed Harry toward his cab. Transportation was not a huge issue on the island. For the most part, autos weren't a necessity on St. Carlos. There were really only two neighborhoods. The resorts, a few pricey private homes, and condos on one end, and the rest of the town across the island where most people lived and worked.

All in all, it was about ten blocks between them. People generally traveled by bike, golf cart, or simply walked. Unlike the other islands, which had at least one export, St. Carlos was still basically island jungle with resorts tacked around a massive cove on the south, and the rest of the town to the north. The only other major trade on the island was banking. This was a favorite destination for off-shore accounts and hidden money coming from the drug business and wealthy Americans seeking a tax dodge.

As we rumbled along slowly, Tomas explained the history of the island. The Indians were on St. Carlos for centuries before the Spanish arrived and took over the island as a port. The cove on the south side of the island offered their ships refuge in storms. The indigenous people lived along the ocean to the north. The island was sold to the French for a short time, but the Spanish took it back. When the slave trade became a full-fledge business in the 1800's, St. Carlos was a port stop before heading into the United States. The slave traders loved St. Carlos because if a slave jumped ship, there was nowhere to run except into the jungle. The traders could hunt the runaways down with relative ease or kill them and let the jungle animals take care of their burial.

Some of the Africans who escaped were able to survive and hid in the jungles, actually forming a hidden colony. It wasn't until the early 1900's that they assimilated with the islanders, which by then consisted of the Indians, Spanish settlers, a few French and British, and a gaggle of American ex-pats.

When Harry told Tomas exactly where we wanted to be dropped off, Tomas's eyes shined knowingly. Tomas actually remembered Tami's grandmother. He told us that when he was young Tami's grandmother would pay him a nickel to help her carry her groceries home from the store. And she would give him peppermints, which for an island boy was a rare treat.

Harry recognized that area as soon as Tomas pulled to the curb. The small house was gone, replaced by a two-story office building. It was relatively new, built within the past ten years, but was manufactured to give the appearance of a structure that had blessed the island for a century. It housed a real estate lawyer, a tiny bank, and at least a half-dozen small investment firms. When Tami's grandmother passed away, her home was purchased by a British citizen who lived on the island. He promised to keep the house as it was, but once the other two properties on either side became available, he had all the homes demolished and erected the office building in their place. Progress.

As we stood in front of the building, Harry described Tami's grandmother's house. It was a small, white clapboard structure with soft blue shutters and an immaculate garden teeming with flowers. The house had a stone walkway that led from the cobblestone street and a front door painted a welcoming shade of red. It only had two small bedrooms, one bath, a kitchen with an attached dining nook, and a grand room. The whole place couldn't have been over 800 square feet, according to Harry. Tami's grandmother had added on a small sun room in the rear of the home that overlooked the amazing garden in the back. Behind the garden, a breathtaking view of the sea was visible from the rear of the property.

Tami's grandmother, Emma, had traveled to the island on numerous occasions while writing a book about a sixteenth century pirate name Gustallo and had fallen in love with its simplicity and beauty. Back in the 1950's, St. Carlos was only a bud of the resort island it is today. Emma bought the small plot of land and actually had the house built. It cost over $15,000 to build the house, which, by island standards, not to mention the time, was an enormous amount.

As I listened to Harry, for the first time I felt a twinge of recognition that he and I existed in the same world. That there was something we held in common besides a loved one who had died. Both he and I were captives of a memory we were trying to figure out how to deal with. Stepping back, moving forward, rushing by without glancing up, we were both clamoring to find some way to exist with a new reality. Releasing Tami would be a part of it. A beginning, I hoped. Or, at the very least another baby-step in the right direction. Harry and I were aiming in the same direction, but I knew we would have to take very different roads.

I didn't interrupt Harry as he recalled good times his family spent here. Being back on this narrow, cobblestone street again, Harry was surrounded by the aroma of a past that made him smile. As he continued to present tales of vacations with his wife and daughter, sharing with me nostalgia about Tami as a young girl – how many of the islanders referred to her as "the little American beauty with sand for eyes" - Harry stood taller. His eyes opened wider, and with the light dappling across his face through the leaves of the trees, he actually seemed younger and happier than I had ever seen him before.

We walked around the little neighborhood of six blocks by six blocks. Harry pointed out where things once stood, a park he took Tami to when she was a baby. There was no swing set, slide, or jungle gym, just an open grassy area and a sandpit for the children to play in. But Tami would play there for hours after she came back from the beach. "She seemed to like the park better than the beach. Tami never did like salt water until she was older," Harry reminisced.

Talking relieved some of the pressure that had boiled up inside him. All he had left were memories and reliving them in his head allowed him a few moments of solace. I don't think

Harry much cared who was there with him as he recalled snippets of stories and times past, he just needed to verbalize them. Make them real for himself one more time because he knew that, afterwards, they would be neatly folded and stored in that place inside his heart where cherished history was safeguarded.

As we rounded the block at the back of the office building where Emma's house had once stood, Harry looked at me, his eyes squinting. His demeanor changed immediately, and he stopped talking. He realized he had shared far too much with a guy he didn't even like. The man who would never be his son-in-law. Hard to believe that Harry and I came so close to being kin. But at that point it was all horseshoes and hand grenades. In the end, the reality was that Harry and I only had death in common.

"Where is this place Tami told you about?" he questioned in an abrupt tone that actually startled me.

I pointed down the block. I remembered Tami telling me about the spot and the directions from her grandmother's home. I believed I could find Tami's special place from the landmarks she'd described, as long as the streets hadn't changed.

Harry and I made our way to where the street ended and a small trail began through a piece of jungle. And jungle it was. The trail was overgrown, as if without the houses on the blocks, it became an obsolete memory.

I don't know why I hadn't noticed before but Harry was hardly dressed for a trek through the jungle. Maybe because he was wearing exactly what he always wore. A short-sleeved, button-down shirt, creased slacks, and these brown slip-on shoes that weren't made for hiking over anything more rugged than Berber carpet.

Harry never impressed me as a big outdoorsman. He was more the Barcolounger and remote kind of guy. I couldn't even imagine that even in his youth Harry had much liked the camping and hunting thing. He was probably very happy he had had a daughter and not a son. I'd stake some cash on

Harry never being very adept at football or baseball, though I had witnessed him screaming at the television while watching a Bears game, chiding the professionals about how to play the game better.

"There's no way you're going to hike through this shit in your Hush Puppies," I commented, pushing under the overgrown branches and stepping into the shadowy jungle.

"What about you? You think you'll make it through in a pair of shorts and those silly looking basketball shoes?" he retorted.

Point taken. But I wasn't about to let him know that.

"I could make it," I smirked, knowing that the only way I would ever attempt to cross through that thick jungle was drunk. And thankfully, I still passed that test. "But I'm telling you this, if you fall I'm not picking your ass up. I'll take Tami from you and leave you there for the animals to eat."

Convincing Harry that we had to redress him if he were to survive this excursion - and figuring I'd rather be safe than sorry and find some more suitable duds - we discovered a small general store that we had passed earlier as we walked around the neighborhood. I found us both long-sleeved shirts, long pants, hats, and a couple pairs of heavy shoes. Unfortunately, the pickings were slim, so everything - the pants, shirt, hat, and even the boots - I bought were the same color.

"You got to be kidding. You're going to dress us exactly alike?" Harry questioned, mortified at the thought.

"What choice do I have, Harry?" I answered, not hiding my own lack of joy.

"I hope to God no one sees us," he sneered.

"You think I'm happy about this? For Christsake, we're hiking through vines and shit. It's not like we're going to be out there posing for pictures, so get over it," I snapped, shoving the clothes in his arms.

Harry grumbled but pulled on the shirt and pants, then laced up the boots. He grumbled even louder when he paid 'island prices' for them.

It wasn't until we were dressed that the full impact of just how silly we looked smacked me. We resembled one of those awful family photos where the father and son dressed in exactly the same Christmas get-up. Say cheese!

I yanked the hat down as far as I could over my face as Harry kept a step behind me, grumbling, hoping no one would notice. But they did. The locals pointed and snickered, which was humiliating enough, but when a tour bus rolled by from the resort and the guests spotted Harry and his "boy toy" in our identical outfits, the laughter could be heard until they rounded the corner and disappeared from sight.

Bullseye, God.

Lumbering through the dense trees and vines, we pushed slowly forward, unable to see any light at the end of the thickly-entwined vegetation. "Are you taking me out here to kill me?" Harry questioned, tripping over the fallen branch of a tropical tree.

"The thought had crossed my mind," I said, branches snapping under my weight, as we marched on.

"You don't have a clue where you're going, do you?" Harry badgered.

Of course I didn't. It wasn't like Tami handed me a secret treasure map before she died and whispered, "bury me on the X." I was winging it off of a conversation Tami and I had had while lying in bed after sex. Not the best time for an accurate recollection of anything. And the last time Tami was there was when she was eleven. Things change. As I can sorely attest to.

"Just keep walking," I sighed, "and keep your eyes on the trail."

"This isn't a trail. A trail has markings. And a path. Do you see a path? I don't think anyone's been through here in a hundred years," Harry complained, holding onto my shirt, Tami's canister tucked safely under his arm.

"You're not in Chicago," I snarled, "things grow a little quicker here because it doesn't get twenty below zero every winter. Do you want me to hold onto the container?"

Harry wrapped his hands over the canister to protect it, as if he were smuggling explosives through customs. Short of death, he was not letting go of it. And even then I believe his sweaty, little hands would be permanently stuck to the canister, hardening their grip around Tami so he would never let her go. Harry refused to let me control the canister. It was his daughter, he paid for the cremation, he paid for the container, he was holding on to it. Fine. Let him stumble around in that pain-in-the-ass thicket. I was just trying to be nice. And look where that had gotten me thus far.

Harry remained silent for the next few minutes and then suddenly began talking about Tami's mom, Winifred. "A most unfortunate name for a woman of that generation," Harry added with a shake of the head. I wasn't sure if he were talking to me, himself, or to anyone. Hiking in this bug-infested canopy of vegetation was scary and maybe he just needed to hear his own voice. Remember someone he loved. And Harry had clearly adored "Winnie." I sensed as much as I adored Tami. But Harry confided that they fought a lot. Sentiment and her illness turn memories more benevolent, Harry said.

The more he spoke, the more it became clear that Harry was still dealing with these memories. Unfortunately for him, the memories never turned him benevolent enough.

Marching forward, I finally saw a clearing. Even I was getting worried that we were heading into the jungle never to return to civilization. We would probably find a slave or two still hiding out. But finally, through a crack ahead, daylight. I picked up my pace, leaving Harry to fend for himself, wrestling with the vegetation with his one free arm.

Stepping through the vines into the sunlight, it took a second for my eyes to focus. I could only imagine Tami, as a little girl, fearlessly rushing down the overgrown trail, through the sliver of jungle until she hit the sand again.

And then I saw it. And I comprehended exactly why that little girl believed it was the most special place on earth.

The jungle led to a clearing with reed grass blowing in the sea breeze. This gave way to sandy dunes that dropped down to a very private strip of white sand tickled by the ocean. It raced up in white fingers and then disappeared back into the endless waters in the distance. Maybe in my life I had seen a more beautiful place, but at that moment I couldn't remember a single one. What I felt as my eyes took it in was what I was sure that little girl felt; that I was the very first person to ever see this exquisite place. And it was suddenly mine.

Harry crawled from the jungle into the clearing, mumbling to himself and cursing at me. Once his eyes caught sight of the glorious vista, his mouth shut, and he stood tall and allowed himself to take it in. He clutched the canister tightly to his chest, as if hugging Tami for allowing him to find her secret place.

We stood. All of our senses were alive with the sights, sounds, and smells of this stunning, secluded, sliver of beauty that Harry quickly dubbed, "Tami's place." The moniker fit perfectly.

As stupid as it sounds, I never wanted to leave. I could have sat down and let day turn to night over and over. This was a place you would never tire of. The view was a painting and you sensed it changed every day, brand new with each dawn. I couldn't get past the image of a little blonde girl running through the grassy reeds, rushing her hands over the seedlings, releasing them into the breeze to race into the blue sky and dance into the jungle behind. That little girl could have been Tami, she could have been our daughter. But I'll never know.

"Let's do this," I said, breaking the long silence between us.

Harry didn't even return my look. His arms slid tighter around the canister, pulling it into himself.

"Harry," I voiced, assuming he was daydreaming, not unlike I was, probably seeing the same little girl in his mind, wondering if it was his daughter from the past or the granddaughter that would never be.

But again Harry ignored me, his eyes focused on the surf.

"Harry, it's time to release Tami's ashes."

Slowly, his head shook. He refused to look at me. His arms continued to wrap even tighter around the canister, locking it to his torso.

"I can't," he said in an injured, timid voice.

I felt sorry for him. I didn't want to let go of the last tangible dust of the woman I loved either. Sending her ashes into the wind was officially saying that not only was she dead, she was over. Gone. But it was what she wanted. And I needed to let her go, to own that tiny splinter of peace that would come with knowing I had granted Tami her final wish.

"Harry," I responded as softly as he had spoken, not wanting to turn this into a confrontation, "This is what Tammy wanted. This is why we are here."

I gently reached for the canister, but Harry shifted his body, giving me his back. This was not going to be easy, and I refused to wrestle the son of a bitch to the ground and pry my girlfriend from his arms. There was no way I was going to rip off the lid to the canister and fling her into the air without so much as a tear or a goodbye just to keep Harry from stopping me from fulfilling her wish. That was wrong in a million different ways.

I tried again to retrieve the canister from him, but Harry wriggled around further, vetoing any chance of me touching it. Every time I reached around him, he hunched over further until he was nearly in a ball around the container.

"Goddamn it, Harry, this is nuts. Give me the canister! This isn't fun for me either," I snapped.

But it wasn't happening. If I was going to free Tami from his grip, it would only be with a fight. I just couldn't. Fucking bastard was completely freaked out over letting her go. How do you stop a man from feeling that fear? I was for certain not the man who was going to relieve Harry's dread over letting Tami go. Right at that moment all I wanted to do was punch him in the back of the head and walk away.

I stopped trying to maneuver around him to pull the canister from his arms. If I was just a bit more lubricated, I'd probably have tackled Harry and ripped the canister from his arms, screaming, "Fumble!" Then raced deep into the ocean where he couldn't swim out and yanked the can open with my teeth, just for effect.

But I did not have it in me. Either the emotion or the alcohol. I sensed my rage mushrooming every second I stared at his back. I shoved him hard from behind, causing him to stumble a few steps.

"You are so fucked," I spat out. "This is not about you and your pathetic desire to hang onto your daughter forever. We came here to do this for Tami! She's gone, man," I continued with more fury than I had intended. "You can hold that can for eternity. It won't bring her back!"

There was another attenuated silence between us. Harry didn't turn around, he simply continued to huddle over the can.

"Find your own way back," I said, turning toward the jungle, and began walking until I reached its lip once again.

"You spread her ashes without me, I will kill you," I called to Harry, meaning every word. "I will fucking kill you deader than dead."

And with that, I disappeared into the trees, leaving Harry in the sandy clearing.

As I got into the jungle, I began to run thought the vines, shoving through like a feverish ape. The faster I ran, the more I felt the frenzy percolate inside me. I couldn't believe Harry had dragged me out there and played that bullshit game. There were so many painful moments over the past six months for which I truly hated Harry Everett. But not a single one topped the furor churning inside me then and there.

I wanted the whole thing to go away. I wanted Tami to be where she wanted to be, so I would feel better about where I wanted to be, which was on a bar stool getting shitfaced and picking a fight. Because right then a fight sounded even better than getting laid. My head throbbed as I pushed through the branches and stomped over the dead trees and leaves that covered the jungle floor. I was sobering up from my morning and I didn't want to sober up. I preferred to crawl into that hell and stay there for a while. Yeah, it was destructive, but so what? Hanging onto a can of ashes isn't destructive? And sick? Stupid, old man. He stowed away on this trip to do one thing. Why couldn't he do it? Why did he have to pull this crap? Let it go!

Snapping off the last few branches and yanking down the vines, I escaped the jungle and trotted down to the sidewalk. Where I bent over and threw up.

ONE HUNDRED PROOF

Since I hadn't eaten all day, all that came up was scotch. I'm not a guy who heaves much when he drinks, so this was about something else making me sick. Or more accurately, somebody else.

I walked back to the resort, which wasn't more than a mile away. I needed time by myself. I really hadn't had any since I had begun my ill-fated journey and purging my misery to Kat earlier only made that desire stronger. I thought I would be spending as much time alone as I desired, but once Harry horned his way in, that dream exploded and I grew a second head, a mutant hump that always seemed to be looking over my shoulder. The little time I did escape Harry, I was hanging in the bars answering ridiculous questions about an occupation - and I use that term loosely - that I didn't have or fending off come-ons, snickers, and smarmy carnal glances. I was never going to outrun this past week when I was constantly reminded of it. Any chance I had of putting at least a piece of this behind me, Harry cheated me out of because of his parental-psychosis. Goddamn, was everybody more nuts than me? I'm no poster boy for mental stability but daily it seems I meet people far more messed up than I am. That alone is reason to be scared. Reason to want to be by myself.

As this swelling madness ulcered in my gut, I knew I needed to be extremely careful. I was one punch away from six months in the St. Carlos jail. Falling on the bed in the suite, I rolled over and popped open the tabernacle. Restocked. Praise the Lord. I grabbed all the little bottles and tossed them onto the bed spread. Gazing out at the ocean through the open balcony doors, I unscrewed the little caps and heaved them over the ledge. All I needed was a wafer as I guzzled down my sacramental tonic. Damn, if I had just taken that brunette's offer a moment sooner, Harry wouldn't have found me. He would still be wandering the resort, trying to figure out where the hell I'd disappeared to while I was locked in a room with a woman's legs locked around my waist. An entire afternoon of carnal amnesia. And with any luck the icing would be when her old man came strolling in early and caught us. I could have vented some of this incredible rage defending myself as he came at me. Allowing myself to pound the shit out of someone in a knotted cloak of twisted justification.

Things happen for a reason. I cannot tell you how many people had whispered that little ditty to me in the past week. Yeah, thanks for the eye-popping revelation. Now can any of you tell me the reason? I thought not. I knew the reason Tami had stepped into my life. To save me from myself. But now bad Todd was back, guns blazing. The Universe screamed at me loud and clear that a prick like me didn't deserve to keep something as wonderful as Tami. It needed one of us to go so it wouldn't unravel. Only the Universe screwed up and took the wrong one.

I raised my little bottle and drank to that.

Harry slipped into the room, the canister still in his arms. He had a few scratches on his face from wandering back through the jungle.

I didn't bother to ask him how he was. I didn't say anything. I didn't care. He was controlling Tami even after she was dead. As he placed her back in his suitcase, wrapping her up again in the sweaters and locking the bag, he glanced up at me as I tossed another bottle cap over his head at the mirror.

"We'll spread her ashes on my last day here," he said, "I just can't do it now."

Whatever you say, Harry. You can spread them on toast and serve them to everyone for breakfast for all I care. You're P.T. Barnum. You control the Tami Show, so do with her remains what you will, when you will, if you will. Just leave me the hell out of your psychodrama. I got my own demons dancing around, ready to burn me at the stake. I don't have the energy to deal with your shit.

He knew I didn't want to talk to him. And he knew I wasn't about to relinquish the bed. I tried making my silence as directly uncomfortable for him as possible, in the hope that he would leave me the hell alone. But instead, not really sure what to do with himself, he snorted, "I don't care what you think of me," as he waddled out onto the balcony.

"I've never given a rat's ass what you thought of me either, Harry," I replied. "The thing that pissed me off was your never-ending bullshit in trying to turn Tami against me. But she never believed an ounce of your crap. You ended up being a joke in her eyes."

I believe more drinkers die of foot-in-mouth disease than of cirrhosis of the liver. And I could have died from the look in Harry's eyes. But once the scotch has worked its medicinal magic, whatever inappropriate thing is rolling around my head is inevitably coming out of my mouth. "You know what Harry," I said, tossing myself off the bed, leaving the empty bottles, "all the shit you told her about me. What kind of man I was. How I was never good enough for her. I was trash. I was a prick. Well, I'm going to spend the next eight days proving you right." Hurricane Todd. "You can go home with the souvenir you always wanted; being right about me."

I was so tired of caring. Of helplessly standing by while everything in my life fell apart. If my life was going to crash and burn, I was going out fighting, with a scotch in one hand and a naked chick as a hostage in the other.

Eyeing myself in the mirrors that lined the elevator walls, I put on my game face. It was late afternoon, and I knew the bar would be hopping with couples having cocktails. There had to be at least a few single women who wouldn't mind bumping hips with a faux-gigolo. If the brunette was still around, she would do. It didn't much matter anymore, just as long as I was drunk and she was warm and willing.

I could feel all eyes turn on me as I strutted into the club bar and plopped my ass down at the bar, opening my wallet and yanking out a wad of twenties. Kat simply glared.

The bar wasn't as crowded as I had hoped, but there were a few couples dotting the place, mainly at the tables. The mood was island lazy, with resort patrons stepping up onto a small stage to screech through karaoke. Especially at a resort, you forced to endure cheesy bar festivities.

Ordering a Cutty neat, Kat put a glass on the counter, poured it. The way she walked away told me she was done with me. Didn't want to hear any more of my whining about the life that got away. And certainly didn't want to listen to me yammer on to some needy middle aged woman about the fictional occupational hazards of working on your back. I knew she thought every word I spoke about Tami was a lie. Maybe that was all the better. She seemed like a pretty nice woman, all things considered. Staying away from me was something I'm sure her better sense had warned her about the moment I sat down at the bar the first night. She should have listened.

I was still wishing I could find a better sense.

As the crowd chit-chatted, I enjoyed the fact that I was distracting everyone by my winning presence. Guess there wasn't anyone at this place who hadn't caught wind of my "occupation" or my "sugar daddy." I had two choices. Either get pissed off, which certainly wasn't out of the question, and maybe get the chance to pound some dork trying to impress his chick by taking a poke at the big drunk, or I could play it off for my personal enjoyment. And although I was wired enough to get into a fight, I had my priorities.

"If you're all going to stare, one of you assholes could at least buy me a drink," I announced to the entire bar, figuring why be coy about my needs, and gratefully interrupting some young woman straining her way through "Wind Beneath My Wings." Hell, they should all be happily buying me rounds for stopping her musical massacre of that horrible dirge.

But everyone turned away, either pretending they didn't hear me or choosing to ignore me. Even Kat didn't bother looking up from what she was doing. What the hell is that about? I can get that kind of reaction back in Chicago when I'm drunk. You people are vacationers. Lighten the hell up, for Christsake. Hmmm. I guess if I weren't me, I wouldn't want to make eye contact with me either. But by the end of the night I intended to be cross-eyed enough to do just that.

Grumbling, I threw back my drink and waved another twenty at Kat. She walked over, poured the drink and said, "It worked. You're covered."

When I asked which benevolent soul had so generously opened his or her wallet, Kat shook her head and walked away. Either Kat loathed uttering another word to me or I had an anonymous admirer. Or at least an anonymous benefactor. Either way, I was more than happy to accept the charity. I raised my scotch and saluted the room, but still no one came forward to claim responsibility. Or even guilt.

My resort infamy was paying off. So far that day I had saved myself over twenty dollars drinking on someone else's dime. Why that trick hadn't occurred to me earlier in life, I'll never know. Think of the money I could have saved pretending to be interesting characters, letting kind folks buy me drinks while I entertained them with colorful stories of my falsely fascinating life. I'd actually have a 401K worth talking about.

As the bar filled, more idiots got up and sang karaoke. Either my reputation or vibe kept anyone from sitting on a stool near me. They say you should never drink alone. I now say it's the only way.

Feeling the presence of someone standing behind me, I closed my eyes. That little freaking shit was back, I was sure in some lame attempt to make up for his wussy behavior earlier in the day. Harry was going to try and save me from myself. Exactly what I didn't need. I felt my buzz immediately simmer as I took a long slug from my glass and then spun around, my hostile game face on.

It wasn't Harry. It was some guy, around my age, give or take a few years either way. It took me a vague moment to recognize him. He was the one I'd heard talking about me as I entered the elevator after my night on the beach. I had flipped him and his friend off.

"What?" I asked, surly enough to warn him that this better be good.

"Hi, uh, I'm Ian," he said with a weak smile as he thrust out his hand to shake mine.

I didn't. Ian fumbled for a moment, unsure what to do with his hand, which then went through his hair nervously. He chuckled to himself and then shrugged, searching for a way into a conversation. But I was giving him nothing.

"My friend and I want you to do us a favor," Ian finally blurted out, having no other choice.

A favor. Yeah, that'll be happening real soon, Ian. Let me get out my calendar so I can write down the date and time. Being the gay gigolo is only fun until you have to put up or shut up. Time to shut up. "Not interested," I stated sharply, turning around and giving him my back.

"I don't mean to bug you," Ian insisted, not taking me ignoring him for an answer, "we'll pay you."

"Dude, go the fuck away, I'm not interested in you or your boyfriend."

"No, no...not for us, not that way," he continued, punching the sentence out in one breath, "we're straight."

"Join the club," I muttered under my breath, still not turning around as I gulped down the last of the scotch in my glass.

"It's for my friend's wife, Cheryl, she's sitting over there," Ian said, surreptitiously pointing her out.

I don't know what made me turn around, but I was interested to see what Cheryl looked like. She was young. Couldn't have been over twenty-four with a nice, tight body that she obviously enjoyed showcasing. Her auburn hair was piled up on her head, and she had been working a might too hard on that suntan as her shoulders were more red than brown. She wasn't looking in my direction; she was listening to another resort patron yell her way through Midnight Train To Georgia, so I gathered that whatever old Ian was here to ask me was meant as a surprise for Cheryl.

I spun further in my chair and glared directly through Ian. I wanted him to know that if I didn't like what he was asking, I was going to get up and break him into pieces. Being bigger than most guys does have its advantages.

"My friend and I will pay you a hundred dollars if you get up there and sing "Just A Gigolo" to her, maybe come down and dance around her a little bit, you know, come on to her, make her uncomfortable," Ian said, his eyes lighting up at the thought of the prank.

"Now, why would I want to do that?"

"Two hundred dollars. I can't give you any more. See, she did it to us one night at a club, you know, bought us a dancer. But it ended up being a transvestite. This would be a good way of paying her back."

Sober, I wouldn't have entertained that clown for this long. Lucky for Ian, I wasn't anywhere close to sobriety. As I mulled this offer over, I continued my hard stare at Ian, mainly because I could tell it scared the shit out of him, and that tickled me. Just to see what kind of reaction I would get, I threw my hand at Ian as if I were going to punch him. He jumped back with a gasp, nearly falling over himself. When he regained his footing, he looked at me wide-eyed. My hand was out, waiting for him to shake.

"You got a deal," I said, my hand still sitting out there in space. Hell, this sounded like fun. Stupid, obnoxious fun.

Ian smiled nervously and took my hand, shaking. I wrapped my fingers around his tightly, not letting go. "But," I began, yanking him a little closer, "I don't dance for less than 250, sorry." I wanted to see if I could frighten a few more dead presidents out of the lad. See how bad he wanted this and if he was willing to take the chance of pissing me off by turning me down.

"Two-fifty...okay, okay..." Ian said, simultaneously pulling his hand free and his wallet out. He quickly counted out the cash, stuffing it into my hand.

"Her name is Cheryl. We want to embarrass her big time." He smiled wickedly, as if he had just made a deal with the devil and got to keep his soul. And his teeth.

I watched a guy step on stage and sing some old Neil Diamond song. Off-key. What the hell, I couldn't do any worse than all the rest of these losers. I knew I couldn't sing a lick and wasn't about to pretend I could. But I certainly could chart my way around embarrassing a woman. I'd practiced that most of my life and prided myself on being a professional.

I weaved my way through the tables and up to the lip of the stage. There was a DJ who was setting up the karaoke, and I told her what I wanted to sing.

"Great choice," she smiled knowingly. My reputation hadn't escaped her either.

Stepping onto the stage, I recognized the mistake I was about to endure. There were actual people sitting in this place, getting more crowded by the minute. I didn't like giving presentations at work much less stand in front of all these honeymooners and other assorted couples attempting to embarrass this woman by singing. For weeks before the wedding I would get short of breath every time I thought about reciting my marriage vows to Tami in front of our friends and family. I wasn't sure I was drunk enough for this, especially for two hundred and fifty lousy dollars from some asshole name Ian. As I took the microphone in my hand, I could feel the perspiration push from my pores. It reeked of scotch. I was sweating out perfectly good scotch.

I should have asked for 500, goddamn it.

My Jockeys felt like they were strangling my balls. No amount of liquor could make me do this in my real life. But this wasn't real life. It wasn't even my life. Todd, the male escort, stood on the stage. And he was not afraid of anything, especially when it came to being out in front of people. And there was crisp cash involved. Come on, I would never see these freaking people again after that week. I wouldn't remember a single one of them. But they'd be talking about me for a long time. And at least my new pal, Ian, didn't request I warble "Like A Virgin" or something proportionately humiliating. Granted, a David Lee Roth song isn't high art, but if my splotchy memory serves me, he couldn't exactly sing opera either.

So I sang. More like screamed, but it's all relative in karaoke. After the first verse, I lost a fair amount of the fear that was pumping through my body. Everybody in the place was watching, most were laughing. Not at me but with me. And in a room full of fools, I will always try and be the biggest and loudest among them.

When I jumped from the stage and began strutting through the tables, some of the women screamed excitedly. That made me laugh. One woman ran at me and stuffed a dollar into my pants, which brought applause from everyone in the place. I continued barreling through the song as I maneuvered my way toward Cheryl. Once she realized that she was the victim of this prank, her mouth fell open and she tried to look away. But that wasn't happening. She shot both her husband and Ian a dark look as they doubled over with laughter, clapping along to the music.

Before she could bolt for an exit, I was on her. I straddled her, pinning her to her chair. I was tall enough that when I stood up her face was at crotch level. Embarrassed, she couldn't look anywhere but down, so I slid down her body and brought her head up so she had to look at me. I'd like to say it was all in fun, but this chick was hot. And I wasn't going to waste the opportunity to do a little grinding as I slipped and dipped around her tight body, making sure she knew my attraction wasn't all work and no play.

The entire room was cheering me on, especially the men. Bolstered by their approval, I stood Cheryl up, took her in my arms, and pressed my body tightly against hers. I was over a head taller than her. I held the microphone in one hand and wrapped my other tightly around her small waist. Dancing her around the room while I sang, she just held on for the ride figuring she had nothing to lose by playing along. Suddenly, her hair fell down and flipped around, her hips swaying back and forth, and I could feel her grinding herself into my crotch.

My cock stirred. Hello. You're awakening the dragon, darling. And I knew she felt it reaching out to her. Her eyes came up and met mine with a hot, come-fuck-me glimmer. Neither of us gave away the secret, continuing to dance around as I finished the song. The room erupted into applause. I kissed her hand politely and escorted her back to her chair.

"We got you, we got you," Cheryl's husband, Tim, a tallish, thin guy with a wisp of chin whiskers and frosted tips in his hair, repeated a few times, pleased with himself.

Cheryl smiled coyly. "You got me."

Tim invited me to sit with them for a drink. Another free drink. I was there. Slipping into a chair at the table across from Cheryl, Ian and Tim flanked me on either side. Most people don't realize how easy it is to make friends when you make an ass out of yourself. Folks love a good ass. Even when they're big ones, like me. Tim asked me what I was drinking and waved down a cocktail waitress. They were all imbibing those dorky tropical drinks that smell like suntan lotion.

My scotch came as another couple exited the table next to us. They both walked past, patting me on the shoulder with laughing smiles. Seems my celebrity at the resort was rising. Now, I was the drunken male whore with the wicked sense of self-deprecating humor. And that's a mouthful for someone who's sucked down as much as I had.

Tim and Ian were best friends from college, blah, blah, blah. Friends for ten years, blah, blah, blah. Tim then blathered on about Cheryl. When they met, when they married.

The only other tidbits I recall was that Cheryl ran a nursery school, and that Tim and Ian were both some kind of lawyers.

"The three of you came down here together? That's sort of kinky, isn't it?" I asked Ian with a shit-eating grin.

Ian quickly explained that he had a girlfriend but she'd been sick since arriving on the island. Ian continued to pass along stories of his and Tim's annual trips which they'd been taking since college. Aspen, Hawaii, Fiji, Austria, blah, blah, blah. Thank God I had a drink in my hand. It made it a lot easier to listen to a lawyer recount his yearly vacations with his frat brother. And they thought I was gay.

Glancing across the table, I could see Cheryl's eyes glaze over as Ian continued to prattle on about holiday after holiday. I wondered how many times she had heard these stories. Probably every time Ian and Tim met someone new. The two men laughed with each other, pushing each other playfully as they recalled events that only they seemed to remember as good times.

"Here we go again," Cheryl huffed out under her breath, rolling her eyes dramatically, knowing that neither her husband nor Ian were focused on her. I shot her a knowing smile, but the boys were too busy to notice, laughing with each other; bosom buddies, lifelong friends. I never had a male friend like that. So, it was as hard for me to relate to as it was for Cheryl, who probably believed her husband was more in love with his best friend than he would ever be with her.

I wasn't sure what that feeling was at first. A tickling in my balls. I was beginning to catch glimpses of Dr. Buzz again, but he had never affected my nuts before. Then, I was sure of what it was. Toes. And they certainly weren't mine playing with my cajones. Without an ounce of surprise, I glanced up at Cheryl again. She held the same blank look on her face that she had since the boys began blabbing about their vacation stories. But under the table she was massaging my crotch with a vengeance. And I will say, if she ever wanted to give up running nursery schools, she has other, more lucrative talents.

This was childish and dangerous. But I loved it. I let
Cheryl work her sorcery on my crotch, and she brought me to
full mast. My crippled judgment gasped its dying breath about
how wrong this was. Luckily for my crotch, my judgment
flatlined before it traveled that far south.

Tim and Ian finished their stories about the time I
finished up my scotch. I thanked them, shaking Tim's hand
and then Ian's. I stood, making sure my loose shirt covered my
crotch, and shook Cheryl's hand, telling her I hoped that I
hadn't embarrassed her too much. "I know how to take a
joke," she said with a wide smile, her eyes sliding over in Tim's
direction. "Besides, Tim knows I'll get him back."

I excused myself, telling them I needed to use the head
and wandered out of the bar, with Kat watching me go, her
eyes announcing she knew exactly where I was going and why.
There was no disapproval in her look just exhaustion with me.

I often have that effect on women. Well, on everybody.

Waiting in the hallway which lead to the resort's
kitchen, I lingered around the bathrooms for a few minutes.
Two women slipped past me, heading into the women's room,
both smiling warmly and laughing. Yes, thank you, ladies, I'll
be performing here at the resort all week. As yet another waiter
passed, I realized that I had misjudged the situation with
Cheryl. She had teased me. Got my engine revving. Game
over. I'd been dissed. Not like I needed it, but it was another
reason to get drunk.

Heading back to the bar, an odd movement caught my
eye. There was a small linen closet shared by both the dining
room and the bar. The door was slightly ajar. As I passed, the
door opened further. Cheryl stood there with a nasty-ass grin.
"Time to get back at Tim," she said, her hand reaching out and
taking mine.

There was no joy in her face, this was business. Cheryl
needed this as much as I did. I peered around. No one. I
slipped into the closet and pulled the door shut behind me.
The place would have been tight for even a small man, but I

barely fit into the room. All the better for the situation.

I buried my head into her shoulder and slid my hands under her strapped T-shirt. She wasn't wearing anything underneath, something I already knew from sitting across the table from her. My hands cupped her arched breasts, working the nipples to a quick, full erection. Cheryl wasn't shy either. Her hands were under my T-shirt and it was over my head and off quickly. Her mouth went to my chest, as I slid my hand under her tiny skirt, up her thong, and began massaging her. She moaned softly as I worked her body. Her hands slid around my cock, and she tried to get the zipper of my shorts down. I knocked her hands away and got my pants down in a flash. Since it was the tropics, underwear was optional as far as I was concerned, and I chose the option of not wearing any.

She yanked down her skirt and thong in one swift move, giggling as she did. Grabbing my manhood, she climbed aboard as I lifted her up. Holding her hips, I slammed her back into a linen shelf to prop her up. She grabbed hold and hung on for the ride.

I'd like to say this was about something other than release, but it wasn't. I just wanted to fuck. And this hot, little woman seemed to be in the same frame of mind. If Tim were my spouse, I'd want to fuck other people too.

I was not prepared for her to be a screamer. As she got hotter, she moaned out in breaths that grew in intensity and volume the closer she came to coming. I ripped down a tablecloth from above her head and shoved it into her face. She buried her face in it so as not to draw any more attention to our closet rendezvous than we already had, given the walls were shaking as if the island were being hit by a tsunami. Fuck it. This was a resort. We couldn't possibly be the first two vacationers to have our pants around our ankles in their linen closet.

As I got close, I flipped her around and she held onto the shelves, allowing me to go even deeper. Cheryl screamed into a stack of napkins, and as I came, I buried my face into her back, letting go with a triumphant war whoop, wanting to drain the last of my energy.

Awesome. Now this is textbook meaningless sex.

Since the space was so tight, we had to help each other back into our clothes. There was no nervous chatter in a pointless attempt to turn this tryst into anything more than a quickie in a closet. I was just glad to be of service. I was beginning to like Todd, the male stud. I had forgotten about everything else for the past twenty minutes. "I knew you weren't gay," Cheryl said as she opened the door, glancing out. She said nothing else before sliding out and disappearing.

I pulled my T-shirt back on, thought about straightening up the small room, but there were tablecloths and napkins tossed everywhere. As I slid through the door, I nearly mowed down a waiter with a tray. He gave me a dirty look but kept moving. Probably not the first person who had almost knocked him over coming out of there. And he knew what a mess had been left behind. Touristas.

As I sat back down at the bar, I looked over at Cheryl, who was back at the table with Tim and Ian. Only now she was part of the conversation, laughing and touching her husband warmly. See what a good boning will do for someone.

Turning to wave down Kat, a handsome black man with the whitest teeth I'd ever seen stood behind the bar. He informed me that Kat was off. Something about her child being sick. A kid? That fractured the image of carefree, ex-pat bartender that I had created in my head. You learn something new about people every day. God knows she had about me.

I ordered another scotch and congratulated myself on being back to pre-Tami form. It's not something most men would be proud of, but considering my life recently, this was a good place to circle the wagons. Burying myself in the physical pleasures of sex in an effort to keep myself from feeling anything else was a warm, well dug cave for me.

At about one in the morning, two rich girls in their early twenties dragged me out onto the dance floor. They had arrived without boyfriends, believing it was a single's resort.

And since I seemed to be the only guy in the place who didn't have a mate, they zeroed in on me like kamikaze pilots aiming at a lone battleship. They giggled a lot and weren't too bright. I was drunk off my ass. It was a match made in heaven. They double-teamed me, dirty dancing, grinding me, kissing me, working me up into a male froth. My sweat smelled of scotch and Cheryl.

The two single chicks slipped out of the bar at about two, disappearing. I thought maybe I would get a two-fer but they had had their fun with me and then dogged me. Maybe they thought I was too loaded to be of any ministration to their needs. Whatever. I'm sure they were laughing at the big dork they had worked into a lather and then abandoned. But I wasn't about to let that bother me. All in all, it was a pretty wreckless night. Old Todd wreckless.

Staggering back upstairs, I was whipped. And I had no idea where I was sleeping, since I was sure that Harry had already claimed the bed for himself. I guess it was either that thin sofa or the floor, unless getting naked and crawling into bed with Harry would chase him out of it.

Stepping off the elevator, I turned the corner toward my room. As I passed the room closest to the elevator, the door swung open and I was yanked inside. The two girls I had danced with downstairs were staying on the same floor as I was. And they came prepared to party. Since they were both only wearing bras and panties, I knew I was about to be taken advantage of sexually.

Sweet.

Two women. Three in one day. I hadn't done that since college. I was only hoping that I would be able to perform, my veins surging with an abundance of scotch. It had never affected me before, but I was out of drinking shape. When I was with Tami, I cut my alcohol consumption was down to one or two drinks at the most. Which for me was next to nothing. But that day if I had had ten drinks, I'd had twenty. Who knew? I was completely shitfaced, but when you're standing in a hotel suite with two adorable hard bodies wearing nothing but body-hugging underwear, your job is to come through in the clutch.

I don't remember how I ended up on their bed with the two of them on top of me. I either stumbled there, which was likely, considering I could barely stand, or they dragged me over and pushed me onto the bed. I didn't struggle, and they yanked my clothes off of me, getting limbs stuck but still able to pull my shirt and pants off without me feeling much.

The brunette crawled onto my chest, sitting there, her knees pinning my biceps to the bed. I lost sight of the other girl but I could feel her on my body behind the brunette. "Can we ask you a question," the brunette asked through her giggling, which made her breasts bounce.

"Considering you have me pinned to the bed, do I have much of a choice?" I asked, noticing her light treasure trail that lead down into her white panties.

"How many guys have you slept with?"

Oh man, they had heard about me. Did they just bring me up here and get me naked to question me? I wasn't drunk enough to enjoy that.

"None," I said, closing my eyes, "I don't sleep with men. Never have. But if I liked men, I would have slept with every man I could."

The brunette glanced back at the blonde, who peeked around her, looking at me with a nod.

"I told her you weren't gay. I can always tell," she stated, with an authority into which I didn't put an ounce of credence. She gave me a confident smile and quizzed, "So, how many girls have you slept with?"

"Many."

"Have you ever been in love?" The brunette piped in as she stared down at me.

I didn't need that. If they wanted to fuck, fine. They could have used me anyway they wanted. I was here, I was naked, and I didn't care what they did to me.

"Once," I replied against my better albeit impaired judgment, hoping that would end the questions and we could get down to business. I was still inebriated enough to not put up much of a fight.

"Did you marry her?"

My body seemed to collapse even further into the mattress, sinking away from the two girls. I could feel the blood instantly race from my erection and collect in my head. I was supposed to be lying in bed next to my wife. Holding her, smelling her hair as it fell across my face during the night. Feeling her skin, still warm from the sun that day. What the hell was I doing with these two girls, whose names I still hadn't bothered to ask, on top of me, playing multiple choice about the woman I loved? A tidal wave of conflicting feelings ripped through me like the glass from a window pelted with buckshot.

In a heaving move, I sat up, dumping both of them off my body and onto the bed. My legs slipped over the edge as I sat up, my head dropping into my hands. The erupting emotions were bombarding me so fast I couldn't arrange them in any order to even make sense of them. Anger. Immense sadness. Embarrassment. Self-pity. Rage. Complete, endless emptiness.

The blonde came up behind me, her hand tentatively slipping onto my shoulder. "What's the matter? Are you okay?"

"I'm so goddamn far from okay I don't know if I'll ever get back even for a short visit."

I stood up and found my pants, sliding into them.

"I'm sorry. Find another guy for this tonight. I've fucked up enough today. I'm not...I'm not...being around me just isn't a good place to be right now."

They curled up together on the bed, both dejected and unnerved at my manic flip-flop. I eyed at their nearly naked bodies intertwined as they held onto one another, their touch seeming to keep the other calm. The two girls seemed so comfortable with each other. The blonde glanced up at me and smiled softly.

"Whatever it is, I'm sorry," she said.

The hollowness of my stare frightened them as they clung tighter to each other. My eyes narrowed.

"You two love each other, don't you?" I asked.

The girls traded secret smiles, answering my question.

"She's my girlfriend," the brunette nearly whispered, more to the blonde than to me. "Yes. I love her."

I wished I could have smiled for them. Shown some acknowledgment of their happiness. But I couldn't.

The brunette then turned to me. "We love each other but we like sex with men better than with women. It's complicated. So we pick up guys."

"That way we can be together and...." the blonde added, then paused, "you know, have the emotional connection with each other and the physical thing with a man."

I felt even more lonely. They needed a male body, any male body. And it struck me like an acute migraine that that was all I had left to give anyone. My skin. Everything else I possessed had been eroded in the acidity of death. Seeing them knotted together on the bed, their skin against someone they loved, I would have cut off my arm to have that again. To fall asleep with someone I loved. To fall asleep in Tami's arms and be able to dream.

There was little keeping me from running headlong through their balcony door and throwing myself off.

Slapped back to soberness, I exited their room without another word and made my way down the hallway, pulling on my watch and running my hand through my hair, which had been cut short for my wedding. I entered the suite quietly, so as not to wake Harry. But he wasn't sleeping in the bed, he was on the sofa. As soon as I turned on the light, he bolted upright with a gasp.

"Didn't mean to wake you. I thought you'd be sleeping in the bed."

Harry shifted around, finding his watch, checking the time. He then sniffed as I walked past, his face souring. "You stink like a French soldier coming out of whorehouse," he announced. "What have you been doing?"

"Don't ask questions you don't want an answer to, Harry," I responded, walking into the bedroom. My head was about to burst.

As I began to undress, I felt him behind me, standing at the door to the bedroom. I thought maybe if I didn't look at him, he wouldn't bother me and go back to the sofa. But he wouldn't budge.

"Were you faithful to my daughter?"

I turned back around and focused directly into his eyes.

"From the day I met her," I said.

"Then why couldn't you wait at least a week before you slept with another woman? You can't see that it's wrong?"

"I don't care if you think it's wrong. I don't have anyone to answer to anymore."

"What about my daughter?"

"She's in your luggage, why don't you ask her."

As soon as the remark left my lips, I knew it stung. Hell, it shocked me, and that's not easy to do. Harry took a deep breath through his nose, his chest puffed out, his head raised high. If he was only a few feet closer to me, I'm sure I would have another print of his knuckles on my jaw. Biting his lip, he sneered darkly as his eyes narrowed to slits. He searched for something to say, something cutting, painful. He needed to hack me off at the knees and dance around my writhing body.

"Fuck off."

Those words weren't easy for Harry. He prided himself on being a gentleman even in battle. For Harry, uttering those two words, that flew out of my vulgar mouth without thought or hesitation, was epic. I knew that, again, I'd rattled him to his essence. And it was about time he shoveled a little of it back in

terms I could understand. I knew I deserved it. I more than
deserved it, I earned it! Hit me, Harry. Hurt me. Do
something. Because I am feeling nothing except this raging
nastiness that now occupies every inch of my corpse. And
that's all I am now. Goddamn it, I was begging for him to lay
me out.

I sat down in a chair across from him with a
questioning shrug. "Have you ever had a life, Harry? You
keep finding a reason not to. I think that's why I hate you so
much. Tami was everything to you. I loved her more than
myself, but I still couldn't compete with the adoration you
poured all over her on a daily basis. And I wanted to. I wanted
to prove to her that I loved her more than you did. That I
could take care of her better than you. Be more to her." I
shook my head in disgust. "But I couldn't."

"Damn right, you couldn't," Harry sniffed, "you don't
have it in you to truly love someone."

"No, Harry," I said without a trace of resentment or
anger, "I couldn't compete with you because you loved her
wrong. You have that kind of love that drowns a person. That
takes their soul away so you can own it. You did everything to
smother her and possess her, and I still wanted to compete
with you."

Harry's shoulders slumped. He leaned back against the
wall as the sides of his mouth turned into an injured frown.

"She was such a smart kid," Harry shook his head. "I
don't know why she couldn't see through you." Harry's eyes
fell from my face and he slipped into a nearby chair.

"Even when she was little, there were just some things
she wouldn't let herself believe," Harry spoke in a voice only
slightly above a whisper. "When her mother got sick, I tried to
prepare her for what was coming, but she was determined to
deny it. She would not allow herself to entertain any notion
that her mother was going away. She fought me over it. She
refused to listen when I tried to talk to her about it. Just like
when I tried to warn her about you."

Harry leaned back in the chair. "I used to get so frustrated. I never knew how to get through to her when she got locked on something. She was always a strong-willed girl."

Harry recalled that when Winnie passed, Tami searched the house for her mother every day for a year. Believing with all her heart that her mother was there, somewhere, and just couldn't be found.

"I let her look. What could I do?" he asked, his head shaking at the bittersweet memory.

His eyes then locked on me again. "No one could smother a girl like that."

It dawned on me that Harry probably wasn't always the monumental nudge he had morphed into over time. I would bet that once Tami's mother passed away, Harry crumbled on the inside at the same time as his crustiness hardened on the outside. A feeling I could now completely embrace. Harry became the sole provider and protector of his little girl and for the slivers of memories he had with his wife. Harry hulked into this gigantic pain in the ass to protect himself from the pain that traveled with the death of someone you love too much and the aftermath of emptiness.

"The problem is, Harry, you tried."

I got up and walked out onto the balcony. The air was sticky with the smell of the ocean. I listened to it crash onto the beach a few times before Harry spoke again.

"I feel sorry for you. You don't know the first thing about love," Harry stated flatly, as if it were fact.

I was beginning to wonder that myself.

"I loved your daughter. She is the only person I ever loved," I admitted without turning around to face him.

"You act like you're proud of that."

I shook my head. Hardly. I should have loved my mother and father, but they didn't love me. No sympathy. Because I don't have any for myself. That's life. Some kids don't get those breaks. I was a big kid, I took care of myself. I never went without clothes or a meal, just love. It wasn't until Tami walked into my life that I had any conception of what love actually was. Stupid as that sounds, I didn't have a notion it could be that overwhelming, that omnipotent. Tami took over my life in almost every way and changed me into a new man. Her love was that profound. It was that strong.

But when an extreme love escapes into the ether, it turns into a noxious gas. It wipes every living thing under its cloud.

That Todd, the one Tami had wanted to marry, died when she did. He was gassed and fell over where he stood, his eyes wide open, saliva trickling from his mouth, unable to move. The feeling drained from his body, leaving him paralyzed until his lungs no longer inflated, and he couldn't breathe. He couldn't even close his eyes while he died. He had to watch himself go.

"I'm not proud of much in my life," I said, finally turning around towards Harry, "except loving your daughter. No. No, loving her was easy. I am most proud that she loved me."

"Then why can't you respect that memory?"

"Because I won't live for a memory. I'm scared to hold onto them. Jesus, Harry what fucking good does it do me to remind myself of something so wonderful that I'll never, ever have again?"

Harry's look shifted as I realized what I had admitted. A painfully truthful confession from that tiny place inside me that holds the puddle of genuineness. I try not to touch that place too much. It's delicate. And I am not. I batter everything I come into contact with. Tami was the only object in my life I didn't damage.

"You don't think you'll ever fall in love again?" Harry asked, with what registered to me as real concern.

I sat for a long moment, not moving. No, I didn't. But could I tell him? Or would he give me another disapproving look, squinting up his face like a rodent eating a persimmon. Fuck it. When did that become his goddamn business?

"No," I heard myself saying.

Harry's eyes wore a sad heaviness.

"Out of all of this," Harry spoke cautiously, "that could be the saddest thing of all, Todd."

Harry never used my name. Throughout the time that Tami and I had been together, he avoided it, as if by never recognizing me by name, he stole my validity and maybe I would vaporize. But hearing him say it now echoed inside me and only made me feel more vacant.

I felt tears wash over my eyes. This was the last fucking thing I needed, to cry. But I couldn't stop myself. Because it was true. I knew, knew from deep in my bones that I would never, ever fall in love again. I had had the best love ever. How do you match that when you're pretty much incapable of manufacturing it for yourself?

I let myself cry.

Wiping the tears from my eyes, I could see the sympathy in Harry's eyes. He knew exactly where I was. At that moment, I recognized how intimately alike Harry and I actually were. It went beyond the kinship of deep loss. Though I knew I would never like Harry, never forgive him for the hell he put me through in trying to keep me from marrying his daughter, I understood him better than he knew. And as he had from the very beginning, he knew exactly who I was and what possessed my soul.

"Harry," I uttered slowly as I stood up, "I came down here to lay waste to every moral fiber of my being. To drink and fuck and fight and hate the world. That's what I do when I'm trapped. And I've never felt more trapped. You may think this means I never loved Tami. But the truth is, I loved her with a capacity that even I had no idea I was capable of. And that's left me in a hole so deep I don't know if I'll ever be able to crawl out of it."

"You're going to kill yourself," Harry said.

"Maybe. I'm certainly going to test the limits."

LAYING WASTE

When I woke up, Harry was on the phone with the airline.

"So you're completely booked again today. And tomorrow," he said, frustration thinning his voice. "Can you tell me how many standby passengers got on yesterday?"

He sneered. None.

The Harry I had shared a heart-to-heart with the previous night was gone, replaced by his evil twin.

As I watched Harry berate the agent on the other end of the phone I wondered if he remembered our conversation from the night before. Even with the amount of liquor I'd ingested, the emotion of the night overshadowed my ability to forget. Harry and I had reached a new level of honesty with each other. I hoped I wouldn't live to regret it.

"Now what kind of idiot would I have to be to stand around the airport all day to wait and see if I can get on the flight? No, a better question is what kind of idiot are you for suggesting it? It's ridiculous and you shouldn't treat customers this way," Harry added before hanging up.

"No luck," I rasped as I sat up, needing water.

Harry grimaced. "Did it sound like I had any luck? Damn third world airline," he complained.

I was already beginning to regret my tete-a-tete with the good Harry. I didn't want to get too close to this man. My sentence with him would be over soon and I never knew which Harry I was waking up to. He knew which Todd he was waking up to. I only had one personality. It had varying degrees of surly obnoxiousness, but it was pretty much the same asshole that had gone to bed the night before.

I pulled myself from the bed, scratching my balls until I noted Harry glowering. I gave him a limp smile. "They itch, what can I say?"

I realized all those deep furrows around his mouth and on his forehead were not from concern or worry, but from constant frowning. If he wasn't frowning, he was searching for a reason to frown.

"I also burp, fart, and leave the toilet seat up," I muttered, walking past him and into the bathroom.

"Thank God Tami's mother never met you."

"She would have loved me," I responded through the bathroom door, "It's only you I enjoy pissing off, Harry. Right now it's what's keeping me alive."

Once I'd showered off the skanky sex smell from the previous night, I felt at least partially human. It was already after noon, and I was hungry as a bear. When I drink, I have a tendency not to eat. But now I needed sustenance, real food, the kind that comes on a bun with onion, tomato, a slice of cheese, and a side of fries. Cashews from the minibar weren't going to cut it.

Coming out of the bathroom, Harry ambushed me. "Do you want to go back to Tami's place? Take her ashes?"

Was he really asking this? Do I have 'complete idiot' tattooed on my forehead? I was hoping that the minor bit of progress Harry and I had made the night before would last at least a full twenty-four hours, but as soon as he asked me to trek across the island again, I knew I was going to blow that all to hell.

"There's no way on God's green earth I'm doing that again, Harry," I stated, heading into the bedroom to throw on some clothes.

"I will release her ashes this time. Yesterday was just too..." he searched for the word, "final."

"I'm no shrink, but you're not going to let her go until you absolutely have to. And I'm not marching through the jungle again. Especially dressed in our matching safari outfits. If we go through what we went through yesterday, one of us is not coming back from that beach. And it ain't going to be me. So choose your time wisely, grasshopper."

Harry shot me an acid glare.

"You think I'm joking, man? Try me."

I was surprised at the amount of people who were still firing me the stink eye. As I wolfed down a plate of chicken and pasta in some Caribbean sauce, everyone in the place gave me what I was sure they believed were subtle glances. They weren't. Neither subtle nor mere glances. My escapades from the previous night must have sizzled along the resort grapevine. Or some must still believe that Harry and I were performing The Odd Couple in matching leather jockstraps up in the honeymoon suite. The fact that Harry and I had rarely been seen together since we checked in should have given everyone a clue that what they believed wasn't anywhere near the truth. Who the hell knew what they thought? More to the point, who the hell cared?

Harry was never going to get off the island until our scheduled flight. There was an outside, three-point shot that if he waited on standby he might get on a plane, but there wasn't a chance he was going to do that. Harry didn't wait well. He was a man of sure things. I was stuck with him in my suite for the rest of the week.

Harry seemed completely ill-at-ease at the resort. It wasn't like he was going to put in eighteen holes before breakfast or sign up for a tennis lesson. Harry wasn't going to do shooters with the young couples nor dance the night away in the disco with some chick in a short skirt and halter top. Harry was a Holiday Inn sort of guy. No point taking him somewhere where he would actually enjoy himself. He had no capacity for that. Even when he was having a good time, Harry seemed miserable. He'd been in a snit for so long, being uptight was a safe place for him to stay.

All the better for me. Having Harry hibernate up in the room gave me free run of the resort without another pair of eyes peering over my shoulder. There were enough people watching my every move. Infamy does have its price.

Wandering around the pool deck, I found an empty lounge chair. I ordered a scotch from a poolside waitress, yanked off my T-shirt, and collapsed in the chair to catch some sun and start a drunk.

As I took the first sip of my drink, something grossly white and wrinkly was standing in front of me.

"Who's sitting next to you?"

You've got to be kidding me. I didn't have to look up to know from whom that nasally whine emanated. My eyes moved up from his waist to his chest and then up to his face, which was half hidden under a hat that had "Lake Michigan" embroidered across the front.

"What are you doing here??!" I protested, pushing Harry out of my sun.

"What am I supposed to do? Sit in the room all day?"

"Yes!" I bellowed almost before he finished his sentence. "It has worked for you so far. Go. I don't want you here."

"Why not?"

"Consider this my territory," I said, waving my hands around to include the pool and bar area. "Take a tour or go deep sea fishing. You're messing up my action."

"Action?" Harry sneered as he took a long, mocking glance around at the inactivity that encircled me. "I don't see any action."

"My potential action," I fired back

"Potential action for what, pray tell?" he asked, continuing his derisiveness.

"Potential action for avoiding you for the entire day. Whatever I can find that can do that will work for me. Now scoot," I said, waving him on.

Harry plopped his ass in the chair next to me. "I am not going to sit next to people I don't know," he declared, really enjoying being a bug up my ass. "What would I have to talk about with them?"

What would he have to talk to me about? And I'm sure the other vacationers would have loads to discuss with Harry. Most of which would cause Harry to turn six shades of purple before the blood vessels in his head exploded and he died there on the pool deck. Which wouldn't be a problem except that I didn't know the combination to the lock on his suitcase. I simply wanted to lay in the sun until I was appropriately buzzed. Then head into the bar and embark on another day of searching for meaningless sex. But my 'boyfriend' was ruining my chances and causing tongues to wag, after I had worked so hard to dispel the rumors, other than the ones that worked to my advantage.

Harry wasn't going away. Worse yet, he was clad in a silly beach jacket with matching shorts, which I am sure had been hiding in his closet along with his leisure suit and hip huggers. Did this guy ever hear of the Salvation Army? Perhaps I should have agreed to spread Tami's ashes at the secret place? Positive that he would not let them go yet again, I could then have justifiably smacked the crap out of him. Because seeing him planted in the chair next to me, wiping on the sunblock like he was painting a house, I surely felt like it now.

"Harry, look," I said, shifting over to face him, "we got a problem."

"Just one?" he asked, amused by his own witty repartee.

"One you aren't even aware of," I began, trying to ease my way into a conversation I really didn't feel like having right then. Or ever. "Look around. Look at all these people. You see a theme?"

Harry peered side to side, his "thinking frown" stuck on his puss. He shook his head and went back to slathering on the sunscreen.

Great. Now we were going to have to play the guessing game. Come on down Harry, you're the next contestant.

"Take a harder look, big guy. You'll notice a little something about everybody else BUT us."

After he finished rubbing the sunblock all over his face, he yanked on his sunglasses with a shrug. "They actually like each other?" he retorted to his own bemusement.

Nothing bugged me more than Harry being bemused.

I made a buzzing sound. Game over.

"They are couples, Harry. Twos. Like Noah's Ark. Ninety-nine percent of the people here are with their partner," I pointed out. "Wife, husband. Boyfriend, girlfriend. Newlyweds, newlyweds, newlyweds."

Again, Harry scanned the pool area. Most of the chairs were pulled together in couples. He couldn't miss it now that I had pointed it out to him.

"Hmm," Harry muttered rather ambiguously, not catching my drift.

"Harry," I sighed, wishing I didn't have to spell this out for him in crayon, "This is a COUPLES resort. And here we are, you and I..."

He still didn't grasp the big picture.

"Me and you..." I signaled that there was more coming, but still no registration. I lounged back in the chair and looked up at the blue sky. "Harry. The people here think we're a couple. They think we spend our nights crawling up each other's asses."

A Godzilla-like gasp tore from Harry's lungs. He look liked he had swallowed a Japanese blowfish at a sushi dinner and then found out it was poisonous. He shook his head, but no sound came from his mouth as he tried to form words. Any words.

Finally he scrunched up his face like a Shar Pei and sputtered out, "Ewwww."

"Pretty much my reaction when I found out, too," I said, as Harry glanced over his sunglasses to see which couples were eyeing us and whispering to each other.

"These people think that you and I are...here together," Harry stammered, starting to shake.

"Not really a couple," I said, enjoying watching Harry squirm in the lounge chair, "they think you're an old, rich guy, and I'm the male stud you hired as an escort." I let the words sink in before I added, "And seeing how you're dressed right now they're probably reassessing the 'rich' part."

"Oh, my God," Harry barked out loud enough for everyone around the pool to hear, and then repeated "Oh, my God!" a few more times before wrapping his narrow, little mind around that truly wacked-out concept. "People think I. You. Paid. To come with me and that you and I are..."

"Uh-huh," I smirked.

"Waitress!" Harry screamed at the cocktail waitress as she strode past.

He quickly ordered a double vodka tonic. He could barely control the tremor in his hands. I had no idea that this disclosure would completely fritz him out. It was more than I could have hoped for. For grins, I thought about laying a big wet one on his lips, but that would result in a severe meltdown from which Harry would never recover. His wide eyes continued to circle the pool deck, pinpointing each couple he was sure was ogling him.

"Jesus, Harry," I whistled, surprised at how bent out of shape as he was, "if I knew you were going to zonk out like this, I wouldn't have said a thing."

"You would have left me not knowing what people were saying about me?" he questioned with gross indignation.

"Is it that big of a deal? Shit, it's not like you're trying to pick up chicks. Think how this situation has hampered my odds with the ladies."

Harry grimaced. "Not like it stopped you last night," he said. Then his eyes widened. "Oh, Lord, please tell me you didn't have relations with a man!"

"Good Christ, Harry, are you that fucking nuts?!? I had sex with---" I stopped myself. Why the hell was I telling this lunatic? He's a shade past loco! Neurotic and paranoid.

Harry yanked his hat lower on his head. "We can't stay here another night," he stated, ready to pack up and swim off the island if he couldn't find another way off.

"Maybe you can't," I laughed, "but that big room is paid for. I'm not wasting it. I don't care if these people think I'm doing small farmland animals."

"Don't you have any morals?" Harry asked indignantly.

"It's not like we're actually doing it, Harry. Good Lord, it's gossip. Get over it."

"Tami is turning over in her grave."

"Tami isn't in a grave. She's canned up in your suitcase."

Harry breathed through his nose, his lips clenched tight.

"Don't get smart," Harry snapped. "This is not funny. Not at all."

No, it really wasn't. At least not until then. Although at that moment, I was finding it all pretty goddamn hilarious.

"Damn, if I knew this was going to tie your underwear in a knot, I would have brought it up earlier. Maybe you would have worked a little harder to get off this island."

But Harry wasn't in the mood to laugh. Mortified, Harry threw some money at the waitress when she returned and quickly sipped his vodka. I had never spied Harry drink anything other than a glass of wine with dinner. Once. He coughed and sputtered through the entire glass of vodka, his hands still shaking, his eyes continuing his search for anyone on the pool deck who could be secretly talking about him.

Lying in that chair next to Harry was only going to push my buttons as he continued on his freak out. No way. Not there. Not anymore. I pulled myself off the lounge chair and dove into the pool. After cooling off, I climbed out, grabbed my shirt, and slid on my flip-flops.

"I'm heading to the bar. Don't follow me."

As I passed our cocktail waitress, I handed her a twenty and told her to treat Harry to a few more double vodka tonics. And to really spill a little salt into the nightmare, to tell him they were from a young guy who loves a hot 'Daddy.' That ought to wig him out even more. She smiled with a sweet laugh as I muffled a chuckle, strutting toward the bar.

The place was nearly deserted, except for a few people having early afternoon cocktails. Kat was back at work. I gave her a weak smile, almost apologetic though I wasn't sure what I was apologizing for.

"How's your kid?"

She fired a look that held more surprise than she intended. "Problems at school. Bullies. He's skipping out rather than dealing with them," she remarked as she poured me a scotch.

"He got a father?"

"What he has is a huge jackass who causes us as much hassle as he can. My ex- is the reason I took my son and moved down to this island," she said, shaking her head before adding, "I've always had a thing for the bad boys. How do you think I could smell you coming as soon as you stepped into the bar?"

"Then I'm guessing you don't want me to teach your kid how to defend himself..."

"Yeah, that's exactly what he needs. You're such a role model."

"Well I tried. I could teach your kid to run away. But seems like he's got that down pretty good already," I added just for a little flavor, which caused Kat to move away from me with a cool smirk.

I smiled and not just because I was submitting to the cozy clutches of the liquor oozing through my veins. From where I sat I had an excellent view as the cocktail waitress set down another drink next to the unnerved Harry. He tried to give it back to her, waving it off, but she was adamant and left it on the small table next to his lounge chair after giving him my mysterious salutation. Harry worked to ignore the drink, his eyes scanning the pool deck for his anonymous admirer, which only seemed to unhinge him even more. Finally he succumbed to the vodka's calling and picked it up, taking a hard gulp.

"Just for the record---"

"Which I'm sure you have," Kat piped in.

"I do. But no felonies. And only one arrest, thank you. But what I was going to say is that everything I said to you yesterday was true. No bullshit."

Kat's eyes widened into a shocked gaze. Not the reaction I was expecting.

"So that little man out there causing the scene is actually your fiancée's father," she asked as I realized she wasn't looking at me but peering directly over my shoulder.

I spun around on the chair as my glass slipped from my hand. As it shattered on the tile floor, I jumped up, staring through the ceiling-to-floor windows. A bad dream was happening right before my eyes.

Outside, Harry was standing over some young, buffed guy and his hottie of a wife, screaming uncontrollably at the both of them, his hands waving frantically, like the robot in "Lost In Space." The man had clearly had enough of Harry, the psycho, and was starting to climb from his lounge chair, flexing his long, muscled limbs like a peacock fanning his tail. As his hands balled into fists, I knew that the day was going into the crapper.

My first inclination bent towards ordering another scotch to replace the one I had dropped and pulling a chair up to the window to watch the young buck kick Harry's ass. Harry hadn't caught a clue and wasn't backing off. He was still in this guy's face instead of ducking for cover. The young guy was ready to rearrange Harry's mug, as his shapely wife crawled off her chair and stood behind her husband for support.

But if anything would turn Tami over in her canister, it was me standing by while her father got his lights punched out. Besides, it hardly looked like a fair fight. This kid had some muscle like he'd spent hours pumping iron and doing some kind of taebo bullshit. I could tell by the way he held his fists that he wasn't much of a fighter. So at least he couldn't pummel Harry to a bloody pulp before the cavalry arrived.

And this messy situation was partially - yes, partially - my fault for plying Harry with a few cocktails from his secret admirer.

Young buff guy took a poke at Harry. Harry didn't
exactly dodge it as much as fall backwards when the fist
brushed past his face. Unfortunately, Harry had nowhere to
run. Penned in on one side by a retaining wall, and caged on
the other two by lounge chairs and people fleeing out of the
way, Harry's face was an open target as the young guy took
another swing at his beak.

The punch landed somewhere around the top of
Harry's head, so no major damage there. The one advantage of
having a thick skull. Harry's "Lake Michigan" cap flew up into
the air, and he flipped ass-over-tea kettle, rolling back over one
lounge chair and onto another, knocking into two women and
spilling their drinks.

Great. It was now a full blown scene. Could the police
be far behind?

Blood shot from his nose. No, not Harry's. The young
guy's. Just after he punched Harry in the noggin, I stepped into
the young, buff guy's face and grabbed him around the throat.
I had always found that to be an extremely effective way to
punch someone. Usually their first reaction is to grab for the
hand clamped on their esophagus, leaving me open to plow
their face with my free one.

My second punch sent Young Buff Guy reeling into the
swimming pool. His wife began screaming obscenities at me,
whaling on me with her arms, landing blow after harmless blow
to my chest and shoulders.

"Stay the fuck away from Jim, you fucking gorilla!
Don't you fucking touch him again or I'll have you fucking
arrested," she screeched at me, still attempting to beat on me as
I grabbed her wrists, keeping her back as I stood at the edge of
the swimming pool, glaring at her husband, letting him know
that climbing out of the water wasn't in his best interests.

"Maybe Jim shouldn't be punching men old enough to
be his grandfather," I exclaimed, settling her into a lounge chair
before reaching out to the embarrassed and rattled Harry,
yanking him off the two ladies he had fallen onto.

"He's a nut case," Jim countered, holding his head back and pinching his nose to stop the flow of blood that was dripping into the pool.

Like I didn't know that. Come close to being an in-law, dude, then you'll get the real picture. The jackass is six bricks short of a load. If that was reason enough to punch him, I would have taken out a license.

"We were just sitting here, and he went fucking crazy, fucking screaming and yelling at us," Jim's wife screamed at me.

"Where did you get your vocabulary, lady, a truck stop? Shut the hell up and stay out of the way," I snapped at her, focusing back on her husband, hoping to mellow out this scene and squire Harry the hell out of there.

"Your sugar daddy attacked us," Jim nasalled, still holding his nose.

"I don't even know what that means!" Harry yelled, then glared at the crowd that had gathered for the deck show. "Quit talking about me, I am not a homosexual," Harry protested to any and all, his entire body now shaking.

I tried to grab Harry to get him out of there, but he kept slipping from me, screaming at one person, then another, bobbing and weaving through the amusedly terrified crowd. I was trying to keep Jim's wife on the lounge chair and Jim in the pool. I didn't need a pissed-off Pilates king climbing out of the pool and pounding on me while I was trying to wrangle in Harry.

Harry would not shut up. His words were thick on his tongue, and he was ranting incessantly, shoving the mess from bad to completely fucked up. After a couple quick vodkas, he was lubricated like a Ferris Wheel axle. Too much tragedy, too much liquor, too much sun, too much gossip, and Harry had finally snapped. Couldn't this have happened while I was asleep?

"Goddamn it, Harry! Shut the hell up," I screamed at him, finally grabbing hold of the slippery rascal. I yanked him with me, keeping one eye on Jim and the other out for resort security. My benign prophesy of spending my days rotting away in an island prison were vastly more real now that Harry had blown a gasket.

And if there really was a hell, Harry and I would end up cellmates.

By the time I got him back into the building, Harry was hysterical. His body quivered, and he futilely battled more tears. "They were all talking about us! And that man and his wife were laughing at me. My God, what kind of place is this? Who would think that you and I are...are..."

"Drunk?" I finished his sentence harshly with the truth.

"Having that kind of relationship," Harry wheezed, choosing to finish his own sentence with his own truth.

I was very frustrated, but I wanted to laugh. That was the sort of insanity in which I was usually the culprit. Besides, what else could I do at that point? Just more shit tumbling down on top of me. But I recognized that laughing at Harry in his overwrought, unhinged state of mind would fuel a fire I was incapable of extinguishing. Harry hardly needed to be pushed toward the brink when he already had a leg over the edge of Mount Nutbag.

"I go to church. I'm an usher, for heaven's sake. If my wife were alive she would be mortified. If Tami were alive, she would be so ashamed that all she could do is cry."

Tami would cry over this all right. Cry from laughing so hard. She would never let me live down the fact that people thought her father and I were butt buddies. But she would feign hurt indignation to her father, treating his absurd mania with kid gloves. Harry wasn't a man you joked with even on a good day. He required remote respect and to be taken seriously especially when he was upset. Which often made it even easier to laugh at him.

Then Harry leaned against my shoulder and cried. Oh, shit. What else could I do but put my arm around his shoulder as I led him to the elevators? He balled uncontrollably, like a five-year-old who had wet his pants at a sleepover. Every time I wanted to hate the little rat bastard, he showed some pathetic vulnerability, a crack in his rigid veneer, and I knew that Tami would truly have been heartbroken if I hadn't taken care of him.

"Take a shower and sleep it off, Harry. When you get up, we'll take Tami's ashes and spread them. You need to get the hell out of here."

"I should never have come," he said over and over again, as if those words had become his new mantra.

No shit, Sherlock. Not under these circumstances. And not with me.

The entire trip I had wanted little more than to torture him. I didn't want him coming along in the first place, and if he hadn't blackmailed me with Tami's ashes, I would have rather died myself than have Harry on my honeymoon. Consciously, and probably even more viciously in my subconscious, I toiled hard to make him feel like crap. I'd like to blame it on Tami's death. Death makes you feel like utter shit. And you want everyone else to feel it, too. Harry owned as much pain as I carried on my back. But that didn't stop me from burrowing deep to add a new layer of dung to his anguish.

He needed to go. Harry needed to return to the tatters of his life. Harry's chore was even greater than mine. He had to figure out how to slop himself out of the pen he'd been mired in for the past twenty years and make a life for himself without Tami.

And I needed to get on ruining my life with excess, without a moral conscience 'tsking' in my ear at each debase action I participated in.

Snoring bounced off the walls of the suite. It was a deep, full-bodied, sound that only came from a hard-earned drunk. God knows Harry had merited that one. It forced me out onto the balcony to escape the vibration, where I lined up little bottles on the balcony railing.

So far there had been no repercussions from my scuffle with young, buff Jim. He was probably too embarrassed to file a complaint. I knew I should apologize to young, buff guy. But that wasn't about to happen. I was sure he was pissed off, but an apology would only add fresh vinegar to his bloody nose.

Harry slept. And I waited. I thought he would sober up and rise in the late afternoon, and we could set out to release Tami to the island, say our goodbyes, get Harry packed, and somehow, some way, get his ass on a plane, off the island, and out of my life. But as the sun set deep over the ocean in multi-shades of orange, through shreds of clouds that hung on the horizon, Harry was still sawing logs.

Tami would remain locked in his suitcase for another day.

BAD MOJO

In no way was I going to spend my night parked in that room watching Harry snore and fart, and make whatever other unnatural bodily noises he was producing. Does that happen to everyone when they get old? Their body makes involuntary sounds, like death is creeping in and taking residence. Thank God you're asleep and can't hear them, or they'd certainly cause a heart attack.

I had ripped through the last of the tiny scotches. I enjoyed those little bottles. Drinking from them with their small opening was like sucking a nipple. And I'm not sure which I liked more. Since my body was at just the right temperature and the cupboard was bare, it was time to head downstairs and finish off my nightly drunk in the bar among the vacationers, who would now be even more frightened by my presence.

The club was crowded with bodies. More packed than it had been since I had arrived at the resort. A lot of new faces. Which meant a slew of people who hopefully hadn't caught wind of my viral reputation. I wanted to go into the night fresh, no celebrity that I would have to live down. Or play up. That night anonymity would be a blessing, especially when it came to getting my groove on. After being pent up in my room, waiting for Harry to awake from his drunken coma, I was overcome with the anxious need to get nasty with a bad girl in the worst way. Only the sounds of sex could drown out the noise of Harry's snoring, which was still rattling around in my brain.

I had to wait for a seat at the bar where Kat was now working one end and the black man with the great teeth the other. I didn't want to take a table. I always hated when some lonesome asshole sucked up a table when groups were waiting. A stool at the far end away from Kat would be ideal. Without getting any disapproving glares which would make me second guess my wicked yearnings, I could scope the room and pick out a not-so-innocent victim. See if she was drunk enough to want to go home with a story. Great thing about people on vacations, they feel they have license to misbehave when they wouldn't imagine the same behavior on their home turf.

After a woman who was being crowded by some loser left her stool at the end of the bar, I laid claim to the territory. My shoulders barely fit back there against the wall, but I adjusted, sitting ajar on the stool, facing out so I could lean back against the wall and leer at the dance floor, where couples were gyrating to the sounds of Janet Jackson.

Darting to my end of the bar, the bartender with the smile pointed at me. "What can I get you?" he asked quickly, rushed by the crowd.

"Scotch. Double. Neat."

He poured a couple shots into a glass and slid it down to me, his eyes narrowing.

"You that guy that popped the dude at the pool today?"

I nodded reluctantly.

"Saw that. I was working the cabana down on the beach," he smiled. "That'll be eight bucks."

I slid him a twenty, signaling him to keep the change and keep his mouth shut about the day's escapades. All I wanted from him was to keep my glass full.

Watching the people slide around the dance floor and the colored lights pulsate off their bodies, I felt safe in my corner. Protected with my dear, old friend Dr. Buzz. I caught Kat's eye only for a moment, but, with orders being bellowed at her from every side, it was far too hectic for her to pop down and say hello. There were more women in the club that night, more singles. They must have wandered over from other hotels and resorts in the area. Some were pretty good-looking. I hadn't had the chance to scope out the other night spots on the island yet. But I had the rest of the week. And I'd had enough of that place, which was predominately couples. I could get more action in other clubs. And a lot less assumptions, which after that day had gone completely off-the-chart. But right then I had my seat to watch the action and see what wandered past. Another great thing about the islands, the women have no inhibitions about wearing very little.

As I licked the last of the scotch from the glass, I waved over the busy bartender. "I'm going to make your life real easy," I said, slipping him a fifty. "Bring me five more doubles and line them up." I wasn't in the mood to jump around every fifteen minutes or so, trying to get his attention. He set the glasses up in front of me, as the others sitting at the bar tossed worried looks at the future drunk.

After I had emptied the first two, a very hot blonde wandered up. I vaguely recognized her, but my head was only clear to partly cloudy by that point, so I couldn't pinpoint the location of our encounter.

"I'm sorry about today," she said.

Still I couldn't put my thumb on it; yet, not wanting her to make a hasty exit, I nodded like I knew exactly what she was talking about.

"There was probably a better way to handle it. I mean he was an old guy and pretty small," she said. "Jim just doesn't like people getting in his face," she laughed.

Jim? Young Buff Guy. Punch. Bloody nose. Pool. Right, got it. Perhaps if she had used the word 'fuck' in there as a noun, a verb, an adjective, or an adverb, I could have nailed our rendezvous a little sooner.

"So please accept my apology. Jim and I can both fly off the handle sometimes," she smiled.

No shit, sister.

"Yeah. I can relate," I nodded again, noting for the first time how truly beautiful she really was. Earlier, there hadn't been much time to assess her attributes, especially as she was beating on my back. I knew she had a good body and nice face, but this broad was a hottie, with shoulder length blonde hair and large breasts pressing against the thin material of her tight T-shirt.

"I just didn't like that he took a swing at Harry," I said, sort of making an apology but not really.

"He really isn't your fucking boyfriend, is he?"

I shook my head. "I don't know how that bullshit got started," I responded, noticing Kat watching me talk to the woman from the other end of the bar. "Harry and I are...well, we were almost related by marriage. It...it's a long story. But no, he and I aren't anything to each other besides a burr in each other's ass."

She chuckled. There was more than amusement in that chuckle. Attraction? Interest? The need for a spanking?

"I sort of figured that," her hand casually slid onto my knee. "I'm Debra."

"Hello, Debra. Where's your husband tonight?"

"Jim is...he's not around tonight. That's my long story."

Oh yeah? The conversation had just gained momentum.

"I won't push. Life's short and long stories take up too much time."

"Let's just say that Jim and I have our time together and we have our time apart. I know that doesn't work for everybody, but it is very good for us. We'd probably kill each other if we didn't take a break from one another now and then."

"Even on vacation?" I asked, testing where this was going.

"Especially on vacation," Debra laughed again. "So, what's your story? Why are you here, drinking all alone?"

I handed her a glass of scotch and picked up the other. "I'm not alone now. But I could make up a story. Hell, I'm loaded with those."

"I think you're just fucking loaded," Debra laughed, taking a sip.

I joined her chuckle even though I didn't find it that funny. But I was interested in seeing this conversation go further. There was something incredibly enticing about this woman on a lot of levels. All of them carnal. And laughing at her inane jokes was a small price to pay for a chance at the possibility of climbing onto Debra's very hot, naked body later on that night.

I really dug this girl. And not only because she had her hand on my leg, but because she had big breasts, a beautiful face, and a husband that I not only didn't like, but who was out of the picture that night. I respected that Debra was honest enough to accept that much of what had happened earlier was her husband's fault for going after Harry while the old man was having a meltdown, instead of calling him a few names and then walking away. I knew I wasn't blameless by any stretch. But at least she wasn't wagging her finger in my face and berating me with four letter words again.

And she was drinking scotch. A girl after my own heart.

I downed mine in a few gulps, as Debra daintily sipped hers, which was a mild surprise for a woman who talked like a career soldier. She didn't seem interested in finishing the drink any time soon, and if this chance meeting was headed in the direction I was hoping, I'd be a happier man if she downed the drink. I always looked better to a woman when she'd been drinking.

Making a move to push her way down in my direction, Kat didn't get very far. There were just too many people tonight for her to take time out to lecture me on what bad form it would be to have sex with the wife of the man whose nose I bloodied earlier in the day. Not that I would have listened anyway.

Debra set her half-drunk glass down on the bar and put both her hands on my legs, stretching.

"Thanks for the drink. This place is too crowded, I'm out of here."

I grabbed her wrist. "Where you going?"

"I don't know. I hate this music. Maybe a walk on the beach. Somewhere quiet."

She locked eyes with me as the backbeat pounded between us.

"Want to come?" she asked.

Come? Was she using this high school double entendre on purpose, or was it just my foul mind? Either way, she didn't have to ask me twice. I emptied the scotch left in her glass as we stood. Debra gave me a smile that was hard to read, as if she were sizing me up. Then she slipped her fingers around my hand, and we made our way to the exit.

Glancing over my shoulder, I could see Kat was frozen for a moment, watching. God, did she have to turn into my mother? That is if I had had a mother who actually cared. Couldn't she understand that this was all about forgetting? And fun? And no one needed that duo more than me. I turned back quickly, giving Debra a sly grin that let her know exactly what I was expecting. I felt her tiny fingers wrap even tighter around mine.

Score!

The night air was thick with the aroma of the beach. The stars were a massive jigsaw of sparkles, as wisps of transparent clouds clung to the air below them. Rain was coming. You could smell it. I followed Debra across the pool deck, where couples had come to escape the loud music or to sit under the stars.

"Why don't we hang here, it's pretty quiet," I said, happy to be out of the bar but less thrilled about hiking on the beach. Even with this gorgeous woman. If this was leading to the conclusion I was hoping for, I wanted to be near a bed, not digging my knees or my ass into the sand.

"No. I feel like walking. You can stay but it's a gorgeous night…" Debra said, letting go of my hand.

She was playing with me. Didn't take a sex therapist to figure that out. This was a woman who liked men chasing after her. She was used to being desired. By more men than just the one who had married her. I sensed that I wasn't the first man she had led on just to see how far she could take it. But I wanted to close this deal and if it meant a walk and talk along the ocean's edge, so be it. The clock was ticking on my one-hour charm limit, so I was hoping she was talking about a short stroll and not a marathon.

Debra crossed to the stairs leading to the sand. A young couple was making out around the corner from the stairs. The guy broke the kiss and looked at me. We shared a smile as he glanced at Debra who was pulling off her shoes, knowing that she and I were soon to be in a clench not too dissimilar from the one he shared with his girlfriend.

I have to say that if I was going to get lucky with any woman that night, there could have been no one more perfect than Jim's wife. It was the icing on the cake after the jackass had punched Harry. When I planted the flag, in my head I would be calling, "Viva La Everett!"

Catching up with Debra, she turned to me with a sly grin. "Come on...I promise I won't bore you with my husband problems if you promise not to bore me with any of your own."

Since I was running from mine, I nodded quickly and answered, "Deal."

She took my hands and pulled me with her to where the surf lapped up onto the sand. Kicking off her shoes, she let the water wash over her feet.

"I love this," she said and then turned to me, the light from the resort glimmering in her eyes. "Hey, have you gone skinny dipping since you've been here?" she asked.

I shook my head. But at least now I knew she and I were on the same page.

"So?" she shrugged.

This was a no-brainer. And I was more than drunk enough to have no brain.

"Come on," she said with a playful giggle in her voice. She jogged further down the beach, where the light from the resort dimmed into the darkness of the night. I watched her luscious body move and then sprinted after her to catch up. As I caught her, I stumbled forward, grabbing hold of her body. My face dove in for a kiss, but she turned away with a laugh.

"Fuck, you don't waste any time," she said, "I like that."

I suddenly sensed that Debra and Jim's necessary time apart didn't include the caveat of extramarital sex.

As we disappeared into the darkness near a few beached kayaks and surf boats, she pulled up her shirt up, revealing a set of breasts that surpassed my expectations as much as they defied gravity. Her nipples pointed at me with excitement and anticipation. Jim was a lucky man. But that night all the luck was finally rolling my way.

As I yanked my shirt up over my head, ready to answer those anticipated nipples with my raging hard-on, I saw Debra pull her shirt back down over her tits, her smile disappearing.

The liquor fogged my mind and the blood was traveling into my shorts, not my head, or I would have caught the clue. Even before the first hit cracked me in the skull from behind, I knew this was going to hurt.

With my shirt over my head and knotted around my elbows and wrists, I was defenseless. I buckled at the knees but didn't fall. Yet.

I was smacked again from the other side, and I felt blood soak through the shirt right above my left eye.

I coughed out a breath as I was racked in the gut by a board, and then felt it break over my back, which dumped me into the sand. The shirt came down far enough for me to see through the tears that rimmed the bottom of my eyes and the blood that squirted down from further up my face.

Jim stood over me with three other guys.

All I could do was bring my arms up over my face to try and protect my head as they battered me with boards, punched, and kicked me. Every breath I took felt like my lungs were on fire. If I wasn't so drunk it would have probably hurt a lot more. But it hurt plenty enough.

I grabbed somebody's leg and bit into it, literally taking a chunk out of his calf as he screamed. But another kick smashed my nose causing more blood to volcano down my face. These fuckers intended to kill me. Or at least come close.

I had to get to my feet and make a run for it. But between the liquor and the beating, I couldn't even tell which way was up and which was down. I saw stars for a moment, and then another kick came, and I was breathing sand.

With everything I had, I rose to my knees and gave a yell, trying in vain to tackle one of the guys. They laughed as Jim stepped up, holding a shiny metal pipe that glimmered in the light. He brought it down hard on the back of my head. I felt it for only a split second, and then I saw the stars again, only I don't think they were the ones in the sky.

Images. Shattered. Punched. Kicked. Shooting Pain. Salt water. Cough. Tami. Another cough. My cuts screaming. Tami. No air. Water.

Tami.

Holding me in the water, her soaked wedding dress clinging to her body, Tami asked me to make love to her. But I couldn't. I couldn't move. She cried, the lapping of the water rushing over her, as she held my head up just enough so I wouldn't drown.

"I thought you loved me," she whispered through her tears, her eyes pleading with mine for an answer.

But I couldn't speak. I tried to make her understand from the anguish in my eyes that I loved her more than I loved my own life.

"Then why do you do this?" she asked, her fingers running down my face over my wounds.

Because you left me, damn it. I now lived in hostile territory, and everything in it was my adversary. You don't rip away my most precious possession and not expect me to fight for survival. I didn't care if I won or lost, but I was going to do battle. Life was war. And in war nothing is fair, but everything is fair game.

Tami cried harder, burying her face into my neck. I could smell her perfume, feel her wet hair drape across my face.

"You can't come here," she said, sobbing so hard I thought the world would shake apart.

Tami laid me back in the water, slipping around behind me, holding my head just above the surf as it washed in. Her face was so close to mine as she peered down, tears dripping from her eyes. She kept hold of me as I closed my eyes. I could feel her, but I sensed that she had drifted into the night sky, vanishing among the stars. I couldn't see her. I couldn't open my eyes. I could only feel her. Touch her fingers as they wrapped around mine. Sense that she was protecting me, never allowing the salty waters to wash over my face and rinse the blood away. I could hear the tears with each rush of the surf.

Tami was with me.

WRAPPED GIFTS

When I woke up, Harry was holding my hand.

If it was that bad that it had come to this, take me now, God.

My head ached and I had trouble seeing, my vision doubled and blurred. My hand went up to my nose, which was bandaged. Looking down, I could literally see the purple swollenness around my eyes.

"Shit," was all I could mutter, my throat so dry that swallowing was an impossible chore.

I waved my hand at the pitcher of water near the bed. Harry was up swiftly, pouring me a cup, which I drank as fast as my tight throat could gulp it down.

"Slow down, you're not supposed to drink that fast," Harry said, standing over me, assisting in holding the plastic cup.

Even before I came back to all my cognitive senses, I noted something different in his eyes. Less judgment. His ire muted. Was that glimmer actual concern?

Wow. Those guys must have jacked me up bad.

"Do you know who you are?" Harry asked.

I nodded

"Do you know what happened?"

"I got a pretty good idea," I slurred.

Harry nodded. "Good. They thought you might have brain damage."

I forced myself to sit up a little more. My entire body throbbing as I did. "Could you really tell?" I asked.

Harry let himself smile. But it didn't last long.

"You were lucky, Todd. If we hadn't of found you when we did, you would have drowned."

"Tami," I said.

He eyed me oddly, not saying a word.

"She held me. Kept me out of the water."

His eyes arched with sorrow and disbelief.

"I know you think that's the brain damage talking, but it's what I remember."

I glanced up at a bag that was attached to a needle stuck in my arm.

"Morphine drip?" I asked.

"You're hurt pretty bad. If you didn't have it, you'd be a real mess," Harry stated, still holding my hand.

Too late. I was already a real mess. It was just that my exterior now matched my interior.

"How did this happen?" Harry quizzed, concern seeping into his voice, as he stood over me so I wouldn't have to twist around to look at him.

Relaying to Harry what I remembered, the pieces of my major ass whipping came without thought. Harry nodded through all of it, making a mental checklist of the information I revealed. He then gave me a smug sneer as if he were the only man who knew where the life rafts were kept on a sinking ship.

"I knew that little pants-crapper had something to do with this," Harry averred solidly, much to my surprise. "You're lucky that bartender came to the room and got me."

I shook my head, not understanding.

"The dark haired one. Pretty girl. She came up to the room, told me you left the club with that son-of-a-bitch's wife and didn't return," Harry didn't look happy as he spat out the information. "Figuring you got yourself in some kind of mess, she got some of the hotel staff to look for you. Seems she knows you pretty well too."

I didn't say anything. I guess I did have more friends than I thought. At least one. Besides, I think Harry liked me this way, beaten to near silence as he continued on about his Columbo routine after my beating.

"I slipped the desk clerk a few bills, and she told me the blonde and her husband were supposed to stay through the week but suddenly checked out early morning. I had him and that whore of his detained at the airport," Harry said proudly, then snickered, adding, "The dummies were waiting standby to see if they could get off the island."

Harry leaned closer to me so as not to be overheard. By whom I didn't know, since we were the only two people in the room. "I also slipped the Constable here on St. Carlos a couple hundred dollars and told him I was sure they had had something to do with the attack."

I smiled. Even that hurt.

"You sly dog, Harry."

"Whatever it cost me, I'm going to make sure they cool their tanned keesters behind bars for quite a while."

"And I figured it'd be my sorry ass that ended up in pokey down here," I mumbled, trying to stifle the laugh I knew would rip at my guts.

Harry didn't respond. Guess he knew I didn't have any brain damage because I had already returned to smart-ass mode.

I pulled my body up high enough in the bed to gander into the mirror across the room. Holy shit. Though I couldn't see clearly, which concerned me, I could tell that those ass wipes worked me over good. My head was shaved, and there was a row of stitches in the back to repair the fracture. My nose was broken, with three more stitches across the bridge. My eyes were swollen black and purple. I had a gash over my eye that had also been stitched closed.

Under the silly hospital gown, an incision on my right side had been stapled closed from my ribs down to my stomach. Harry told me they had to go in and relieve some internal bleeding, as well as take out a piece of shattered rib that had punctured my lung. They also had to pump my stomach because of the amount of salt water I ingested -- along with, as Harry needled me, "an exorbitant amount of scotch." I still had the taste of brine and Cutty Sark in my mouth. Not a mixture I recommend.

In spite of looking like, well, like I got jumped by four guys, I sensed that I was pretty lucky. I had been in plenty of fights in my life but never got my head kicked in like that.

To come out of it with my life, my teeth, and my memory was remarkable. I don't think it was Jim's wish that I come out of this alive. Vindictive son of a bitch, wasn't he? All planned because I bloodied his nose and knocked his sorry ass into the pool in front of his hard-bodied minx of a wife. Guess that was more of an attack on his fragile manhood than he could handle.

Doctor Haybert, a tall Brit with fingers so long they looked almost extraterrestrial, explained that I had to stay in the hospital for another couple days for observation and to make sure that I had completely recovered from the surgery. When I asked him if he could have me wheeled outside so I could tan while I recuperated, he didn't crack a smile. I'd blame that on the sad state of the British humor, but Harry didn't find me funny either.

Screw them both, I was on a morphine drip and they weren't.

The next morning after a hearty meal of lime Jello and chicken broth, the Constable showed up. He was a slender black man with big features and a Cruella De Ville streak of gray in his otherwise remarkably-black hair. He drank. I know drinkers. I have parked my ass next to many over the years, and I was sure the Constable was a regular at the local watering holes. Roped veins of blood crisscrossing his dark eyes and lines in his face that didn't come with age distinguished him as a lifelong boozer. My guess, whiskey. Maybe rum.

I reiterated the saga of my ass-kicking to him. He never wrote anything down, just simply nodded. I guess he had had a lot of practice in the mental notes department. "Do you think you could identify the other men who were with him?" he asked in a strange accent that clashed Caribbean with the Queen's English.

I told him that one of them would have a distinguishing mark. A chunk of meat missing from the son of a bitch's calf. A piece I took with me into the ocean.

As he walked out, Harry talked with him closely. They shook hands and I saw Harry slip him more cash.

The next two days drifted past mostly in a drug-induced haze. The drip in my arm kept me stupidly content. Kat was the only visitor I had besides Harry. I wasn't exactly cogent when she sat down in the chair next to my bed, her head shaking involuntarily at the sight of my wounds. I vaguely recall patches of our conversation. Me thanking her. Kat telling me she was sorry. Not about the beating...that I deserved that to a certain extent. But about Tami. Harry had corroborated my scotch-induced tale of the misery we had suffered the previous week.

I slept a lot and slurped a truckload of Jello and soup. That's all they would give me, and Harry, bastard that he was, wouldn't sneak me in anything resembling real food. All the soup did was make me want to pee. Thankfully by the time I was ready to leave, there was no more blood in my urine.

Doctor Haybert gave me a prescription for Vicoden and warned me sternly not to mix it with liquor. I nodded in compliance, but I could tell by the way he looked at me he didn't believe I would and figured he'd be seeing me soon to have my stomach pumped again. Harry snapped the pill bottle from my hand and promised the good doctor that he would control my daily dosage.

Harry as my caretaker. If I died under his watch, no one would bat an eyelid.

On the way back to the resort, Harry had Tomas stop at a tourist shop where he purchased me a big hat and sunglasses. I looked like something out of a creature feature with all the stitches in my head and my face swollen and purple. The pain that shot through my side with every step caused me to trod like The Mummy. I was my own fifties horror movie.

I sat on the balcony of the suite, fighting my gnawing urge to raid the minibar. Without that drip pumping juice into my arm, the pain was far more acute. And with Harry doling out the painkillers, I was no longer a happy traveler. I tried to doze, but every time I did, images of Tami shimmered into my dreams. I don't put much stock in metaphysics and all that new agey mumbo jumbo, but I knew what had happened to me when they dumped my half-dead ass into the water. No one can ever tell me that it was not Tami who held me and kept me from drowning. Logically, I understood that it was probably a hallucination. When you get whacked in the head with a board a few times that's a common aftermath. But logic isn't something I step into with both feet either. If I had, my life wouldn't have been as screwed up. And I'll believe what I want to believe. My love for that woman was strong enough to keep me alive.

Having so much time to think now that I was laid up, I bent my head around the question of what I could learn from all of this. Other than never trusting a woman who uses a form of the word 'fuck' as her only adjective and never getting your ass kicked by four guys, I couldn't derive a single life lesson that I could take away from this beating. Not that I'm big on discovering life lessons from events I survive. I haven't from Tami's death. And I'm pretty much a blank when it comes to this one. Life doesn't hold that many mysteries or secrets; you just roll with what's thrown at you and hope that it doesn't cave in that soft spot on your head. I'm sure from the outside there are plenty of people, Harry included, who would tell me this was a sign to clean up my act. But that wasn't an option. When you have nothing to go back to, you don't go back. As soon as I healed, I would tumble back into my comfortable bad behavior. Even Tami asking me not to from the grave wouldn't cure that illness. The fact that she was in the grave was reason enough to keep my annihilative conduct on life support. I saw no reason to be the man I had been with her, without her. Tami was the sole dynamic that made me want to be better. Nothing else in my life ever gave me any impetus to lean in that direction. And lightning doesn't strike people more than once without killing them.

Harry had never not had a project. Tami was his twenty year project, and damn if he didn't raise that girl into a beautiful, loving, magical woman. I applauded the son of a bitch for that. Not an easy thing to do. I'm living proof of that; my parents couldn't have done a worse job with me. And if I had never turned a 180 when Tami entered my life, I still wouldn't have a clue how to be a good man. So for Tami to possess so many rare qualities, Harry should take a bow. That shit doesn't happen in a vacuum.

When I got my head beaten in, Harry discovered another project. Me. And I witnessed firsthand how he worked. Greasing the palm of the local authorities to crucify the jackasses that jumped me, Harry was making sure that justice would be served. And served cold. He may not have been a man of stature, but he could be as mean as a junkyard Rottweiler, guarding his dinner bowl when push came to shove. The nasty part of Harry I sort of enjoyed; his mollycoddling though might as well have been someone drilling screws into my eye sockets. I was his James Caan and he was my Kathy Bates. Thank God my sentence was only another couple days, unless he crippled me in the middle of the night with a sledgehammer.

But I wasn't Tami. I was an admittedly pissed-off adult with issues, not a five- year-old girl. Harry was lucky there were no sharp objects within reach, or one of us wouldn't have made it out alive. Between my ass itching from sitting so long and Harry doling out my medicine like a gnarly prison matron, I found myself grinding my teeth in frustration. As long as I could stay medicated and swipe a bottle from the minibar when Harry was in the bathroom or down in the restaurant, I held onto hope that I could make it through Nurse Harry's shift.

Harry needed to acquire his own life and drop the projects. Or at least find a project his own age to play with. I knew that once he returned to Chicago, Harry would walk back into his house and an oppressive blanket of loneliness would wrap him up like a cocoon and he would never escape it. No butterfly would emerge. Not even a moth. Harry would stay huddled in his own sadness, unprepared to venture out and have a life. Hell, he had forgotten how. Who wouldn't after twenty years?

Just like I had never understood what it was like to be a good man until Tami took my hand and lead me on that journey, Harry never ventured an avenue to his own happiness, busying two long decades of his life by making sure his daughter found happiness instead.

That party was over.

I recognized that I was the only person who could hand Harry back his life. It wasn't that I felt generous or obligated for his deviant revenge against the fuckers who bashed my head in, though that was pretty cool. This was a man thing. Harry was alone. As best I could tell, he didn't have many friends. And with Tami gone, Harry had lost his sounding board. Tami respected and loved her father but she never hesitated to set him straight when needed. Why I had to do it was because I didn't love him and had little respect for him. Tough love would come a lot easier for me. And be more pleasurable. That son of a bitch needed permission to live again. And it had to be done now. Once we returned home, he and I would seldom make contact. Maybe we would run into each other catching a meal somewhere and give a cursory nod. Maybe we would phone each other on Tami's birthday or the anniversary of her death. Although even that was doubtful. We would return to where we had begun the relationship, as strangers.

I had never given Harry much other than a cold ration of shit. But I couldn't let him go back and die without a fight. Harry needed a kick in the pants. He wasn't flatline yet, and there was a lot of life still left in that old fart. If Jim and his hired gang had killed me, no one could say that I hadn't lived a life. I'd lived a couple. Most of them pretty rotten but rotten is better than none at all. Harry needed to know he could still get in there and mix it up. I was actually proud of him when he had a few drinks in him and he went off on Mr. Gold's Gym and his miserable bitch wife. And more proud that he was making them pay-up for my beating. Showed he still had a pair. Even though they had rust on them, his remained brass.

Recuperating in the hotel suite gave me ample time to plot but prevented me from putting the machinations into action. And with Harry, the hawk, watching me, it was all the worse. Whatever gift I was going to bestow on him, I was seriously limited in my ability to pull it off. With my options narrowed, I had to rely on all my many friends that I've made since I arrived. Not a party many would RSVP for.

"Goddamn man, go eat some food, leave me the hell alone for an hour," I bellowed at Harry.

"Why? What do you want to do? I'm taking the Vicodin with me," he answered with equal surliness.

"Stuff it up your ass for all I care, I'm just tired of you hovering around me like a bee I can't swat. Get away from me," I continued my tirade.

"Don't go near that minibar. I'm warning you. I'll have them come up here and take it out of the room," my nursemaid responded.

"If you don't get out of my face, I'm going to pull my ass off this bed and throw myself over the goddamn balcony! Now go so I can beat off or something!"

That did the trick. He curled his entire face into a tornado of disgust, grunting with repugnance. Mumbling under his breath, he grabbed a pass key and split. I grabbed the phone to call my one ally.

Even with Kat's help, making it to the lobby was nothing short of miraculous. My body screamed with every step I took down the hallway. I leaned against the wall of the elevator to catch my breath, all the while she kept asking me if I was going to make it.

"I'm not going to let a few broken ribs, a damaged lung, and like a billion stitches in my head get in the way of me doing something stupid. You should have at least figured that out by now."

Once I got to the lobby, I fell into an oversized cane chair with a harsh moan and waited. Couples passed me, some giving me a knowing look. They would whisper to each other once they passed out of earshot. I had no idea what the prognosis of my reputation was now. Dupe. Hero. Deserving victim. The resort had sent flowers up to the room when I returned from the hospital, and Harry had made some deal with them to pay all my medical expenses and reimburse some of the money, threatening to name them in a civil lawsuit, which they would have no doubt won but didn't want to go through the hassle of entertaining, especially when Harry told them he would file the charges back in the States. Harry watched a lot of Court TV.

Reassuring me that there was only one person on the island who could aide me in my devious, Vicodin-flavored plot, Kat focused on the front entrance as I kept an eye out for Harry. We didn't need him sneaking up on his own surprise party. As our contact came slowly striding in through the glass doors, his dark gaze fell upon Kat and I. Not like I was hard to miss in my baseball cap and dark sunglasses, futilely attempting to camouflage my black eyes and broken nose. Realizing who he was, I glanced up at Kat with a dry smirk.

"Why shouldn't I be surprised?"

"This is an island," she responded, "We all need a few jobs to survive."

He stepped up and settling into the cane chair across from me, his dark, bloodshot eyes holding on Kat for a long moment before his pupils slid in my direction.

"Mr. Cartwright, Miss Murrow tells me that you need a favor," he said without so much as shaking my hand.

"I'll leave you two alone to discuss business," Kat said as she turned to him and respectfully nodded.

We both watched her go. Her backside as pleasant to watch as her front.

"That girl's got a lot of demons. Unlike you, most of hers are real. Her ex-husband found out where she was hiding and made a visit to the island about a year ago," he spoke in a near murmur. "It took a bit of...persuasion, but I made sure that he'd never take another vacation to this island again."

This certainly was my guy. Either that or he was going to kill me.

"Well Constable ---"

"Gabriel," the Constable cut me off. His hard eyes never blinked as he then waited for my request.

"Gabriel," I repeated with deference before launching into Operation Save Harry's Sorry Ass. As I went into detail about what I needed to pull off the ingenious strategy I concocted while Harry was annoying the crap out of me in the suite, I slipped a couple tiny bottles of minibar whiskey from my shirt pocket and set them on the table between us. As the Constable listened, he picked one of the bottles off the table.

"I see Miss Murrow coached you in how to get my attention," he said, uncapping the bottle and downing the amber liquor in a covert gulp. "But Mr. Cartwright, for what you're asking, you're going to have to do much better than this."

Time for the big guns.

"Maybe your tastes run more in this direction," I uttered, palming another shot bottle and setting it on the table.

This one had a hundred dollar bill rubberbanded around it. Gabriel stared at the money without blinking, the red veins that decorated his eyes thickening as the whiskey made his way into his bloodstream. His eyes wandered up to my battered face.

"That's not nearly enough to quench my thirst," he stated, not a hint of humor in his voice.

I set out two more bottles. Both with hundreds wrapped around them.

"That's all I brought. I can get more if you'll help me up to my room," I said.

He picked up the expensively decorated bottles, slipped

them into his pants pocket, and then stood up, towering over me. Gabriel offered me his hand.

"A little advice, Mr. Cartwright," he murmured in his deep, cockeyed, island-accented voice, "Next time you punch a man, don't try and fuck his wife the same day." And then he smiled widely and laughed.

I joined him, even though it nearly splintered my ribs again.

Kat returned to the lobby and helped me out of the chair, never asking about my conversation with Gabriel. I suspected she pretty much knew how it went down, having asked him for a favor in the past. She had done me a big one. Actually a few. It was time I at least repaid the interest.

"How far is your car from here?"

Kat shook her head. "Why?"

"Take me for a ride. There's something else I need to do."

Pulling up in front of the long building with the odd, low slung roof, I expected the structure to be bigger. But, as Kat kept reminding me, this was an island. As we hunkered down in her car, staring across the street at the building, Kat mumbled over and over how insane this was, debating whether she should restart the car and drive away before I did something else truly, inspiringly stupid. But damn it, I was on a roll.

As the bell rang from inside the building, she turned to me. "Are you sure this is a good idea," she questioned with a gulping hesitation locked in her voice.

"Are you kidding me," I responded as I pushed open the car door and heaved my body out of the cramped space with a groan. "I wouldn't know a good idea from a bad one if it bit me in the ass."

Kids rushed from the school building, dashing for their bikes and scooters. Kat leaned against her tiny French-made car, her arms crossed across her chest, finally pointing at her son as he darted from the building, his head down in an attempt to keep a low profile. Guess he was looking to keep from receiving another ass whipping. Earl, who Kat regrettably named after her own father, was a handsome kid with a mop of brown hair that had been kissed by the island sun. The freckles that dotted his nose and cheeks were a road map to a forthcoming time where this kid's good looks would break the hearts of a slew of young girls. Now I understood why the other boys wanted to kick his ass. It was pay forward for a future when Earl was bigger and far better looking than they would be and Kat's boy would be stealing their girlfriends at will.

As I stepped up to Earl, towering over the seven year old, he took a long, drawn out gaze up at me, his blue eyes widening as he hiked a giant step backwards and quickly sized up an exit strategy.

"Point out the boys that have been picking on you," I commanded.

Either Earl didn't register the question or was so freaked out by having some hulking man with dark glasses and a hat, futilely attempting to disguise black eyes and stitches, glaring down at him, he didn't answer until he saw his mother behind me.

Kat nodded. Earl pointed.

There for four of them hanging together near a bike rack giving a ration of shit to another smaller kid who was hoping to unlock his bike and get out of there without getting punched. The bullies were around eleven or twelve with the leader of the pack inordinately big for his age. I could relate. He was me back in grade school. And I did exactly what Baby Huey did, torment every kid that was smaller than me. Now if someone had done to me what I was about to do to him, maybe my life would have been different. Who knows? But I was certain that after today these kids would never pound on Earl again.

As I marched up to the pack of small wolf pups, I pulled off my hat and sunglasses, revealing the entire gambit of stitches that crossed my skull and the blood that still filled the whites of my black eyes. I looked like I'd died and come back for revenge. And that was exactly how I wanted them to remember me.

"Hey you little shits," I darkly bellowed from deep within my gut. "You the little bastards that have been picking on my good friend, Earl?"

For a brief moment there was a shimmer of defiance in the biggest kid's eyes. His first reaction was to save face at all costs. But he was about to lip off to someone who once stood in his shoes and he seemed to sense it. That was the difference between he and I when I was his age. I would have done it. Smarted off with something ridiculously juvenile and then stood my ground while this big, scary asshole ripped my head off. This big turd was smarter than I was at his age. He kept his lip buttoned as I pressed my finger into his chest.

"I'm only going to say this once so turn your dirty little ears in my direction. If I ever, EVER, hear of any of you even looking funny at Earl, much less touching him, I'm coming back, and I'm going to drive my fist into your chest. And before you die I'm going to make you watch as I eat your heart."

Yeah, I know, way over the top. But hell they were kids. They were easy.

"Is that clear?" I yelled in their terrified faces, making the veins in my neck bulge for effect.

As they cowered, nodding in horror, I achingly lifted my shirt exposing the stitches that ran up my side. I thought the skinny kid with the first signs of bad acne was going to hurl his lunch.

"I killed six men last week. Taking out you little pukes will be dessert for me," I spat out with a menacing laugh. It's a delight being a moronic prick when it's for a good cause.

As I shuffled back to Kat and Earl, I was breathing so hard I thought my bad lung would collapse again. Kat shook her head, grinding her teeth together to keep from laughing as Earl stood next to her slack jawed, unsure of what just happened but thrilled he got to witness it.

"You'll be lucky if you don't get your sorry ass arrested," Kat said, climbing back into her small car with Earl.

"I just bribed the island Constable to land a prostitute. I doubt he's going to slap the cuffs on for causing a few bullies to shit their shorts."

On the ride back to the hotel, Earl sat stuffed between Kat and me, grinning with wicked glee. I could tell by Kat's reaction that it was the first time she'd seen that smile in a long while. I was proud of what I had done, believing that Earl, who in essence had no father, was excited to have a male role model stand up for him. But what shot him over the moon was not that I was a quasi-father figure. No, in his eyes I was far cooler.

"You know Mom, I'm the only kid at my school who has his very own monster," he boasted with such buttered delight that even the mortified Kat had to scream with laughter.

And I certainly knew how to take a compliment.

"Thank you," Kat stated as she delivered me back to the honeymoon suite.

I shook my head. "No. Thank you," I panted, still out of breath from the walk down the hallway. It'd been a long day for me.

Kat held her silence for a moment and after the painful excursion back to the room, I actually had tears in my eyes, so I couldn't read what she was thinking. Not that I'm a pro at that on a good day. Not sure, I trudged further, wanting a response.

"Just so we're clear, I'm thanking you because I couldn't have done everything today without you. I mean, I couldn't have even made it down to the lobby. I'd be in a crumpled heap somewhere near the elevator," I added, hoping to prod her into giving me a sign of what was smoking through her head.

But Kat stayed on my face without a word.

"I'd offer a penny for your thoughts but I just gave all my money away to the Constable."

Kat shook her head. "I'm just surprised," she said.

Shaking my head with one of those 'duh' looks on my face, she finally smiled. "That you called me to help you out with this in the first place."

"I didn't have anyone else. Been a problem most of my life actually. But when I needed help, you know how it goes, certain people come to mind. You came to mine."

"Even though you were procuring a hooker, I'm taking that as a compliment."

Laughing hurt. "Do," I said.

She opened the door to the room for me and waved me in. "You lay down. You've had enough of a workout for today," she declared before adding, "I mean, helping my son the way you did and making a friend out of me. That can't be an easy thing for you all in one day."

I turned and looked at her. We didn't need to speak another word. It was true. Kat was a friend. Or as close as I have ever made on my own. Certainly in this short amount of time. It's amazing how close you get to someone you've insulted, badgered, and tipped well for a few days and how much tighter you get in an attempt to get someone else laid. Maybe it's being on an island. Maybe it's that beggars can't be choosers. Maybe she just gets me on some level that I can't quite figure out. I learned with Tami that men never quite figure out women. They are smarter. Not in any way you can register. They just are. But whatever the reason was, it was nice to have a friend. Tami would have been proud of me.

Harry slipped back into the hotel room about twenty minutes later. I sensed by the way he ignored me that something other than munching on a ham sandwich happened when he went to eat.

"Where'd you go?" I quizzed.

"Downstairs."

"Bullshit," I responded quickly, letting him know he was a lousy liar.

Harry pulled open the doors to the balcony. He took a deep breath of the salt air and said, "Went to the jail. Check on that little punk, Jim, and his wife. That woman has a mouth like a sailor."

"You talked to them?" I asked, surprised.

"Yes, I spoke to them. Well, I didn't much talk to her. She called me a few obscene names so I wished her well and said goodbye. My God, if my daughter ever spoke like that..." Harry shook his head. "But I spoke with him."

Harry had my attention. Damn, this guy was like a feral cat with a cornered rat. He wanted to bat it around before killing it.

"He begged me to talk to you. About not pressing charges. He's got a lawyer but they won't let him out of jail. He begged me not to leave him here on this island to rot in a cell," Harry stated.

I couldn't tell if Harry was laying this on me to elicit sympathy for the guy or if his tone was derogatory.

"He kept pronouncing his deep regret. He's sorry. He's sorry. He's so sorry. Said he never meant to kill you. Just teach you a lesson."

Granted, I'm not a man who learns anything the easy way, but I pretty much understood the depth of his unhappiness the first time the board smacked me upside the head.

"What did you say to him?" I asked almost reluctantly, attempting to suss out where Harry stood in this sticky mess now that he'd had a face-to-face with the enemy.

Harry scrunched his lips tightly and shook his head. "Lying little bastard. Didn't believe a single word of it."

Harry was nothing if not consistent.

"I told him that if he didn't mean to kill you the beating would have stopped before he dragged you into the water and left you there to drown."

Harry then announced that he was going to make sure that Jim and his wife were prosecuted for attempted murder.

"You don't think he was being even the slightest bit honest with you?" I half-asked, half-stated, knowing that even I, self-proclaimed heartless jerk, would feel some remorse if I had done this to someone else.

Again, Harry scowled and shook his head as he sniffed up a breath. "Yeah, I think he really wanted me to try and convince you not to press charges. And for about a second I was feeling a little bad for the bastard. But the more he rattled on about how sorry he was, his fear of being imprisoned on this island, and what could possibly happen to him, it dawned on me. Not a single time during his entire speech did he once mention his wife. Never tried to lie and say she didn't know what was going to happen to you. Never asked me to talk to the Constable about reducing the charges against her, because after all, you DID try and sleep with her. Never asked me to contact anyone for her." Harry took a pause and frowned, "Hell. Even you would do that."

I leaned back on the bed with a smile and gave him the finger.

"That's the thanks I get," Harry replied. "I thank my lucky stars that my daughter never fell in love with a creep like that. Actually made me realize that there are worse men in the world than you," he tossed off, before stepping out onto the balcony to watch some distant sail surfers, leaving me in the room with a huge grin on my face. Even though he had to coat it in an insult, that was Harry's way of acknowledging that my love for his daughter was far deeper than most men ever have for a woman. It bolstered my resolve that what I had planned for Harry was not only the right thing to do, it was a hell of a lot better thank-you than a box of chocolates and a note. He would be more content with either of those, but it was time to push him out of his comfort zone.

About ten minutes to nine that night, I again told Harry he was on my last nerve. And it wasn't a lie. He had been lecturing me about how I needed to take care of myself once I arrived back in Chicago. "I'm telling you now, you're not going to be completely healed for quite a while," he said, for what seemed like the hundredth time. That alone was enough to make me homicidal. But I had other plans. For Harry. And they didn't include me. I announced I was taking a walk. Harry rapidly and thoroughly forbade it. The doctor had not okayed me moving around. I was still mending. I could rip open my stitches. The more Harry spit out the list of reasons why I was not to leave the room, the easier this facade became. I announced that I was out of there. I needed to get out, away from Harry, away from this room. "I'm sleeping on the beach tonight," I told him, finding a clean T-shirt and pulling it over my bandaged body.

Harry completely freaked out. Which, of course, was as I had figured. "This is possibly the dumbest thing that's ever come out of your mouth. And, Todd, that is saying a great deal! Even you can't be that stupid," Harry ranted, seemingly unaware that the more he continued the monotonous lecture, the more he sealed the deal. Even if I didn't have ulterior motives, sitting with Harry for another night was more than I was psychologically capable of. He had given me a headache. Or maybe it was the Vicodin and scotch I mixed. Whichever. I didn't think my brain would ever stop throbbing with Harry's whining voice surging through it like an over-amped electrical charge. My gray matter was like a moth fluttering into one of those plug-in bug killers.

ZZZZZZZtttttt!!!

"You are never going to heal," Harry screamed at me, as I slammed the door to the room behind me.

No, Harry, probably not. So you first.

As I made it to the lobby, I witnessed a woman enter. The proud stride, the bouncing hair, a skirt that flowed, a blouse that clung. I knew immediately who she was. When I explained my scheme to Gabriel, I wasn't sure if he was ready to applaud me or walk away. If I wasn't in such bad shape and didn't have a perception of the Constable's dubious ethics from watching Harry work him, I would suspect he would have told me to make my own plans. I explained why we had come to the resort, playing the sympathy card early in the game. Plus, Kat advised me that plying Gabriel with liquor would up my odds of keeping him around through my sorry tale.

Harry needed to get laid. I spelled out the many reasons for Gabriel as the whiskey mellowed him, and he cozied into the cane back chair. My guess was it had been about two decades since Harry had twisted in the sheets with a woman. I couldn't be one hundred percent positive about that, but I probably wasn't off by too many years. And I was absolutely sure that he hadn't dipped his wick since Clinton had been in the White House. And with less frequency than Haley's Comet.

If Harry had even a whiff of suspicion that I was procuring him a hooker, it would result in another terrifying meltdown of Chernobyl magnitude. He was an usher at church, after all. I wouldn't have to worry about him flying home, he would try to swim back to America in a purifying ocean re-baptism. And I wasn't in any shape to be chasing him down. So I needed a woman who had half a brain and was a mistress of seduction. Because an anvil would have to fall on Harry. He was so out of touch with the rules of sexual seduction, short of the woman flinging herself on the bed and throwing her legs in the air, Harry wouldn't get it. And even then I feared he'd assume she was having a seizure and call 911.

The woman would also have to be over forty. Harry wouldn't give a young woman a second look. No fool, Harry would be keenly aware of who was out of his league. Besides, she would remind him of his daughter and that would kill any romance well before the bed slats started squeaking. I knew I was seeking something rare, but I needed an attractive woman of a certain age, with a sense of class and charm, who could take an out of practice, old schooler who had long forgotten the rules of the road, grease his axles, and rock his fucking chassis until he was humming like a classic T-bird cruising route 66.

Gabriel nodded at me without a word. "Oh, and once she gets him into bed," I continued, "I want this broad to be a complete and utter freak."

That got a visible rise out of the Constable. "Remind Harry of what he's been missing all these years," I added with a smile.

"Regina," was all he said. I took a stab that if there were a call girl operation on the island, the Constable had his fingers in it, at least financially.

After watching Regina enter the lobby, striding right past me in the same chair I had sat in earlier that day talking to Gabriel, I knew she was physically everything I had described. Hell, if Harry wouldn't bed her, even in my shattered state I'd give it a whirl. Now I had to hope that she could work some island voodoo on Harry and turn him into a sexual zombie. I wanted a door opened to Harry that had been locked tight for far too long. I couldn't give him much, but this was something I knew with all my being was necessary if Harry was to survive without Tami in his life. He had to be willing to let a woman in and accept her love. And her freaky-deeky. The power of a great lay is amazing medicine to any man. And, I would assume, to many women. But for someone who has exorcised that gigantic piece of being human from his life, awesome sex can be a real miracle.

The first time Tami and I had made love, she taught me in one night what it was to be a real man. I hoped Regina would remind Harry that he was one.

Harry came down for dinner, making eye contact with no one and carrying a paperback book he had bought in the gift shop. Some mystery series he buried himself in. Regina was going to have to get Harry to surrender the novel, which was no easy trick. Too embarrassed to so much as greet anyone, he had long since stopped looking at people after I revealed that all the guests thought we were buggering each other.

After Harry was seated, Regina came in from the lobby bathroom. Her gait was so incredibly sexy it demanded that every man within eyeshot turn and pay attention. This was a woman who moved with a reason. She was on a mission.

I'd like to say that I didn't spy on them. No, I wouldn't like to say that at all; I had to know that at the very least she got him to put down the damn book. From a corner near the entrance to the restaurant, I watched Regina work her alchemy. This broad was a hottie. My guess, she was a well preserved forty-five. She pointed out Harry's book and began talking about it. Harry was shy but chatted with her. Every time he looked as if he were going back to the book, she effortlessly volleyed something else into the conversation. Harry was confused by this kind of attention from a woman; it bewildered him. And a bewildered Harry is a suspicious Harry. But this woman was gifted. I guess after years of seducing men, she had amassed an immeasurable bag of tricks. And she just might have to empty it to get Harry upstairs.

I took great interest, and at least a selfish delight, in watching Harry interact with a woman. I had never witnessed it before. And I would hazard a guess that Tami hadn't either. This was a different Harry, warmer, even a bit jovial. He may not have dated in a ridiculously long time, but there was a subtle charm to the weasel. It didn't hurt that the woman was a sure thing, but I could see that my gut feeling was dead on. Harry craved human contact. More accurately, female contact.

Regina coyly suggested she join Harry at his table. Harry froze in his chair for an awkward moment, then nearly knocked his water glass to the floor he was so fidgety flustered as he cleared a space across the table from himself for Regina to sit. He actually stood up and held the chair for her. Harry, you old, saggy-assed, balding fox, you. I kept trying to peek around the corner unnoticed, but there was no vantage point for me to hang out and see how Regina coaxed her way upstairs. But I would have paid another three Ben Franklins for her to clue me in the morning after.

If there was a morning after. Dinner is one thing. Getting naked with this woman was still a long road to travel for Harry.

I had to find someplace to hang for the night. Normally I'd go straight to a club or bar and put a full court press on whichever chick I sensed was in need. Kill two birds with one stone. I'd get laid and then crash in her bed for the night. But that night I didn't have a shot in hell of luring a woman up to her room. As banged up as I was, I didn't even qualify for pity sex. I shot back upstairs to get my Vicoden. If my ass was going to be married to a lounge chair for the night, I would need something to kill the pain. A sliver of a smile crossed my lips as I wondered who would be more achy by morning, Harry or myself.

I was hoping it was Harry.

Sitting out on the pool deck, I stared up at the honeymoon suite. The lights were still off. Over an hour had passed. I knew Harry and Regina had to be done eating. What was taking so long? A million scenarios danced in my Vicoden-addled mind. Maybe she failed. Maybe she took Harry somewhere else. Maybe they were still talking, Harry stalling, searching for a polite way to end the night. Maybe someone recognized her and blew my whole plan straight to hell. Maybe I was just being impatient. But I wanted to know that my effort did not go unrewarded. I had no 'Plan B'.

Finally, the lights came on in our honeymoon suite just before ten. If that son of a bitch is in there alone, I thought, I'm going to drag my ass back upstairs, kick him downstairs, and tell him to find that hooker and get my money back.

The balcony door slid open. Harry stepped out. Alone.

"Dammit," I muttered out under my breath. Perhaps Regina wasn't as capable as I had assumed. Harry probably freaked out when she touched his hand or sidled up a little too close. I imagined him dashing from the table in a flurry of fear, leaving the startled Regina sitting there, as he sprinted for the elevators and the safety of the room where he figured I'd be waiting.

But then Regina stepped out behind Harry into the night air.

Yes! Yes, yes, yes! I wanted to jump up and thrust my arms into the air in victory. But I stayed huddled in the darkness, peering up.

I have to say that as the sea breeze ruffled Regina's dress, from my point of view, this woman resembled photographs my old man had of Rita Hayworth. If that didn't appeal to Harry, nobody would. They stood close to each other and stared out at the ocean as it crashed onto the beach. They chatted and laughed. I sensed Harry's nervousness, which he gallantly strived to hide. But who wouldn't be nervous if it was your first time at the plate in two decades?

This woman was worth every penny. Enjoy, Harry. Enjoy.

SWEET DREAMS

I'd like to say that sleep came easy once I had done a good deed, albeit not one that would never earn me cloudspace near St. Peter. But I was attempting to snooze on a deck chair. With broken ribs. And without being drunk. Hell, I'd like to say I slept at all. But I didn't. I dozed throughout the night but never actually succumbed to real sleep.

Every time I passed from this consciousness to the other, Tami appeared. I'm not a man who remembers dreams. Ever. If my recollection is correct, the last dream I can recall was a nightmare when I was six. Right after my parents split up, which unfortunately didn't stick. I was living in a shit hole apartment with my Mom. And when I ran into her, she told me to go back to bed. Dreams couldn't hurt me.

Maybe they couldn't but seeing Tami again it simultaneously alarmed and comforted me. The vividness of the dream, the exquisitely textured detail, caused me to feel that I had stepped into an alternate life. Even if it was in my head. And since I would doze and wake, I had only fractured pieces which I couldn't add up to much. They were disjoined fragments of a puzzle. A life together we would never have. A house. Kids. The boy was the spitting image of me. My head on his little body. And in every dream, I could hear Tami laugh. I wanted to wrap myself in that laughter and have it hug my body and keep me strong. It was so unbelievably real.

Every time I woke, I would take a few deep breaths, reposition myself more comfortably, and wait to doze off again. And each time she was there. We danced together in one, were on a sailboat in another. There, Tami actually knew how to sail. Something I had no idea if she knew how to do or not. I never much liked boats of any kind. But in the dream I was right beside her, completely at ease on the water, one arm around her waist.

I must have woken and fallen back into semiconsciousness at least six times during the night. She waited for me each time. It was the best night sleep I ever had not sleeping. If I could only be with this woman in dreams, I would take it. Knowing that Tami would be there when I shut my eyes ebbed the feelings of rage and loss.

Sometime around dawn, Tami told me she had to go. She was in the house, packing for a trip, frazzled that it had come up so suddenly. I never asked her where she was going. I seemed to accept that she had to go. As she folded clothes into a suitcase and shut it, she looked up at me and asked, "So what are you going to do now?"

I stood there in the bedroom, our dream bedroom, and blinked. I didn't understand the perimeters of the question. I had no answer. What was I going to do? I was completely clueless. Seeing how lost I was, she smiled. "Don't be mad," she said. When I asked her at what, she giggled that laugh that always told me I was being dense. It was her polite way of saying, 'figure it out.' But I couldn't. I just stood there, knowing I didn't want her to leave but unable to express that to her.

Tami moved to me, taking my hand. She kissed me deeply as I slid my arms around her, climbing into the kiss with everything I had. I was not going to let her go. And she seemed not to want to leave either. We collapsed onto the bed and continued to kiss, our hands searching one another's bodies. I opened her blouse and buried my head against her chest. The passion was fiery and complete.

I made love to my wife.

Throughout the aftermath of this crushing tragedy, this was the best moment. It may not have been real, but it was mine.

As I woke, the morning sun was beginning to cast angled shadows over the pool deck. Early morning swimmers were repetitiously freestyling their way back and forth through the water. Achily I sat up, reaching into my pocket for the Vicodin. It wasn't there. My hands shot to my shorts, but the bottle wasn't there either. Shit. Patting myself down, I couldn't locate my survival pills.

"Looking for these," Harry said from behind me, causing me to turn...painfully to see him rocking the pill bottle between his fingers.

"Goddamn, Harry, give me two of those little bundles of joy and get me a glass of water."

Harry popped open the bottle and dropped two into my hand. He searched for a glass, finally stopping a waiter changing the linens on the patio table and bothered him for water, pointing over in my direction.

Harry pulled over a lounge chair next to mine and sat down. Examining his face, I sought out any signs of sexual bliss. But Harry looked like the same old, squinty faced, unhappy man that I had barked at the previous night before leaving the hotel suite.

As the waiter retrieved me a glass of water, I popped the two pills into my mouth and washed them down. Come on, fellas, work your magic, my entire body hurts like it had been buzz sawed.

Averting my eyes, I tossed off, "So, how was your night?" with enough chilled snarkiness, hoping he wouldn't assume I had anything to do with Regina and that she was a forgone conclusion.

Harry squirmed in the chair as if his old body hurt all over. I turned away quickly so he wouldn't see the juvenile grin on my face that came and went, and then returned to work on sustaining my faux-pissiness. Harry turned to me, slipping his dark glasses further down his nose so he could stare at me eye to eye. And in those eyes, something had changed. Hot damn, there it was, twinkling in those bloodshot orbs. This son-of-a-bitch got some! I wanted to let out a humungous war whoop, but not only would that have divulged my master scheme, it probably would have blown out all my stitches and left me curled over on the pool deck, screaming out in unearthly pain, as he let me bleed to death. Come to think of it, it might be worth it.

"I want the truth," Harry stated, no leeway in his voice, "did you have anything to do with that last night?"

"With what?" I asked blankly. "What are you talking about? What happened?"

As I've mentioned, if I have any gift, it's looking completely stupid at any desired moment. And this was the instant to look as vague and innocent as I could possibly muster without sending it over the top. I leaned into Harry, my eyes wide with the desire for information. My mouth hung slightly open as if awaiting a surprise. Being as big as I am, that only makes me appear even more lummoxical.

Harry shook his head. "Nothing," he said, sliding his sunglasses back up his schnozz, and turning away from me.

"Nothing?! What the hell is that, Harry? Something happened?"

"You need to learn to mind your own business," Harry muttered, sitting back in the chair, allowing the sunshine to hit his ray-deprived body.

"Coming from you, Harry, that is a joke. Besides, you brought it up."

"Why did you sleep out here last night?" he asked, still suspicious.

"Because you make me crazy, and this is where I fell asleep."

Again, Harry shook his head. "I'm going to take a little nap," he stated.

"Then I'm going back up to the room," I said, attempting to pull my big butt from the chair and stand.

"No," he blurted out, grabbing my arm.

I fired him a look but Harry turned away, not wanting to make eye contact.

"The room is a mess. Let the maid clean it up first," he said more evenly, as if that would quell any inquiry.

"What did you do up there, old man? Please don't tell me you got drunk again last night and acted like an asshole. Is someone else and his friends going to kick my ass?"

"Nothing happened. Nothing like that," he let slip.

"Ahhhh," I said in my best, albeit pathetic, Charlie Chan impersonation, "then something happened, Mr. Everett. And you are going to tell me what it is."

Harry stared straight ahead for a long time. But I wasn't going to let him wriggle out of the bowl that easily. So I stared, waiting, not going anywhere until I got details. I wanted to hear from Harry's mouth that he had done the deed, and that my money was well spent on a little sexual healing.

I already had the answer to both those questions. Harry wanted to hide it, but I could tell it was the night of his life. Or at least the best night he had since disco was king. His posture in the chair alone was more regal, less frumpy. He sat up like a man. Harry had forgotten how to be a man. His title was 'father' and that was the role he had assumed for way too long, sublimating the other aspects of his life so he could become an all-star of parenthood. And he had. If there were a hall of fame for raising children, they would dedicate a wing to Harry. The roles we play often overtake our lives. We become single faceted. Idiot savants. I should know.

Harry, the man, was reanimated. Awakened from his slumber by a kiss from Princess Charming. And if my guess was accurate, it was a kiss with a little tongue action involved. As he lay in bed with Regina, I imagined him with his little woody tenting up the sheet, screaming at the top of his lungs like Dr. Frankenstein, "It's alive! My God, it's alive!!!"

There's no mystery to sex. Relationships are a mystery, but sex is easy. We like to believe sex is mysterious and elusive because of the puritanical fear of getting naked with another body. Sex is base, animalistic. And as humans we're expected to be above all of that. Well, welcome to being a Homo sapien. Lord of the animal kingdom. We may not drag our knuckles on the ground anymore, but that's certainly no requirement for getting your horns trimmed. God bless mankind!

Harry still didn't turn to me as he began talking. If he would have looked at me through this confession, he would have either clammed up swiftly or burst into flames. I would never have gotten him speaking again. He began by saying he met a woman at dinner. I knew if I got excited or ribbed him in any way, he would have withered back into his shell. I sat back and let him talk, not making eye contact with him either. This was his confession and I shouldn't know who was in the booth telling me their sins.

He met this woman and she joined him for dinner. She was beautiful and had read the series of books that he was reading at dinner.

No she didn't, Harry. I clued the Constable in that when you went to dinner you would take your mystery novel. You've read it at every meal you've had on the island. Even the ones you shared with me.

They discussed the books and music they liked. Harry didn't know any modern music really, he was stuck back in that hazy area when Sinatra was morphing into Bob Dylan. When Tony Bennett was being replaced by the Beatles. But she knew all kinds of music, even though she was "younger, much younger," he said. And then Harry added proudly, "It was the most interesting adult conversation I've had in a long, long time."

I guess talking to me was neither scintillating nor adult.

After dinner she came up to the room.

"I didn't want to go up because I didn't know if you would come back or not. But she said she would leave if you did. She wanted to see the view from the balcony. She's not staying at our hotel," Harry continued. "I had one drink. One. There's nothing wrong with having a nightcap on the balcony with a friend."

Friend? I like that. I made a few of those at the resort too. And dare I say one real one.

Harry was far too shy to say he was on the balcony with a gorgeous woman, whether or not she liked to read. That would sully the memory he was creating for me. And I dug that he was being romantic and sort of dewy. That side of him was a rarity to me, so I enjoyed it when it snuck out of its turtle shell and peeked its little head around.

"I didn't want it to go any further but this woman, she, well, I was really comfortable with her. She was so sweet. Here on vacation. From Florida," Harry relayed, a generous smile on his lips, "And well, after we had our drink, we went back into the room. I wanted to sit on the sofa but she moved over to the bed."

Harry turned to me. "That's a sign, isn't it?"

"Pretty much," I responded, not wanting to interrupt the flow.

"Yeah. I thought so. It has been a while. I'm not a young man any more. A little out of touch with all of this...dating stuff."

Dating. So that's what you kids call it these days.

"She patted the bed for me to come and sit next to her. I didn't want to be rude."

And then Harry stopped talking. I almost blurted out that he wasn't shutting me out now that he was closing in on the nitty gritty. The dirty talk I paid for. I wanted a few sweaty details. Did she dance naked above him? Grab the ceiling fan and swing around? Did she climb on his face and command him to lick? But when I glanced over at him I could tell it wasn't that he wasn't holding back, he was reliving. He was back in the moment. Raise the Bismarck.

Regina was a pro. She knew what she came for and how to make that happen. I didn't press Harry anymore. And I was actually happy for the weasel. He'd rediscovered a piece of himself that he had buried out of goodness. Out of deference to his wife and to raising his daughter. I knew that I could never have done that, which made me respect it that much more. I'm not a total heartless bastard; I just behave that way most of the time.

"So it was a good night, huh?" I asked, flowering it up a little, so Harry would know I was not trying to get too personal.

"It was a good night four times," he announced, without even an ounce of bravado.

Damn, Harry, you horny, little pitbull. Four times! Guess there was a lot of sperm built up in there waiting for the dam to break. They may have been past their expiration date, but that doesn't mean those squiggly tailed, little suckers can't still swim.

"I remember..." he stumbled with his thoughts, then tried a different tack. "This was different. This was," Harry paused, selecting his vocabulary carefully, "ferocious."

I couldn't help but turn and fire him a look. Damn! I actually felt a twinge of jealousy. I tried to remain calm, though I really felt like standing up and high fiving the old bastard.

"Vacations. People are freer. More open," I added.

Especially if they're professionals paid to get their groove on.

"I had forgotten what it was like to have a woman sleep in my arms," Harry said, a hint of regret and nostalgia in his voice.

"Yeah," I muttered, my mind going to Tami and my dream.

I wondered how she would have reacted if she knew I had bought her father a hooker. That he made love all night. Would she suddenly have seen her father as a man, or would she have blanched at the thought? Tami wasn't here to judge. She lived in my head. Visiting only in my dreams. And I can't answer to dreams. My methods may not be the most upstanding, but seeing the expression of content manhood on Harry's face as he sat in that lounge chair catching rays, told me I had done awesome. Fuck right or wrong. That had shot out the window a week earlier.

I muscled my body from the chair, wincing, the Vicoden still short of kicking in. I looked down at Harry, and without a shred of cynicism I said, "You're my hero, dude."

As I walked away, I could see Harry sit up proudly in the chair. An aura of masculinity replaced the nebulous neutered vibe he had going on before. Right on, Harry. When he got back to the States, there was hope for him. Watch out women of Chicago, Harry's coming back.

The maid gave me a knowing look as she left the room. Those sheets must have been super funky. She's probably seen worse, but hell, this was a sixty-something year old guy getting nasty. Unfortunately, she probably thought he had been doing the deed with me.

After I showered, which was fairly painless with the drugs finally pulsing through my veins, I dried off and stared at myself in the mirror. I was going to have a few scars. The one across my nose would be tiny, the one above my eye would be camouflaged by my eyebrow, the one on the back of my head would go unseen forever --- God willing I didn't get my grandfather's hairline. But the one down my side and to my stomach would be a daily souvenir of my trip to St. Carlos. I was already working on a better story about how it happened, one that was sure to get me laid. The purple around my eyes was already fading, the swelling receding enough that you could actually see my eyes. My face was starting to look like my face again. Even my head had nine o'clock shadow as my hair began to grow back. In another couple weeks I would be back to resembling the photo on my driver's license.

Harry returned to the room while I was dressing. I had a hard time getting the shirt on over my head, and he assisted.

"Where are your shoes?" Harry asked, searching the room.

I waved him off. "I'm not an invalid for Christsake," I said, digging my flip-flops out from under the bed.

Harry moved over to his suitcase and unlocked it. Pulling out Tami's canister from the pile of clothes, Harry held it up. For a moment, he didn't speak.

"Should we?" he finally questioned.

I sat down on the bed, actually tired from wrestling my clothes onto my stitched, stapled, and bruised body. I would never again take for granted lifting my arms over my head and pulling on a T-shirt. Nor would I take for granted lifting my arms over my head and trying to pull it off. Which is what got me in this predicament in the first place.

"You gotta promise me you will not change your mind. I am not up for a romp through the jungle only to have you back out again. Physically, I'm in no shape to kick your ass..." I paused, feeling he needed to hear a little truth from me, "And emotionally, I just couldn't deal with it. Not today."

Harry's eyes wrapped around me. I sensed his response before he spoke.

"It's time to let Tami go," Harry said carefully but with more assurance in his voice than ever before. "She needs to be at peace."

"Yeah, she does. I could use a dose of it too," I muttered as I stood up, kicking off my flip-flops and scooting over to the boots I had bought the first time we took Tami's ashes to the beach. Looking Harry dead in the eyes, I added, "Don't let me fall in that jungle, Harry, because if I end up face down in a pile of bird guano, I don't care how much pain I'm in, I'm going to drown your ass in that ocean."

Dressed again in our matching jungle garb - which made it loads of fun to cross through the resort lobby - Tomas drove us back to the end of the block where the road ended and the jungle started. Harry and Tomas both had to assist me from the taxi. Not a good sign for what lay ahead. Harry still wasn't secure enough to let me hold the canister, but in the shape I was in that was all the better. I needed both hands to pull my way through all the vines and branches.

Staying right by my side, Harry kept me moving through the overgrowth. I was hoping the Vicodin would keep this excursion as painless as possible. No such luck. Every time I stumbled or lost my balance, I felt every staple in my stomach pull and the skin rip. That hike had been no picnic the first time. But in the shape I was in this time, the haul was just short of suicidal.

The most dangerous element of this insane expedition was that I had Harry assisting me every step of the way. Harry had a hard enough time keeping his own footing, bitching and moaning as much on this attempt to cross the tangle of trees and vines as he had on the first. And with every step I took, he told me where to take my next. How to place my foot. Watch out for the limb. Careful with that vine there. Don't step on the leaf pile just in case it was a snake nest. Harry was becoming the father I never wanted. If I had only thought to bring earplugs. And perhaps a flare gun, which may have come in handy if I fell on Harry or needed to shoot him.

By the time we made it to the clearing on the other side, I was just short of tears. A couple tumbles that had sent me into trees really did the trick. It hurt twice as much as I thought it would and was twice as fucked logistically even with the medication steaming in my pipes. All it did was slow the pain impulses to my brain, which were firing so fast and furiously it didn't matter. The thud was dull, but it was still a thud.

I leaned against a tree and stared out. The view was so incredible I almost forgot my own physical suffering. A vista without parallel, Tami's secret place is where I want my own ashes spread when I pass on. Not only to be with the only woman I will ever love, but because if I were to be released into the wind there, it would bring me peace. I remember joking with Tami that if I died before her, I too wanted to be cremated. Only I was leaving a list of people I didn't like, and I wanted her to throw handfuls of me in their faces.

She never found that as funny as I thought it was.

But since visiting that unequaled beauty, I knew that it was where I would rest once I passed. And spend eternity mingled with Tami.

"Are you all right?" Harry asked, as I leaned up against the tree, allowing the pain to subside.

"Dandy, Harry. We couldn't have let Tami go the first time, you had to wait until I'm half-broken and then march my ass back through the jungle. Who the hell are you, the Viet

Cong?"

Harry slid his body against my good side and helped me walk through the high grass that lead to the sand and then out to the calling ocean.

"Where should we do this?" he asked as I huffed and puffed.

I pointed to a spot where the high grass tangled with the sand. There, the ocean's surge tickled its froth as high up on the beach as it could reach. Harry nodded. Sensing we were both feeling the same thing, not another word passed between us. There was an olio of sadness, excitement, and finality. The moment was here.

I unlaced the boots and wrestled off my socks, allowing the ocean to rush over my toes, burying them in the warm sand. I hadn't spent a lot of time in the ocean since arriving on the island, other than being left there to die, and having the sea water dance around my toes was a sensation I will never forget. But I didn't want to forget anything about this moment. As difficult as it was, letting Tami go was what we had to do, and I wanted to remember the moment for the rest of my life.

Harry's tired eyes held onto the canister, a panorama of emotions washing across his face. Each one more crushing than the next. Each one cutting deeply. Without a doubt, freeing Tami to this island was the hardest thing Harry would do for the rest of his life. He had suffered through so much death. His wife's. His only daughter's. I don't know how one survives that much loss. I proved incapable of dealing with half of it. It sets deep shadows on your soul. I looked away, knowing that his anguish would become mine very quickly, and I was already struggling to keep mine in check.

Harry held out the canister to me. My eyes met his. Tears in both.

"She loved you," Harry said, directly and with admiration.

This was the disease that Harry had struggled with since Tami and I met. That she and I were in love. Even while we were making plans to be married, he never acknowledged the love that existed between us. As if he could prevent it if he kept denying its existence. And here he was stating it out loud. So that I would recognize he was not only aware of that intense bond that Tami and I shared, but that he had come to accept it.

I couldn't take the canister from him. I grit my teeth hard in a vain attempt to rein in the throbbing emotions I grappled with, not wanting to sink into the wet sand and sob. I couldn't take the moment from Harry. Tami had been mine for almost a year. The greatest and yet the worst year of my life. She had been his for twenty-four years.

"She loved you long before she loved me, Harry," were the only words I could get out before I started to cry. I balled hard, feeling my bones aching each time my body heaved. But the sharp pain only intensified the fervent blaze in my heart.

Harry stepped toward me, struggling to put his arm around my shoulder. He held out the canister.

"Open it."

I reached out and popped the lock holding the canister closed. Nodding at me, Harry silently directed me to remove the lid. Following his order, I pulled it off, revealing the thick powder inside. Both of us took in the ashy dust, trying to reconcile it with our memory of Tami. This was her. Reduced to cinders. It made it easier to let her go. She was already gone to us. This was just a formality, a final wish granted.

I nodded my head and Harry took the canister and began shaking it. The heavier pieces tumbled onto the sand and into the ocean, the dusty powder caught the breeze and blew back, covering us in a gray sheen of ash.

"She just can't let go, can she?" Harry remarked wryly, causing us both to laugh, as he tried to wipe the residue off of himself.

Harry and I bathed in the ocean water, cleaning the ashes off our faces and arms, letting them mix with the surf and be carried away to an awaiting ocean that welcomed her.

"I love you, Tami," I said under my breath, wiping the dust off my chest.

"Always, honey, always," Harry almost whispered, finishing my thought.

Standing in the water, Harry and I stared out, knowing that Tami was free from us. Now in every way. I took the canister and threw it out into the surf to let it be carried out to sea. Tami's tomb was free to become the home for a crab or tiny fish. Perhaps protect them from being eaten by a larger predator.

I could have stood there forever, staring out at that gorgeous site, allowing myself to become part of it. But a family emerged from the jungle, locals who knew the secret of this amazing island oasis. The children laughed as they ran, their tiny feet leaving pale dents in the white sand. They rushed around Harry and me, giggling joyously as they fell into the surf, splashing and swimming.

I smiled at Harry.

"Time to go."

He turned and started out of the water. Once he got to dry sand, he waited for me. I joined him as the children's parents greeted us.

"It's special here," the father said to us in his lilting island accent.

"More than you know," I said. "Have fun."

Harry put his arm around my waist and helped me back through the high grass to the far edge of the jungle we had to cross.

"Are you ready for this?" he asked.

"I've survived worse," I responded.

As we started into the overgrowth, Harry took a deep breath and looked at me. "You know, I like you a lot more now that you're not marrying my daughter," he said.

I laughed so hard I almost peed down my leg.

HOME FIRES

Sleep was at a premium. I had swallowed the last of the Vicodin earlier in the day and figured I was strong enough to make it without them. But the incision up my side had begun to itch terribly as it healed, and I still suffered from a dull headache. Of course there was always scotch. But it was two in the morning and I had a hard time imagining myself sitting in the dark sipping from a little bottle. Even a drunk such as myself has a line he doesn't like to cross. Makes me feel superior to the other miserable sots who are doing exactly that.

But something else concerned me, something I couldn't dispel. The next day was our last full day on St. Carlos. And there was this gnawing, clinging awareness that I didn't have a clue as to what I would be walking into once I got home. I had gone down there to escape my life, spend ten days getting drunk. But certain events and people bludgeoned my plan all to hell. Life never works out like you think it will.

In my abstinence, I had far too much time to think. To assess. That's the bitch of being sober and cognizant, you are constantly living in your head. A dangerous place for me to exist. We try and create logic out of living, which is specious if not downright insane. If I had stayed drunk, I would have staggered back onto that plane without having put any energy into appraising the worth of my lot. Maybe somewhere over Arkansas it would have hit me that I was returning to a physical and psychological black hole. But short of throwing open an emergency door and being sucked out in mid-flight, there would be little I could do about it.

Sure, there was a job to return to. There were people who cared about me and certainly many who cared about Tami. I was sure there were bills stuffed into the mail box that needed to be paid, and a dining room table piled with wedding gifts that I needed to either return, toss away, or donate to some charity. I could stay busy. Thoughtlessly so.

But the idea of stepping back into my condo, now filled with Tami's furniture, her mountains of clothes stuffed into my closet, her perfume sitting on the dresser in my bedroom, wafting with memories of our nights together making love, scared me to my core. I would rather have endured a thousand beatings like the one I'd received a couple nights before than return to a museum of what would never be. On a good day, I'm defensive if not retaliatory with my feelings. This homecoming would beat me up again. Daily.

How many times did I have to survive that? How many times could I?

At about 4:30 a.m., I climbed out of bed and tried to stretch. It hurt to reach too far in any direction, and I really didn't feel like popping the staples out of my side. I wanted to heal. Harry was snoring lightly, snuggled onto the sofa, wearing plaid pajamas. I would bet my last dollar that Harry hadn't slipped into those Martha Stewart-looking things when he was cuddled up with Regina. I pulled on a pair of pants and a long sleeved shirt and painfully bent over to tie the laces of my boots. I crept quietly out as Harry continued to saw logs.

Standing at the end of the street where it met the jungle, Tomas looked at me with concern and asked if I wanted him to stay. I patted his shoulder and tipped him another couple bucks. "I'll make it," I added. The sun wanted to break over the horizon but didn't quite have the angle, though it was light enough now to vaguely see where the hell I was.

Once in the jungle, it was another story. Even in the blazing sun, it was shadowy with pockets of complete darkness. But now I was walking almost blind. Carefully, I pulled my way along the trees, keeping one eye out for any night scavengers that would be returning to their burrows. Running into jungle creatures wasn't high on my priority list at any time. But on that morning, I wouldn't stand a chance against an opossum or whatever other gnarly creatures populated the island.

Forced to rest a few times on my trek through the claustrophobic canopy of vines and branches, my body ached from the wounds. Without the painkillers I was feeling every step. It may not have been the brightest idea I had had all week. Then again, I hadn't had but one or two that were anything more than half-baked since Tami died, so I could score this one right up there with the rest of the ridiculously fucked-up things I'd done. After pausing a third time to catch my breath and let my body rest, the only thought that kept me marching forward was that if I stopped, no one would find my body in the jungle until it was half-eaten by the local carnivores. That image didn't sit too well with me.

You'd think for as many times as I'd tromped though that stretch of terrain over the past week, we would have trampled down at least the outline of a trail. But that insidious vegetation seemed to grow before your eyes. Finally, though, I saw the light of morning peeking through the trees, and if I had thought I could stand up afterwards, I would have fallen to my knees and thanked the gods.

The sun was coming up on the other side of the island, casting long shadows over the ocean. I stood and stared out at the water that had swallowed Tami and made her one with the elements. I pulled off my boots and pushed my feet into the sand, snailing my way towards the shallows of the morning tide. It was the first time I had been at Tami's secret place alone, and I found it even more awesome at that time of the morning, with no sounds but those the island creates when she too is alone.

Sitting in the shallows, I struggled my shirt off over my head and tossed it back with my hiking shoes, safe from the gentle waters that rushed between my legs, covering my toes with soggy sand. I laid back and closed my eyes. I needed to be there. With Tami.

Like I've said, I've always been a believer that people don't change; they just become more of themselves. It takes a radical bolt of lightning to truly change the sum and substance of a man. Finding Tami resuscitated a joy in me that I didn't even know I possessed. Losing her just as abruptly was a horrendous jolt too. But it was more like sticking a fork in an electrical outlet; I stood there and shook, smoke rising from my charring skin, unable to let go, slowly smoldering to death.

One is an act of fate, the other one of sheer pointlessness. I could live with fate. But it was hard for me to live with senselessness. Mine or anyone else's.

Now I found myself walking the plank, heading into the predatory shoals of emptiness, never again holding in my arms what I had had for too short a time. Or holding instead the sword of drinking and reckless behavior that I certainly would fall on sooner rather than later.

A choice of not if I will die, but how.

The white ball of fire continued its ascent into the sky over me, and I could feel the subtle difference in the tide as it did. The way the waters moved around my body. Minnows danced around my toes, every so often brave enough to test them as breakfast. The water was now flooding my ears, making murky the sounds of this special place, except for the sound of the surf which only magnified into a bass profundo of power. Eventually the water would completely cover my body, and I would have to wriggle my way further up the sand to keep it from rolling me out with the tide.

Being alive and possessing a reason to be alive are different islands kept apart by rough waters. Waters I had no idea how to navigate. I could no longer piece together the shreds of my life. Who do you talk to when you don't have a goddamn clue as to why the hell you are alive? With the tough, bullheaded, bastard life I'd cultivated, everyone knew me as the man who could drink his way out of any problem. And I hardly desired for the people around me to start checking off all the wonderful justifications for my existence. I didn't need anyone lying to my face or becoming a cheering section for the 'choose life' campaign. Nor did I need to hear that age old chestnut about having my whole life ahead of me. Buck up, boy. You'll get through this. You know, even the kid that picked on you in grade school cries. The captain of the football team can't get a hard-on every time. Women who wouldn't give you the time of day sit home alone more Saturday nights than all of their friends.

I hate having these heart to hearts with myself. Self-reflection has always been an icky, creepy feeling. I never send myself an invitation to my own pity party. I grew aggravated with anyone who offered me condolence. Why the hell would I be any more tolerant of it when it came from within? All my life the cards fell where they fell. No complaints. I wasn't always happy about it, but I learned how to zig, I learned how to zag. Bottom line, I dealt. But for the first time in my life, I couldn't just muddle my way out of the deep, dark box I'd crawled into. Hard to deal when you don't know what you're dealing with.

As the day progressed, my skin turned reddish-brown from the island rays. I stared out at nothing on the horizon. There was no rescue boat coming to take me home. There was no throwing me a life buoy, buying a vowel, or catching a clue. It was a revelation for me to be lying there, seeing absolutely nada. And still stranger, an oozing feeling swelled up in me that this was the moment that would define the rest of my life.

Talk about scary.

From the well of my body, I bellowed at the sky. Every ounce of rage was bursting to be set free. But it was muffled by the water that covered my ears. I could feel the scream but not hear it. And when it was over, the dominant roar of the ocean dwarfed whatever power I had inside me. Why the hell would I go back to the life I had had before Tami? Or to a life without her? Yet I couldn't lay in that water forever.

I felt her before I saw her. She was there. As I opened my eyes, Tami stared down at me, her wedding dress heavy from the surf that had soaked the bottom.

"How many times do I have to save you?" she asked.

"Why didn't you let me drown?" I responded.

"Because saving you is a challenge, Todd," Tami answered, lying down next to me in the shallow water, "You don't make it easy."

Her answer made me grin. No, I don't make it easy. Even for her.

"Was it worth it? I'm suffering like a dog lost on the Interstate."

"Todd, I saved you twice. I can't do it again," she said, leaning up on one elbow in the surf so she could look right at me. "It was so easy for you to give me everything with your love. Why is it so hard for you to give any of it to yourself?"

I didn't have an answer for her. I judged my behavior, albeit most of it bad, as being about myself. My life was a long sentence of doing what I wanted. Isn't that giving to yourself? Making sure everything went my way. Most of my needs were remarkably base, but they always seemed to come first.

"That's not the same, honey," Tami stated, peering over at me with a sad look on her face.

"I didn't say anything," I answered her, fairly certain I hadn't spoken what was rattling around in my head.

Tami reached over and pushed me with a giggle that had always made me weak- kneed. "I know everything you're thinking, Todd," she continued, smiling. "I chose to be part of you after we met. That will never change. I can't share with you the life we planned, but I am a part of everything you experience. Every adventure you brave, every person you love, every breath, I am a part of it. Your laugh makes me smile, your pain brings me to tears."

Silenced by her message, I instinctively caressed her face, wanting to touch her. I needed to feel Tami again, still afraid that her words weren't true, that this moment would disappear and I would be alone again.

"Todd, when you give your soul to someone, you do not get it back when you die."

Tami sat up, climbing atop, straddling me. Her finger ran along the incision on my side, drawing her eyes up to mine as she looked down.

"I can't live life now except through you. Do you understand that? I'm giving you permission to live. So do that for me. Even if it is just for me. Do everything, everything, so I can feel it again through you."

She lied down on my body, hugging me.

I held her body against mine, closing my eyes. As the waves washed over us, Tami dissolved into me, until there was only her white dress lying on top. Sitting up, I realized her white dress was the ocean's foam that had rolled in with the tide. But it was clear to me now why she had to come to me. To save my ass for the third time. My life meant something because she meant something in my life. The kaleidoscope of experiences that would make up my future would each be colored by the prism she had given me, by loving me. Without me even realizing it, before she left me, Tami had designed my soul.

I pulled my big ass out of the surf and stripped out of my pants. I then ran out into the water and swam out as far as I could in the waves. There was no panic that I wouldn't be able to return. I knew I would. Knowing Tami was with me, I felt free again. If she was a part of every adventure I would have, I wanted her to have a full, fantastic life. I wanted her to experience everything, including love. Because she was the one that had taught me how to love.

And I would love her forever because of it.

I swam for the next couple of hours until I was completely exhausted. Pulling myself up onto the warm white sand, I fell asleep deeper than I had in the past week.

"Mister, you're not wearing any clothes," a little kid said to me with a wide, gap-toothed grin.

I sat up, shaking myself awake. Surrounding me were a gaggle of neighborhood boys all snickering at my nakedness. I signaled them all to turn around and wandered down the beach to collect my pants, shirt, and boots. But everything was gone.

"Very funny," I said, turning back around, but the kids were dashing off, waving my clothes as they disappeared into the jungle.

"Goddamn it," I muttered, wondering whether anyone would find me if I stayed put.

"You wanted an adventure..." I said to Tami as I trudged toward the trees, knowing I was going to have to traverse that jungle with my manhood swinging in the breeze and nothing under my feet.

I arrived back at the hotel, wearing a white cotton sheet that I had found on a backyard clothesline where the town backed up to the jungle. I snuck around the neighborhood in the sheet until a man hauling flowers to the other side of the island let me sit in the back of his truck. My feet were hacked to pieces and bleeding. Damn kids. Not that I wouldn't have done the same thing to some naked stranger when I was their age.

Harry was just short of panic. I had not woken him up, sneaking out, and he didn't have a clue where I had disappeared to. "Someone already tried to kill you once down here," Harry reminded me. "And that's even taking into consideration what stupid thing you might just do to yourself," he added. Now that he knew I was alive he was even more angry. Ranting on, he pointed out that it was now nearly evening and I "hadn't bothered to even call."

Sorry, Harry, I didn't have a cell phone stuffed up my ass for those just-in-case moments.

Harry had spent the day in the suite waiting for me. And trying to track down Regina. Luckily, he wasn't able to find her, and the hotel she'd mentioned she was staying at told Harry that she had checked out. A standard line to Johns in search of the hooker they had hired the night before, but what did Harry know.

I never wanted Harry to find Regina. Harry held an illusion of his night with her that shouldn't be compromised by reality. It would only cause him to rethink the dramatic alterations in his life, which he had previously been willing to travel. Nothing like a great lay to make you wonder about everything in your life. But these were vastly positive changes, a man reemerging from his cave, transformation from 'Daddy' to 'Who's Your Daddy?'

Harry assumed that Regina had returned to Florida and was quizzing me on how best to track her down. I stood in the shower allowing the water to wash away the salt that had dried on my body and the blood that had dried on my feet. As Harry hypothesized how he could reunite with the woman who revived his manhood, I gently suggested to him that he let go of the thought of reuniting with Regina. As I dried off, I told Harry that he would be better off discovering a woman closer to home, someone he could flatter with the attention he had once doted on his daughter. There were so many mature women who would climb over each other to find a man like Harry. Women who had been left by shit-heel husbands, forgotten by men, and who now felt invisible to the opposite sex. Harry would make them feel that they were the most important thing in the world. "You're a catch, Harry," I told him, "it's time you wake up to that fact."

Harry smiled. Little by little, the snail was sticking its head further out of its crusty, old shell. He may not cross the road in a blur, but he'll get there.

Harry graciously announced that he was taking me to dinner. I should have gotten him laid when Tami and I had first started dating. But if he wanted to pay for my meal, who was I to stop him? Besides, between being gone all day and coming off the Vicoden, I was ravenous.

Every meal I had eaten on the island, that didn't include Jello, I had taken at the resort, so I coaxed Harry into trying something new. I handed Tomas a healthy tip and stated, "I want you to take us somewhere off the beaten path. Somewhere we could sate a mean hunger and imbibe on a few spirits." Tomas gave me a knowing nod. "I know just the place, my friend."

My only trepidation was that we would run into Regina. Even worse, Regina on a 'date.' But escaping the resort in search of something a little more exotic was worth the gamble.

Tomas spun us around to the other side of the island and dropped us off at a dingy shack with a ripped screen door. Harry refused to crawl out of the taxi, demanding Tomas squire us back to civilization. But I gripped him by the arm and yanked him out.

Some guys just don't go easy.

"I thought you were starting to live a little, goddamn it," I poked, firing him a look that roughly translated into, "don't be a big wuss."

He took a deep breath and shut his eyes, following me in through the screen door. Guilt is such a beautiful thing.

"If I have diarrhea on the flight home, I am not going to be happy," was all Harry said, as he stood behind me, peering over my shoulder at the dining area which was a long room with tables smashed together to jam as many bodies into the place as possible. And with reason. The restaurant was packed. Whatever spices were bubbling in the back filled the room with a tangy effervescence that masked the sweaty heaviness of the humidity that also occupied the room.

A tall, attractive woman glowing from a thin coating of perspiration exited the kitchen, spotting us standing at the door. She raised her long arm in our direction.

"You two. Here," she said, her deep Caribbean accent tickling my ear over the din of the enthusiastic crowd and the Latin rhythms pulsing underneath from speakers in every corner of the room. We pushed through larger groups that were waiting and dodged the tables to make our way to where she waited for us. She gave Harry a big smile, pulling out a chair for him.

"You sit here, let the big man sit against the wall. I feel he has more enemies than you. He should never have his back to the crowd."

Harry slipped me a sliver of a grin. "You two must have met before," he added slyly, plopping into his chair.

Viola welcomed us to her restaurant. She was happy to have a slice of the tourist business. This regal, handsome woman explained that since she doesn't grease the palms of the cab drivers and hotel workers, they seldom bring her island visitors.

"You don't look like you're starving for business," I said.

She smiled, her hand landing on my shoulder. Each finger bore a one-of-a-kind, hand-crafted ring.

"I ain't never not busy," she stated proudly. "I treat my people right, and they repay the service by returning."

Listening to this woman, Harry sparked up. Dining in a funky, local hang was entirely alien to a man who ordered the same meal every single time he went out to eat. Chicken-fried steak. Happily, I could tell that wouldn't be on the menu. Harry would never have thought to wander off the resort property and take a chance on a local restaurant, but since I was with him, he didn't have to do the heavy lifting and could enjoy the ride. If it sucked, it was my fault. If it was great, he made the right decision.

The menu contained a list of Caribbean delicacies. Or so Viola told me. What the hell would I know about Caribbean delicacies, or anything about food, for that matter. Fish glazed in exotic sauces, pork smothered in homemade gravies, fowl garnished with local spices and fruits. From the tang floating from the kitchen, I wanted to sample everything. But spying plate after plate flying out of the kitchen with mountainous portions, it didn't look like I was going to go home hungry. Harry's eyes widened every time the tangy spices that doctored the air passed over him.

Viola sashayed herself back to our table and stood over us.

"Time to order, boys."

"You pick," I resounded, "Just make sure it goes well with whatever firewater you serve, and know that I haven't had a decent meal in days and am hungry as horse."

Her eyes narrowed as she smiled. "I know just what you need," she said with a tickle of a laugh.

Harry threw up his hands and to my shock added, "make it two."

Viola took the menus, as she walked past Harry. "Daring," she whispered, her hand stroking his neck as she passed him.

Before Harry and I could begin a conversation, the couple at the next table got up and began dancing. I don't know what provoked this unrestrained urge but no one else in the place seemed to be plussed by it. Just a typical evening at Viola's. The couple moving sensually together in the small space between the tables ballooned the already heady spirits of the restaurant. More couples followed, all jamming into the small aisles between the tables, swaying erogenously to the Latin rhythm that vibed through the restaurant.

Taking in the joyous spontaneity, this instinctive desire to express their feelings so artfully, almost religiously so, froze me. I realized that I was holding my breath so long I had to pant to regain it. Four older women at a table across the restaurant stood, and they too joined in the dance. I didn't know if all these people knew each other or just didn't give a good goddamn; it was what they felt like doing, an expression of thanks to Viola for supplying them with a great meal and an open environment.

As I glanced over at Harry, the flicker of the candle on the table added a symbolic fire to his eye as he perused all the dancers admiringly.

"Get up and dance," I said to him.

His eyes widened even more, and he shook his head. "Are you out of your mind?"

"You've known me long enough to know the answer to that, Harry."

I stood up.

"What are you doing?" Harry asked, his first reaction to reach out and try to pull me back to my seat.

"What Tami wants me to do," I replied, as I slipped around and began dancing with a couple at a table behind us.

Harry watched, still not ready to take the leap. But the smile on face said he understood what I was doing.

I danced until the music waned and the crowd applauded. Everyone went back to their tables with appreciative nods to all the other dancers. Slipping back into my seat, I used my napkin to wipe a glisten of sweat that had broken out on my forehead.

"You're going to rip those stitches right out of your body," Harry warned.

"I'll heal."

"We both will," Harry said, without an iota of cynicism.

I didn't need to respond. We would make it. It wouldn't be easy, but somehow we would find our footing and move forward. I had Tami keeping me together. And giving me permission to live as the man she was responsible for me becoming. Believing with all my heart that she was present in my soul, truly a part of me, unburdened me to live again. I still didn't believe that I would ever fall in love again, not in the massive, incredible orbit that I had when I met her. That breed of love is rare. I had it. Or, should I say, I have it. I possess what most people never hold even for a brief moment in their lives.

I am a lucky man.

Never in my life had I eaten food with such explosions of taste. Harry surprised himself by gorging on the chicken and fish drizzled with an amber glaze made from local fruit juices. Twice more through the meal, people got up and danced. I joined them both times, but was unsuccessful in luring Harry from his chair. He did participate though when the entire restaurant clapped to the beat of a local musician. I danced with a young woman, swinging her through the tables. She was graceful as a feather floating on an updraft, as we made our way around the restaurant and through the other dancers.

I was lost in this place where no one knew me, where I sensed no judgments. I could have danced away the night in that restaurant, elated to be part of something new. Even more, something completely foreign. Tami wished for me to have adventures to feel joy, so she too could feel it. And now I understood. She allowed me to open myself up, to actually be in a moment and realize the treasures that were right there in front of me. I never wanted to miss another opportunity because of my anger. I could not be sad any longer. Whatever rage I had locked inside me would be saved for when it was necessary, not spread out daily. Before Tami, I never understood what it was like to truly embrace a woman, that moment when your lips lock, when her supple body melds into yours with the steel of passion. Now I had to embrace life with the same notice and power. There was no more looking back. Tami was with me. Whatever was to come was out front, and I had to grab it with both hands.

Arriving back at the resort, Harry yawned, announcing that it was time for him to get some sleep. We were traveling back the next day, and it would be a busy one.

"One drink, my treat," I offered.

Before Harry could send up any kind of protest, I held up my hand, stopping him. "It's our last night here. You can accept one drink."

Acquiescing, Harry shrugged and signaled that he would follow.

The club was crowded, music pumping through the bodies on the dance floor. There were no seats at the bar - especially on Kat's end, but just at that moment a small table opened up in the middle of the room, and I pushed my body over and grabbed it.

"Kismet, Harry. Do you believe in fate?" I asked as we sat.

"I'm not sure. Too much has happened to me in the last week to even guess at that," he responded. "But a lot does happen that's strange."

Amen to that.

I cleared a path to the where Kat was toiling behind the bar. She gave me a knowing grin, two cohorts in crime. Focusing on her as she tipped bottles and drafted beers, it struck me that the most outlandish and unexpected surprise of everything that had occurred in my life lately was that it was women who had taken over and become my life guides. The greatest woman I had ever known instructed me on how to truly love, a language I could never speak until I held Tami in my arms. And now Kat had tutored me in trusting a friend. Females. Teaching me. Who the hell would have thought? Maybe it's not only fitting but oddly symmetrical. I'd lived my entire messy life on massive doses of testosterone, but it wasn't until I opened the door just a crack and allowed in a whiff of estrogen that my life truly changed. Anybody who knew me prior would say it was for the better. And fuck it, I'm man enough to admit it too.

"You look like you're doing better," Kat stated, setting the drinks on the bar top.

Setting cash near the drinks which she waved away, I added, "Minute by minute. Thanks again for helping me out."

"Which time," Kat beamed.

"You sound like Tami," I said before thinking.

Kat's demeanor wavered as if I were seeing her across burning asphalt. It didn't grow dark or weary as I expected but bloomed with greater empathy. Even though there were people waving money at her, Kat's eyes remained drilled on me.

"Are you still seeing her," she asked.

I reluctantly nodded.

"I think that's a good thing," Kat voiced over the din of the crowd.

"You don't think I'm crazy?"

"Of course I do. You're completely certifiable," Kat responded with a snicker, "But that doesn't make it any less powerful, Todd. You love her."

That I do. Forever.

Kat tilted her head and leaned over the bar, drawing me closer to her. "You've changed," she said softly.

I wanted to back away, to look into her face but something told me not to.

"You don't remember," she stated. "You and I met before. Eight years ago."

This caused me to back away. Holy mother of God, was she kidding? This could not be good.

Kat smiled. "Bloomington, Indiana. You were there for a training program or something like that, if I recall correctly."

My mind flipped back through calendar pages until I remembered being in Bloomington. Winter time. Cold as a bitch. It was my second job. Working group insurance sales for Met Life.

"I was a cocktail waitress at a club. Remember Hot Coals? You drank at one of my tables every night," Kat continued but still elicited nothing but a fuzzy gaze from me. Then she dropped a dirty bomb that sent shrapnel scattering through my memory.

"You and I had a thing."

I felt my heart plunged somewhere down near my gonads, hiding. 'Shit, shit, shit' was all that ran through my mind for what seemed like minutes until I could harness my thoughts and drag them back from the edge of the cliffs like a wild stallion running aimlessly towards his death. Vaguely, I remember having great sex with a very hot woman who worked in a club. I swore I had feelings for her, vowed to see her again, that we were meant to be, all in a perverted attempt to keep her coming back night after night while I was stuck in that town. I could never remember her name so I covered by always calling her 'sweetheart'. She bought my bullshit with no money down and a very low interest rate. I knew plain well that once I cut out of Indiana I'd never call her, much less see her again.

And just to prove myself right, I didn't.

My eyes widened as I searched for some excuse to make her believe I was never in Bloomington in my life. Didn't even know where it was on the map. But it was too late for that. And an apology seemed nearly a decade too late.

"I'm sorry. I didn't put two and two togeth---"

Kat put her hand on mine, stopping me from finishing the sentence. Taking a deep breath, she whispered in my ear, "I told you I've always had a thing for bad boys. My curse."

Stepping away from me, Kat hastily filled a half-dozen orders. I stood, frozen in the past, my hands wrapped about the two glasses of scotch in front of me.

She returned to me and placed both hands on the bar. Eyeing me with acute directness, I could see converging thoughts cascading inside her. Finally, she nodded just once and voiced, "You've changed, Todd. Whatever Tami did for you, it was damn close to a miracle. Don't lose it. Don't go back. I may love bad boys but I like you better with a little of the asshole rubbed off."

She leaned in and kissed me on the cheek, a brief smile crossing her lip.

Kat returned to work. Her words felt like someone had fired all five pinballs in the machine and they were rapidly smashing into every vital organ I hadn't already damaged. But I knew it all good. Somehow it was all very good.

As I returned to Harry, he was glancing around, still uncomfortable being out in public at the resort. I could feel him tensing up the more his eyes worked the room.

"People are staring at us again," he huffed, unable to hide his embarrassment.

"Who gives a shit? Let the bastards stare. I don't get why you give so much power to a bunch of drunk strangers."

He looked directly at me, my words breaking through and actually making sense. A satisfied smile inched across his lips. More progress. Prior to this, I believe Harry would have excused himself and dashed away, heading back upstairs to hide from the crowd he believed was talking about him. As the drinks were delivered, I raised my glass to him.

"To you, Harry. We may never be best friends but we both carry something special with us. We were both loved by a great woman. That never goes away."

The rest of the tension in Harry washed out of him in a flood of emotions. He tapped his glass off of mine and took a sip as he repeated just loud enough for me to hear, "It never goes away."

As we slugged our drinks slowly, a girl in tight jeans and a loose blouse bounced over to us, leaning in so we could hear.

"I don't mean to be rude," she said with breathless speed, "but I think it's so cool that you two would come down here and be together and all that. I mean after the hard time everyone's given you this week. But you have a right to your relationship just like everyone else."

Harry shifted in his chair, and I thought he was going to leap up and run, but he was just turning to put his hand on the girl's and said, "You're absolutely correct. We do have a right to our relationship. Thank you."

"Well, you have my vote for cutest couple here," she said before dashing back to her table.

Harry and I locked eyes.

"Damn right we're the cutest couple," Harry nodded.

I raised my glass, and he slammed his off of it, both of us laughing.

As Harry took another shot from his drink, I set my glass down on the table. "What would you say if I told you I wasn't going back, Harry?" I asked.

He didn't speak. Instead, he took a long moment to assess my demeanor. Was I pulling his chain? Fishing for sympathy? Leading into something even bigger?

None of the above.

"Where did that come from?" Harry asked with almost parental concern in his voice.

I could only shake my head. Hell, I didn't know. I just felt that there was no point in returning to who I once was. Tami and I needed adventures, to feel life. I knew it was certifiably insane. But so the hell was everything else that had happened.

"Where would you go?" Harry asked.

"Here. For a while. There are a lot of other islands. A whole world of people I haven't met. Things I haven't done. I feel that right now it's time to get out there and live whatever crosses my path."

"Young, dumb, and full of cum," he fired back. When I gave him a goofy look, he smiled wider. "It's a thing we used to say in the army about new recruits. Guys who were going to experience the world for the first time. For many of them they had never lived anywhere but with their parents," Harry said, leaning back in his chair, his glass cradled in his hands. "You know Todd, life goes so fast. Look at me. I don't feel sixty-three. You always see yourself as a kid. Because there's still so much we haven't learned. There was a lot I didn't do, but I've seen a lot. And felt a lot. Hell, who would have thought I would bury both my wife and my daughter?"

He stopped speaking, a melancholy pallor rising over the moment, before he looked back up at me and asked, "What would you do?"

"I'm a man of many talents. I know how to mix a drink, add and subtract, and God knows I am a people person," I answered, getting a laugh out of him.

"Yeah. And these bars down here need bouncers. They'll let in just about anyone," he snapped off.

I smiled and nodded. "There you go."

But Harry's grin washed off his face. "Todd, you don't think you'll ever find a woman to love you again, do you?"

"Not like Tami loved me."

"No. Not like Tami loved you. I could never figure it out, Todd, but my daughter adored you. She saw something in you, that for the life of me, I didn't understand. Well, maybe a little now."

"I would have given her the greatest life imaginable."

Harry nodded. "That I never doubted." He took another sip from his drink and leaned across the table, closer to me. "There will be other women who will love you. They may even see in you that man that Tami saw."

"That would be something."

"Don't let them down. Tami would be hurt."

I choked back the tightness in my throat and reached across the table, offering Harry my hand. He gripped it hard, and we shook. As I was about to pull my hand away, Harry startled me by pulling me toward him over the table. I went with the moment, and he hugged me. Reflexively, I wrapped my paws around his back and held on. He sniffled once and then let go.

As we sat back down across from each other, I sensed the entire room peering at us. And I knew he felt it too.

As the music in the club slowed, it hit me. A big ass grin plastered on my face. I stood up.

"Fuck these people, Harry. Let's dance."

His eyes saucered, his jaw slacked open. "What?" was all he could ask.

I grabbed him and literally lifted him from the chair.

"We're dancing," I proclaimed, and before he could register any protest, I was dragging him toward the dance floor.

He tried to pull free of my grip, but I had him tightly by the forearm. As I said, some people just don't go easy.

"Fight me, Harry, and I'll throw you over my shoulder. This is our last night, and I want to freak out these idiots," I stated, spinning on him, going face to face. "Now are you in or are you out?"

Harry searched for the words, a million pounds of fears ticking across his eyes. He just couldn't come up with what was racing through his head until he finally blurted out, "I'm older, I lead."

Fuck yeah!

We climbed onto the dance floor and into the middle of the crowd and began to dance together. Everyone stared. People literally stopped moving and watched us dance together. They didn't know whether to be insulted, angry, or to accept. Harry stood stiffly, protecting his dignity. I was in complete 'fuck you' mode, moving like a panther. And the more I moved around him, the more a strange resolve seeped into Harry's body. It took almost the entire song for Harry to release his inhibition and fling off his cloak of embarrassment. He began to move. Slow at first, head high, looking past everyone. Then the dam broke. He stopped me in my tracks. "I told you I'm leading, damn it," and suddenly he was twirling around like a demented Barishnikov, dancing with me, dancing with a group of young girls, dancing with anybody who would make eye contact with him. I was afraid he was going to try to break dance or maybe attempt a few Rockette high kicks and hurt himself, but he was content filtering through the bodies and picking up a partner here and there, and then working his way back to dance with me as I followed his lead and danced with whomever was available and willing.

We closed the bar that night, Kat joining us after her shift ended. The three of us sat with a bottle on the table as they mopped the floors around us, Harry prattling off advice to Kat on how to handle the problems with her son, Eric. At the end of the night, Kat kissed Harry good-bye and then turned to me.

"I hope to see you again," Kat said firmly, her fingers tenderly gliding down the side of my face, before turning and walking away. I watched her go, each step fading her into the darkness of the damp night. From the shadows, I saw her turn and give me one more wave. If I wasn't absolutely sure it was Kat, I would have sworn it was Tami. But the eye sees what the eye wants to see.

The next morning, Harry chucked a few aspirin down his throat, complaining to me that I had devoured all the Vicoden, leaving none for him when he was in critical condition from all the dancing. As we both packed, Harry offered to take care of things back at home: my condo, the furniture, bank accounts, whatever I needed done. He explained that he would want to stay very busy for a while, settling into his new existence without a daughter he loved and an asshole son-in-law he didn't.

I promised him I would keep in touch. Let him know where I was. What I was doing. He gave me the standard 'be careful' speech, and I agreed not to do anything too stupid. But he knew he could never hold me to that promise.

Outside the hotel, Tomas waited next to his cab ready to take Harry to the airport for a flight he was sure to make. My honeymoon with Harry was over. Now it was time for the two of us to get on with our lives. I knew that it was very likely that we would never actually see each other again. But then again, we were different people, and I have learned never to say never. If a woman can change me, any damn thing is possible. It is all a journey.

"Goodbye, Harry."

"Goodbye, Todd."

We hugged one more time, no words passing between us. He gave me a sanguine smile before climbing into the cab and Tomas shut the door. I didn't wave as he pulled down the driveway of the resort, vanishing from view. I had learned that disappearing from view doesn't mean you're gone. The heart has a reality all its own. If you listen closely, it can take you on greater journeys than your mind or body is able to understand. As I picked up my bag and flung it over my shoulder, I walked into that for the first time in my life.

And I wasn't alone.

Made in the USA
Charleston, SC
11 December 2012